"One of Durrell's most fascinating novels"
—(London) *Sunday Times*

"A truly memorable experience. . . . The same superb sense of place, the same sensuous imagery that distinguished 'The Alexandria Quartet' are present here in a haunting novel within a novel."

—*Publishers Weekly*

"To read any of Durrell's mature novels is like eating a bowl of Devonshire cream—a delicious form of entertainment. I found this one, for nearly its entire course, exhilarating."

—*Newsweek*

"A unique and brilliant novel . . . loaded with opulent detail and fascinating incident."

—*Chicago Tribune*

"The mixture is as pungent and teasing as ever. . . . There is some insidious power in him that keeps one reading."

—*The Observer*

FARISHIAN

MONSIEUR
was originally published in the U.S.A.
by The Viking Press.

Books by Lawrence Durrell

Acte
The Alexandria Quartet
   *Justine
   *Balthazar
   *Mountolive
   *Clea
Bitter Lemons
*The Black Book
Collected Poems
*The Dark Labyrinth
Esprit de Corps
The Ikons and other poems
An Irish Faustus
Lawrence Durrell and Henry Miller:
   A Private Correspondence
Monsieur
*Nunquam
Pope Joan (translation)
Prospero's Cell and Reflections on a Marine Venus
Sappho
Sauve Qui Peut
Spirit of Place
Stiff Upper Lip
*Tunc (first in a series with Nunquam)

*Published by POCKET BOOKS

Lawrence Durrell

Monsieur

PUBLISHED BY POCKET BOOKS NEW YORK

MONSIEUR

Viking edition published 1975

POCKET BOOK edition published March, 1976

Standard Book Number: 671-80304-2.
Library of Congress Catalog Card Number: 74-4925.
This POCKET BOOK edition is published by arrangement
with The Viking Press, Inc. Copyright, ©, 1974, by Lawrence
Durrell. All rights reserved. This book, or portions thereof,
may not be reproduced by any means without permission of
the publisher: The Viking Press, Inc., 625 Madison Avenue,
New York, New York 10022.

Printed in the U.S.A.

For Ghislaine de Boysson

Contents

Monsieur

"Outremer"

The southbound train from Paris was the one we had always taken from time immemorial—the same long slowcoach of a train, stringing out its bluish lights across the twilight landscapes like some super-glowworm. It reached Provence at dawn, often by a brindled moonlight which striped the countryside like a tiger's hide. How well I remembered, how well he remembered! The Bruce that I was, and the Bruce I become as I jot down these words, a few every day. A train subject to unexpected halts, unexplained delays; it could fall asleep anywhere, even in open country, and remain there, lost in thought, for hours. Like the swirls and eddies of memory itself —thoughts eddying about the word "suicide," for example, like frightened tadpoles. It has never been, will never be, on time, our train.

These were the reflections of the lone traveller in the lighted third-class compartment at the rear of the train. In the tarnished mirror this man is watching himself. It had ever been thus in early spring, he told himself—even in the early student days of the old PLM. By the time the train had cleared echoing Dijon it became all but empty in this season. He was try-

1

ing to remember how long it was since he had last visited the city; but sitting there in his corner, half asleep and half awake, it seemed to him that in reality he had never been away. Or at least some part of him had always been present in its shady streets and quiet shabby squares.

But this was a strangely different return to it; crawling out of a northern winter into a nascent spring at the summons of a blue telegram. And an awful season for such a journey! In the north a flurry of snowstorms had all but paralysed rail traffic; but down here the spring had almost decided to unfreeze the land. Once across the green mulberry belt and into the olive zone, one becomes reassured, for even in the grey winterset of early dawn the gold tangerines hang in thriving loads as if in some Greek garden of Epicurus. His eyes rested unseeingly on the flying landscapes through which they passed.

The late traveller was myself, Bruce, and the journey was none of my choosing. The telegram which had summoned me southward from Prague was suitably laconic. It told me of the suicide of my oldest and best friend, Piers de Nogaret; more than friend indeed, for his sister Sylvie was my wife, though the telegram was signed not by her but by the family notary. It had reached me at the British Embassy to which I had been attached for the last few years as a medical adviser. "Bruce Drexel, M.D., at your service"—but now how insubstantial it sounded, like an echo of far-off certainties which had taken no account of the revenges of time! The man in the mirror stared himself out of countenance. The train rushed and rumbled onwards.

He must be trying to objectify his thoughts and emotions by treating them as one would in a novel, but it didn't really work. As a matter of fact, in Rob Sutcliffe's famous novel about us all, things began in exactly this way. I was strangely echoing his protagonist, summoned to the bedside of a dying friend (this was the difference) who had important things to reveal to him. Sylvie was there, too, in the centre of the picture as she always has been. Her madness was touchingly described. Of course in a way the characters were travesties of us; but the incidents were true enough and so was Verfeuille, the old château in which we had lived out this adventure between our voyages. Bruce was now identifying a little with the hero very much as Sutcliffe himself was, and about whom the writer once said: "Reality is too old-fashioned nowadays for the writer's uses. We must count upon art to revive it and bring it up to date."

Yes, but what about real people as opposed to paper figments? Dying, one becomes out of date; but it brings one's friends to their senses, or should. I so often wondered about this—how to splice the real and the imagined—when I read his book. Now he too was dead, and Pia, my sister, had lodged all his papers in the muniments room of Verfeuille, where the whole searing unhappiness of their married life can be studied by the literary historian. It was not that she was a rotten wife, either, for they loved each other to distraction; it was simply the sad story of inversion —it had left him high and dry, without inner resources. People like Rob become too attached, too vulnerable, and in consequence are easily broken on the block. My sister if she read these lines would put her hands over her ears and cry out "No!" But they are true.

In a few more months the three of us were to have met once again in the city of Piers' birth, to resume the thread of this bizarre friendship which had lasted half a lifetime and which had only been slightly disturbed by his last posting to Delhi. We were both due to retire this year and return to Verfeuille together, to live out the rest of our story with Sylvie behind the massive ramparts of the crumbling château. To wall ourselves up, in a way: to retire from the world completely: to develop and enrich this enduring friendship between the three of us which had withstood so many trials and still remained (at least for me) the central experience of my whole existence. Indeed there was nothing else in my life to which I could compare it in fruitfulness and intensity —a three-cornered love, ill-starred only because one day Sylvie lost her reason and almost dragged her brother with her. Piers hesitated and faltered on the very brink. Had I not been there I think he would have slid down the long slopes of unreason, choosing it as a refuge from his thoughts of her insanity. Now everything had changed, abruptly, brutally. Piers was apparently dead, and the man I had become could see no way forward into the future. The disappearance of my friend had overturned reality; yet the feeling of being bereft created a singular kind of tearless detachment in me, a dazed and fearless irony. The mirror recorded a grimly smiling man. Meanwhile, far away, in the green rose gardens of Montford, Sylvie walked in her Chinese shawl, her lips moving in silent conversations with her dead brother. Here Bruce stands up and paces the empty carriage in a fury of resentment and pain like an animal caught in a trap.

Fatigue surely played a good part in this novel feeling of unreality which had beset me. People take time to die and the dead Piers had only just begun to make his claims on the memory of his friends. It was his body, not his memory, which was cold. Each time I was jolted awake I had to re-experience the fact of his death, an angry sting. For a moment there would be nothing, just an empty space—and then memory slid open like a flick-knife and I realised that he had gone, entered into the weird convention of the state of death, about which we know nothing which might help us domesticate the idea, tame it.

I wondered if in dying he had remembered the initiation which we had shared in Egypt long ago—at the hands of Akkad, distilled patiently from the doctrines of the desert gnostics. I know he had been deeply marked by them. In the matter of death, I mean, they were crucial and unequivocal. For after that initiation it was impossible to attach any profound importance to the notion of dying. All individual deaths had been resumed by the death of God! I remember how the idea terrified me at the time! When we said good-bye to tender smiling Akkad he told us: "Now don't give a thought to what you have learned. Simply become it as fast as you can—*for what one becomes one forgets.*"

Obviously this belonged to the other kind of death, the gnostic one which would henceforward always overshadow the death of mere time in man; the death which for Akkad and his sect was simply one form of the body's self-indulgence, a lack of fastidiousness. "Dying can be a mere caprice if one allows it to happen before discovering the big trick which enables one to die with profit," he said.

I repeated his words slowly to myself now as I stared into the flying night. I wondered where Akkad would be tonight. Perhaps he was dead? I felt separated from Piers by less than half a pulse-beat.

And yet we had been lucky, given the circumstances of our occupations and voyages, to have enjoyed an almost continuous association with each other; our initial friendship, which later turned into love, had never withered on the stalk. As a youth I had come into contact with the brother and sister who lived so strange an abstract life of beauty and introspection in their lonely château: and from then on we had hardly quitted one another. Piers became a diplomat, I a Service M.D., yet despite all the vagaries of fate we were, at the very worst, posted simultaneously to adjacent countries. On several lucky occasions we even achieved the same posting, he to the Embassy of France, I to the British. Thus we knew Cairo together and Rome, we shared Peking and Berne, we divided Madrid. Sylvie was our lieutenant, and when we were apart she shared us, moving from one to the other. But always we spent our summer leaves in Verfeuille together. So that despite all the changes of place and person the whole pattern of our lives (and in consequence our love) had continuity and design.

Later I had deliberately married Sylvie because she wished it. It further cemented out fierce attachment to each other. Nor was I sleepwalking, for I knew full well the psychological implications of the act. I also knew that one day the centre might fall out of Sylvie's mind; that she might have to be sent away, sequestered in the green quietness of Montfavet, the great straggling asylum which hovers among the lush streamlets and sunny bowers of the Vaucluse, exhaling something like the kinetic calm of an Epidaurus. On this score I have never had anything to regret. This three-cornered passion has held me spellbound for a lifetime and will see me beyond the grave. I knew I had found my *onlie begetters*. I was reliving the plot and counterplot of Shakespeare's Sonnets in my own

life. I had found the master-mistress of my passion.
Who could ask for more?

I had been walking all winter long in a country of
snow-bound lakes, locked in the steel grip of ice,
where the wild geese hooted all night long as they
straggled south. Thus walking in the grey winter-
scapes one comes, at every turn, upon little bundles
of dispersed feathers—the snow like a rumpled dining
table in the woods. The diner had left already. Sometimes the fox may have spared a bird's head, but
mostly only a clutch of unswallowable feathers. A
walk in the ancient world, I thought, must have been
somewhat similar, with the remains of animal sacrifices
at every crossroads, in green groves, on the seashore.
They offered up a sacrificial death to the gods as later
on men were to offer up the first fruits of their garden plots. I felt that perhaps the suicide of Piers (if
such an improbably thing were true) somehow par-
took of this sort of offering. But I still didn't quite
believe in it. But then, if not by his own hand, then
by whose? Nothing that had happened to us in the
past offered an explanation for this astonishing development. And all the more so because of the gnostic
ideas of Akkad which Piers claimed to have understood and to have believed in. But wait a minute!

A phrase of Akkad's comes to mind. It went something like this: "People of our persuasion gradually
learn to refuse all rights to so-called God. They renounce the empty world, not like ascetics or martyrs,
but like convalescents after suicide. But one must be
ripe for this sort of thing." Suddenly an absurd idea
has entered the sleeper's mind. Piers' self-inflicted
death as being a part of a ritual murder . . . What
nonsense! I had a sudden picture of my friend, quix-

7

otic to the point of innocence, repeating the words after Akkad. He had always been prepared to push things to extremes.

And Sylvie? What might she not have to tell me? The thought of her, up there in Montfavet, ached on and on in my mind, as it had done for the last two years.

And so at long last to reach home, to clatter softly and wearily into the empty station—that historic point of return and departure: but this time alone. It has always afflicted me with a profound love-dread, this shabby little station, because so often when I returned Sylvie was waiting for me on the platform, hand in hand with her nurse, distractedly gazing about her. I was always looking out for her, I suppose. The train sighs to a halt and the rasping announcements begin in the accents of the Midi. I stand paralysed among the lighted windows, gazing about me.

It never changes; it looks so homely, so provisional, so grubby-provincial. You could never deduce from it the existence of the cruel and famous town to which it belongs.

Outside the mistral purred. In the slowly thawing gardens were the memorable flaccid palms set in their circles of moulting grass. There was still snow-rime in the flowerbeds. And of course a queue of rubber-tyred *fiacres,* waiting for whatever custom the dawn train might bring in. They looked half dead with boredom and disgust, the horses and the drivers. Soon they would be sauntered away into the town sleeping, for the next train arrived after eleven. I managed to wake a driver and strike a price. I was heading for the old Royal Hotel. But as we yawed about and made some disjointed lurches towards the battlements I was seized by a sudden counterinfluence which made me direct the driver towards the river. I felt a sudden desire to see it again, its existence seemed to confirm so many things, the old river-god of our youth. So we slobbered and slid along the ancient walls, outside the bastions. It was dark as pitch, one saw nothing. Trees arched overhead. Then suddenly one heard its voice coupled with the snarl of the wind. Like cats making love. I got out and walked beside the slow cab, feeling the wind clutch my shoulders.

In the greyness the water was inky, swollen and curdled with blocks of ice which thumped and tinkled along the banks.

A faint light touched the east but dawn was not yet breaking. You might have thought yourself in central Asia—the cloudy sky in close link like chain-mail and the fading stabs of moonlight. The driver grumbled but I paid no attention. I even walked out gingerly upon the famous broken bridge, clutching the handrail as well as my hat, for here the wind whirled. A frail ghost-light lit the chapel, but there were no worshippers at that hour. A broken and renowned relic of man's belief, pointing its amputated fingers of masonry westward. I thought of Piers. In expounding Akkad once he had said something like: "What really dies is the collective image of the past—all the temporal selves which have been present in a serial form focused together now in an instant of perfect attention, of crystal-clear apprehension which could last forever if one wished." How hollow all these grave lucubrations seemed in this wind-tugged night. Nevertheless they were perhaps appropriate to the place. For a hundred years this shabby village had been Rome, had been all Christendom.

This was, after all, Avignon.

9

Confused messages waited for me at the hotel, but there was nothing to be done about them at this hour. I dozed on my bed until sunrise and then set out resolutely to find a coffee, traversing the old city with affection and distress, hearing my own sharp footsteps on the pavements, disembodied as a ghost. Avignon! Its shabby lights and sneaking cats were the same as ever; overturned dustbins, the glitter of fish scales, olive oil, broken glass, a dead scorpion. All the time we had been away on our travels round the world it had stayed pegged here at the confluence of its two green rivers. The past embalmed it, the present could not alter it. So many years of going away and coming back, of remembering and forgetting it. It had always waited for us, floating among its tenebrous monuments, the corpulence of its ragged bells, the putrescence of its squares.

And in a sense we had waited for it to reclaim us after every absence. It had seen the most decisive part of our lives—the fall of Rob Sutcliffe, Sylvie's collapse, and now the suicide of Piers. Here it lay summer after summer, baking away in the sun, until its closely knitted roofs of weathered tile gave it the appearance of a piecrust fresh from the oven. It haunted one although it was rotten, fly-blown with expired dignities, almost deliquescent among its autumn river damps. There was not a corner of it that we did not love.

I had not given much thought to Rob Sutcliffe until now, sitting in this grubby café, waiting for the clocks to strike eight. After my sister Pia . . . after her defection had become absolutely unequivocal and Rob knew that they would never live together again, his decline and fall began. It was slow and measured at first, the decline from clubman and adventurer and famous novelist into . . . what exactly? From a dandy with a passion for clean linen to a mountebank in a picture hat. His books passed out of public demand, and he ceased to write any new ones. He took dingy lodgings in the lower town, two rooms in the house of an "angel maker" as the ironists of the town called those old crones who took in unwanted or illegitimate children for a small fee, and with an unwritten, unspoken guarantee to turn them into "angels" in a very few months by ill-treating them and literally starving them to ‘death. This old crone was Rob's only company in the last years. They sat and drank themselves silly at night in the den he inhabited in that ghastly house full of hungry children. His physical appearance had changed very much since he had grown a straggling black beard, and taken to a cloak and the broad-brimmed hat which gave him a striking appearance. But he had long since ceased to wash, and he was physically as dirty as an anchorite. He was fond of the cloak because it was impregnated with dirt and spots of urine. He had deliberately taken to wetting his bed at nights now, gloating over the deliberately infantile act, rubbing his own nose in it so to speak. In micturating he always allowed a few drops to fall upon the cloak. The stale odour of the garment afforded him great pleasure. For some time he continued to see Toby, but at last he refused him the right to visit him. All this ostentatious display of infantile regression was all the more mysterious for being conscious. After all, Sutcliffe had started life as a psychologist, and only turned to writing afterwards. It was his revenge on Pia I suppose, but all the stranger for being so deliberate. Sometimes when very drunk (he also took drugs) he would beg a hack from the livery stables and ride slowly about the town, with his head bowed on his breast, asleep: the reins left on the horse's neck so that it took him wherever it wished. Even when it came to the act of defecation he chose to smear paper and fingers alike.

11

The change in Rob was almost unbelievable. It was his friend Toby who told me all this in his low sad voice—the voice reserved for matters of gravity or distress. He had forced the old crone to disgorge all she knew after Rob's body had been recovered from the river into which horse and rider had plunged.

It was strange to sit here in the early sunlight thinking about him, and also about Piers, who had also met his end not two streets away, in the Hôtel des Princes. Why had he not returned to the château, why had he stayed on in the town? Was he waiting to greet me? Or was there some other factor involved—perhaps it was easier to see his sister? All these things remained to be discovered. It would soon be time to take up the telephone and sort myself out. Nobody as yet knew I had arrived. I wondered whether perhaps Toby was already here in response to my cable.

The reaction of the long journey had begun to tell on me; I started to doze in the café. But jumping up I went back to the hotel, where I knew that a hot shower would give me the energy I needed to get through the day—the memorable day of this return to Avignon and to Sylvie.

It is much later in the year now, when I try to reassess the meaning and value of all these episodes on paper: in search of some fruitful perspective upon my own life here in the old château—the queer solitary life which I have at last adopted. Scribbling all this gives me something to do, I am resetting the broken bones of the past. Perhaps I should have begun it long ago, but the thought of the old muniments room with its books and memoranda and paintings, that depressed me. At every point there I am in touch with them all through their diaries and manuscripts and letters. Moreover I myself must hurry a bit also, for a personal shadow has fallen into step with me, a more prosaic medical one which I can hold at bay for a while with the needle. But I am playing my hand slowly so as not to risk deserting Sylvie if I can help it.

I knew that I would have to undertake a few of the official duties in connection with Piers' death, and later that morning I rang up Jourdain at the asylum, the doctor who had been a family friend, and into whose charge Sylvie had always been placed. He was a cheerful man for a neurologist, and made even melancholia sound like something pleasant and enviable to have. "At last!" he said with evident relief. "We have been waiting for you. She has had excellent remissions, you know, and spent a great deal of time with Piers until this extraordinary business came about. Yes, I am as puzzled as you must be. . . . Why? They talked of nothing but your arrival and the new life you were going to start together in Verfeuille. Naturally she collapsed, but it's not a total relapse. Some twilight, some confusional states, but the picture isn't entirely hopeless. And now you are here you can help me. I am holding her under fairly heavy sedation at the moment. But why not come out to Montfavet this evening and dine? We can wake her together."

I said I would do so. Apparently Toby had given no sign of life either. I wondered if he had received my cable.

That afternoon, to fill in my time, I took a short cut across the part of the old town which lies inside the fortifications and climbed past the ugly palaces of the Popes; I climbed the green-fringed ramps which led up into the marvellous hanging gardens of the Rocher des Doms. From this vantage point one can look down on three sides to see the loops and curls of the Rhône carving out the embankments of its bed in the carious limestone, sculpting the soft flanks of the nether hills. A frail sun shone upon distant snowlines leading away towards the Alps. A little island lay below this cockpit, frozen, like a wild duck trapped in frost-glittering sedge. Mount Saint Victor stood up in the distance, erect as a martyr tied to its stake of ice. But the wind still blew steel, although the faint sunlight had coaxed out some fugitive perfumes, orange or thyme, upon the air.

Here we had so often wandered, Sylvie and I, moving from one panorama to the other. And repeating the journey now I seemed to recapture many fragments of our old conversations. Events had given them an entirely new resonance. They had become part of past history, that part of time we had shared with Piers. I saw us now as figures—rather as in Rob's novel—projected anew by the force of memory upon this vernal landscape. Sylvie's dark-lashed eyes, "borrowed from the thrush" as her brother used to say, and the black hair with its violet blackness shining like carbon paper. Yes, the past now had attained a curious nervous density, a weight which was not composed (as one might suppose) of multiple nostalgias. It was full and rich, plump as an autumn fruit. It had been so fully lived that there was nothing about it one could dare to regret. The feeling of fatality, loneliness, and so on, were constituents of the present. Up here spring was scratching at the door like a pet.

I walked absently about the garden in the cold afternoon air, retracing in my mind the slopes and contours of these ancient conversations and wondering what the future held in store for me in this bereft world.

Sylvie was now the great question mark. Would she, I wondered, ever come to herself again enough to resume some sort of life with me? Funny how confident I had been that the presence of Piers would somehow make this possible, make her return to reason, to reality. There had been neither more nor less reason for optimism than there was now, yet I had felt it. Now I was not sure—I feared the imponderables of mental illness with its imperfectly demarcated boundaries, its sudden changes of temper and altitude. It was Sylvie herself who once said: "One should always distrust the insane. They are of bad faith somehow and they know it. But they don't know how to alter it, and you doctors don't know how to cure it."

And what if the worst should happen? Why, she would elect to stay on at Montfavet in the rooms which had for so long been set aside for her, trusting only in Jourdain, her old friend and confidant. I sighed to think that she might never roam the world with me again, making one member of that sad trio, husband, wife, nurse: nor even that other trio of brother, sister, lover. How close we had been before all this unhappiness supervened! I kept thinking back to those days. Piers, Sylvie, myself, Toby, Rob, Pia and Sabine with her pack of fortune-telling cards— where was she now? Did she know of Piers' death from the cards?—that would be like her. My slow footsteps crunched on the gravel. Below loomed the sinfully ugly palaces of the Popes in all their blockish magnificence, overshadowing the town which despite the resonance of its name was still hardly more than an overgrown village. The quasi-death of insanity with its small periodic remissions, its deviations into good sense, even into brilliant insight, was almost more cruel really than outright death. In my own case it seemed gradually to have worn me out emotionally —the word castration does not sound too exaggerated in the context. An affect damned and frozen. And of course (doctors are always on the lookout) I could trace the spoor of some deep new inhibitions in my dreams, not to mention my fantasies in which I surprised myself by poisoning her. It is unbelievable when I think of it, yet is true. Standing beside the bed in grim silence with my fingers on her pulse until the shallow breathing filtered away into the silence and her extraordinary marmoreal pallor announced the advent of the rigor. And then the sweet scent rose to my nostrils, the imaginary scent of death which I always smelt: I suspect that it was the odour of morphine. Yet in this dream fantasy it was always Piers who came up and put his hand on my arm to restrain me, to exorcise me.

There was plenty of time that evening. The light was faltering away into moonlit dusk when I set out to walk across the town to the station and pick up a *fiacre*. I wanted to jog in leisurely fashion through the green fields and chestnut avenues, over the rushing bubbling streamlets, to join Sylvie. I had so often done this in the past. I was anxious to see again the little church which had always been our point of rendezvous. Did it still stand in its humble little square planted with tall shady planes? Did the old cracked bistro still have the yellow letterbox nailed to its wall? A small, a fragile point of reference in the incoherent and echoing world of her madness, of her life behind the walls of the great establishment.

I used to catch sight of her waiting for me so shyly among the trees, listening with bent head for the clip-clop of the horse's hooves. Her tremulous anxiety ignited the dark beauty of her face with its luminous eyes and white-rose pallor. And somewhere near at hand always lurked the tall, military-looking nurse clad in her stiff field-grey uniform, her white hair tugged back on her scalp and pinned into a coif. She would remain watchfully in the shadow of the trees while Sylvie advanced on tiptoe to meet me, her arms outstretched, her lips moving. It was like meeting a small child. The queer little camel-backed church was always empty too, smelling of wax and cats and dust. We entered it always with our arms about each other, the ice broken at last by the first tremulous kiss of recognition. And as always we gravitated, as if by instinct, to the little side-chapel marked with a Roman five, and sat down face to face with the large rather anodyne painting which we had come to love so much. Here she always insisted that we talk in whispers, not from respect of the place, but lest the eavesdroppers in the painting should overhear—though why these so manifestly harmless images should menace the endearments of two lovers in the silent church I do not know.

Jogging slowly along now, down these long green avenues already touched by the first spring shoots, I felt the full ambivalence of my thoughts swinging from side to side as the little *fiacre* itself swung. Queer thoughts passed through my mind, the anarchic thoughts which sprang from those unresolved childish conflicts and fears: thoughts I could identify at least. Perhaps out of Piers' death I might extract a horror and sweetness which brought me much closer to her? I, who had never been jealous of Piers while he was alive, or so I thought, managed to surprise myself with such a thought. I would have her to myself! And if she were to become sane again, then why not fecund? It was not too late. . . . But here my mind balked. Once before we had taken this path, and it was a distasteful and dishonourable one. Surprised by Sylvie's pregnancy one spring some years ago, and not knowing for certain whose the child would be, I tried to solve the problem by marrying her, only to have all this uncertainty end in a pro-

17

voked miscarriage. It was cowardly to pretend that her state of mind dictated it; it was our state of mind which should have been called into question. Nobody likes being a homosexual, just as nobody likes being a Negro or a Jew. The marriage was only another mask for the hold I had on her brother through his affections. And yet love is a real thing—perhaps the only real thing in this bereft world. And yet how to achieve the only sort which is viable, enriching—one with no sanctions, no reservations, one without guilt?

It was no longer fashionable to ask too much of oneself; we three must have seemed a somewhat pathetic trio to the outside eye—I think of the mordant phrases of Rob about us. We were old-fashioned, we belonged to the age of piety, and perhaps Avignon was the perfect site for this kind of blind adventure which would leave no trace behind, except for a lot of mouldering papers in the old château which would interest nobody, and one day would be sold for scrap.

Outside, in the shade of the trees, the German nurse in field-grey waited for us, standing upright as a soldier, her arms folded, watching the door of the church from which we would eventually emerge. Once Sylvie had written on the walls of the gutted ballroom at Verfeuille the phrase: *"Quelqu'un en gris reste vainqueur."* And I knew she had been thinking of this tall dour custodian of her reason.

Yes, the church was still there, thank goodness, and the little square had hardly changed. My eyes at once sought the familiar corner under the trees, but now there were only a few aged men stooped over their *boules*. I halted the *fiacre* and went into the nave for a moment, bemused by the sleepy silence, and thinking of nothing in particular. I sat for a while absently in our little side-chapel, staring at the familiar painting which had presided over so many of our conversations. Then I set myself to think hard of her, wondering if perhaps by telepathy I might project some of this sad calm towards her. I closed my eyes and counted the breaths for a while, re-creating her form mentally the while in the shape of a target, an ikon. I conjured her up—all the small-boned litheness which issued in such abrupt but sure gestures: she wore clothes of a slightly old-fashioned cut, and little jewelry. It was not hard to forge her image, her "eidolon," in the grey gloom of the little church. I tried to project towards her that part of a man which is his knowing, thinking and caring part—beyond the ego and the tricks of the mind. Yes, I saw her and another phrase of Akkad came into my mind. I repeated it softly to myself.

"Even death has its own precise texture and the big philosophers have always entered into the image of the world it exemplifies while still alive, so to become one with it while their hearts were still beating. They colonised it." But it was when Akkad said things like that, which had all the air of being quotations from some forgotten gnostic poet, that Sylvie, beside herself with admiration, would spread her hands towards him and say, "O convince me, dear Akkad, please convince me."

Unlike her brother she shared my native incapacity for belief, a lack which prevented either of us advancing very far into the tangled jungle of the gnostic world; whereas Piers took to it at once like a duck to water, and only just managed to prevent himself becoming a bore, a fervent.

Time was moving on, the sunlight was slanting across the planes in a last configuration before dusk. I broke off my reverie and rejoined the little cab. "To *Montfavet-les-Roses*," I said, and the driver looked at me curiously, wondering, I imagine, whether to feel sympathy or not; or perhaps he was just curious. The idea of the roses gave a singular tinge to the notion of madness. Indeed in the vulgar Avignon slang *"tomber dans les roses,"* which had been waggishly adapted from *"tomber dans les pommes,"* signified going mad enough to be incarcerated in the grey institution. We were moving through the cool evening light towards Sylvie. I wondered how I should find her.

You would say that they were simply two old dilapidated rooms with high ceilings and a predisposition to unreachable cobwebs, but they were rather glorious, belonging to an older age, part of the original foundation. But they had always been hers, set aside for her, and now it was as if they belonged to her completely. The authorities had allowed her to move in her own graceful furniture from the château, carpets and paintings, and even a large tapestry rescued from the old ballroom. So that it was always a pleasant shock of surprise to come upon this haven of calm and beauty after traversing the rather forbidding main buildings, and the succession of long white corridors with sterile-looking glass doors painted over with doctors' names. Moreover her own high French windows gave out directly onto the gardens so that she could virtually live in the open all summer. Hers was the life of a privileged prisoner, except when she happened to have a period of remission when she resumed her place in the ordinary world. But the rooms stayed hers, and while she was away they were kept scrupulously dusted.

She worked under the great tapestry with its glowing but subdued tones—huntsmen with lofted horns had been running down a female stag. After the rape, leaving the grooms to bring the trophy home, they galloped away in the soft brumous Italian skyline; a network of misty lakes and romantic islets receding

into the distance along the diagonal; fathered by
Poussin or Claude. The stag lay there, panting and
bleeding and in tears. None of this had changed and
I found the fact reassuring. The beautiful old Portu-
guese writing desk with its ivory-handled drawers,
the rare bust of Gongora, the autograph of Gide en-
larged and framed above the piano. Jourdain stood by
with a quiet sad smile, holding his passkey in his hand,
and giving me time to take it all in. My eye fell upon
a bundle of manuscripts, and a tangle of notebooks
lying about in a muddle on the carpet—as if a packet
had exploded in her hands. "The spoils from Piers'
room," said Jourdain following my eye. "The police
allowed her to carry off some of the stuff in the hope
that she might reveal something of interest. But so
far nothing. She seems to have been the last to see
Piers, you see? Come; we can talk later."

Well, but she had gone away to lie down and sleep
in her vast unmade bed with its heavy damascened
baldaquin holding back the light and neutralising it.
Her eyes were closed but she was not asleep. I could
tell by the movement of her inquisitive fingers—they
were playing something like the slow movement of
the A minor; but slowly and haltingly, as if sight-
reading it for the first time. We made little enough
noise, but I could tell from long experience that she
knew we were there, sensing the fact like an animal.
Nor was there anything mysterious in the fact that it
was I, for she had been expecting me. It was the
purest automatism for me to go down on one knee
and place my finger on her white wrist. I whispered
her name and she smiled and turned; without opening her eyes she kissed me warmly on the mouth,
lingeringly. "Bruce, at last you, Bruce." But she said
it as if I were still part of a dream she was enacting
in her mind. Then she went on in a different register

and in a small precise voice. "So then everything smells of burnt rubber here. I must tell Jourdain." My companion grunted softly. Then she went on at a headlong pace. "I think really that it was his way of eating that repelled me. Toby always ate in that way. Poor Toby." I took her hand, forgetting, and said, "Has Toby arrived yet?" But she only put her finger to her lips and said, "Shh. They must not overhear. He will be coming soon. He promised me." She sat up now in a masterful mood, clasping her hands, but still keeping her eyes fast shut. "Piers' diaries, they are all over the place, and I can't sort them properly. Thank goodness you have come, Bruce." Her lips trembled. "But the smell of rubber and sulphur—I can't tell which is the worse. So now I am completely in your power, Bruce. There is nobody left now who can hurt me at all except you. Do you want to kill me, Bruce, to drive me to it? I must know the truth."

"Please."

"I must know the truth."

She opened her eyes at last and turned towards us smiling—a trifle tearfully to be sure but with a basic composure that was reassuring. It always amazed me that whenever I reappeared after a long absence she suddenly shed her sickness. It was like watching a diver slowly surfacing. After a moment she lay down again and turned her face to the wall, saying, but this time in a confidently rational tone, "Part of the confusion is in myself, you know, but mostly in all three of us at once. It is horrible to be a battleground of three selves." I knew only too well what she meant, though I said nothing, simply keeping my fingers on the precious time-piece of her pulse.

She lay sighing, and then after a while it came back, the sensation that by some enigmatic act of will-power I drew her slowly back towards reality once more. It was still a factor of control over her (which did not always work) that I would have liked to rationalise, to use like a real healer. I tried to explain it to myself by saying that with me she gradually began to forget that she was mad. In ascribing a rational value to everything she said, however confused, I provoked her into trying to provide one for herself. I pretended that it all had a meaning, and of course in another sense it did have one, if only one could have deciphered it. It was indeed literally drowned in meaning, like a flooded boat.

There is nothing stranger than to love somebody who is mad, or who is intermittently so. The weight, the strain, the anxiety is a heavy load to bear—if only because among these confusional states and hysterias loom dreadful probabilities like suicide or murder. It shakes one's hold also on one's own grasp of reality; one realises how precariously we manage to hold on to our reason. With the spectacle of madness before one's eyes one feels the odds shorten. The eclipse of reason seems such an easy affair, the grasp on sanity so provisional and insecure. While I was feeling the weight of these preoccupations she was saying: "Everything seems to have come to an end now, but has it? Three little nigger boys . . . then there were two. I am afraid of you, Bruce, what shall we do?" The question was asked on such a rational note that I took the plunge and asked: "You were with him? How did it happen? Did he do it himself?" She gave a small sigh, and closed her eyes once more; she was fading back into sedation again, that marvellous defence against the importunities of the world; I felt a fool for having adventured such important questions at such a time. Jourdain had the grace not to look quizzically at me. He shrugged. A tiny snore escaped her lips, and the doctor drew me softly out of that submarine bedroom into the study.

I waited there for a long while, suspended as if in a solution of silence, watching her and listening to her gradually deepening breathing as she edged her way towards the dismemberment of a drugged sleep. Jourdain was very patiently waiting too; he was an endearing man and the slight cast in one eye gave him always a sad juridical air, a tiny touch of melancholy which invaded his frequent smiles and inflected them with sadness. He sported dark suits even in summer, when they must have been stifling to wear, and white wing-collars with ties almot broad enough to be stocks. He whispered that he would come back for me at dinner-time and then quietly tip-toed away. I sat beside her for a while longer and then followed his lead. But in the outer room I started to gather up all the litter of papers and notebooks which were lying about on the carpet. It was typical of the sort of jumble of paper that Piers accumulated around him—everything unfinished, down to the last aphorism! One might have thought that a mad magpie had been at work among this heap of old concert programmes, maps of cities, rare pamphlets, notebooks and letters. I did what I could to sort and tidy, but it was not easy. Among the letters, some still in their envelopes, there were a number from me, and a number from Sylvie to me which I had sent on to him—so much did I feel that we were one person and obliged to share each other's lives, both inner and outer.

Then there were some from Piers to her, all written on the notepaper he affected which bore the legend *Outremer*. (I had noticed on her finger Piers' seal ring with the same rebus. He had always ironically referred to himself as "the last of the Templars," and the word expressed not only the family tie, for he was indeed a de Nogaret, but also the Templar pride in the overseas commitment of the order. For such a romantic going to the Middle Orient was a thrilling experience—of a quasi-historical kind. He felt he was returning to the roots of the great betrayal, the roots of all anti-Christian dissent. Piers was a worshipper of the Templar God. He believed in the usurper of the throne, the Prince of Darkness.)

I pondered all these contingencies as I sat in the green armchair, sifting the papers and dreaming. "In the face of such evil, creative despair is the only honourable posture," he said once and was annoyed when I smiled at his serious expression. I turned the pages of a diary in which he jotted down the visits he had received during the days preceding his death. Had he given his sister the seal ring which she now wore, the *Outremer* ring? I shook a copy of *A Rebours* and more letters fell out onto the carpet. One was a note to me from Piers giving an account of one of his sister's relapses. "When these periods come on, Bruce, she hears my voice everywhere, in the woods, in the hot-water pipes, in the drone of a mosquito, crying out always, 'Sylvie, where are you?' Followed by a sudden ominous wail 'I have killed my sister.' She is terrified at such times. What can I do?"

Such periods corresponded neither to the phases of the moon nor to her own physical rhythms. They seemed perfectly arbitrary and unpredictable. If we came to see her at such a time she would recognise only one of us, Piers. And here was a long rambling letter which she had written to me, but dedicated to her brother. "Dearest, you have been away so long. Soon it will be my birthday and I can scent the each-ness of numbers, they mate with such reluctance. I know you cannot come as yet but I pretend. Today

I waited all day for you, clothed from head to foot in a marvellous seamless euphoria. The throbbing of the almond-blossom has been almost unbearable, I cried myself asleep, back into reality again. Now the fruit is forming and I know I love you. Bruce dear, this is Man Friday's sole in the sand, I have it in the carpet now. Even Jourdain says he sees it, so I know that I am not romancing. Piers was a Friday child, remember? My dearest, they say that now you are back from India, and yet no word. Why? You will certainly have your reasons, and everything will be explained when you come. Forgive me if I am impatient.

"I am impatient to hear about India—O how was India; how calm was India? Starving and God-drunk and tattered with dry excrement? I feel I know. Every drawn breath an infanticide, every smile an enigmatic option on inner loneliness. When I was there long ago I felt the moon of my fragile non-being was at full. The smell of the magnolia remembers me supremely. A deep sadness seemed very worth while. But locked up in the first-class waiting-room of my mind I have come to repine. Yesterday they let me pretend and I went down to our Montfavet church to say hullo to the people on the wall. Nowadays at night I seem to hear Piers walking about in the other room, but he is never there when I run to see. This place, this mockery of a place, is full of a special sadness. Jourdain feels it too. He is still here, still talking of retiring, fastidious as a leper; I taste his smoke after he has gone. The taste of iodine too."

I tested each phrase on my inner ear, my inner mind, as I thought of her sitting in the fifth side-chapel of the Montfavet church under the three oil-painted witnesses, so gauche, so awkward. On the wall at her back there was a plaque commemorating

the death of a forgotten priest. If I closed my eyes
even now I could read it off.

ICI REPOSE
PLACIDE BRUNO VALAYER
Evêque de Verdun
Mort en Avignon
en 1850

I was so far plunged in reverie that I forgot the
sleeper next door, and when at last Jourdain came
tapping on the glass for me I wondered who it might
be. I was half asleep I suppose, fagged out after the
long journey. However I sprang up and followed the
doctor to his own bachelor suite at the other corner
of the main buildings. It echoed his lifelong passion
for painting, and I noticed several new additions to
his collection of oils.

In order to emphasise his civil capacity, so to speak,
he had put on an old and cherished English blazer—
to underline I suppose that his stay as a student in
Edinburgh had been a most enjoyable period in his
existence. The wines were thoughtful and tenderly
chambered. The food was slight but choice. And for
a good while we said nothing, which is the preroga-
tive of old friends, but sat sipping our cognac and
smiling at each other. "I was about to ask you if there
was any reasonable explanation," he said at last with
an exasperated laugh, "and I see that you are just
about to put the same question to me." He was right,
I had been on the point of asking him what the devil
had got into Piers. As he was fully informed of our
plans of retirement and so on I could speak to him
quite freely. I had always suspected him of being in
love with Sylvie, but he was a man of great pudicity;
when it was once a case of doing a mild psycho-
therapy on her he passed her over to someone else,

in order, I thought, not to prejudice his doctor's control: or was it because he did not wish to feel the jealousy caused by his probings? "Let me tell you what is what for the present," he said at last as we sat down to the meal. He drew a long breath. "Piers came here on retirement nearly a year ago, and set up shop in the hotel in order to be near Sylvie as he waited for you to arrive. Everything was in order for the execution of your plan, he spoke about it twice to me with enthusiasm. Sylvie herself celebrated the whole thing by several splendid remissions—you would never have thought she had been ill at all. Piers was beside himself with joy, and she spent nearly every day with him, either walking about the town or sitting in his rooms helping him sort papers or playing cards with him—you know his passion for cards. For the last week before this . . . well, extraordinary act . . . he had been in bed with a slight cold, nothing really to worry about. You will see when you look at his diary that quite a lot of people dropped in to see him, but it does seem that the very last was Sylvie. The nurse used to collect her in the evenings around seven and bring her back here to her rooms. Mind you, it was quite appropriate that the last person to see him alive was his sister. What is odd is that she was almost in a state of collaspe when the nurse arrived, so the inference is that he had already done it or had told her that he was going to do it. But at any rate she knew. From then on such facts as she produced must be held suspect, for she went right round the bend. The nurse produced one interesting point—she said that she (Sylvie) was in a fearful state because she thought herself guilty of killing Piers, for she poured out his sleeping draught for him that night and thinks that she made a mistake. The empty bottle was beside the bed, where inevitably those flat-footed police found it, and insisted on an autopsy to settle the matter. Did he poison himself, or did she accidentally do so? That is the question."

"An accident sounds more plausible. I'm reassured."

"Exactly. He gave absolutely no indication of a desire to commit suicide. I was too late to prevent the police having him carved up, but I did get on to the *préfet* who assured me that unless there is very special evidence to the contrary the thing will be treated as an accident. Which solves the question of burial. I have also contacted that strange uncle of his, the Abbé of Foulques, who has agreed to lend a moral support should the police become tedious. You know he had permission to be buried in the family vault at Verfeuille? We should get all the formalities settled by tomorrow evening. Well, that is all I can tell you for the moment." He placed his fingers on the table and reflected deeply. "It may have been Sylvie," he said, "in which case we can absolve her of any ill intent; it could only have been an accident. Yes, it must be so."

I was strangely comforted by this exposé of the situation, which had at first seemed to be so full of ambiguities. At least now the whole matter was plain, and when the police came back with the obvious result things could take their normal course, the funeral could take place. As Jourdan talked, however, I saw in my mind's eye the long casual autopsy slit which stretches from below the breast bone to the *mons pubis*.

"And Toby?" asked Jourdain with a sudden testy note in his voice, "where the devil is he?" It was a question I could not answer for the moment. "We have all cabled him in Oxford. But perhaps he hasn't yet gone up, or is away on a walking tour in Germany as he so often is . . . I don't know." Jourdain nodded; and then with an exclamation he stood up, recalling something he had forgotten. "I completely forgot. I

borrowed the police photos for you to see. They
show the room exactly as it was when the police photographer was called in by the inspector and the
médecinlégiste. Of course in part it is due to the
fact that it took place at the Princes Hotel—what the
devil induced Piers to stay there instead of somewhere like the Bristol? Funds? It's virtually a *maison
de passe*. Perhaps he had special secret vices we don't
know about? Anyway, whatever happens at the Princes
is automatically suspect for the police. Hence these
awkward questions, photographs and so on. Of course
he was an amateur of *quat*—hashish—which delighted
the cops. But there was precious little else of interest."

As he was speaking he was undoing a heavy black
briefcase which had been lying against the sofa; from
it he extracted an official envelope which held a number of photographic prints, as yet hardly dry. The
glossy surface stuck to one's fingers as one peeled
them. They were extremely beautiful, these still-lifes
of Piers' disorderly room. Jourdain spread them out
on a green card-table and drew up two chairs, at the
same time producing a large magnifying glass through
which one could study the detail of the room with
its strange inhabitant, who lay in bed, in the very
posture in which he had been found. I felt a shortening of the breath as I contemplated them. Jourdain
was talking on softly, anxious to give as complete an
account as he could of this strange affair. There were
several sets of prints on the empty bottle here, on
the bedside table. One of them Sylvie's, which is interesting. As you know he took quite large doses
of Luminash, as a sort of sedative as well as a sleeping draught. Presumably this is what they'll find in
the organs."

Piers lay on his side with his knees drawn up—in
almost a sketch of the foetal position; he had thrown
back the sheet and the covers and appeared to be

30

about to get up from his bed. His head was turned round towards the camera, presumably in the direction of the door, and he was smiling as if in delighted and surprised recognition at someone who had just entered the room. It was clearly a smile of welcome. The flashlight threw into relief his pleasant patrician face and the brilliance of his bright blue eyes, which had a sapphirelike luminosity. He wore one of his old white nightshirts with the little monogram on the breast. It was like a frozen shot in a film, and it was difficult to interpret what he might have been about to do; instead of rising perhaps he was just sinking back luxuriously, and smiling goodbye as somebody left the room?

Yet one outstretched hand with its firm fencer's wrist was stretched out towards the bedside table as if to switch off a light, take up a book or a cigarette. I passed the magnifying glass across the field to examine the detail with more precision. A novel lay beside the bed. His wrist-watch and his ebony cigarette holder lay in the silver ashtray on the bedtable. In a second and larger ashtray lay a mountain of cigarette and cigar ends. I recognised the stubs of the cheroots he smoked. For the rest the room was in a state of chaos; everywhere were tea-cups, jars of jam, flowers, packets of joss, picture-magazines and mountains of books and papers. "The room looks as if it had never been cleaned," I said, and Jourdain shrugged his shoulders. "It's the Princes," he said as if that explained everything.

To tell the truth the appearance of his room was, for such an untidy man, relatively normal. Cupboards hung open revealing his wardrobe. Though he had always been a little bit of a dandy his choice of apparel was scanty, but choice, with a distinct leaning towards clothes made for him in London. A couple of medium-sized trunks were enough to house per-

sonal possessions of this kind; but the books were
a different matter—Piers could not live without books,
and plenty of them. This explained the sagging
home-made bookshelves knocked together from pieces
of crate. And there was the oil painting he liked so
much, of the three of us. Sylvie in the dappled sunlight under the planes, sitting in a yellow hammock
her lap full of flowers. On either side of her we
stand, Piers holding her straw hat in his hand, as if
he had just retrieved it from the grass. I stand leaning
against the tree, lighting a cigarette. The sky has
the peculiar peeled look which is conferred by the
mistral only, cloudless, hard as enamel. I went
through the prints with a feeling of weakness, with
a lump in my throat. Yes, there was nothing unexpected here. The only other decoration would be the
famous death-map which he had been compiling of
late and which had a bearing on his intention of writing a memoir on the subject of his own approaching
death. But more of this later. My hand is tired tonight. I must get some order into my thoughts.
Something troubled me in all this. What was it?

Jourdain dropped me at my hotel that evening after
dinner, and grunted as he saw through the glass doors
of the patio the shapes of two men who sat waiting
for me. They sat with such an air of involuntary boredom, smoking patiently, that I almost divined who
they were before he spoke. "That's old Bechet the
notary, and Tholon the police inspector. They probably want to take you to see the room and ask you
for any notions you might have."

I turned and bade him goodnight. "Keep in touch,"
he said as he let in the clutch, and I said I would.
I opened the glass cage and stepped into the patio
with its undusted potted palms and introduced my-

self to the two men—or at least to one of them; for Bechet I had already met some years before with Piers. We exchanged shocked commiseration at the news of his death, genuine enough in his case because he had dearly loved the family. He puffed and blew in his fussy way, and used his hands to say what his tongue could not.

It was unthinkable that it should have been anything but an accident, he told me, more than once. The little policeman, who looked so undistinguished in civilian clothes, did not intrude his speculations upon us. "We must see," he said quietly. "Tomorrow we should have the results of the autopsy, and the body will be returned to the morgue, to the *chapelle ardente*, where his relatives may visit him if they wish." My soul shrank back however at the thought, which was unworthy of a medical man like myself—I know it. Bechet plunged into the details of the funeral which he had rememorised from the will. The details rendered him somewhat plaintive, for Piers was to be taken to the family *caveau* after dark, by the light of torches, there to be placed among his ancestors. But no service of any kind was to be read. "It's awkward," said Bechet, "I don't know what the Abbé will have to say. He will think that Piers was an atheist." Tholon sighed and I gathered from the volume that he harboured anticlerical sentiments. "It's vexing," said the old lawyer scattering ash over his rumpled suit, and on the end of his spotted bow tie. "In a way it was worse," I said thoughtfully, "for he belonged to a sect of gnostics who live in Egypt—and they are certainly not Christians but dissenters. Hence the provision in his will, I suppose." Tholon began to look impatient now and asked me if I would care to see the room in which my friend had died. It was being held under police seal for the moment, but perhaps the contents might give me an idea to help explain the affair. I was reluctant, but felt I could hardly refuse. Despite Bechet's obvious distaste (he was, like all Mediterraneans, superstitious about the death of friends) he allowed his courtesy to rule him and agreed to accompany us on the short walk across the square to the hotel. I had decided to get the thing over and done with.

It was deep night now with a rising moon. The gold lantern with its legend "Hôtel des Princes" swung softly in the light breeze. It was an old hotel and smelt ruinously of dust and blocked drains. We climbed to the first floor and Tholon undid some tapes stuck with sealing wax on one of the doors. The room was a pleasant size but very musty. The inspector crossed it before even turning on the light and opened a door leading out onto a small balcony; then he returned and switched on the electric light within. The bird-spattered balcony gave out onto a corner of dilapidated garden whose withered and ancient trees had long since given up bearing fruit. No doubt Piers sat out here obstinately in the icy evenings of winter to watch the light softly fading over Avignon, watching the city softly tilting into the uncaring twilight like a sailing boat turning its cheek to the wind. From here, across the network of brown clay roofs, everything slid downwards into the massive green river, which itself propelled its currents downwards to Arles with its desolate necropolis, the Alyscamps. His mind, like mine now, would have crossed the river towards the sea and then veered northward once more. . . .

There was not a corner of this magnetic country that the three of us had not explored together, sometimes on foot, sometimes on horseback, or else in a dilapidated pony cart piled high with camping equipment. Often in summer as we sat down round a fire of olive trimmings in some field near Remoulins or

Aramon a moon like a blood-orange would wander into the sky and hang above the river, waiting for our return. Avignon, so small, stuffy and parochial, was in my blood. I shivered and stepped back into the room where the two men stood in sympathetic silence, waiting for me to take it into consideration and perhaps to offer some useful observations on it. But there seemed little enough to be said.

"The body has been removed, but nothing else has been touched except the glasses and the bottle of sedative from which we took our fingerprints." On the nether wall was the so-called death-map compiled by my friend. I saw Bechet studying it in a somewhat nervous way and stepped to his side to explain it as best I could. "All the names were the names of friends who had died. He seemed to attach particular importance to the fact, and used to say that each separate death had taught him something new about death, and that he was going to resume this knowledge in a philosophic essay about dying. It was connected in an obscure way with the beliefs of this sect of gnostics to which he belonged." It sounded pretty lame and stupid as an explanation but it had the merits of filling in an area of darkness. Bechet tutted with anxiety and readjusted his pince-nez. "Well. Well. Well," he said disconsolately, for death was a subject he could not stand—his whole life, constructed of a tissue of routine boredoms, had been designed to shelter him from the realisation that he was gradually approaching death. Tholon was made of different stuff, being much younger. He studied the big yellow chart with gravity. "I have noted all the names," he said, and one could sense that a formidable dossier was on the way to being assembled.

"So they are all dead?" said Bechet with distaste.

"Yes."

35

"But why the singular shape of the map, which looks like a sort of snake?"

"It is a snake—for this little sect death in an individual assumes the shape of a constellation, the Serpent. The snake symbolises process, even time itself."

Bechet almost groaned at these obscurities. He looked quite alarmed, and I realised that it was time to spare him. So much of this must have sounded rubbish to him. "At any rate that is what he explained to me," I said hastily while the lawyer rubbed his long *ultra*'s nose and sighed.

"Perhaps," said Tholon, scenting my awkwardness, "you would care to spend a little while alone in the room? It is difficult to concentrate when one is with people. But alone and quiet you might notice something of interest. What do you say?" I hesitated. I knew that the good fellow wanted to leave me alone to say a prayer for the soul of my friend. I said I would like to stay if it did not upset anyone. To tell the truth I was anxious to see the back of them and eager to examine the bookshelf and the notebooks of my friend. There may have been a manuscript worth saving from the rapacious curiosity of the police. Tholon at once handed over the keys and the waxed tapes which I must affix. "Just lock up," he said, "and I will come round tomorrow and pick up the keys from your hotel." I thanked him. Bechet seemed eager and relieved to quit the place. But he said: "Just one thing I'd like to have an opinion about. In the will he speaks of his horror at the chance of being buried alive, and asks to have a vein severed. Would you be prepared to do that?" I said that there would hardly be any need for the safeguard in view of the autopsy, and he agreed at once, relieved.

They both went. I heard their voices and footsteps descend in diminishing echoes down the stairs; then the uneasy blurred silence of the city fell upon this tomblike room with its disinherited objects. From time to time the susurrus of traffic might be broken by a clattering stammering outburst of a church-bell, but that was all. So this is where Piers had spent the last hours of his life! I sat down on the foot of the bed and put my hand to the turned-back sheet. It was lukewarm. The room smelt very faintly of joss as well as of drains. I pulled back the bedclothes and was not surprised to find the scarlet bedsocks he always wore to match his vivid Egyptian *babouches*. A dozen pairs of socks he had bought to accompany a dozen pairs of slippers—enough for a lifetime, as he exultantly said: "When you find your colour stick to it."

Most of the books I knew; they bore his bookplate and came from the château library. The notebooks were empty, so that I presumed Sylvie to be in possession of any manuscripts of vital importance. Or else the police had already swept them up. There were a few business letters in the bedside table drawers. Bills. Tradesmen's advertisements posted on to him by the Bag Room of the Quai d'Orsay.

The bathroom was in a fearful mess that was all too customary: a crumpled face towel on the floor by the *bidet* bore lipstick marks—a dark crimsonlike tone which reminded me of something, a memory I could not place for the moment.

I went back into the other room and counted the cigar butts in the big ashtray, calculating that the room had not been cleaned and set to rights for at least a week. There was also a toothmug here, presumably without fingerprints, as I could see it had been dusted over with the traditional talc. It smelt very faintly of alcohol—mouthwash, dentifrice, gin or Luminash? Impossible to say. Then I remembered something and returned to the ashtray in order to pick out

37

two or three little cigarette ends from the darker
pile of butts; they were slender and had gilt tips
marked with the same dark crimson lipstick. Well,
Piers did not smoke these, and his sister did not
smoke at all. I pondered the matter for I knew somebody who smoked precisely this sort of theatrical gilt-
tipped cigarette—loading them with dried grains of
hashish after puncturing them with a pin along their
length: then sealing the punctures with a spittle-
daubed finger. Sabine did! My heart leaped up with
pleasure to think that she might have visited Piers
before the end, even that she might still be in Avignon.
For the colour of the lipstick of her preference had
always been, as Sylvie said, the second cousin of arterial blood. I made a mental note to ring up the old
château where old Banquo presumably lived. Perhaps
by now he was dead? But bankers never die. And yet
I had a feeling that Sabine had most probably disappeared as she always did: she could never stay long
in one place, a few days at most. Then she would be
gone like a wind, following the gipsies into Hungary,
or joining the slow caravans which traverse the wave-
worn desert highways of the spice routes. I had not
run across her for years, this enigmatic woman. Perhaps we should meet again here, in the context of
Piers' disappearance?

I stood before the death-map, adopting something
like the stance that Piers himself always took, hands
behind his back, head cocked reflectively on one side.
I tried to think my way into his recent mind. There
were no dates on his map, just simply the bare recorded fact, the name of a human being who had, in
the act of dying, turned himself into a point-event.
But when one saw the whole thing spread out in this
way, in a schematic fashion, one came closer to realising what had been in Piers' mind as on each occasion
he quietly added another name to the fallen. Every-

one must have a personal calendar of death compiled after this fashion. A war memorial, for example, never achieves this kind of coherence, for it gives too generalised a picture of death. Its universality is stressed and that is all. But in this case each separate single death had discharged itself with a throb of grief onto the heart of Piers, and the succession of falling sadnesses, like the grains of sand in an hour-glass, had gradually weighed upon his heart and his memory: until he realised that he was receiving an education for his own death. The realisation of one's own death is the point at which one becomes adult—he was never tired of repeating this proposition of Akkad's. Yes, that was the inner meaning of the map before which, for so many years and months, he had walked up and down, pondering; each name became a whole constellation of memories. From them he hoped to extract the essential philosophic meaning which would, so to speak, enlighten his own coming death and enable him to write of it with insight and truth. It was an ambitious undertaking but one upon which he had set his heart.

Over the years he has sent me small fragments of autobiographical introduction—which was to be entitled "A Water-biography" because he was astrologically a fish sign as was I. One little fragment I carried in my wallet, written out in his own fluent and lyrical handwriting. It went: "If I must try to describe Piers de Nogaret without benefit of mirrors I must begin by saying that his favourite word was *precarious:* whatever he wrote and thought gravitated towards or away from that word, his pole-star. In spirit and intention he was not a sensualist but an ardent Epicurean. Everything, both the best and the worst, came to him because of his sister in the first instance —for he tried to avoid loving her without avail. This was his greatest single experience, and yet he always felt that it conferred a limitation on his growth—until, that is, he visited Egypt and became a gnostic disciple of the thinker Akkad. The only other love in his life was for a man who loved him with a dispassionate singleness of intent—and who also loved his sister. The three of them could hardly tell themselves apart, became a sort of congeries of loving emotions, all mutually complementary. None of this was achieved without a tremendous struggle against their sense of rightness, logic, even appropriateness. They won, but it severed them from the world, and yet they lived a quasi-worldly life for years, which had little reality outside the company of each other. A happy trinity of lovers. Or so he makes bold to claim."

There was little else in the room to alert a detective, but I lingered on a while, luxuriating in the sense of familiarity conferred on me by these friendly possessions. I knew that I would not come back here and that sooner or later the seals would be taken off and all these items find their way back into some barn or lumber-room at Verfeuille, losing all coherence and identity. His death had invested them with a dramatic significance which they did not merit. There were some notes in the back of a copy of Swift, and I recognised the handwriting of Rob Sutcliffe. "Short story about N who to escape his sister foolishly forced himself to fall in love with a Berlin actress, very romantic, who follows him across Europe in her husband's car, dressed as a chauffeur. Shot at him in Zagreb but the weapon missed fire; he felled her with an umbrella. He had come to study the Caballa with an old Jewish sage whose name he had first heard from a psychiatrist in Zurich. She tried to pay him, pulling out a wad of notes as thick as a sandwich. He fell in love with the gesture and took her to his hotel, only to sneak off at dawn, steal the car and head north."

The tone and the matter were typical of Rob, and half the books in the château contained similar brief plots for stories or novels—a practice which annoyed Toby very much for Sutcliffe appeared in the end to make no use of them. They simply came to him as spontaneously as a limerick might. But afterwards he lost interest in the idea and bothered no more with it. I looked to see whether his name was on the death-map. Yes, there it was, Robert Sutcliffe. How soon would it be before some scholar applied for permission to sift through the mass of documents he had left behind in the muniments room at Verfeuille? His fame was still growing.

It was late when I got back to the hotel, but the bar was still open and I was glad of a stiff whisky before going up to my room. I lay in bed for a while in darkness, thinking; slowly the numbness was wearing off, I was beginning to realise that I would never see my friend again.

The next morning early Bechet phoned the hotel, and with hardly disguised triumph told me his good news. We had a following wind now, for the papers had come back as well as the authorisation to proceed with the funeral. Moreover the police had waived their suspicions, thanks to the *préfet*'s intervention, and were prepared to accept the hypothesis of an accident in default of any firmer evidence. The will was in order. Only the provisions for the funeral were irksome, for the coffin was to be followed by nobody. Bechet wearisomely enumerated these stipulations in his singsong accent, and showed concern when I said that I proposed to violate them. I could not, would not, let Piers go to his grave without one friend from this life beside him, ready to see him over the threshold into the next. Duty and inclination were hand in hand, and I expressed the matter with some force. Bechet pondered and then gave in. As a matter of fact he had already had an altercation with the Abbé, who was furious because he had hoped to conduct a service for Piers, and Bechet had warned him that it would be forbidden. "At any rate," he said, "the old man is determined to come, service or no service. I can't forbid him that, nor you. I will drive you over myself. If I could fix everything for tonight would you agree? I think the sooner it is over the better for all concerned. I will try for tonight and ring you back this afternoon about five. I would like to finish with the matter." I agreed, glad to feel that Piers' case was escaping from the stagnant reaches of French bureaucracy. He added: "By the way, another provision: no flowers. At least we can accept that one, can't we?" I knew the reason for this also: because they were ikons for the living soul which the gnostics did not believe in. The only appropriate and permissible flower would have been sea-lavender, then, which is a sort of fossil rather than a plant. Needless to say I did not disconcert Bechet by repeating all this strange lore.

"Sylvie can't come of course?" he asked.

"Of course not."

"All the better in a way."

"I agree."

He rang off and I prepared myself to wait for the formalities to be completed. By now the remains of Piers must be reposing at the morgue. I suppose that I should have mustered the courage to visit him there, but I could not bring myself to do it. It was a contemptible lack of courage really—and in a doctor with a wide acquaintance with surgery—to funk it. But I did. I did.

Yet the thought of getting the funeral over was itself a relief, and I spent the morning wandering round the bookshops and recalling the past. There was no longer a soul in the place who recognised me, or if there was I did not meet one. I was back for an early lunch, still perplexed by the silence of Toby, who by all calculations should by now have reached the town from Oxford. But in case the night was going to be a late one I took the wise precaution of closing my shutters and taking a siesta, for the deep fatigue of the last two days had told heavily on me.

In my dreams I found my way back to the old château, to the Verfeuille of the distant past, that strange catalyst of a stranger love; back to the life of the past with its extra-real flavour. Verfeuille sheltered us, and within its walls happiness became an imperative. Now circumstances had scattered the pieces, an invisible hand had overturned the chessboard. But sleep is merciful. In my dream nothing had changed as yet. I turned the leaves as one turns back a vine to catch glimpses of the old house between the branches. How could we have taken it all so much for granted?

It stands high up on the westward slopes of the Alpilles and from the highest orchards you can see not only misty Avignon in the plains below, but snatches of Arles and Tarascon as well. The winding roads lead steadily upwards towards it with a graceful inevitability, passing through rich olive holdings, the grey-silver leaves ashiver at the least caress of the mistral. The plots around the old house are so rich in springs, and the soil so correspondingly rich and loamy, that the ancients planted oak and plane and chestnut to make a verdant green shade around the house and protect it from sun and wind alike. Colonies of nightingales sing there by day and night to the tune of splashing water, while the hum of the cicada, deafening in August, provided a steady drizzle, as if of strings, as a background. Of the twin lions guarding the gates of the lodge one had lost a paw and the other half of the ceremonial sword he once held so proudly, point downward; as for the massive wrought-iron gates themselves, they had been carried away and melted down as a contribution to the war effort of 1418. The weeds have long since turned the gravel driveway to a mossy causeway where the wheels of a car tend to skid slightly in wet weather. On this unexpected carpet of silence one turns and twines for what seems an age before the house comes into view, perched slightly at an angle in order to take the best of the sun aspects and set a stout shoulder to the northern quarter from where the butting mistral blows.

The windows, so tall and narrow, wear deep stone eyebrows, while the high donjon, a prodigiously strong square tower, dating from the twelfth century, centres the whole mass, giving a minatory touch of fortress to what is now a comfortable dwelling merging into a farmhouse with all its clumsy dependencies —barns and stables, wine-magazines and olive-presses. The noise of cattle and poultry rules here, and the prismatic dust hangs in sunbeams. None of this will ever change. The whole of this heavy mass with its grilled windows encloses the grand central court-yard to which one gains access via a deeply vaulted passageway—an easily defensible feature; this in turn leads to the vital heart of the place, the great well-head with its carved crucifix and its benches. At each corner of the court rises a quaint and crusty little tourelle from which the besieged could keep up a raking fire along the thick walls.

The main portal consists of a set of massive iron-clamped doors whose rusty teeth fold in upon each other—or once did, for nobody in living memory has ever seen them closed. Now they always stood open and the whole courtyard had the placid look of a place given over to peaceful husbandry. Chickens and ducks have taken possession of it, they wander about gossiping; a venerable goat, untethered, meditates in one corner. From the stables come the stamp of horses and the roars and sighs of cattle, or perhaps the mewing of quail in their wicker cages. An army of pigeons skirmishes impertinently about in all this with the noise of wet linen flapping in the wind. Their own headquarters is the squat bell tower, now transformed into a dovecot, with the Roman hourglass fixed to it.

Everything gravitates towards or away from this central court with its well—though its presiding goddess is not, as so often here, a Roman nymph, but merely an old blindfold horse which is started up each morning like a clock and then left to its own devices. Slowly and painstakingly it covers the trodden circle of its duty, and slowly through the hours the cold well-water is dispersed along a chain of stone troughs.

There were in fact several wells—one indeed in the main barn—which cater nowadays for both cattle and men by courtesy of a brisk electric motor. But the slow overflow from the ancient well, splashing into its basin, is channelled away, and conducted to the salad garden to irrigate the plants there. It is through this little garden with its kitchen herbs that one can reach the more extensive formal gardens of the château—for so long fallen into disrepair. They decline southward and westward and are well sheltered from the sudden inclemencies of the Provençal weather. It is difficult to imagine how they must have looked in their heyday. Ever since I knew them they have remained overgrown and unweeded, full of the romantic melancholy of desuetude. Rob used to say, "Very bad for my poetry this; it makes it all crumbly." None of us shared his feelings when we walked here, either by dawn or by moonlight. No; these gardens abounded in balustraded terraces and ornate stone benches perched at strategic points. Here and there you could happen upon a marble nymph or two in a debased and old-fashioned style, though now made really charming because overgrown by ivy or rambler roses. Here were many sheltered corners which one watched covetously for the first violets or the tender spring flowers; while along their length the beehives stood in rows.

Once all this was a profitable and lovely demesne and in the time of Piers' parents its yield represented a very great fortune. But when they died the two children did not know how to make it work and the whole enterprise became moribund from lack of effective management. It was not their fault—they had both pursued their studies in Paris and London, and for them Verfeuille represented simply a divine haven for summer holidays, nothing more. The decline as gradual but sure. Its great army of retainers began to drift slowly away to more lucrative work; war intervened, then the vine plague, phyloxera, and then a malignant drought one summer. Much of the land was sold off, and some mortgaged; the wood was sacrificed in a bad year, bringing in very little. A succession of small shortsighted follies sapped the economy of the great farm and nibbled away at its yield.

Nevertheless the estate, despite all these limitations, remained a very large one, and perhaps more beautiful because of the neglect, though no farmer would have said so. The country was marvellous, for it lay upon the flanks of the Alpilles and extended outwards from the foothills of the range pointing towards the level region where the Rhône valley widens and begins to merge into the valley of the Durance.

On the higher slopes of the land are straggling groups of self-seeded almond trees—what puffs of delicate smoke-white, smoke-pink they emit in February when they so briefly flower, turning the whole mountainside into an oriental wash-drawing. Lower down reign the more formal olive-terraces—a silver-grey sheen the year long, for this seraphic tree sheds and renews its leaves all the time. Then as the hills dwindle away into the plain come the wide vine-yards and the wheat fields and vegetable holdings (once stocked for the greedy Paris market). But the plantations of fruit trees still bear, falling away in one corner to reveal the distant flats of the tedious Camargue with its lime-green ribbon of shallow sea. In my memory it will always be Christmas here, the Noel of 19——, the year that changed the direction and leaning of my life. Nothing had ever happened to me before—or that is how I felt about the events of that year. I had encountered the inhabitants of Verfeuille a year or two previously, but it was some time before, to my amazement and indeed chagrin (nobody likes to be pushed out of his depth), a classical love set in, and with it the long debate about the rights and wrongs of it. One should I suppose feel like smiling when one thinks of the painful solemnity with which we watched this marvellous ogre advance upon us, club in hand. Sutcliffe pities us, or so he says in his book, because we cut such childish figures, were taken so much by surprise. Had we never (he asks) considered the possibilities of a common passion which might sweep us far out to sea? I wonder. I recall Piers' pale serious face as he said one day: "Well then, it must be love." Rob would have laughed out loud I suppose at the tone, which was that of a doctor making a diagnosis—as if one might say, "Well then, it must be cancer."

(I notice the shift of verb tenses in these hasty

notes—they throw my memories in and out of focus, as time itself and reality melts in and out of focus when you dream.)

In those days Piers took his seigneurial obligations rather seriously and felt it very much his duty to be present for Saint Babara's day, the fourth of December—for the old Provençal Christmas begins with the planting of wheat or lentil seed in little bowls which were then set upon the broad window-sills to ripen. Their growth, and other little indications, would give one firm information about the state of the weather during the coming four seasons. At that time I think Piers nourished some ambitions about restoring the property to its old affluence; but if so, they soon declined steadily, undramatically, as did the number of servants. A bare dozen were now left—a few too old for serious labour, and a great many children who were as yet too young to be pressed into anything more exacting than the olive-picking of late November. The relationship had become a much closer one because of this depletion—poverty and lack of numbers had created the bondages of a smaller family.

But there were other factors this year, troubling ones. For Piers had as yet not announced his intention of leaving the château the following summer to follow a career. His nomination had only just been ratified by the Diplomatic Board in Paris, and he was as yet uncertain of his first posting. How momentous for him that it should later turn out to be Cairo! Nevertheless he was full of sadness, the thought of leaving the family home was a dire wrench. It threw into relief the stagnating fortunes of the place, the decayed husbandry of the land, the lack of financial viability. Verfeuille was bleeding to death and here he was deserting it. . . .

Paradoxically, though, a profession would enable him to keep the place going, even if it slowly fell apart. At least this way the property itself would continue to belong to him and to his sister, even though encumbered with debts. He had realised by now that he was no farmer and that in this context the condition of the place was irreversible without heavy expenditure and an increase of staff. It had gone too far. But naturally such a decision, as well as its causes, was very hard to explain or justify to family retainers whose doglike devotion and trust were completely unreasoning. He was aware of the anxiety his announcement would cause. But it had to be so, for he proposed to appoint one of the older servants as steward of the estate in the hope that he might hold his ground at home while he himself was absent on duty abroad. He had gone ahead then, while Sylvie and I had elected to stay on in Avignon, and then pick up horses at the halfway house and ride the last few miles to the château. Our saddle-bags were full of presents, coloured sweets for the children, confetti, crystallised fruit, and little bottles of cognac and liqueurs. Also we had brought a huge family of little *santons* of painted teracotta for the crèche. No Provençal Christmas is complete without these little figures which populate and deck out the family crèche, which itself does the duty of our northern Yule-tide Tree. Originally the cast, so to speak, was a small one, restricted to the Holy Family and two or three other personages who figured directly in the legend, like the kings and so forth; but under the influence of the hardy Provençal sense of poetry the whole thing had flowered rhapsodically and we had found in the shops about forty *santons,* all different. Their verisimilitude might have been suspect but they brought the story up to date with characters out of stock like the village policeman, a poacher, a Camargue cowboy, and the like. All this gear was carefully wrapped against breakages and stowed in our capacious saddle-bags before we attacked the slow winding ascent to the château. The horses were fresh and faced the path in lively fashion. But a misty period had set in and the journey needed a little caution also, for neither of us had done this ride for several years and anyway never in winter; we had all but forgotten the devious and winding bridle paths and the fire brakes which crossed and recrossed the main road as it rose into the hills. From time to time all visibility was reduced to nil, and then Sylvie, who was in a particularly mischievous mood, pushed her horse into a canter, to be swallowed at once in the mist. It was not a procedure to be recommended and the second time she did it I plunged after her and punished her with an embrace that left her breathless; feeling her cold lips and nose against my face, seeking me out. Such was its magnetism that we became fused into this posture, unwilling to detach ourselves from each other. I tried to at last—for I could feel the mist condensing into droplets on the collar of my old tweed coat; but she whispered "Stay" and it was only too easy to obey her. We were not far off our landfall now, in a forest of tall trees which dripped moisture all around. Among those muttered endearments I recorded one or two phrases which underlined her own astonishment at our situation, as well as a doubt which was the twin of my own, and also Piers'. Ah! Later Sutcliffe was to make cruel fun of us three in his book. "They are so happy. They admire themselves. They have invested a wedding cake in each other. A slice under each pillow, O desirable treat. An unholy trinity of romantics, a love sandwich with the perplexed and thick-thewed Bruce making the filling." I was glad that he was later so badly punished by my sister Pia—an ignoble emotion, but these passages were wounding. "I have stolen you from Piers, and he has stolen me from you? What can it mean?" I told her there was no loss to be reckoned out. "Not with lost property—the lost-and-found department had caught up with us three." These sounded like inspired confidences to us: Rob would have thought us mawkish and refused to believe in the reality of our case, our emotions. I was glad that I did not know at the time, it was only years afterwards that the book made its appearance. By that time he was himself going through a bad period and had little sympathy, it seems, to spare for someone else.

He even invented a diary for Piers to keep, describing him opening it each night to make a forlorn entry "by the grave light of two tall-stemmed candles," if you please. And this is the sort of thing he wrote to attach as a literary pendant to our situation. "It was very late in the day to realise, but at last I did. It was imperative to send them away together, my sister and Bruce: or face losing both. For the lovers had moved into such a deep phase that they had become almost alarmed for themselves as well as for me. We were held in a kind of fixity of purpose, the three of us like the rings of Saturn. One can only love like this, to utter distraction, when one is young, altogether too young. A breath of real experience would cloud the mirror. They felt unable to extricate themselves from each other, from the triune bond. In them flowed a sort of tidal sadness—the equinox of a first and last attachment; the advancing and receding waters closed over their heads. And being swept away like this they found themselves drifting towards the falls." All this was entirely imaginary; I have never been in Venice, but as he knew it well, he used a novelist's licence to transplant us there. Our intensity was of another order, less literary. Yet "Even the physical envelope, lips eyes bodies seemed to have become somehow mental contrivances only; the three inseparables seemed to themselves all mingled up, like a plate of spaghetti. But Venice did the trick, Venice exorcised the act. So the three of them were able to walk silently arm in arm among the marble griffins and the swerving canals, or sit silently playing cards on the green tables at Florian's. A strange trio, the brother and sister so lean and dark, like lizards, and their blond captive with his thickset form and rather simple peasant expression. The girl would obviously look a thorough shrew at forty with her long canny Mediterranean nose; the brother was slightly touched with romantic mountebank." So that is how he saw us when it came to give us the definitive form of print. I have never recovered from my astonishment!

And he has the effrontery to add: "Real love is silent, or so they say. But never was the green Venetian silence of the trio so energetic, never did words whispered at night burn so deeply down, guttering like candles in the sconces of memory."

None of this was as yet part of the present kiss, the present cold small nose; she had undone my shirt and placed her icy fingers over my heart. But the horses were restless now, for they had been very patient under the boredom of this long embrace and were longing for the warm stables which they knew must lie ahead, somewhere beyond the mist. Their hooves clicked, and the cold air turned their breath to pencils of spume. What could they care about the meeting of three separate solitudes? Meanwhile the imaginary romantic diarist had written, according to the novelist: "They actually dared to love, then, even though they knew that the end of all love was detachment or rancour or even horror; that it ended in despair, or even suic . . . But I dare not write the word." This at least was a prophetic piece of invention on his part; but it is the only thing that touches the fringes of the truth. The so-called infernal happiness which he attempts to describe is altogether too theatrical to belong to us. We were babes in the wood, innocents abroad.

The horses drew away, delighted by the vague outlines of everything and aching for another canter; we set off down a ride and at that moment, deep in the mist, we heard the shrill but musical voices of children, chattering and chirping. It was so uncanny that, mindful of the folktales of the country, we wondered if we were approaching a band of mist-fairies in the obscurity of the tenebrous forest. "Nonsense," I said robustly in the voice I use to reassure patients with terminal illnesses that they will live for ever. "Nonsense. It's a school excursion." But as we advanced the sound seemed to recede from us so that we quickened our pace in the hope of catching it up. And with the swaying of the horses and the meanderings of the paths the voices themselves seemed to change direction, coming now from this side, and now from that. And despite my hardened rationalist scepticism I confess that for a moment I hesitated and wondered about the provenance of those shrill voices. But on we went, picking our way and listening.

Then, rolling back like a curtain, the mist shifted aside and we came upon another path, at right angles to our own, down which poured a line of flesh-and-blood children of all ages, skipping and chattering, with their arms full of greenery. They were laden with crèche-making materials they had gathered— mosses, ferns, lichens, laurel and long polished branches of holly and mistletoe. The holly they carried like sceptres—the small-berried holly, the one they call still *li poumeto de Sant-Jan* in Provençal, or "the little apples of St. John." With a cry of pleasure Sylvie now recognised the children of the château, and she dismounted to kiss and hug them all and to ask if her brother had arrived safely. They cheered when they knew that we were bringing the rest of the material for the crèche. It was also a surprise to realise how close the house was: the mist had been playing tricks of visibility on us, though we were comforted to find our direction-finding so good.

But now we were engulfed in this happy throng, so that we hand-led our horses—perching the singing children on their backs. And so at last in triumph we came to the main portal of the château where their parents waited anxiously, peering out into the forest from time to time, watching for their return.

The familiar smiling faces were all there—old Jan, clad in his sheepskin jacket, the firelight behind him in the great hall turning his silver hair into a halo. A little behind stood his quiet and sturdy wife Elizo. Marius was their son and the apple of their eye—a man of forty with broad shoulders and sweeping black moustaches. A younger man, Esprit, came out to help us unpack our luggage. Then all the girls streamed out to embrace us, the children and the grand-children with names like Magali, Janetoun, Mireille, Nanoun. Here after the ceremonial embrace we were offered the traditional posset of red wine with its mulled spices, the old warmer-up for winter travellers. In the ensuing babble, with all of them trying to talk at once, we hardly noticed the absence of Piers. But he was far from absent, for when at last we reached the great hall with its blazing logs we saw him standing looking down from the first landing, smiling in shadow and delightedly watching. Then he came skipping down the broad staircase with its carved balustrade, but a trifle shyly, as if to control his ardour, his affection. When all the greetings were given and all the questions answered we were free, just the three of us, to mount the staircase arm in arm and take the long white corridors which led to his room, which lay beyond a small gallery of pictures, for the most part ancestors, smoked black by time and the wood fires. At the end of the gallery, in a somewhat disconcerting fashion stood an easel on which was propped a large cork archery target, plumped full of arrows with different-coloured feathers. Piers spent a good deal of time practising here with the great yew bow he had bought in London. The whipple of the flying arrows sounded throughout the house when he did so. His private rooms, so full of books and masks and foils and shot-guns, had old-fashioned vaulted ceilings. The petroleum lamps and the tall silver candlesticks threw warm shadows everywhere. In the tall fireplace bristled furze, olive and holm-oak which smelt divine. Everything had been timed exactly for the Christmas feast and Piers was beside himself with joy because there were no unexpected hitches or delays. Moreover in two days' time Toby and Rob (the Gog and Magog of our company) were due to arrive and bring with them the lighthearted laughter and inconsequence which made them such excellent company.

We sat now, the three of us cross-legged on the floor before the fire, eating chestnuts and drinking whisky and talking about nothing and everything. Never had old Verfeuille seemed so warmly welcoming. If we had an inner pang as we remembered Piers' decisions for the future we did not mention them to each other. It would not have been fair to the time and the place to intrude our premonitions and doubts upon it. But underneath the excitement we were worried, we had a sense of impending departure, of looming critical change in our affairs—in this newly found passion as well. As if sensing this a little Piers said, during a silence, "Cheer up, children.

Yesterday we went out and selected the Yule Log—
a real beauty this year." He described to me the little
ceremony in which the oldest and the youngest member of the whole household go out hand in hand to
choose the tree which will be felled for Christmas,
and then return triumphantly to the house bearing it
with, of course, the assistance of everyone. It was
paraded thrice around the long supper table and
then laid down before the great hearth, while old
Jan undertook to preside over the ceremony of the
libation, which he did with great polish, filling first
of all a tall jar of *vin cuit*. Describing it Piers acted
him to the life, in half-humorous satire—his smiling
dignity and serenity as he bowed his head over the
wine to utter a prayer while everyone was deeply
hushed around him, standing with heads bowed.
Then he poured three little libations on the log, to
Father, Son and Holy Ghost, before crying out with
all the vigour he could muster in his crackly old
voice:

> *Cacho-fio!*
> *Bouto-fio!*
> *Alègre! Alègre!*
> *Dieu nous alègre!*

> Yule Log Burn
> Joy Joy
> God give us Joy.

And as he reached the last words of the incantation,
which were "Christmas has arrived," a huge bundle of vine trimmings was set alight under the ceremonial log and the whole fireplace flamed up, irradiat-
ing the merry faces of the company, as if they too
had caught fire from sympathy with the words; and
now everyone embraced anew and clapped hands,

while the old man once more filled the ceremonial bowl with wine, but this time passed it about as a loving-cup, beginning with little Tounin the youngest child: and so on in order of seniority until at last it came back to his hand. Then he threw back his head and drained it to the dregs, the firelight flashing on his brown throat. Suddenly Piers, despite himself, was seized with a pang of sadness and tears came into his eyes: "How the devil am I going to leave them, do you think? And what is going to happen to us, to It?" It was not the time for such questions and I told him so. I finished my drink and consulted my watch. In a little while it would be in order to tackle the second half of the ceremony, which consisted in decking out the crèche with the candles and figurines. I was glad of the diversion, for this little aside of his had wakened all kinds of doubts in me—about the future which awaited us, the separations. . . . Sylvie appeared with her arms full of things, dressed now in the full peasant dress of Avignon and looking ravishing. Everyone clapped her. "Hurry and dress," she told us, "before we do the Holy Family."

It did not take long. My own rooms were on the eastern side of the house. Thoughtful hands had placed a copper warming pan full of coals in my bed, while a small fire, carefully shielded by a guard, crackled in the narrow hearth. I lit my candles and quickly put on the traditional black velvet coat which Piers had given me, with its scarlet silk lining; also the narrow stove-pipe pantaloons, dark sash and pointed black shoes—*tenue de rigueur* for Christmas dinner in Verfeuille. Piers himself would wear the narrow bootlace tie and the ribbon of the *félibre,* the Provençal poet. I hastened, and when I got downstairs Sylvie was already there trying to bring some order into the candle-lighting ceremony, which was almost swamped by the antics of high-spirited children flitting about like mice. She managed to control the threatened riot and before long they were all admiring the colour and form of the little figurines as they were unwrapped one by one. Soon a constellation of small flames covered the brown hillsides of Bethlehem and brought up into high prominence the Holy Family in the manger, attended by the utterly improbable kings, gipsies, queens, cowboys, soldiers, poachers and postmen—not to mention sheep, ducks, quail, cattle and brilliant birds. Then came the turn of Piers, who exercised a bit more authority, to unwrap and distribute the wrapped presents, all duly labelled, so that nobody should feel himself forgotten on this memorable eve. Great rejoicing as the paper was ripped and torn away; and so gradually the company drifted slowly away to dinner. This had been laid in the great central hall—the long table ran down the centre with more than enough room for the gathering of that year. We three were seated at a cross-table which formed the cruciform head with Jan and his wife on our right and left respectively. Candles blazed everywhere and the Yule Log by this time had begun to thresh out bouquets of bright sparks into the chimney.

It was not a place or time easy to forget, and I had returned to it so often in my thoughts that it was no surprise to relive all this in my dreams. I must have unconsciously memorised it in great detail without being fully aware of the fact at the time. I know of no other place on earth that I can call up so clearly and accurately by simply closing my eyes: to this very day.

Its floor was laid with large grey stone slabs which were strewn with bouquets of rosemary and thyme: these helped to gather up the dust when one was sweeping, as well as things like the bones which were often thrown to the hunting dogs. The high ceiling was supported by thick smoke-blackened beams from which hung down strings of sausages, chaplets of garlic, and numberless bladders filled with lard. More than a third of the rear wall was taken up by the grand central fireplace which measured some ten feet across and at least seven from the jutting mantelpiece to the floor. In its very centre, with room each side in chimney corners and angles, stood old wicker chairs with high backs, and wooden lockers for flour and salt. The mound of ash from the fires was heaped back against the back of the fireplace, which itself was crossed by a pair of high andirons which flared out at the top, like flowers, into little iron baskets, so often used as plate-warmers when filled with live coals. They were furnished with hooks at different levels destined for the heavy roasting spits. From the mantelshelf hung a short red curtain designed to hold the smoke in check when the fire became too exuberant, as it did with certain woods, notably olive. Along the wide shelf above the fire were rows of objects at once utilitarian and intriguing because beautiful, like rows of covered jars in pure old faïence, ranging in capacity from a gill to three pints, and each lettered with the name of its contents—saffron, pepper, cummin, tea, salt, flour, cloves. Tall bottles of luminous olive oil sparked with herbs and spices had their place here. Also a number of burnished copper vessels and a giant coffee-pot. And further along half a dozen tall brass or pewter lamps with wicks that burned olive oil—as in the time of the Greeks and Romans—but rapidly being superseded by the more modern paraffin-burning ones.

To the right of the fireplace was the wide stone sink with rows of shelves above to take a brilliant army of copper pots and pans—a real *batterie de cuisine*. To the left a covered bread-trough, above which hung the large salt and flour boxes of immediate use together with the bread-holder—a sort of cage or cradle in dark wood, ornamented with locks and hinges of polished iron.

On the opposite side of the room was the tall curiously carved Provençal buffet, solid and capacious, and shining under its glossy varnish, the colour of salad oil. Then, to the left of it, the grandfather clock —a clock which was so much of a martinet that it assertively struck the hours in duplicate. Some old rush-bottomed chairs stood about awkwardly—for there was no real thought about luxury or even comfort here. The order of things was ancestral, traditional; history was the present, and one did not conceive of altering things, but simply asserting their traditional place in life, and in nature. As well try to alter the course of the planets. Beyond the bread-trough hung a long-shanked steel balance with a brass dish suspended by delicate brass chains, all brilliant with scouring by soap, flour and sand. Then among a straggle of farm implements standing against one wall was an ancient fowling piece resting in wooden crutches driven between two broken flags. The walls were heavily decorated with sentimental lithographs and oleographs, depicting scenes from the local folklore of the region; and, inevitably, with numberless old family pictures, now all faded away into a sepia anonymity—faces of unforgotten people and events, harvests, picnics and bullfights, tree-plantings, bull-brandings, weddings and first communions. A whole life of austere toil and harmless joy of which this room had been the centre, the pivot.

But the wine was going about now and the most important supper of the whole year was in full sail. By old tradition it has always been a "lean" supper, so that in comparison with other feast days it might have seemed a trifle frugal. Nevertheless the huge dish of *raïto* exhaled a wonderful fragrance: this was a ragout of mixed fish presented in a sauce flavoured with wine and capers. Chicken flamed in Cognac. The long brown loaves cracked and crackled under the fingers of the feasters like the olive branches in the fireplace. The first dish emptied at record speed, and its place was taken by a greater bowl of Rhône pan-fish, and yet another of white cod. These in turn led slowly to the dishes of snails, the whitish large veined ones that feed on the vine-leaves. They had been tucked back into their shells and were extracted with the aid of strong curved thorns, three or four inches long, broken from the wild acacia. As the wine was replenished after the first round, toasts began to fly around.

Then followed the choice supporting dishes like white *cardes* or *cardon,* the delicious stem of a giant thistle which resembles nothing so much as an overgrown branch of celery. These stems are blanched and then cooked in white sauce—I have never tasted them anywhere else. The flavour is one of the most exquisite one can encounter in the southern regions of France; yet it is only a common field vegetable. So it went on, our last dinner, to terminate at last with a whole anthology of sweetmeats and nuts and winter melons. The fire was restoked and the army of wine-bottles gave place to a smaller phalanx of brandies, Armagnacs and Marcs, to offset the large bowls of coffee from which rose plumes of fragrance.

Now old Jan's wife placed before the three lovers a deep silver sugar bowl full of white sugar. It lay there before them in the plentitude of its sweetness like a silver paunch. The three spoons she had placed in it stood upright, waiting for them to help themselves before the rest of the company. The toasts and the jests now began to subside, sinking towards the ground like expiring fireworks, and the time for more serious business was approaching. By tradition every year Piers made a speech which gave an account of the year's work, bestowing praise or censure as he thought fit. But this time his news was momentous and would affect the fate of everyone in the room. I could see that the idea worried him as much as it did his sister, who glanced at him from time to time with affectionate commiseration. After many hesitations—for he changed places more than once to have a private word with this person and that—he rose and tapped for silence, to be greeted with loud applause and raised glasses by the very people whom his speech would sadden.

He stood, resigned and a little pale, while he allowed it to subside, before beginning with the Christmas wishes. He then went on by saying that he had been a trifle sad and preoccupied that evening because of the news he had to give them. Not that it was downright tragic, far from that; but all change made one sorry and sad. "But before I speak of the journey I must make let me speak of the new arrangements which will come into force when I leave. First, I raise my glass to old Jan, closer to me than my father. He will become the *régisseur* of Verfeuille while I am absent *en mission*." The whole speech was most skilfully executed, and touched everywhere with feeling and thoughtfulness. He reassigned the role of each of the servants, stressing the increase in their responsibilities and according each one a small rise in pay. This caused great joy and satisfaction and much kissing and congratulation followed each announcement. It was a good augury for his diplomatic role to follow—for by the time he came to the sad part of his speech his audience was cheerful, fortified by all this Christmas bounty. This enabled him to come firmly and honestly to the root of the matter and explain without equivocation that the choice before him was to find a financial way of keeping on the property or else to sit and watch it slowly swallowed up by debts. He had decided to seek a post in a profession which he knew, but, he added, there was one promise to be made. We three would always come back to Verfeuille in the summer, to spend whatever holidays we got there. Everyone cheered and approved these robust sentiments, but for my part I foresaw that we might be forced to separate, for my medical finals were coming up that autumn, and I did not know what the future might hold in store. It would not have been possible to foresee the extraordinary fluke that landed me in the Foreign Service post within three months of passing them. At that moment I was possessed by a deep, numbing nostalgia for the land where I had spent the happiest hours of my life—in Aramon, say, among the cherry trees, on green grass, with summer round the corner; or Fons or Collias, or a dozen other spots where we had camped. A sombre sadness possessed me as I watched the preoccupied face of Sylvie.

A short and thoughtful silence fell upon the banqueters as they took in the full import of the words; as if in their minds they were trying out the absence of Piers, to see how it would feel without him. At that moment there came a light but peremptory knocking on the door of the room which made us all look at each other and wonder who could knock at this time and on this evening. The rapid knock was repeated after a pause and old Jan rose and clicked across the flags to throw open the door into the hall.

Outside it was shadowy, but framed in the winking firelight was someone whom I took to be a gipsy for she wore the motley patchwork of one, with a brilliant headscarf and cheap but very heavy earrings; nor was the supposition so far-fetched for Avignon had a large gipsy colony encamped about its walls, Salon was not far away, and today would be a suitable day to beg for alms. . . . But the apparition moved a step forward into the light and said huskily: "Piers, I heard you were back." The deep voice and the cultivated accent at once belied the trappings, and excited one's curiosity. Her feet were bare and dirty, and one ankle had a grubby bandage on it. Hers was a massive head with small black eyes and a long nose—at first blush one would say an ugly face. But the mobility of expression which changed continuously and the thrilling deepness of the voice were magnetic, startling. There was something authoritative and superb about the woman. Piers embraced her warmly.

This was my first glimpse of Sabine, about whom I then knew little enough; indeed I only knew her name when Piers used it and Sylvie repeated it as a greeting. Later I learned to know her and to admire her—but never as much as Piers, who had a regular passion for the girl. She was the daughter of Lord Banquo, the Jewish banker of international repute, and their château was at Meurre, a dozen kilometres away. After brilliant studies the girl had abandoned the university, and had all but taken to the roads with the gipsies on whom she professed to be basing an ethnographic work. She disappeared for long periods only to reappear at the château without any warning, and resume her old civilised life of a well-groomed and well-spoken only daughter. Her mother was long dead and her father lived from one mistress to the next, for the most part minor actresses. He tired of them rapidly, and replaced them frequently. He was always delighted to have his daughter back, largely for selfish reasons, for she was an excellent hostess and he entertained a great deal. From time to time, when she was in trouble, she turned up at Verfeuille and asked Piers' help and counsel. They had met out riding.

She was an unforgettable sight that first evening and

I watched her curiously and rather jealously, so evident was Piers' attachment for her. On this occasion, as in the past, it was something to do with the gipsies, I do not recall what, but some sort of trouble concerning a man who was then lurking about in the grounds as far as I could gather. After listening to her low voice for a moment, Piers, without a word, took up a lantern and gestured her to lead him out into the forest. They disappeared with startling abruptness through the front door. I noticed that the prudent old Jan went to the gun cupboard and produced a short carbine which he loaded before he too went to the door and stationed himself to wait there, peering out into the night, waiting perhaps for a cry for help. But none came. We could hear a sort of altercation between two male voices; then the deep voice of the girl. At last Piers reappeared swinging the lantern. He was alone. "It's all right," was all he said by way of explanation. "He won't harm her."

By now the old man had discovered that it was nearly time for the village mass. "We will have to hurry up," he said consulting the old clock, "we must set a good example on the day of the days." The company donned hats and scarves and we straggled out into the night with its washed-out late moon trying to guide us. Our feet scratched the flinty path which led away to the tiny hamlet of Verfeuille, whose ancient church was now so ablaze with candles that the whole fragile structure seemed to be on fire. I walked arm in arm with the brother and sister, silent and preoccupied and wondering about the future—the future which has now become the past.

The telephone beside the bed shrilled. Bechet was as good as his word. "Everything has been arranged for this evening," he said in his fussy-complaisant manner. "And I myself will drive you over if you will be ready for me about six. Wait in the hall, please, because of difficult parking on that narrow street." I drowsily agreed. There was a comfortable margin of time in hand which would enable me to have a bath and dress in leisurely fashion. I lay back on the pillows for a moment to recover from this welter of ancient memories—a patchwork quilt of history and sensation. And Sylvie? I rang through to Jourdain and told him what was afoot. He was surprised and also very glad that Bechet had acted promptly and that the authorities had decided to co-operate. As for Sylvie, there was for the present nothing to be done but to let her rest. Nevertheless I promised to come up and visit her on the morrow when everything to do with the funeral had been taken care of. On the one hand I felt a certain elation to think of everything formal being over that very day; but on the other hand I felt certain misgivings, for after all this . . . What? I had decided on nothing, what was I going to do with the rest of my life? I was living from moment to moment. Half my mind was plunged in the past, and half contemplated the future with a sense of disorientation and blankness. And Sylvie?

Much of this passed once more through my mind when at last that evening I sat beside Bechet in his stuffy little car, watching the twilight scenery unroll along the valley of the Rhône; the same opalescent packets of mist about which I had dreamed in the afternoon brimmed the lowland fields. Darkness seemed unduly late for the time of the year but as the time of the ceremony (or non-ceremony) had not been specified there was little cause for anxiety on this score. The old Abbé was driving up in his own car from some village further to the east. Bechet rather dreaded the meeting because of this infernal injunction of Piers about a religious service. "I have put it to him most forcibly," said the lawyer more than once, "and it is my duty as a lawyer to see that his last wishes are complied with. And I shall do it. If he so much as mutters a Hail Mary . . ." He made a vaguely threatening gesture with his chin and drove on with his features composed in a martial expression. As a driver he was a slow and jerky one, and was obviously rather concerned about mist.

It would perhaps have been more reasonable to dwell on the existence of frost on the roads which started to climb upon the steepish flanks of the Alpilles, but this did not seem to enter into his calculations at all. I think the capricious visibility played a little on his nerves, or else perhaps his eyes were weak and old. And at any rate we jogged along, carefully verifying our safety at every corner, while he engaged me in a string of commonplaces about the weather and the probems of motorcars in winter. The tricks of the mist were certainly dramatic—as dramatic as in the dream-memory I had just dreamed —and in one of these sudden snatches we suddenly came upon a sleek black hearse which was ahead of us, and moving in the same direction. Bechet expelled his breath in a whistle and said in a superstitious sort of voice: "That must be the body of Piers being taken up to the château—the hearse belongs to the morgue and they gave me a rendezvous for seven." My heart did a double somersault at this ominous and dramatic vision. We now began to play hide-and-seek with the hearse in the shifting mists as we climbed. There was no frost but a deal of wet, with swatches of sodden leaves clinging to our tyres. The forest grew up round us, sombre and darkling. It was eerier to follow Piers like this, sometimes losing the hearse in the mist only to recover it again at a corner. Once or twice we were right on top of it and Bechet let out a sort of exclamation, at once exasperated and concerned. As a Frenchman from the south he would have had a superstitious nature and might have read something ominous into this long pursuit.

But darkness had already fallen now, and in the frail glow of our headlamps the country looked forlorn and all but deserted. Bechet's anxiety had increased in inverse ratio to his speed. Once or twice cars came in the opposite direction and he shied like a frightened horse and came almost to a standstill. The road had become narrower. I think, too, that he deliberately slowed down his pace in order to lose the hearse, and I was glad of the fact, for its presence afflicted me with a foreboding which was not less unpleasant for being, I knew, senseless. Halfway up the ascent he asked permission to take a rest and a cigarette, drawing the car off the road and halting it while he smoked. The darkness which descended on us when the headlights were switched off was not reassuring either; a deep thawlike night declared itself and the trees dripped moisture on the canvas roof of the car. Bechet did not speak, indeed seemed suddenly weary and distressed as he puffed his thin cigarette. The reason perhaps was that he did not quite know what to expect up at the château, and he wanted to give the mutes time enough to deliver the coffin and take their wretched hearse away before we arrived. At any rate the halt was not too badly calculated as matters turned out for by the time we sneaked and skidded down the last reaches of the avenue leading to the house the black car had already unloaded, and was backing to tackle the return journey to the morgue, its mission accomplished.

But the scene outside Verfeuille was an unusual one, not lacking in colourful strangeness. A tall fire of logs had been lighted—almost the height of a pyre,

of a stake, on which to burn a martyr. It contested
the warmth with the wet night sky. One would have
thought it the eve of Saint John—the only occasion
in the year which is celebrated thus—but this was
not the case. The logs were red-hot and noisy, loosing
a thick column of hot air which drove a broad trail
of sparks up into the canopy of forest trees which
were grouped around the main porch like silent on-
lookers. The front doors of the house were open and
inside there were bright lights; but also wide open
were the doors of the barns and stables on the left,
and they too were brilliantly illuminated within.
Against these complementary flamelights moved a
group of rapt figures thrown into deep silhouette
by the dark which stood between us, and which the
feeble headlights of Bechet's car could do little to
qualify. Their movements seemed slow and laboured
—almost hieratic; and the object they so clumsily
manipulated seemed very heavy. For example, a
farm cart of the old-fashioned sort, with brightly
painted sideboards and a long wooden tongue which
took a double yoke, was being man-hauled out of the
barn. An object more fit for a fair than for a funeral,
one would have said; perhaps there was nothing else
which would do? One figure turning, though standing and watching the work without helping, identified itself as a thin man in priest's robes. Briefly, too,
in that jumping light the painting on the side of the
cart came into view—a picture of angels ascending
into a blue empyrean, their dark curly heads and
olive eyes conspiring with each other as they threw
their appeals upward, skyward; their little white un-
trustworthy hands were raised in tapering fashion to
form poses of prayerful propitiation. Hoof thunder
followed this tableau, as a gigantic farm horse was
backed out of the obscurity of a barn into the light,
to be harnessed and blinkered by a hissing shadow.

The fire made it nervous, it rolled its kind eyes and agitated its carefully plaited tail. It had been polished all over for the occasion like a grand piano. It moved awkwardly from one large hoof to the other as it submitted to the last ministrations of its keepers.

A group of figures, four or five, were busy about the cart now, arranging the couplings. Something black and damascened—a sort of scrolled blanket—was thrown over the cart and then a smaller one over the horse. The priest had taken up a pose like a golfer about to drive off a tee—he had a prayer book in hand. Bechet swore and jumped smartly into action. It was obvious that the peasants could do nothing against the venerable figure of an Abbé, even supposing them to be in the know about Piers' will and his last instructions. There was a brief but sharp little altercation in which the Abbé came off worst, for he hung his head and put away his book; but Bechet was quite out of breath and red-cheeked from the intellectual effort, and I was amazed to see that he had, after all, a backbone.

But he was not in time to prevent the manufacture of this home-made hearse by old Jan and his staff, and it would have been cruel to make them change it now. They had managed already to take possession of the coffin and push it onto the back of the cart; and now somebody ran up with a glossy black plume and fixed it to the crown of the horse's head. What a religion to be buried in, no wonder Piers had renounced it! Nor could I coax up more charitable feelings by glancing at the thin foxy face of the priest as he scornfully watched the proceedings; then he bowed his head defiantly and appeared to sink into deep prayer. I glanced at Bechet to see whether he had noticed this illegal performance or not; but he was looking the other way. I vaguely recognised old Jan, walking about in shaky fashion, but still very much in charge of things, giving orders in a low voice, and setting everything to rights. The flames rose higher, shining on the sweaty peasant faces and great paws sticking out of dark Sunday suits.

A slight powdery snow had begun to fall, but was melting instantaneously in the hot column of sparks from the fire. Cumbrously the cart was reversed now and set square upon the gravel path. The priest woke from his intercession with the forces of darkness and moved towards the cart; I caught a glimpse of a long deceitful face, narrow as a dog's. His lips were drawn back over yellowish teeth He was very tall and skeletonic, and must have been in his seventies. The whole set of his face suggested contemptuous vexation—presumably due to the lawyer's insistence. Bechet now stepped within the pale of the firelight and introduced me. I received a glance like a sword-thrust. He must have known of my existence to look at me so keenly. Then his priest's face went hard as a rock and he turned away. But by now all was in readiness. Out of the front door came shawled women *endimanchées* and Sunday men, all the retainers of the place in fact, and we formed up behind the towering farm cart in a sad procession.

We set off into the darkness, away from the crepitations of the fire, with only the music of the huge hooves to guide us. We had one or two lanterns and by common consent they headed the procession. Jan walked holding the horse's head, his own lantern held aloft to light his path. So we crunched across the gravel and then onto a wide mossy pathway which led to the family vault which had been built in a secluded part of the forest, thick with sycamores and planes. During this slow descent I somehow managed to make myself known to Jan and his son, while two of the women darted at me to take my hand and press it to their wet cheeks. We spoke hardly at all, but there was a note of reproach in their voices which was not hard to interpret; it was as if this perfunctory burial were robbing not only death of its proper dues, but also them of their time-honoured rights as mourners. This was not a fitting way to do things. What would become of the spirit of my poor friend if his body was rushed to the grave without any religious rites to smooth its sad way? Had the place and time permitted they would have interceded with me on this score, I knew that; and I was glad that we had delayed our journey. Now it was too late to change things. As we approached the vault in the deep woods we were joined by other little lantern-led groups of neighbours and friends. Jan waved his old warped hand to them bidding them join us, and gradually a long glowworm of light followed the cart.

Soon we were walking down a pathway bordered by a broad canopy of shrubs on either side; they met overhead and sheltered us from the powdery snowfall. I found all this a winding and gloomy walk to the burial place. The sky above us was silent and void of stars. We came at last to the site of the vault with its dilapidated urns, crude *putti* and detestable cypress trees, which had always made my heart contract with distress—even before, I mean, there was any association involving Piers. I hated them as Horace had once hated them. Here we halted irresolutely, the place was in darkness; but old Jan had the key and he now addressed himself to the task of opening the iron grille. It was a bit rusty, and I stepped out to give the old man a helping hand. After much coaxing the thing yielded. By the light of the lanterns which had been placed on the ground, we descended the flight of broad steps which led to the door of the vault. This by contrast was quite new and the lock had recently been changed. Pushed gently, it opened on blackness. We turned back for our lanterns. It seemed to me that the place had not been swept out for some long time; dead leaves littered the floor, and there were dead snails curled up in one corner. But all this was quickly remedied for one of the women had brought a straw broom with her and, while the rest of us were busy manoeuvring to get a purchase on the coffin and convey it down the shallow stairway, she set to and swept out the vault at full speed.

Now there was light which enabled us to look around a bit. It was a musty enough place but larger than it had at first seemed. There were tombs of several periods and not a few cobwebbed side-chapels; but there were several blank, unoccupied emplacements, and it was towards one of these that we headed with the covered coffin. Shadows by lantern-light bobbed and danced; figures suddenly became giants or diminished to dwarfs. Here normally Piers should have lain at rest for a whole night and a day, while his friends and servants filed by for a last look at his quiet face before leaving the chapel to be bricked in by the masons. But now the absence of a formal ceremony created a peculiar hiatus. By the light of lanterns on the ground everyone looked at his or her neighbour, then crossed himself and muttered a prayer. From the Abbé's point of view this unorganised praying was little short of scandalous. He stood motionless, chin on breastbone, as if in deep meditation. In an unvoluntary and sheepish fashion we had formed up behind him in the posture of a congregation, waiting until he should return to this world and give us permission to depart. It was awkward. He stayed thus for what seemed an age; then slowly turning round he gazed at us with a vague and abstracted eye, as if his thoughts were far away. He opened his mouth as if to say something and then appeared to think better of it; he closed it again and shook his head, uttering as he did so a profound sigh. "So we must leave him," he said and turned round on his heel.

For no reason that I can fathom this ordinary remark touched off something in me, an irrational feeling of self-contempt—perhaps because I had been too cowardly to go and visit Piers in the morgue. At any rate I was seized by a kind of panic as I saw one of the farmhands advancing with a screwdriver and a fistful of brass screws. I must, I felt, look once more, for the last time, on the face of my friend before the coffin was screwed down and the embrasure irremediably bricked up. I had noticed that the coffin was of the continental kind with a hinged lid to reveal the face in the case of a lying-in-state. I stepped impulsively forward to put my feelings into practice —I had almost pushed back this section of the coffin —when they laid firm hands on my arm. Priest and notary on either side of me prevented the execution of the deed with a sudden alarm which was hard to understand. "But why?" I cried angrily as they forced me slowly back. But they were as incoherent as they were adamant. Against my will I submitted and allowed myself to be gently pushed back to the grating, and finally up the steps. It was astonishing; but of course this was no place and time for violence or an altercation. What struck me was that Bechet and the Abbé both participated in this restraining action. Their vehemence as well as their unity of purpose struck me as highly irrational. What could it be to them that I should take a last look at Piers before they closed him down? I was furious and also puzzled, but I swallowed my resentment temporarily and stood for a while on the steps gazing into the yellow pool of light and reflecting. The wind whimpered in the trees. At last there came the tapping and the screech of coffin-screws being sunk into place.

Then one by one the stragglers assembled once more in the dark holding their lamps and lanterns. On the way back to the house the procession slowly dissolved as we traversed the dark woods. Bechet walked beside me with the Abbé on his right. For a while he said nothing and then, feeling no doubt that silence without a platitude to ornament it would make us uneasy, gave a sigh and said: "Human life! How short and how precarious it is." But the priest said nothing as he trudged on with a kind of dogged misery. Nothing!

Inside the hall of the house a good fire had been stoked up, while the pyre outside was slowly being put out by the drizzle. It offered some warmth and cheer on such a gloomy evening. The priest and the notary (those two infamous figures of French life) settled down at a table at the far end of the room and addressed themselves to a sheaf of papers which Bechet extracted from a battered suitcase: attestations of death, burial or whatnot I supposed; or perhaps the last will and testament. At any rate they seemed much preoccupied with the business, whatever it was. I betook myself to the far corner by the fire, where old Jan brought me a jug of mulled red wine and sat down beside me in the chimney corner which we shared with Elfa, the favourite gun-dog of the house. For a while now we sat, saying nothing. From time to time Jan gazed sideways at my face as if about to speak, and then renounced the idea—as if he could find no words to do justice to his feelings. The familiar silence of the house settled about us, except for the scratch of pens and shuffle of paper in the far corner. On a sudden impulse I said: "Jan, tell me why they did not let me look upon Piers in his coffin—or for that matter any of you? Eh?" In a sense the question was rhetorical, as I did not expect an easy answer from old Jan; I was simply airing a grievance, that was all. But he looked at me with a new incredulous expression, as if I was asking a silly question to which everyone must know the answer. I stared at him in a puzzled way and repeated "Why?" And he continued to stare at me with the same expression; then he said: "You know very well there was nothing to see. The body had no head. The men from the morgue said so. Surely you knew that—and Monsieur the lawyer? Surely he knew?"

The information was like a thunderclap. The words fell upon my ear like a deafening report. No head! "That is why they restrained you," the old man continued. "They thought you had forgotten about it." He gazed at my dumbfounded expression with sympathetic concern. It took a moment or two to get back my self-possession and accustom myself to the thought that we had been burying a headless man. But *why?* But what on earth could such a charade mean—if both Bechet and the priest were in the know why had they not told me? On the other hand perhaps it was all rubbish—perhaps old Jan had got hold of the wrong end of the stick, misunderstood a chance remark, muddled up a conversation in that old head of his?

An idea struck me; and I asked: "Did you see it with your own eyes?" He looked at me sadly and nodded. "So you are quite sure." He nodded again in a surprised way. I drank a long draught of wine and reflected. "Then how do we know for certain that the body was that of Piers?" I asked. It was his turn to look astonished; clearly the doubt had never crossed his mind. Then his face cleared, the explanation had come to him. "By the right arm," he said, "the wound."

I knew then what he meant. He made the gesture of drawing back his sleeve as he said: "They exposed the arm for all to see." Not many years ago Piers had had a very serious skating accident in Davos which resulted in a gash along the length of his right arm—it severed tendons and created a permanent disability, enfeebling his grasp with that hand. The cicatrice of this old wound was quite unmistakable. Obviously when they came to lay out the headless body they had drawn back the sleeve to expose this irrefutable mark of identity. Old Jan, in describing the fact, used a Provençal expression which is used by poulterers in describing the procedure by which rabbits are skinned in such a way as to leave their ears as a form of identification. The use of this word gave me gooseflesh.

I suppose that at this point I should have turned savagely on Bechet and demanded some sort of explanation. After all, the truth could have been quite ordinary, quite banal, and easily explicable. I should have asked but I was seized by a singular sort of constraint, almost a *pudeur*. Instead I went to the lavatory and was violently sick; while the two muttering men pursued their long conversation at the far end of the hall.

It did not last very long, for presently Becket stood up and signalled to me his readiness to depart. I went up to them to bid the priest goodbye; he wore a haggard and sorrowful expression, and gazed at me curiously. Becket flapped and flurried about snow on the pass and mist along the foothills. Why did I not tackle him directly there and then about the burial? I do not really know. I followed him tamely out into the darkness, having first embraced old Jan and other members of the clan, promising them that I would return soon to stay in the château. They made all sorts of extravagant promises about the place, but I knew it would never regain its solvency; and it was inexpressibly painful to think of coming back here all alone. We regained the car, and a moist fog swirled about the headlights, but this was a good sign for it smelt of a thaw, while here and there one felt a small push of wind from the northern sector. The merest puff of mistral along the Rhône valley and everything would become cold but clear as glass, with a blue sky to crown it.

"I'm glad it's over," said the little faded man as he manipulated the wheel of his ancient car, "in spite of the undignified rush. I must say, I loved Piers very much but I was often mystified by him. And as for the château I don't know how they will keep ahead of the tax people. Piers had no head when it came to figures, no head at all." The association in the metaphor emboldened me to put to him the question which had been on the tip of my tongue, but without giving me a chance he went on. "And talking of heads, my dear friend, I took one liberty without consulting you —in the interest of speed, of despatch. I have ordered a *caput mortuum* to be cast. You will have it tomorrow." So that was the explanation! "You will, I hope, pardon me for the haste. Many motives impelled me. First, I felt it was a good thing to get it over, specially for you; then, on a more selfish plane, I wanted to get the papers and certificates in order as I am going on leave tomorrow for a whole month, to Sicily. I hate unfinished business, and in my profession you know how things can drag on and on. . . ." He puffed at his cigarette and gave me a friendly sideglance. "I hope tonight you will get some real sleep," he added, "because now all is in order." I suddenly felt very old, and fragile, and exhausted.

Back in Avignon the streets were wet and the rainy vistas picked out with lights trembled as if seen through gauze. I could hear the sour tang of the clock on the Hôtel de Ville as we drew to a halt under the trees in the main square. I was glad to be set down here, and to have a short walk to the hotel. I wished him a happy vacation and shook his hand. It was a relief to be alone again and I turned up my face to the sky to feel the warmish rain on it. But it was already late when at last I reached my objective and I climbed the stairs heavily, exhausted and dispirited. I had already reached the first landing when the night porter awoke and came after me with a message. A gentleman from England had asked for me; he had taken a room but at the moment he was in mine. He had ordered soda and whisky and was waiting for me. It could only be Toby, and my heart leaped up exultantly to think that at last he had managed to get here.

I hurried up the next flight and along the gloomy corridor to my room to verify this certainty and found that giant of a man spread over the foot of my bed, snoring lightly. His spectacles had been pushed up onto his forehead and were in danger of falling; his detective story bought for the journey had already slipped out of his grasp onto the floor. Ah, those spectacles! Never have glasses been so often dropped, sat upon, kicked, fractured, forgotten. They held together by a miracle, and every fracture was carefully put in splints with the help of electrician's tape. "Toby!"

He stirred, but then plunged back deeper into his sleep, his lips moving. His huge form bore all the familiar characteristics of the bachelor don—the untidy raincoat whose belt had long since vanished, the shoes like boats, their rubber soles curled up from too hasty drying in front of gas-fires after long muddy walks. Indeed his desperate trousers had traces of yellow clay at the extremities which suggested recent walks in limestone country—as well as perhaps a reason for his silence after my telegram. He had been away on a walking tour. Since he seemed to have no luggage with him save his detective story I presumed that he had first secured a room for himself, dumped his luggage, and sat down in mine to wait for me. His sleeping likeness to Rob Sutcliffe was almost uncanny; if they were not doubles, they could at least have been taken for brothers. For us they were Gog and Magog, two huge shortsighted men with sandy unruly hair and colourless eyelashes; specialists in laughter and irremediable *gaffes*. While looking down at the sleeping Toby I was also seeing Rob Sutcliffe.

Toby smelt of spirits but there was no trace of a glass in my room; but when I examined the bathroom I found a half-empty bottle of whisky, and a toothmug still half full—which went some way towards explaining his present porcine slumber. In order to celebrate his arrival—my spirits had risen with a bound since I knew he was at my side—I drank off the measure of whisky in the glass and returned to the bedroom to wake him and claim my own bed. But his sleep was still of the deepest and I had to repeat his name twice before there was any reaction at all. "Wake up, Toby!"

He appeared to stir in coils like a python—various parts of that large anatomy changed disposition, unrolled themselves, without the sleeper himself being aware; he then scratched his thigh, groaned, half sat up, only to relax again and deflate like a punctured balloon. The eyes opened at last and examined the blurred ceiling with its scrolls and cherubs with unfocused attention, seeing everything and nothing.

It was clear that he was puzzled, that he did not know where he was. I was charitably inclined to suppose that fatigue as much as alcohol played a part in this state of utter bemusement. "Toby. It's Bruce." He now woke up with such an exaggerated energy that it seemed he might levitate and go right through the ceiling. He struggled to his feet, grasped my hand in both of his, and said in rapid telegraphese: "I suppose I am very late? Telegram was at college—been walking in Germany—was completely bowled over—and yet somehow expected something like it—didn't exactly know what—but this is it—now recognise the whole thing—the suicide—typical—damn it all."

"It's a bad dream," I said.

He nodded and went into the bathroom where he threw some cold water on his face to wake himself up. He then re-emerged vigorously towelling himself and, snorting like a carthorse, sat down on the edge of the bed and stared at me. "Suicide," he said at last, as if that were something he had never properly thought about. Then he wagged a thick finger and went on. "Bruce, you never really took all that stuff seriously, did you? I mean Akkad and all those wretched tenets he was always stuffing down our throats. You never took them at their face value—but I always did and I was always full of misgiving to see Piers go overboard for them."

I felt it necessary to apply a brake to this kind of free speculation, if only in the interests of poor dear Akkad. I said: "Toby, even if we haven't got a precise reason for this act of Piers I don't feel we have the right to jump to the conclusion that the Egyptians have anything to do with it—and I mean most particularly Akkad. They were dead against self-destruction, and Akkad never ceased to emphasise the point."

"But you didn't go as far as Piers—you were always on the fringes of the thing, Bruce. So how to know?"

"And you didn't go anywhere at all—so how dare to speculate?" I felt angry, aggrieved. It solved nothing to have idle theories spun about something so cardinal and definitive as Piers' death. "Sorry," said Toby like a sad elephant, and bit the end of his thumb as he sank into a deep reflection. "I was only trying to think of a reason, but of course there doesn't have to be a reason. Just depression or illness could account for it."

"Of course."

"He had a medical check in the autumn—I mean, suppose the sawbones found something slow but fatal like a cancer or like Hodgkin's? It could easily . . . But I am making you impatient."

It was true. It was also a little unjust on my part. I realised that I was simply trying to work off a little of my shock and hysteria on him. I apologised and he grinned affectionately and said he quite understood. It paved the way for me to bring him up to date, to tell him all that I knew, and to describe my visits to Sylvie and to the funeral at Verfeuille. He listened to all this heavily, and with an occasional sigh. But he still shook a doubtful head. "Rob used to say something like: 'There is always a philosophy behind the misadventures of men, even if they are unaware of it.' And that's what I feel about this. Don't be angry with me. It smells purposeful."

Hence the smile on Piers' face, I thought to myself; but I was heartily glad that Toby had arrived too late to inflame the police mind with his theories. I fished out the photographic dossier I had been lent with the police enlargements. He spread them slowly over the bed and bent over them, obviously touched to the heart for he solemnly blew his nose in a grubby red handkerchief. But there was nothing more of significance to be drawn from these things now. The enigma of the welcoming gaze towards the door perhaps. I don't-know. One tended to think up mysteries where none existed. I thought of the gold-tipped cigarette ends, and I thought of Sylvie and her distress on the evening of the act. Presumably these factors too would be explained when Sylvie recovered her reason again, if ever she did.

I finished my drink at last. Then I drew the curtains to watch the dawn come creeping up over the wrinkled river and over the muddled rooftops of the town where already the lacklustre pigeons were beginning to flap. Sour bells clattered the hour. "We must get some sleep," and Toby rose yawning and stretched. I felt as if I were making my first steps in a new world, a world where all the dispositions had been changed abruptly, all the proportions altered.

We agreed to meet at ten in the hall, but I slept so heavily that I did not hear the maid's knock, and when I did get there it was to find a message from Toby to the effect that he had gone out to the Café Durance for a *croissant* and a cup of coffee. It was not hard to follow in his footsteps and find him there, in the early sunlight, half asleep at a table, gazing with deep affection at his own personal corner of the city, the corner that meant the most to him—the main square. Ah! That romantic square with its horrible Monument des Morts festooned with its mangy tin lions, so typical a fancy! All squared off by the beautiful mature trees sheltering the intimate little fringe of cafés and restaurants where one could dawdle away whole days, whole holidays, whole lifetimes. I can never see it now without seeing the phantom of Piers cross it, limping to the *tabac* for cigarettes with his slight suggestion of wolf-slink; and as often I see Sylvie walking there with him, arm in arm and pressed tight to his side like a scabbard. She had that special walk with him, pressed snug to his side, proudly. In the Greek islands one has seen little seahorses walking like that, innocent, sensual and upright. . . . My friend was dozing; or rather he was in the benign stupor which overcame him always in his favourite city. "Ah! Avignon!" he said quietly, as much to the sky as to me. So one might have exclaimed "Ah! Childhood!" Today was just one day added to a long tapestry of days woven by memory. At every time, and in every season, he had known the town, by summer and winter, perhaps better than any of us. For while we had so often been far away Toby had spent several months each year working on the documents in the château. Piers had put at his disposal an enormous cache of original material which had a bearing on the history of the Templars, the subject of Toby's *magnum opus* —"a work which will deflower the detestable Professor Babcock, and secure me the throne of medieval studies at Garbo College." It was to be understood that Babcock held diametrically opposed views about the Templars and their mysterious history. But the old man's fate was sealed, for the great three-volume work of Toby's was almost finished, and it made use of much unpublished material which he had found in the muniments room at Verfeuille. Toby as a victim of the historical virus could not look at the town without seeing it historically, so to speak—layer after layer of history laid up in slices, embodied in its architecture. There was no corner of the place which did not conjure up for him delicious reveries, vivid associations.

"Will I see Sylvie?" he asked softly at last, "or would you rather not at the moment?" On the contrary, I said, he was expected and a visit might do a great deal of good. "We can go up this evening if you wish. I only have to telephone Jourdain and let him know." But at the thought I felt weighed down again by the prehistoric depression caused by her plight— and my own. Here was time running away with us and still we were plagued by these fearful misadventures of the reason and the flesh. Moreover here I was in roughly the state of an orphan—I mean that I had severed all my ties with the outside world and had come here to settle. The few personal possessions I owned were on their way to join me. The crates of books and paintings would not be long delayed. I should soon have to make up my mind about the future—stay here, hobbled by Sylvie's plight, or go away, somewhere far away, using some medical excuse? Cowardice, I know, but when one is desperate one toys with desperate solutions. Toby suffered from no such doubts. "Oh course you will have to go back to Verfeuille now," he said stoutly, "you can't leave Sylvie—unless you took her on a long sea voyage or something like that."

But I hadn't the strength to undertake a long journey in which I should have to nurse her night and day, with always the danger of a *fugue* staring me in the face, or a complete relapse into something like catatonia. Would I be forced to stay, then? (Walking alone at night, when thoughts won't sift properly, down dark roads in the rain, in the roaring northern rain which brimmed over the edges of the world, I had been over and over the problem of Sylvie. Months of solitary walking.)

I ordered wine. It lay before me, glinting in the sun. It was hardly done to drink Tavel so early in the morning but I could never resist the colour or the taste; Toby, true to form, gulped at an *anisette*. His ample presence comforted me no end. Perhaps I might consider a return to the château if he himself were going to stay there and work for a month or two. His company would help to make me acclimatise myself perhaps?

So we sat and watched little scenes from the life of the Midi enacted before our eyes—a delight because they confirmed the unchanging character of the place and its inhabitants. Some workmen were trying to mend the defective machinery of the old Jaquemart without success. At last the little waist-high couple of figurines gave a spasmodic jerk or two and advanced a little in order to strike midday twice—as a pure concession to the workmen it seemed, who were using extremely bad language, and didn't appear to know how the thing worked. It was a pity. The Jaquemart was one of the prettiest features of the square when they did work—the little man trotting out punctually, to hammer out the hours with his tiny mallet. But from time to time they stuck, and this was at least the third time we had witnessed an attempt to put the machinery to rights, and this time the whole project seemed to be beyond the workmen, for in a while, after a lot of desultory messing about, they started to climb down the tower. They were halfway down when, as if in derision, the little figures jerked into their curving trajectory and without prompting struck midday (or midnight). The men shook good-natured fists at them and shouted expletives.

It was reassuring in its amiable futility, this operation. Clearly the task was beyond them, and a specialist would have to be summoned to deal with the problem. We walked back to the hotel in silence, strangely reassured by this trivial scene, by this cold but benign snatch of sunlight, by the taste of good wine. I rang up Montfavet and spoke to Jourdain. He was quite delighted to hear of Toby's arrival—as I knew he would be. "She has been speaking about him quite a lot, and complaining that her rooms smell of his tobacco. Let him smoke a pipe tonight as a mark of identification. No; there is no marked change for the time being. What else have I to tell you? Yes, the morgue people have sent me round a plaster cast of Piers' face, taken by the *médecin-légiste,* or someone assigned by him, I will hand it over to you when you come."

Things were beginning to sort themselves out—or was that just an illusion born of the friendly presence of Toby and the fact that Piers' funeral had become an accomplished fact, was over? At any rate I felt much calmer as I spent the morning with Toby walking round the town, visiting the bookshops and the more immediate historical antiquities. He always felt the need to reverify his city, to make sure that it was still there, still insisting on its poetic role in the world

which had by now so far outstripped it. We walked
and talked regardless of the hours; then returned to
our rooms for a short rest before the affairs of the evening. At dusk we jogged up to Montfavet in a *fiacre,*
Toby obediently smoking his foul shag in a bull-nosed
pipe and speculating on what the future might have in
store for us.

Well, she was dressed in rather a haphazard fashion
—in a long, old-fashioned hobble skirt and a number
of brilliant scarves of different colours and materials.
Eccentric, if you like. But she gave her evident disorientation a sort of tropical brilliance, like a bird of
paradise.

It was depressing, it hurt, because it was such
a close parody of good reason. The capricious evolu-
tions of a child, say. Yet it was not. She seemed to be
expecting us or at any rate me—perhaps Jourdain had
told her something? At any rate she wore a red velvet
carnival *cagoule* through the slits of which her eyes
looked at us, unblinking or perhaps glittering with
malice. Who can say? "There you are!" she cried, and
went on: "There is no need to speculate on my identity," giving a little gesture which was somehow a forlorn caricature of an imperious one. She was like an
amateur actor in a difficult play. Standing up now she
said: "After all, it is all mine to do with it whatever
I wish, no?" Toby lumbered up to her like a bear saying: "Of course it is," and took this velvet animal in
his arms. "I recognise you," she said, "because of the
smell of your tobacco. And you, too, Bruce." This was
a great encouragement. But it did not change the constraint we felt, I suppose because neither of us quite
believed it. Then she surprised and encouraged us by
quoting a phrase of her brother's. "Here comes Toby,
with shoes like boats, and a handshake as hot as a

busby." This at least showed that she knew who he was. Laughter. We were both delighted, and Toby, in search of patterns of reminiscence which might, like grooves, familiarise her back into phase, went over to the piano and began to pick out tunes with one finger. This had a surprisingly calming effect: she laughed and clapped her hands, and sitting down at the card-table dealt herself a hand of solitaire. The evocation of Verfeuille in winter was perfect. Toby has just returned wet through from a walk in the rain. He sits on one side of the fireplace, literally steaming. On the other side Rob Sutcliffe. Both smoke infernal pipes. Piers lies asleep on the sofa—too much wine at lunch and a late night. The rain swishes down in the park, teems on the window-panes, brims the gurgling gutters. Piers sleeps; the two giants argue with acrimony about the Templars. I whittle a stick. The gun-dogs snore and tremble. It is one of those long afternoons where imprisonment by the weather becomes delightful. She deals herself a hand of solitaire. Propped in front of her is a notebook of Rob's from which she occasionally reads out aloud, though nobody pays any attention to the words. "Identity is the frail suggestion of coherence with which we have clad ourselves. It is both illusory and quite real, and most necessary for happiness, if indeed happiness is necessary." Toby, in the act of blowing his nose, cries "Bad Nietzsche!" over his shoulder. This was the scene which we were now busy re-enacting except that Piers was gone and Rob was gone. It was a frail thread to hang on to, but it held. With bowed head and concentrated air she played on, listening to the dislocated one-finger noises of Toby on the Pleyel. "Do you remember Akkad? He used to say to us: 'Hurry. Hurry. The minutes are leaking from the clocks and as yet we have only brushed the Great Cryptics.' Well, Bruce dear, I tried to hurry like he said, but I missed my footing somehow. Anyway it was always approaching me, what Piers called 'the old fern-fingered neurasthenia,' and now Jourdain thinks he understands a little but he doesn't. It's the merest presumption of medicine." I knew that only too well. In a while she got up and walked about as if she were trying to rehearse for a play. She had unmasked herself now and her eyes were full of mischief. She poured out an imaginary drink, added soda, and took it over to Toby, who thanked her and drank an imaginary mouthful before setting it down on the piano. Then she lighted a real cigarette, but almost at once threw it into the grate. There was a fire laid there, and the gesture drew my attention to the fact—also I seemed to recognise some fragments of manuscript in Piers' hand. "Are you burning Pier's papers?" I said, and she suddenly stopped dead in her tracks, hand on her heart. As if recovering full possession of herself she fell on her knees before the grate and, bursting into tears, began taking out the crumpled papers and smoothing them in her lap. "Why did I do that?" she cried. "When there was nothing to hide, nothing at all to hide?"

No, there was nothing to hide. I took the crumpled papers from her and sat down to sort them while she returned seriously to her game. They were by several hands and not all by Piers as I had surmised. Sutcliffe's large florid feminine hand was very conspicuous, as were the brilliant inks he used. His loose-leaf notebooks were always exploding and letting their contents tumble about in hopeless disorder.

Meeting on the threshing floor to wrestle with death and with love like Digenis

A railway strike produced strange things like this mountain of motionless roses laid up in a siding

Intuition has no memory, it jumps off the spool, it eludes thought memory and also causality

another tiring dream of grave allegorical figures, of sleep, cathedrals sitting in blue water on canals with wet shoes at night

a letter to Pia written in my sleep by braille

out of this tremendous chaos, Pia, I am trying to build my new and perhaps my last book. The studio floor is littered with fragments of this great puzzle

when the age gets swept out to sea and dispersed by the tides what remains will be the result of the purest accident; one-fifth of Anc. Greek Drama one-tenth of Elizabethan is all we have left so why worry?

Infants are smooth and lack all swank They only have themselves to thank.

Language is all very fine and we cannot do without it but it is at the same time the worst invention of man, corrupting silence, tearing petals off the whole mind. The longer I live the more ashamed I get.

Sorrow is implicit in love as gravitation is implicit in mass.

The mechanism of causality is mighty and mathematically quite inexorable even for mental phenomena.

I sat there among these fragments of the great puzzle of Rob's unfinished novel whose dismembered fragments littered the muniments room, and heard Toby picking and picking out his one-fingered tune, merciless as a woodpecker. "Sylvie." She raised her dark head and gazed at me abstractedly, her eyes still full of playing cards and their magic. "Did Piers tell you . . . ?' It was stupid of me to broach the subject at this moment, and Toby gave a grimace of displeasure. But she behaved as if she had not heard. But a moment later she said: "He had considered every possible issue before deciding that he must stick to the rules. His heart was set on it."

"On what, Sylvie?"

She produced a sad little smile and I could see that she had slipped, so to speak, off the time-track again and into the solipsism of childhood. I put the papers on the table and she read off a phrase from one of them in a low voice: "Me he will devour in the next life whose flesh I eat in this." I wondered where Piers had found that quotation for his commonplace book; also a verse by a forgotten Elizabethan:

> And so it grew and grew
> And bore and bore
> Until at length it
> Grew a gallows that did bear our son.

It must have struck his mind as a reference to her child, Sylvie's child. She shook the hair out of her eyes and said: "Remember the song the Templars sang?" I shook my head, but truthfully, for I did not know what she meant. In a small ghostly voice she sang "Oranges and Lemons, say the bells of Saint Clements." A well-enough-known nursery song, though I had never heard that it was originated by the Templars. She was very earnest now, and very solemn in her dreamy way, and as the words of the song flowed out she began to enact the scene of the nursery game which we had all played when we were little. "Here comes a candle to light you to bed, here comes a chopper to chop off your head, chop, chop, chop, chop . . ." With joined fingers she executed a long line of children—guillotine fashion. Then she stopped dead, entranced, gazing at nothing or perhaps only the projection of her private thoughts on the white wall. Then she said: "Everything that happened began at Macabru, you know that. Piers knew it. Macabru changed everything."

I waited painfully for something further to emerge from this unsatisfactory meeting, but nothing more came; and soon the nurse came with her medicines and the little trolley with the frugal dinner of the patient. Jourdain, too, came and reminded us that we were his guests that evening. He was delighted to see Toby again. But Sylvie was now withdrawn, silent, in the Trappe of her private mind. "In the perspex cube of an unshakable autism." I stroked her hair and said goodbye, but she did not even look up.

In Jourdain's study, on his desk, lay the smart black velvet casket with the death-mask. It was at once like and unlike Piers—as though time had played tricks on the image like it plays on memories, distorting them. I think these thoughts might have passed through the doctor's mind as well for he said: "There always seems to be a shrinkage after death, which has puzzled me repeatedly. The image withers up. I have even tried weighing several people after death to see if this is imaginary or real. Does the personality actually weigh something? Because when it is emptied out a vast disorganisation starts, and the first sign of it is a kind of diminishing. But this is an illusion, the weight does not change." He was right, for the face of Piers looked shrunk, famished, reduced. Jourdain closed the casket with a snap and said: "Well, there it is. It's yours." I thanked him for having thought about the matter. No doubt one day, in the fulness of time, when we had got over the pangs, the first gnawing pangs of his death, it would be pleasant to have him there, in a favourite corner of the room, on a writing desk, in sunlight. I thought for a long moment about the equivocal and enigmatic quality of love, and a phrase from a novel by Rob came to mind —Piers had.copied it out. "In our age too much freedom has destroyed the fragile cobweb which gave the great human attachments their form and substance— their truth. Health rages in us like a toothache, but fine styles in living, as in writing, have been overtaken by loutishness."

And what of Macabru?

Macabru

The four riders, one of them a woman, who set off that noon from the Canopic Gate were as young as their mettlesome long-legged horses. The party was guided by a decrepit one-eyed Arab on a somewhat capricious white camel. They were heading for an oasis called Macabru which lay some way to the east of Alexandria. Yes, we were all four somewhat new to the place, and as yet very much under the spell of its skies and its vistas of many-coloured desert—here and there smoothed out so like curls freshly combed: here and there so like fresh snow, bearing the perfect imprints of animals' paws and of birds' claws. As a matter of fact Sylvie had only recently arrived to stay with her brother at the French Legation, while I was putting up our friend Toby, who was on his way back from Palestine to Oxford after a spell of disappointment with his Bible studies. "The more I learn about Our Saviour the less I like him. I am not going to take that sort of Holy Orders anyway." This was his most recent theme; but in fact already his addiction to drink had marked him down as rather a questionable candidate for the priesthood. When tipsy he was capable of saying anything to anyone, and if it happened to be one of his examiners? At any rate he was one of the four riders—the most amateurish I would suppose, sitting his horse gracelessly, with splayed bottom and toes turned out. He was a very large young man, his face burnt beetroot by the sun, his ears sticking out steeply—which gave him the air of trying to overhear what was being said a mile away. Thick spectacles broke up his features into reflecting planes. His sandy hair stuck out or fell down in his eyes when it needed cutting. He smelt of Lifebuoy soap and exuded a clumsy but effervescent goodwill which was contagious. Only in this case he protested a bit, feeling that he had been let in for a long and exhausting ride to little purpose. It is difficult to see why, for in his disappointment with Our Saviour he had turned his sympathetic attention to the heresies of various sects which had departed from the strict canons of Christian theological dogma—so that in some ways he was much better informed about the activities of Akkad than we were.

In the case of Piers, who rode a little ahead with his beautiful sister, the question was different—he had fallen under the spell of this strange man. The views of Akkad—for Piers had encountered him quite often at parties in the city during his first few months *en poste*—seemed to him something like a revelation. "I seem to understand everything he says, and I feel I am hearing something absolutely truthful for the first time—so it's all quite orginal for me, quite pristine. For the first time, Bruce, I can *believe* in something, a proposition about myself and the world which holds water. It satisfies me, it's like falling in love." This is the point at which Toby would groan, but Sylvie would turn her face to mine and kiss me softly. "O to hell with you," said Piers spurring his horse.

In those days there were no real suburbs—the desert began almost at the gates of Alexandria and with it of course the damp enervating heat which soaked and bathed one, until one could feel the sweat trickling through one's clothes into one's very saddle. Our breathing was laboured. There were small villages giving (so many were the mirages) the illusion of being fictions; their reflections rose in the air or settled into the ground. Purely fictitious lakes with minarets surrounded them, turning them into violet islands. Finally one got to disbelieving one's own eyesight and waiting for the truth to emerge—the sordid truth, for the villages were all decayed and fly-blown, and now in the noonday sun for the most part deserted.

In one the Arab guide beckoned us to follow him, with a sort of cheeky grin, as if to promise us an agreeable diversion. There was a naked old man chained to a block of wood set deep in the ground. He seemed dead, but the Arab turned him over with his foot as one turns a strange beetle over. No, he was alive, but mad. He mopped and mowed, smiled and salaamed and mumbled. He was as thin as an insect, but was brimming over with an insane gaiety— the blissful amnesia that all excessive suffering brings. We heard his story. He had been chained here as a punishment for some crime by the local pasha. But time passed, the nature of his crime was forgotten by the village, even the old pasha himself died, and the criminal went slowly mad with the heat and the thirst. But his madness took the form of a tremendous and exalted happiness. He submitted to everything happily. He was in a state of perfect bliss, whatever happened. Perhaps it was due to this that he survived, for the villagers brought him food and water, first out of sympathy and lastly because they felt that he was really a saint. The truth broke upon them.

Now he was cherished and fed, and people came to visit him as if he were an oracle. He had indeed become a saint, and would when he died give the village a yearly festival. Only they had no authority to free him, that would take a great deal of effort and documentation, and there was hardly anyone in the village capable of examining the legal situation or undertaking the necessary paperwork. Meanwhile he was euphoric. He kissed Piers' toe and went on muttering. The sandheap in which he lay was full of ants, and there seemed no shade for the poor man. But packets of food lay about, and having had a hearty laugh at his compatriot's plight the Arab guide suddenly turned pious, made him a deep obeisance and then went to fill a pitcher of sweet water for him. One felt helpless and thoroughly disgusted. Normally one bought out one's horror and embarrassment when face to face with such a spectacle (a beggar covered in sores, say), but in this case what good was money, what good our etiolated town-sympathy? It was hard to know how to curb one's fury, too, against the guide for having thought up this pleasing little spectacle for us. Suddenly Egypt hit us all like a hammer.

It was a sighing relief to quit the hamlet for the pure desert again. I have said there were no suburbs of the modern city and this is true—but everywhere outside it in the sand of the desert, half buried, were the extensive remains of ancient buildings, shattered archways, smashed causeways and musing lintels, and what often seemed to be partly demolished statues. So that we had some truthful inkling of the original dream-city of the boy Alexander which, according to Pliny, had had a circuit of fifteen miles and had housed three hundred thousand souls. It had gloried in palaces, baths, libraries, temples and gymnasia without number. But we were latecomers to the place, modern scavengers of history upon a scene which had, it seems, long since exhausted all its historical potentialities. It was with something of a melancholy air that Piers (who loved guide books) had read out the preamble to the article about the city in Murray. "Alexandria is situated in 31° 13' 5" north latitude and 27° 35' 30" longitude, near Lake Mareotis, on an isthmus which connects with *terra firma* the peninsula that forms the two ports."

Repeated historical earthquakes have dashed down the monuments and engulfed the place time and time again; at the time of the French invasion the population had declined to some eight thousand souls. But an infusion of new blood and a long world war restored to it much of its lost importance, and by now its central parts had become almost opulent again with villas and gardens in the French Riviera style of building, shady public squares, museums, banks and galleries. Its swollen Arab quarter was now nearly as varied and picturesque as that of Cairo; its brothel quarters were as extensive as well might be in a port which was now used to the regular visits of so many foreign warships. But the past had quite gone, and much had vanished with it. Turning slightly left towards the foaming sea line now through the tinted afternoon light it was only possible to imagine the marches of Alexander through such a haze of shimmering silence, broken only by the curses of his guides and the curious lumpy shuffling noise a camel makes in the dunes. "And yet," said Piers, to whom I can attribute this sentiment, "and yet the outer furnishings of his world are still here—palms, water-wheels, dervishes, desert horses. Always!"

"Mirages," groaned Toby, "and oases."

"Some people say that it was not Siwa where he was proclaimed God, but Macabru; that is why I jumped at the invitation of Akkad."

"Romantic," said Sylvie.

"Not at all," he said, catching her wrist with a little pleading gesture. "Can't you see how marvellous history is? The presence of other people whose actions and thoughts seem to still hang about in the air? Don't tell me you can see the Nile delta without a thought for poor Euclid who obviously worked as a clerk in the Ministry of Waterways? How boring his life must have been. What a hypotenuse everything must have seemed, even love, to a poor civil servant, married with nine children, all isosceles in shape. . . ."

"Enough, Piers!"

Gradually as we advanced the fatidic afternoon relinquished much of its fearful heat, the colour began to fade into evening; objects began to take up new positions in this dying sky as watching silhouettes. This would be most pronounced on the Nile itself—wing of a felucca sailing southward into darkness! But we had to reckon with the part of the sky which hung over the blue-brown sea. "Another mouth, sicking out its alluvial muck," said Toby, and Piers said rather primly: "Once there were seven mouths, and seven cities built upon them. Now even the ashes of the ruins . . ." But they were buried completely in silt or washed out to sea. A wild sea drubbed and hummed upon these desolate beaches, beating like a fateful drum or a bassoon of sadness. The sand was full of shattered shells and dead crabs, and the colour of dirty flour; our horses sank, and in order to coax them to a gallop we had to look for firm surfaces right at the sea line. Here at least we managed to let our mounts have their heads, but only for half a mile or so. The stout wind precluded all but smiles. Thick fingers of current rinsed back the bays while the undertow noisily macerated the occasional beach of pebbles. Woe to a poor swimmer on these beaches! We passed an old withered man on a mule. He seemed sunk in a trance of fatigue, but he croaked the guide good-day. This seemed to spark off a talkative vein in our own Arab. Coming alongside us with his slower

animal he said: "Him very old. You don't see people
very old in Skanderia. Die young, Egyptians." The
observation was a true one, but he did not elaborate;
I would have liked to know whether he thought this
was due to the climate, the diet, or simply malefic
djinns. The latter I presumed for I had been told so.

Now the shore became rocky and firm and we came
upon the buried and crumbling remains of what looked
like a tidy-sized necropolis, but as it was not marked
on Piers' maps we had no means of telling what it
really was. It tilted seaward, sloping like the floor of
a theatre, and with open mouth as if it were really a
stone quarry. But Toby voted it a hypogeum, I suspect
because he liked the word and not because he knew
what it meant; no more did I. But exposed as it was
to the north it must have been filled with waves and
spray whenever it blew a gale. It appeared to consist
of corridors, now open to the sky, radiating out from
what might have been a central courtyard. Bats flew
squeaking up to the echo of the pebbles we dropped,
in trying to determine its depth. But there was no time
to play about as our guide was fussing about the distance still to be covered before we came to Macabru.
There was a ferry to be crossed with these capricious
steeds and the white camel—and even I had learned
that camels are bad-tempered and inclined to bite
when under stress.

When we struck the mouth of a small but violent
river we turned abruptly inland and followed its
course, sure now to connect with the ford which offered
the only link with the further desert and the small
oasis which was our destination.

But with every advance the visage of nature
changed; Canopus, that desolate city, once erected
about the tomb of Menelaus, lay far behind while
ahead of us glinted more miles of unbreathable desert
where nothing moved save little bands of swallows

skimming to and fro. Clambering through the waste in which the sand drifts were in some places blown up into heaps and in others spread out into vast mattresses, where our animals sank a foot deep, and in others again, water-covered and reduced to black mud, we gradually made dogged headway under a changing sky. It had become leaden and dark with clouds in the fading daylight, a sky full of winter tones. An obstinate wind, now turned colder with the dusk, kept up its pressure on the ear-drums, and in this dull twilight the further desert looked anything but inviting. Rather it was dreary and desolate beyond all expression.

But we persevered and when the night seemed not too far off we came to a jutting little promontory with a sad little jetty barely holding its own with the boisterous snarling waters. The river was wide too at this point, and for a while we felt some real doubt as to whether we were going to achieve a crossing. From time to time, in the lulls of the wind we could hear our stirrups clink, or the dull stabbing screams of a gull, or the rasp of a heron. But night was beginning to fall. There was no sign of the ferryman on the opposite bank. We stood our ground, deliberating, while enormous crabs issuing from the holes in the river bank advanced to greet us, frightening the horses. The guide was in an ugly despair. We all shouted and yelled but our calls were swept away in the wind, and no answering voice came to offer us the promise of a passage. We felt half mad with disappointment as we saw our hopes of visiting the oasis withering away. It was in this Stygian situation and mood that I had the idea of firing off my revolver, and surprisingly enough this seemed to do the trick, for a portion of the thick dusk stirred and it was not too long before we heard a voice hailing us. And behold, the ferry boat in all its glory rounded a little spur of sand and came swaying down to us. It was quite an exciting manoeuvre, the whole embarkation business, but fortunately both the horses and the camel behaved with exemplary good sense.

From then on a last village and we advanced into the desert and into the darkness; there was nothing to be seen save the desolate dunes stretching away on every side—and now visibility was foreshortened by the absolute dark. Yet the sky had cleared. We asked the Arab if he steered on a star, but this he did not seem to understand, yet he seemed quite confident of his direction and plodded mechanically on, while I took a reading from my little oil-compass just to see that we were not being guided in circles, or even back by mere accident to the river. No, he was certainly on a course, which was somewhat reassuring.

Another hour or so of this sturdy riding on uneven surfaces and we suddenly found the sky growing much lighter, as if with a false sunrise about to break through the soft horizon line to the east. Objects seemed to define themselves more clearly, and with a soft phosphorescent glow. Later we were to discover that this was due simply to the as yet unrisen moon shining against banks of soft cirrus. Everything seemed to be clearing, and it had become very much cooler. We were out of the wind now, exchanging glances with the stars which began to prickle above us on the dark carpet of heaven. Softly, with the faintest whirr of engines—indeed with far less noise than the average bus—a light aircraft rustled slowly over us with all the lights glimmering in its cabin. It made a slow turn eastwards and began to descend. The guide gave a croak of relieved triumph. The aircraft was Akkad's and it was ferrying some of his guests; there was apparently an excellent natural landing strip in the desert quite near the oasis. As a matter of fact we had been offered a trip in this fashion but being young and romantic had declined the invitation, preferring to ride. Nor had we anything to regret in the matter. But now our spirits rose in us with the confirmation that our course was a true one.

Insensibly we quickened our speed, and even the horses seemed to feel something of our urgency and began to make an effort to carry us faster. We wound laboriously up a particularly large dune and were at last rewarded by a light—a soft unwinking glow in the desert some way before us. It floated, a warm rosy emanation, upon the tumultuous desert floor, promising a point of fixity in the midst of desolation: a land-fall. And so we smiled at each other in darkness (there was a smile in our voices, in our banter) as we hastened over the sand.

Macabru was simply a shadow which dawn's light would break down into objects and planes; for the moment all one could say was that it was not part of the desert. It hovered on the edges of the warm light, re-serving its beauties for the coming moon. But the light as we approached now broke down into many separate points, and we saw that we were approach-ing something like a desert encampment—the bivouac of some huge army. All was mingled and muddled by the darkness—distances, volumes, angles, objects. But as we came to it it looked not unlike another large Arab city, but this time all lit up against the darkness. It was only when we were on it that we glimpsed a slender tulip of minaret, and a patch of water rip-pling like a mirror—the size of a lake or the arm per-haps of the river which we had just crossed? We reined our horses on the edges of the nearest light—a fire of straw burning in a field—and here a rider came up to meet us on a great black mare.

"A seneschal," said Piers, thrilled to the core not only by the word but by the medieval formality of this meeting. I knew that he was thinking of the Crusaders

—how often they must have met with this kind of Moslem reception. The tall thin man, face bearded and nose aquiline, asked us who we were in Arabic, but immediately broke into sound French when we announced ourselves, politely dragging off our light but cumbersome Arab burnouses which had been stifling us with heat throughout the ride, but which we now surrendered somewhat reluctantly for the evening had turned cool. Instantly the messenger turned his dancing horse and led us down into the lighted township. Akkad had already described to us most accurately what we would see.

It was not only in the towns and bigger villages that one met with the tombs of holy men, or those who had achieved a posthumous sainthood and conferred it on a place, signifying it with a yearly feast day. Often, and throughout the country, they stood in deserted and solitary places, and usually had a fountain or small date grove adjoining, where a wandering dervish might pause to pray and meditate after performing his ritual ablutions: or where indeed the ordinary traveller might simply quench his thirst and enjoy cool shade on a journey. Macabru had begun modestly enough with a shrine and a fountain—but it was a real oasis with a sheet of lake water, crystal clear, where the clouds floated by day or by night. Tall reeds fringed the holy lake.

Around the tomb of the saint had grown up a small chapel consisting of one square apartment surmounted by a dome most handsomely fluted. Outside was a magnificent marble fountain of filigreed workmanship which had been donated by the local pasha, who had also endowed the place so that regular religious observances could be supervised by the three gloomy, pious resident dervishes. How well we were to get to know the curious flat dusty smell of these places, the smell of brackish water on well-washed stone; and the peculiar disorienting effect of churches with no central altar, no point of focus, save only the hanging gonfalons with their grand script invoking the blessings of the Moslem God. And always the same sparse furniture of mat, water-jug, and a coloured chest to receive the donations of the passing traveller. And thus once a year the oasis came to life in honour of the saint. A bazaar sprang up around the central palm-groves where the camels were tethered, streets mapped themselves out, a hasty but useful drainage system was dug in the sand and partially solidified by water. Even a frail system of electric lighting with myriads of coloured bulbs crossed and recrossed the streets which were now lined with multicoloured stalls selling every imaginable thing, for the fair (or *mulid*) as it had developed over the years was half secular and half religious in inspiration. Of course we saw little of all this in detail at our first entry into Macabru—just the thrilling bazaar crackling with life and roaring barter, and the lights which led back in a sweet diagonal shape towards the central chapel, which was one of some consequence. And behind the hum of human voices and the snorting of mules and horses from the dark groves beside the lake we could hear the festive beat of the little drum and the squeak of fifes. Some of the painted stalls were of wood or light wattle, but most were mere tents of soiled and tattered cloth. At the end of the provisional village (for that is what it became for three days every year) we came to a great striped marquee with hitching posts about its entrance where we divested ourselves of our horses and, delighted to find that Akkad had not yet arrived, plunged back into the bazaar, which for us was one of the most exciting places we had ever seen.

It was indeed marvellous in its comprehensiveness, our admiration was really justified, for not only were there stalls for sweetmeats, copperware, camel gear, calendars and so on but the provision market was as handsomely stocked as the big markets of Alexandria —from which I supposed much of this stuff came either by land or water. There was no refrigeration in those days—or at best heavy and rudimentary ice-boxes which were not easily transportable. Provisions were ferried by camel in stout sacks of gunny with blocks of ice packed round them; a herculean task. Once the destination was reached commodities like bottles were sunk down wells by the basketful, or left in the lake to keep cool. But here were exposed various kinds of meat, fresh and dried fruits, vegetables, herbs, fowls, game, fish in abundance, very fine bread, milk and fresh eggs. The country round about produced little or nothing, so that all this sophisticated fare must have come from Rosetta, Alexandria, perhaps even from other villages in lower Egypt. We wandered speechlessly about in a daze of admiration for the colours and the scents and sounds. There was a lot of rough cookery going on, and a good deal of barter for cheap jewelry. There was also a kind of sand-ring where villagers were playing at single-stick, but in mockery, amidst laughter—a version of shadow-boxing: only wielding these huge iron-shod sticks gracelessly, keeping time to music like dancing bears. This sort of sham fight seemed to be very popular to judge by the crowd. The music however was supplied by the followers of some ladies of easy virtue who had also come no doubt to celebrate the saint's day in their own fashion. They watched the tournament, seated on horseback, heavily painted in ghoulish fashion and bedizened with feathers, grease paint and necklaces of onions and garlic. The master of ceremonies for this group was a clown who sat back to front on a mule with his face white-washed. He carried a monkey on his shoulders dressed in a coloured cap and re-minded one of the court buffoons of the Middle Ages.

His sallies were obviously rather double-edged and provoked roars of laughter.

We were all so absorbed by the marvellous spectacle that we did not know for a while that Akkad himself had joined us and was walking smilingly amongst us; true, he had put off his town clothes and wore an old and much darned abba and a soft fez. But there he was, this much discussed merchant-banker, who was equally at home in four capitals and four languages. I did not share the deep fascination of Piers, but on the other hand I found Akkad a most surprising and attractive man, with quirks of behaviour and speech which always seemed to be leading him away to the darker corners of his own thoughts—it was as though in order to speak at all he had to wake himself up from a trance of inner meditation. Much that he said was scattered and disconnected, and much I frankly did not understand—or is that true, I wonder? His physical presence was also intriguing for he sometimes looked heavy and fat, and sometimes thin and ascetic. I have seen him driving across the city in those inevitable dark glasses, with a growth of unshaven stubble on his chin and his hair parted on a different side—and I had the impression of a fattish sluggish pasha, wallowing in riches like a Turk. At other times, at his town house which was splendid with statues and fountains, built round an interior courtyard which abutted onto the shady and silent gardens of the Museum, I saw another Akkad, the cocktail version, so to speak. Beautifully dressed by London with a buttonhole and a silk handkerchief planted in his sleeve as if it might sprout something. He still kept the glasses of course, but his face seemed narrower, more goatlike, his hair finer and more sparse. Of course he sometimes abandoned these fads, taking off his glasses to talk—and then one suddenly saw his eyes. They were so deep, so sea-green that they filled you with inquietude; and the faint suspicion of a squint in them increased the feeling of disorientation, for he never seemed to be looking at you so much as looking into or around you. Porphyrios Akkad! "I know what you feel," said Piers once, after a long thoughtful silence. "You find Akkad too articulate, he doesn't quite carry conviction to you, so consequently you are on your guard. But those eyes, Bruce!"

"I know."

"And that mind!"

"You are talking like a schoolboy!"

There was no need to reply to that, for I had frankly acknowledged that I was out of my depth for the greater part of his strange "expositions"; even later, when I read the texts of them at leisure I only half-saw, half-agreed. . . . For his "sermons" were recorded and Roneo-copied for the benefit of absent members. In Piers' hotel room at Avignon there was a ton of these fascicules, some of which I could even remember having heard him deliver in those far-off days. As for Piers, Sabine once said of him: "It is pitiable. He has a thirst for belief. Almost anything might do to satisfy it." Poor Piers was deeply wounded by this remark, as he was by mine.

Akkad was so charmed by our tremendous attraction for the oasis-bazaar that he refused to leave us and rejoin his guests, saying: "They will forgive a little lapse. Come, I insist. I will show you round myself." And this he faithfully did, explaining everything in that calm melodious voice so full of tenderness for these colourful aspects of his native country. It did not really take all that long, but here and there he stopped to exchange greetings or banter with an acquaintance, or listen to a whispered complaint and promise redress for the complainer, so that it was about an hour before we came to the last man, the water-seller with his special little rituals. This one was distributing free water on behalf of a rich man who had been to Mecca and who was known for his charity. The seller, who propped the dark slobbering skin across his shoulders, held out to us the gilded cup from which we all drank, and also held up the mirror to our faces to remind us that we were mortal and must die. An elderly sheik shared this little ceremony with us, and afterwards benignly gave the waterman a coin and made him spurt scented water on his face and beard. So we came at long last, and in leisurely fashion, to the brilliant marquee among the supplely swaying cypresses and clicking date-palms—a really enormous tent about the size of a regimental mess-tent, though the company was not so inordinately numerous.

We were about twenty or thirty people in all, I guessed, and extremely various, both as to race and colour. There were two pretty Chinese ladies, some old Turks, and then a sprinkling of more modestly dressed people who looked like minor university professors or post-office officials. Some we already knew, like Casimir Ava the tragic actor with his pale eunuchoid-velvet complexion and studied poses. The stagecraft of suicide meant everything to him, and everything he read or acted seemed to hint at it; it infected his moods and physical attitudes. You could tell at once that it would end like that, just by looking at those deepset burning disabused eyes. He was Werther. He would win his own title to extinction! None of this did I know at the time; and Piers himself told me little enough about the long private sessions he had with Akkad.

There was Anne Dunbar the Ambassador's daughter, Angelo Tomasso the great surgeon, Spiro Harari the jeweller, Jean Makaro the policeman, Luther Fox of the Military Mission, Ahmed Osmanli the banker, and several others whose faces were unfamiliar. Later we were to get to know them well. The general atmosphere was that of a relaxed and pleasant cocktail party in the desert, softly lit and silently served to us by numerous servants, white-gloved and impassive Nubians.

There was no special suggestion that all the guests belonged to any particular religious or political persuasion; it was simply another social occasion. Conversation was free and unstudied. Introductions took place, people met for the first time—or so it seemed. Banter and low laughter swayed about the huge tent, swayed among the shadows thrown by the brilliant candelabra pendant on their inverted stems above the white napery of the central table. The night smelt of jasmine and hot wax. The sandy floor of the desert was hidden by a thick pile of magnificent carpets which insulated us against the slight evening damps; an elaborate series of dishes, both hot and cold, found their way onto the buffet—all in the best traditions of Egypt. The finesse and the organisation of the feast in such an out-of-the-way spot could not help but set one musing. And so the evening gradually condensed itself harmoniously and prolonged itself through the wines to the coffee and cigars without anything untoward having taken place. I myself, touched by the ardour of Piers, could not help feeling regretfully that this was perhaps all that we were going to be shown of the group's activities. I don't know why, I had not much faith in the reality represented by such breakaway sects as gnostics, and I was on my guard against the spuriously romantic. In Egypt it seemed dangerously easy to succumb to the folklore of the place— and this my friend appeared to have done. "Ah! Piers," I said, looking into his pale and impatient face. "You are in for another disappointment I fear." He clutched my wrist and shook his head; he was in a

110

fever of excited anticipation, and his eyes followed Akkad everywhere. I loved him most when he was like this—I could read the moods of Sylvie written in his youthful eyes, which kindled almost vengefully under the spur of his emotions. "Patience," he said, pleadingly, and added: "Here comes Sabine again." Akkad was talking earnestly to a tall man in uniform.

Sabine disengaged herself from the rest of the company and came slowly towards us with that air of simple insolence which was perhaps merely a by-product of her costume—for she was clad again like a sort of gipsy, and had travelled into Cairo with a caravan from Tunis. Her hair and palms were stained with henna and her eyes were dazed and stupefied-looking from belladonna and badly applied kohl. Her feet were bare and dirty, her toenails broken. I felt that she somehow enjoyed disgusting people—there was no reason for wearing fancy dress at such a gathering. She also seemed somehow heavier, more obese, but perhaps this was due simply to the lapping of quilted petticoats which covered her. At any rate she looked very much the crafty gipsy of the oriental fairy-tales, and the glass of champagne in her hand seemed almost out of place. She stood before us, smiling from one to the other for a moment, and then asked: "Is Toby with you? He said he'd come." I made a vague gesture in the direction that Toby had taken and she moved off to follow him, shaking her dark stone-carving of a head with a little gesture of impatience and determination. I had never really cared for Sabine, and Piers knew it; he watched me watching her with an amused irony. "Say it," he said at last. "Why don't you say it?" I sighed at being found out.

"Very well, I shall say it. Now that I know her, her very pretentiousness irritates me—thrusting her profligacy down our throats all the time . . ." Piers laughed softly at my sanctimonious choice of the words. "A desert father," he said with his tender yet teasing eye. "Come, my dear fellow." I felt called upon to justify some of the irritation I felt with Sabine. "I am not," I said, "the only one she irritates. Ask those Jewish merchants who travelled with her in the caravan." Piers nodded, with a certain indifference. "Moreover," I went on, "she came and asked me for a consultation, and I found that she was being treated for syphilis with herbs by a camel driver."

"Why not?"

"It's a waste of time, you know perfectly well why not."

I think really that it was her utter indifference to her condition which most infuriated me; or was it because of Toby? At any rate I had told her what I knew about 606, and asked Akkad to send her to a specialist. In those days I was in the full flush of my scientific knowledge—unaware that the dogmatic theology of science was itself a kind of folklore, and that even the most perfect specific sometimes failed to work. Youth inclines towards the absolute in everything. I continued my complaint as I watched her dark saturnine head moving among the others, hunting for my friend. "Although she was still highly infectious she took Toby away to the Fayum for a week."

"You are wrong about her," said Piers, "simply because you don't know all her qualities. I asked her what she thought of Rob Sutcliffe and why she did not marry him, and she said: 'I have never been able to envisage a love without jealousy and exclusiveness, and have never dared to risk the business.' I then asked her if that did not make us seem suspect to her and she said yes it did. 'You are not real, you are figments of yourselves, love on all fours, *amour à quatre pattes*. The conventional *ménage à trois* reversed.' I admit this wounded me. Then she went on, 'But then love doesn't need decoding like a cipher.' "

"She was wrong," I said. "It does. Like a cipher or a riddle to which the answer is always ambiguous in a Delphic way. Besides, did you think I was not jealous?"

Toby had told us that Rob Sutcliffe was planning to sketch us into his new novel and I wondered vaguely what his verdict on us might be—in the light of all the freshly turned earth thrown up during his stay in Vienna. My sister had been unsuccessfully psycho-analysed there during a long moment—which was quite sufficient to enable Rob to acquire a bit of the prevailing jargon which made life so distressing for everyone, and conferred such an air of knowledgeable impertinence on the devotees of old Freud. A little knowledge is a dangerous thing, and these findings about the penetralia of sexual life gave the writer a sort of justification for a native acerbity. Afterwards, when love left him in the lurch and he became the wounded man who was such a trial to us all, he took refuge in a laughter and cynicism which were far from his real nature—a secretive one. He had at last discovered that love had no pith in it, and that the projection of one's own feelings upon the image of a beloved was in the long run an act of self-mutilation.

In the flicker of light from a dipping faltering candle I saw that slightly sardonic, slightly disdainful look, and it seemed to me full of a certain enigmatic maturity. Sabine was older than the rest of us—not in years, to be sure: but in judgement and insight. Her voyages and adventures had forged her mind already while we were still upon the threshold of our emotional maturity. The word I was looking for, I suppose, was "sphingine"—I thought of the baleful prehistoric smile of the Mycenaean women. She drew her shawl about her with a sudden gesture of dismissal, of renunciation, and shrugged her strong shoulders. Then she leaned forward to kiss the cheek of Sylvie with a humble gesture and to smile into her eyes. All at once there was something heart-appealing about this strong girl in her buoyant fancy dress—it was the warmth of a burning and candid intelligence. I saw what Sutcliffe had seen.

Much later of course I came to "recognise" her as one who, in her inner life, had thrown over the intermediaries of convention and reason which might have shielded her social self, in favour of direct vision, direct apprehension. This was the secret of her courage—of everything that made her seem so often *outré,* unconventional, out of scale. The small-minded found her simply rude and inconsiderate, whereas she was quite simply unaware of the fences they had set up about the notion of conventional behaviour. It was like being colour-blind, say, or tone-deaf. Once one realised this about her it was possible to make allowances, and to arrive at different conclusions about her. But it wasn't easy. For example, even now, dressed as she was . . . And then once she went outside and blew her nose in her fingers to the horror of the servants. But Akkad loved her, Akkad accepted her fully. I once saw them meet, put out their hands like antennae and touch softly, sighing both and smiling with the kind of joyous feeling normal in lovers— which they were not. Yet he loved her because there was never any need to tell her anything, to explain, to expound. At least this is what his looks sought to convey. While in his presence she seemed to become younger and shyer, less assertive, more humble. For her part her meek looks seemed to be saying: "He knows everything, he understands everything—but best of all, he knows that it is of no importance whatsoever. No need to plead, no need to convince."

Piers followed my glance as well as read my mind

as I formulated these thoughts. He said mischievously: "I think that you really envy her, because she makes love *à tous les quatre vents* without ascribing an absolute value to the act: whereas we three are in the grip of an infatuation which goes on and on. How strange to have lost one's taste for other people—like losing one's sense of smell almost: why is there no word for it in English? We have deaf and blind, but nothing to describe the lost sense of smell . . . or the loss of the other thing for that matter."

Akkad was slowly making his way towards us now, and one could feel a sort of leisurely intent in his movements; nor was I wrong, for he came up to take Piers tenderly by the sleeve and place his other hand upon my own arm. "In a little while," he said, drawing us both together, "we shall invite you to come into the shrine of old Abu Menouf with the rest of us for what will be something like a religious service—or a reading of the psalms. I will be doing the commentary and the exposition. If you get bored, do not hesitate to leave and come back here. No offence will be taken. It is understood that you could be potential members of the group though as yet not set in your resolve. There will be others like you also, so do not feel that you are all alone. It should not be more painful than one of the traditional lectures on the Koran that you have heard, given by a venerable old sheik in Cairo; but of course the subject will be heretical from all points of view." He laughed soundlessly, and spread his hands out in a gesture of quaint helplessness. "What would you have us to do—sit down under the great lie and accept the rule of one we call the Prince of Darkness?" The tone in which he said this suggested more the deliberations of a stockbroker than the lucubrations of a bigot.

He went on in a lower tone: "It is not a question of making a small compromise on behalf of happiness

—it cuts far deeper. Once you see the truth the way we see it you simply cannot refuse to accept. You are surrounded, cut off, severed forever from the world as you have been living it, lost, sunk, foundered . . ." His tone remained wryly quizzical, sardonic, but his eye was very much alive, with its strange glaucous movements. As for myself, this very absence of a definitive attitude, this shying away from the mantic or the vatic, filled me with misgivings. I was young and anxious to be carried away, to be swept off my feet—just as much as my friend. But in this domain mere logical arguments, mere theological prevarications didn't seem to me to be what I was looking for. If the sort of conviction that Akkad implied was what we desired, why then rational argument was not the way to foster it. Romantic? Yes. We had every right to be. We dreamed of a perfect conviction of the truth of being which would be independent of arguable proof. Akkad stood before us in his much darned abba—the one he wore to paint his vivid water colours—and smiled his jubilant and dreamy smile. No, it would not do—at least that is how I felt. If the whole sum of human knowledge had to be put to the question then only a prophet of wrath, a poet of wrath, could do it, and could carry us with him over the rapids into the new country which was, according to our friend, waiting to claim us. Something of all this —doubts, hesitations—may have been visible on our faces for Akkad hesitated once more before resuming his more solemn manner. He looked at his slim watch and made an almost imperceptible sign to the major-domo, the tall aristocratic Arab who had met us on the black horse at the entrance to the oasis. The servants began slowly to bring in light silk prayer-mats and small cushions—the colour green predominated. These we placed over our arms as we prepared to leave the tent for the shrine. But we were not as numerous as I had surmised—a full third of the company appeared not to belong to our group, and not therefore to be in the secret of our private congregation about the sepulchre of Abu Menouf. It was, then, an ordinary holiday cocktail party on to which Akkad had grafted the members of his little sect. It was, so to speak, a small intermission in the general celebrations of the Moslem fair, the noise of which we could still hear reverberating outside the brilliant walls of our enclosure. So gradually, without prejudicing the pleasant atmosphere of the party, we sidled towards the entrance, following Akkad, who waited a while at the door and then turned to lead the way.

A brilliant moon poured its molten light into the lake where the tall reeds, turned ink-black or pure quicksilver according to angle, stood rooted once in their own reflections, then twice in the light clay floor of the depression. The sand of the desert could have been snow. Still as plate glass the whole world, except where here or there an insect incised the glowing surface with its struggles, and sent small wrinkles shoreward. The sky was cloudless—the moon rolled across the surface like a lamb searching for its dam. The desert air struck chill as we wound along the palm-groves towards the shrine. A dim light could be discerned from it, shining through the windows covered in painted wax paper. In and out of darkness we were moonsplashed so that one had little unaccustomed glimpses of each other's faces. I saw Akkad turned by such an accident into a grim mummy, Sabine smiled with white monkey's teeth, Casimir Ava shorn of his hair by a trick of the light looked like an old lady at prayer. I had the illusion that our numbers were swelled, not by candidates from the cocktail party, but by other unknown people who had been waiting outside in the darkness, and who now attached themselves to our procession.

The two dervishes, unkempt and forlorn though they were, held the door open for us, watchful as mastiffs. They gave the impression of knowing exactly who belonged and who did not, but this must have been an illusion for they did not know us, for example, and yet they signalled us to pass with the rest. A dark narrow stairway led us into the body of the little mosque—into a large central room very dimly lighted by tiny night-lights floating in saucers of olive oil. Because of the darkness the domed ceiling seemed as high as the sky outside, and by consequence our figures appeared diminished, and as if they were rapidly melting back into the darkness from which apparently they had been summoned.

The form of the ceremony was easy enough to discern—it was, as he had said, exactly like a Cairo sheik delivering a theological lecture in a mosque. Akkad was to be seated in the middle of the floor upon a carpet and cushion with a low table of inlaid wood some distance before him. Placed to his right and left were other tables and cushions placed for his two acolytes—one an old blind man in a white robe, the other a swarthy and bearded man of middle age in a crumpled lounge suit, but with no collar. He looked like a retired postmaster. In his hand he held a bundle of texts and a book, which he consulted, and he had the air of a stage-prompter; while the old blind man looked like one of those itinerant "singing" priests, beadles or sacristans, who can always be summoned to chant verses from the Koran in time of need. These dispositions taken up, we the auditors formed a circle at a distance round the trio, being all seated with the greatest regularity upon the ground, and while nobody actually marshalled us in any particular order we felt that an order had insensibly been conformed to: the inner circle consisted of those who were more or less the real initiates of the group and the circles moved outward until they came to us, who were simply "on-lookers with intent," as Akkad called us.

For his part he sat himself down in the sheik's place, removed his glasses and clasped his hands before him as he gazed dreamily up into the darkness of the mosque. We knelt or sat in silence. The blind man waited with his chin on his breast, breathing softly, his hearing tuned, it seemed, to concert pitch, waiting for a sign. The other scruffy individual consulted a pile of texts and then, clearing his throat, coldly announced a reading from the Pistis Sophia—but for all the world as if he were announcing a reading from the weather almanac. A further silence followed. Akkad appeared to pray now, for he extended his long fingers and held up his clasped hands. Then he leaned forward and tapped with a fingernail on the little inlaid table. The old blind man drew a joyous slow breath, and with a smile—looking upwards now with an expression of great sanctity—started slowly and melodically to recite. All three smiled at the familiar opening phrases—as musicians might smile as they joined forces to interpret a piece of music long known by all and loved. But the recitation was in Greek—somewhat to my surprise; and while only the old man uttered the words the lips of the other two men moved caressingly over the polished and familiar phrases. If I say I was surprised at the Greek it was because (knowing nothing then of such matters) Akkad had given us to understand that the Pistis Sophia was a Coptic text written in that language. This was indeed so, but the Coptic of which he spoke was itself a translation from the Greek, so that we were hearing was the original from which the Coptic translators had worked. Piers, whose scholarship was really quite profound, later claimed to have followed nearly the whole reading with tolerable accuracy. Myself not. But the asides of Akkad were delivered in French or English and served as a quite

spontaneous commentary upon the text, uttered with
too great an informality to suggest prayer, but with the
deep reverence one accords to great poetry or great
music. "And it came to pass when Jesus had risen from
the dead, that he passed eleven years discoursing with
his disciples, and instructing them only up to the regions of the First Commandment, up to the First Mystery, that within the Veil, within the First Commandment, which is the four and twentieth Mystery without
and below—those four and twenty which are in the
second space of the First Mystery which is above all
Mysteries—the Father in the form of a dove." (Later
I came upon the translation of Mead, and others, from
the Bruce Codex and similar sources and was so able
to document myself a little bit about this weird post-
resurrectional history of Jesus.)

The odd thing about it was that it sounded not at
all oracular, but in a queer way perfectly intelligible,
perfectly sound as sense—when quite obviously if one
doesn't know the terminology, as we did not, it is the
purest gibberish. I could not judge either in what precise degree the rest of the sect interpreted this monotonous chanting. Their heads were bowed, except when
Akkad broke into the recitation with a dry staccato
observation speaking often with a kind of restrained
passion which was foreign to his ordinary comport-
ment. Such as "The more you know of man the less
can you condone the human situation under the
Prince." A fearful act of duplicity had overturned the
rational order of the universe—that is what he meant
I afterwards realised. The interloper, who had replaced
the original monarch of the ages, had thrown into confusion the workings of cosmic law. Since he came, the
Black Prince, everything had to be reordered, reap-
prehended, reshaped; the whole of reality therefore.
"The Greeks said 'All this is untrue but it is beauti-

ful.' But beauty is no excuse. Beauty is a trap. We say 'All this is untrue but it is real.' "

It was much later that I realised what he meant—to be of this persuasion was to remain truthful to the fundamental despair of reality, to realise finally and completely that there was no hope unless the usurping God could be dethroned, and that there seemed to be no way to do that. Had I understood more at this first encounter with the gnostics I should have been filled with the same despair as they presumably were. The implacability of process would have haunted me, as it came to haunt me later. What Akkad himself called "The very death of God," for the usurping prince had made away with the original king whose reign had been an illustration, not of nature's discord, but of nature's harmony and congruence. Under him birth and death had been fully realised, spirit and flesh, animal, insect and man were joined in a creative symbiosis of light and justice—such as we had not dared even to conceive since the date when the Prince of Darkness took his place on the throne.

I cannot say that all this did not confuse me, for it did; yet in a strange sort of way I felt that from time to time things deviated into profound sense. It is as if someone were reading to me in a language I knew but imperfectly; little patches of meaning floated out to me, sandwiched in between long passages of meaningless sound. Akkad's oracular interventions were often apt and indeed beautiful. "Who are they, then, these people? They are those who are born and re-born again unlike the Many. They recognise each other when they meet without a word being exchanged. They belong to the vertigo of nothingness, having emerged from the root of all dissent. The thrust of their souls is towards the moon of non-being, their God is he who no longer exists. How can they hope to make themselves understood? Reason is powerless—for this kind of understanding can only be soundless, wordless, breathless. Its meaning is as precarious as reality itself." Strange to read these words many years afterwards and to remember the circumstances of their delivery with such vivid accuracy. Without even closing my eyes I saw him, sitting there in his shabby old abba, looking suddenly very much older and moved almost to tears by the message he had to deliver. All the beautiful women listened, silent as fruit, some in evening dress, some in coloured shawls, all with apple-calm minds.

Part of it was litany and part ritual for once or twice the man who seemed like a prompter blew out the candles and relit them, as if to mark a distinct pause in the proceedings. He also proposed texts, uttering the first line in a solemn twang and waiting until the blind man recognised the passage and then, lifting his head like a dog, joined in on a higher register. Piers was rapt and attentive, and at the same time disappointed, I could see that; while his sister had closed her eyes and let her head fall forward, as if she were listening to music. "Thereafter there cometh a receiver of the little Sabaoth, the Good, him of the Midst: He himself bringeth a cup full of thoughts and wisdom, and soberness is in it; and he handeth it to the soul. And they cast it into a body which can neither sleep nor forget because of the cup of soberness which hath been handed unto it. But it will whip its heart persistently to question about the mysteries of the Light until at last it find them through the decision of the Virgin of Light, and so inherit the light itself forever."

I was far away as yet from "seeing" in the gnostic sense that night—of acquiring that penetrating vision which could turn us all to masks and caricatures of reality with names, mere labels; each one of us nevertheless with an "eidolon" or signature, a disposition, a proclivity visible to the naked eye of the intuition only. Within each of us struggled man, woman and child. Our passions were packed in the cool clay of our silences, ready for the oven, ready for the mystical marriage feast. . . . In this sense, and in this sense only, did I find a perfectly satisfactory rationale which subsumed my double relationship with Piers and with his sister. It was through this experience with Akkad and his sect that I at last managed to gain a foothold in that part of reality which was probably my own inner self. It may sound strange, but I now understood the nature of my love—and also the nature of human love as a whole. I saw quite unmistakably that man had set astray the natural periodicity of sexuality and so forfeited his partnership with the animal kingdom. This was his central trauma, and it also signalled the final loss of his powers over the matter—that was coming . . .

Yet despite the apparent informality of the proceedings which amounted almost to laxness one could feel underneath the structure of a method. I had the impression that something was being conveyed to me as a sense impression, and not being made rationally explicit in order not to indulge my natural faculty of ratiocination. After all you cannot ask a perfume or a sound to explain itself. By the same token I simply inhaled all this lore without trying my mind on it, trying to reduce it to some sort of canonical formula.

All this and much more was borne in my consciousness on that strange night; despite my misgivings and my distrust of hocus pocus. . . . The incident of the snake and the mummia and the wine when it came seemed absolutely natural and not a mere seductive folklore to gain adherents or convince doubters. One of the dervishes brought a large flat wicker basket which he placed at the feet of Akkad, who lifted the lid from it and disclosed a very large snake—a species of cobra which I had not seen before. It was very much bigger than the ordinary Egyptian cobra and could have perhaps been Indian. But its colour was extraordinary—a kind of nacreous pink shading into violet underneath its body. It appeared as domesticated as a household pet. It looked about with its forked tongue flicking softly in and out of its cruel white mouth; its hood was not fully inflated. A saucer of milk was placed for it with some dead flies floating in it and it leaned forward delicately to lap like a pet; indeed to facilitate the meal it slipped out of its soft basket giving us a chance to marvel at its great length. Akkad stroked it in familiar fashion, and it accepted his caress as a cat might, flattening its head and extending it for the touch of his palm. After a pause the recitation went on, though all eyes were now on the snake. When the reptile had finished its meal Akkad took it up softly and came towards us holding it in his arms, draped around him, curled, oozing, swaying. We were each of us to stroke its head, so he told us; and in spite of our fear and revulsion we made an effort to do so.

Piers and his sister passed the test easily but in my case and Toby's the snake appeared to hesitate and ruminate, and when we put out a hand it uttered a slight hiss. "Insist quietly," said Akkad, "and don't be afraid of it." It was easy to say, and we did our best to comply with his instructions, but I did not feel that the perfunctory pat on the head I gave it amounted to very much. When it came to Sabine's turn Akkad simply emptied it into her arms, and snake and woman seemed to sink into a complete embrace. She murmured the sort of endearments one might reserve for a favourite kitten, stroking its head and winding it around her body. It took some time to complete this little ceremony for everyone had to touch it in turn; but when it was completed Akkad took it back to its basket and coaxed it to resume its position inside it—erect and ever-watchful however. Now some batons of incense had been lighted by the dervishes and clouds of aromatic perfume rolled about the dark corners of the mosque, obscuring outlines and transforming faces and forms. The recitation with its melodious but twanging Greek shifted key, moved in the direction of greater emphasis, as if kindled by the waves of perfume on the dark night.

Akkad sat listening, his head now bowed, like a man under a waterfall; but it seemed that he was waiting for a particular passage or a special break in the litany, for suddenly he raised his finger and the reciters paused. "Now let us partake of the holy mummia," he said in commanding tones and the dervishes advanced towards us humbly bearing large silver trays on which were a number of small bowls with pieces of mummia—or at least I presumed it was mummia. Dried mummy-flesh had been a standby in medicine for centuries, and as a doctor in bud I was curious to taste it. But dark Sylvie shuddered. The little strips of flesh were quite dry, quite dehydrated. The consistency was that of the dried fish known as Bombay duck; but the colour was a dark red, almost crimson, and the taste was faint and tenuous. I tried to place it, and found myself thinking of a faint perfume of celery. It reminded me a little of French froglegs, or the dried locusts I had once eaten in the desert outside Cairo. I despatched a wafer or two of this magic comestible without undue anxiety and watched the quantity gradually diminish as each one of us in the circle took up his portion. Akkad watched it all solemnly; but there was no specially ritual aspect of this part of the ceremony. When everyone had partaken of the mummia the dishes were taken away and Akkad, once more interrupting the recitation, said: "Now let us partake of the wine."

Flagons were now brought made of some strange

pottery, and in each flagon there was perhaps a tea-cupful of a wine mixture which tasted salt and tepid; we waited until the whole company was served and then, in response to the same gesture by Akkad, raised our receptacles in an attitude of toasting before draining them. This was the point at which I realised that some of my misgivings had been soundly based—for the wine was powerfully drugged, and one instantly felt one's senses sag and falter. Everything now began to mix and flow—what with the clouds of incense and the staccato note of the chanting, you could quite clearly feel the sudden distortion set in as the vision changed focus; yet it was not at all alarming, we were all quite at ease. Perhaps we were reassured by Akkad, who said, "It will not last long," as he saw the obvious signs of our struggle against the drug.

He added, sweeping our faces with his glance: "Keep your gaze on Ophis the snake." For my part I stared at the snake with all the wild intensity of a pilot seeking a passage across a fog-bound estuary; it was partly due to visibility and partly to the drug we had taken. Everything now rose and subsided, wobbled and merged and deliquesced. The ancient serpent itself appeared to rear up to twice its height in order to present itself more clearly to us, in order as it were to preside more fully over the ceremony. But anything I say about this part of the evening is subject to caution—for we were so obviously and woefully dazed by the potion. I recall the voice of Toby saying, with a kind of triumphant indignation: "Mumbo Jumbo by Jove." But he said it unwillingly, almost sleepily, as though all but carried away by what he saw despite his native reservations. "The eyes," cried Akkad sharply, "look at the eyes."

I looked at the tiny glittering eyes of Ophis, and it gave back my glance with a queer malevolent glitter, an insinuating flicker of that forked tongue. So staring, I felt that I was rushing towards it, its head became enormous, its delicate hinged jaws open to expose long scimitar-like teeth, so white and clean. A wild revulsion rose in me, and I felt all of a sudden as if I were suffocating; I struggled to free my neck from the collar of the garment I wore, to breathe more freely. Then I shook the vision out of my eyes like someone shaking back clear-sightedness after a severe concussion brought about by a blow on the head.

It was something like a battle of willpowers. The serpent was trying to engulf me, like a python with a hare, and I was quite determined to keep myself free. All this rose to the boil, so to speak, and then burst like a bubble, and as it did so I saw what later I was to recognise as our mentor, the usurping Prince, seated in place of the serpent, staring at me with a kind of bloodthirsty jocularity. How difficult it is to describe this sort of vision; yes, we all have the capacity during a dream to fabricate this sort of thing. But this was somehow different, though I cannot for the life of me explain just how. I saw a snake no longer but a kind of huge dung beetle with the head of a dog; its body was armour-plated like a saurian, with black polished scales, like the body-armour of a Japanese swordsman. A single goat's hoof was visible outside the snake basket, standing on the flags of the mosque. This whole vision kept dissolving and reappearing in the vast clouds of incense. Yet it was not quite a vision—it was certainly a Thing of particular consequence to me. I could not just dismiss it as a piece of reality distorted by a drug or a dose of alcohol. I was profoundly impressed and depressed by it, and I had a nagging feeling that nothing would ever be the same again for me. Absurd, of course, absurd.

Looking so fixedly at this strange machine-like

animal-bird-insect I felt as if it were talking to me, felt it had the sort of significance which one cannot render clear by words, a deep symbolic significance of something which by-passed causality. The alchemists apparently have to deal with this sort of symbol in their work; but I was no alchemist, and I knew little enough about orders of knowledge which were not rudely scientific. I also shared a good deal of Toby's dogged scepticism. But there was much of which I was then unaware—and for example, at this very moment I was unaware that I had let out something between a shout and a shriek and tried to leap to my feet and advance on the snake. Toby heard me faintly and told me later on. Yet all movement was impossible—I was paralysed. Moreover I was all of a sudden exhausted, racked with sobs; the current turned itself off with a magical suddenness, and just as if I had depended upon it to sit upright, I found myself falling forward upon my hands. I felt my cheek touching the cold flags of the room as I came to my senses, slowly, trembling all over. When at last I raised my eyes it was to see that almost everyone in the company was in the same case, lying utterly exhausted on their carpets, tremulously breathing and gasping. It had lasted a very short time, the visionary incident. It had drained us of our attention and then left us stranded like objects on a beach at low tide. I have seldom felt so physically exhausted.

But there was one exception to the general state of exhaustion—and that was constituted by the behaviour of poor Piers which differed completely from our own. He was plainly choking, with both hands trying to tear an invisible serpent from his throat; he rose to his knees, writhing, fighting, gasping with weakness. He rolled over on his side, still struggling—and his miming of the snake, something huge like a boa, was so lifelike that for a moment one almost saw the reptile sliding round him, squeezing the breath from his body. As I say, all this was so very lifelike, and his distress so great that I started feebly to try and rouse myself to go to his aid, but Akkad smilingly bade me desist; in fact he looked highly delighted by this mimic battle and by the deep anxiety of my friend. Later he was to tell me, for what it was worth, that it confirmed the initiation of Piers, and his inclusion without further probation into the sect. He had been granted the particular sign of the snake-covenant. Myself I was reminded when he said this of the Aesculapian snake and the *incubatio* in the white colonnades of Epidaurus where the doctors interpreted the first night's sleep according to the snake-dreams of the patient. Yes, there were many connections which Akkad helped me to work out during the short time I was in Egypt with him, many resonances and affiliations.

Piers had gone so white and still that he seemed dead. But to tell the truth everyone showed the same signs of blank exhaustion in varying degrees, and presently at a sign from Akkad the servants appeared with soft wraps which they laid upon the recumbent forms. The great snake disappeared. Somewhere a door opened and a cold whiff of desert air entered to chase the columns of incense and bring a breathable atmosphere into the mosque. But we were all utterly dead with sleep, all of us; myself I lay in a state of dreamy half-convalescence like a child at breast. I felt the soft material draped over me and the cushion adjusted under my head by an invisible hand, and I allowed myself to founder softly into nothingness, worn out with all I had experienced. When I awoke with a jolt it was early dawn already, and all the other sleepers had vanished, with the exception of Piers, who had crawled to my side and now slept quietly with his head against my shoulder. Sylvie? Toby? Gone! Moreover everything was silent save for the hum of insects in the trees outside the mosque. The sun was just touching the rim of the horizon and the whole world was saffron and lion-gold. The cold cut to the very bone of thought. I took Piers' pulse. He seemed perfectly normal now—and indeed I myself felt completely recovered from the mysterious fatigue of the night before. I was full, too, of a physical ex-uberance unusual for me, and also a tremendous mental euphoria—the kind of feeling one gets after having, without deserving it, passed a difficult exam unexpectedly. "Piers," I whispered, "I'm going to have a swim." He did not open his eyes or say any-thing, but a tiny pucker of a smile came to the cor-ner of his lips so that I knew he had heard me.

I went down the stairs into the crisp dawn light; the whole village slept. It looked like an abandoned battlefield. Only an occasional horse was stirring. I walked towards the looking-glass of the lake, eager to see my own reflection in it as if in some curious way I expected to have changed, to have altered in my physical appearance. For what reason? I do not know —only this abstract sense of jubilation and relief dogged my steps, and I could offer myself no reason for it. I broke into a run along the margins of the lake, looking sideways to see my reflection racing through the massed spear-points of the reeds. The sun came up like a bronze medallion and its regal heat spilled over onto the damp sand, swiftly dispelling the heavy night dews. I looked carefully to see if there were any of the telltale black shells in the shal-lows which might portend water infected by the dread bilharzia, but there were none and before I could think it I was up to my waist in the icy bril-liance of the lake water, consumed again by this in-explicable joy. I swam out of my depth and turned over to let the sun fire a million silver drops of pris-matic light onto my wet eyelashes. It was not too long either before a second figure joined me, and then the third—the dark girl whom I could never see like this without a contraction of the heart. I did not say "I love you" aloud, nor did she. Our wet fingers touched and we formed a circle like the corolla of a flower, floating into the silence of the desert dawn with the ancient sun on our bodies. It lasted a long time, this swim which seemed to have some of the qualities of an esoteric act of lustration. We were all somehow too excited to speak or exclaim; only our triumphant eyes met from time to time to exchange jubilant glances. It is true that once I asked Sylvie: "Did you see. . . ?" But she drew her breath and, nodding, cut off my sentence, as if not only had we shared the same vision but also that it did not bear speaking about openly.

Piers smiled to himself. He looked vaguely preoccupied, as if he were making an inventory of his feelings, were documenting something—an experience which threw the whole range of his past feelings into relief, so that he was forced to re-evaluate them all in the light of this new element. *What* new element? *What* had he seen? At this point I recall the coarse stentorian voice of Toby (who was waiting for us on the bank with towels and clothes) as it uttered the words. "Mumbo Jumbo"—but rather defensively, I thought. We who knew him so well could detect something artificial in the fervour of his exclamation. Sylvie smiled. "Akkad is waiting," he added, feeling the water with the tips of his fingers and deciding with a shudder that it was too cold to join us in a swim. "I must take you to him. It's an order."

We three dressed slowly, contentedly, still making no allusion to our thoughts and yet somehow deeply conscious that whatever they were they had become the common property of the three of us. It was like an extension of our loving sort of new tropical flora and fauna, a private country in which we wandered now, luxuriating in all its poetic beauty and variety. No horses attended us here, so we set off to wander across the sand together, led by scarlet Toby, who knew the way and who had orders to take us to Akkad for our breakfast. It was not so very far; we skirted some great silken mounds of dune and came at last to a bare stone plateau, its surface worn smooth by centuries of blowing sand so that even the coloured striations in the rock were smooth-graven, as if by an emery board. I had forgotten all about the little aeroplane of our host. It looked somehow vulnerable and primitive standing out there in the sunlight; like an insect. But bizarrely enough Akkad sat under it in a thronelike barber's chair with inlaid arms smothered in decorations of copper and false pearl: and with a white cloth spread over him. His barber Fahem (we called him the Court Figaro) bent reverently over him to lather his cheeks while a small boy, also dressed in white, kept the already active flies away with a whisk. It was one of the pleasing little opulences of Alexandria for a rich man to have a portable barber; normally businessmen in Egypt did not shave at home. Their barbers waited in the anteroom to their offices with all their instruments. So they were shaved ceremoniously while sitting at their desks and sorting out the morning mail with the help of their secretaries. Akkad had simply extended the bounds of this feudal traditon; whenever he went by plane he took his own barber along. Now he peered at us shortsightedly but with an obvious pleasure—an air almost of congratulation. From the depths of a steaming towel he even said: "Come closer, I want to see your faces." And when we obliged he gazed at us keenly and then gave a sigh. "Yes," he said, "I can see that you saw him; you look so happy. And you, Piers, were accepted at once. It was a cardinal sign, your struggle with Ophis.

132

I can read your heart, and yours too, Sylvie; for you there is going to be no looking back." Then turning to me he said: "The traditions of your education have hampered you a bit but nevertheless you saw what they did, and in the long run your native scepticism will give way to acceptance. It will be slower, that is all. But you will catch them up." Mysterious words! He submitted with a long-suffering comical grimace: to the barber's massage and the wheezing spray of toilet water spurted on his scalp. Toby said stoutly and somewhat surprisingly: "I saw nothing except a lot of smoke. I don't know what the others saw but I saw nothing."

Akkad looked at him curiously and withal in kindly fashion as if he were genuinely puzzled; for my part, it seemed to me clear from Toby's tone that he was prevaricating. But Akkad pondered the question for a long moment with closed eyes, as if he were verifying something in his memory. Then he said: "Yes, but you did see something; I will tell you what you saw. You saw something that looked like a brass rubbing from an English cathedral—the tomb of the Black Prince in somewhere like Canterbury. The vizor of the helmet was up, and you got scared when you stared into the black hole of the armoured head because you thought you saw the glitter of snake-eyes where the face should have been." Toby's jaw dropped and he turned rather pale. "How did you know that?" he gasped, quite forgetting to deny the truth of the allegation. Akkad shrugged his shoulders and adjusted his spectacles on his nose again the better to study his man. "I was puzzled at first," he said mildly. "But now I see why you denied the whole thing; you have confused the biblical Jesus with the post-resurrectional Jesus in the gnostic context. He is simply a cipher for us. He has no connection with what you call Our Saviour (as you say quite rightly one only has to mention his name and blood starts flowing). Our Jesus comes much later in the day, and even he proved powerless to dethrone the personage you all saw last night who has had a thousand names, among them Sathanas and Lucifer. As each one brings a little of himself to what he sees, you brought the trappings of your historic preoccupations, so that Monsieur flattered you by presenting himself with beaver up like Hamlet's father's ghost!" He roared with laughter and struck his knee.

Toby was as confused and discountenanced as any schoolboy; but Akkad took him affectionately by the arm and said still laughing: "Come into the next room, I mean the next dune. I have ordered an absurd English breakfast for you all. After that I shall take you for a ride down to the sea and batter you with a little bit of theology—though not you yet, Toby. You are recalcitrant as yet. Your time will come later." The sunshine was already baking and I was glad of our straw hats which Toby had brought with him; in a cloudless blue sky vultures hovered. We climbed the scarp into the next depression, and really could not help bursting into laughter ourselves, the scene was so surrealist. In the middle of the sand, looking incongruously without a relevant context, stood a long table covered in spotless napery on which Akkad's munificence had caused to be laid out a superlative English breakfast of a sort that only the great country houses might have provided in the past. Leaving aside the sausages and tomatoes grilling quietly in the silver chafing dishes, there were also several kinds of fish, including haddock and kipper, and also, laughably enough, a dish of warm kedgeree with eggs on horseback; the whole was backed up with two kinds of marmalade. We were served (on beautiful plate) by two Nubian servants with gold sashes and white gloves.

Akkad was delighted with our laughter and smiled slyly as he said: "It's not what the others will be getting at all. I thought a sort of confirmation breakfast would be in order. I'm sorry to keep striking this public-school note, Piers, but my upbringing included a memorable English spell at Mournfield which I have never forgotten and which supplied me with a host of affectionate memories and many good friends." So, still smiling over his extraordinary desert scene we took our places and tucked into this breakfast with a will. "Afterwards we will ride," said Akkad. "But just you three and myself. We shall leave Toby behind to look after Sabine until we come back. You see, now that you have seen what you have seen I can fill in the picture a little with more factual things, with texts and little commentaries which relate to your presence here. You see, all this was not an accident—I mean your coming into Egypt at this time, and to me. I saw it happening several years ago during the same period of the year in the same shrine. Of course I did not know your names, but I knew you by sight and I knew your circumstances with tolerable accuracy. I was able to judge what you might do to help or hinder the group in its activities. I was also able to predict the degree to which you yourselves would benefit from the creed of the sect, the tenets of this gnosticism—which seems at first so forbidding." He was silent for a long moment now, smoking a slim cigar and drinking his coffee. "No. It was no accident," he said. "And indeed your circumstances are unlike those of most of the others— the special relationship to sex and the understanding of love in your sense . . . This was what we believe but few of us had ever experienced, at least in the singularly pure form which you seem to have realised. We will speak about that today."

No more was said; Piers hung his head and looked somewhat shy at this reference to sex, for he was always extremely *pudique* about such personal and private exchanges, and shuddered at any kind of coarse allusions to matters which he considered so agonisingly important, so very close to his heart. I think this excessive delicacy used to irritate Sabine, who always tried to puncture what she regarded as an inexperienced and juvenile reserve. But then she had never made love to him—it would have surprised her. But Akkad on the contrary seemed to appreciate and respect this delicacy in him; he would not I think have agreed to Sabine's strictures (so openly and honestly expressed) when she said: "Ach, you and your little sister are overbred and overrefined. You need a streak of coarseness in your lives." She may have been right, she may have been counting upon me to supply the missing factor?

When this baroque breakfast of Akkad's had come to an end a messenger was despatched to summon the horses and bring a small picnic for each of us. "I am going to take you down to the sea, but in a different place where you have never been," said Akkad, who enjoyed putting on a childish air of mystery. "A secret place," he added slyly. And then as we were mounting the horses and trying out stirrup-lengths and reins he said: "By the way, in case any one asks you, you must say that you went to a lecture at Abu Menouf, but not mention the word gnostic. You see the shrine was founded in memory of a great Wali, seer, holy man— but apparently a Mohammedan. Here in Egypt we try never to offend religious susceptibilities, and the dervishes are convinced that what we are doing here is having a quite orthodox religious service in the memory of the saint. So we are. So we are. But Abu Menouf himself was a gnostic, and this oasis being far off the beaten track seemed a suitable place for our gatherings. We did not wish to trouble the authorities with our beliefs which have nothing to do with the social or political situation of the country. We gather twice or thrice a year here for this precise purpose.

Our own patron saint is the Aesculapian snake you
saw, though the dervishes are convinced that the soul
(the Moslem soul) of Abu Menouf went into it when
he died. It would be a nice theological point to try and
establish whether Ophis is Moslem or gnostic. One
day we will ask it.

"For the moment however, we claim it in the name
of Abu Menouf himself, who was an extraordinary old
man, a wanderer over the face of the earth, a great
interpreter of dreams and visions. The snake may well
be his soul revisiting us—they both liked milk, which
to the dervishes is proof positive. For us it is, of
course, a symbol of the caduceus of Aesculapius, of
the spinal column, of the kundalini-serpent of the In-
dians—you will be able to trace the ancestry of the
idea through many continents and many religions. It is
also the sacred phallus of Greece and Egypt and India, as well as the oiled intestines from which one can
perform a divination by entrails as our ancestors did.
All this is an exoteric scale of reference, an explanation: but the actual naked experience of Ophis cannot
as you will realise be properly put into words. It will
be found quite mysteriously fruitful and enriching to
remember as you get older, though you will never be
able to analyse it and discover exactly why. But there
is much you *can* discover, there are many meanings
which *are* accessible to the reason. Now come, as
Byron once said: 'Enough of this antiquarian twaddle.
Let's have a swim.' Only we have to ride about two
hours before I can offer you a sand beach."

Akkad led away on an easterly course and at a
good pace, considering the precocious heat of the sun;
and Toby was left twisting his thumbs and looking
abashed, as if he had been sent to Coventry, though
Akkad assured him that this was no reprisal for his
lack of candour about the ceremony. We faced an
hour of soft riding now, until at last we came upon a

chain of blood-red hills and a large stony valley littered with blocks of stone, of schist, of crystal, it
seemed; the mouth was of considerable breadth, and
it was intersected with parallel lines of rock ravine
where, Akkad said, the gazelles came down at night
in search of dew. This was the entry to a sombre
region of petrified forest which stretched away down
to the edge of the sea. The whole scene was littered
with petrifacts of different sizes and kinds, enormous
trees, weighing tons, bared of their branches, overthrown and turned to stone. It was a weird ride
through this wilderness with its dead petroliths, its
solid vegetation; almost symbolic it seemed, for Akkad
said nothing as he led soberly on, skirting the recumbent tree forms. Some of the tree-trunks measured
about three feet in diameter, and were from thirty to
fifty feet in length! The greater number were of a
species of timber no longer known to Egypt, but there
were also palms here and there melted stone-solid by
wind and weather. The heat was intense here and the
aspect of the place, so wild and abandoned, melancholy to a degree.

With what cries of relief we greeted the appearance of a herring-gull as it hovered curiously over us
bringing us the certainty that we were at last near the
sea; and then with what wild pleasure we heard at
last the stentorian boom of the surf on the beaches
which were awaiting us, lying dazed into pearl-blue
nescience by the lick of the hot sun of midday. Like
phantoms we stripped naked and fell into the bursting
waves, to be swiftly sucked out seawards, out of the
reach of the crashing surf line. The undertow drew
its hissing breaths, dragging at our ankles, but we were
all experienced in maintaining a reasonable distance
from the shore and so we frolicked and swam in the
deafening roaring of the water. It would be impossible
to describe the sense of wild elation which now pos-

sessed us—perhaps it was youth and good spirits, perhaps it was something more. Perhaps it was what Akkad claimed both then and always afterwards, that we had passed through a kind of initiation into a new area of understanding. But so much of this remained to be explained still, and I could see he was rehearsing in his own mind how he was going to approach the subject with us. He had a horror of pomposity.

At last, sea-buffeted and breathless, salt-encrusted and brown as tobacco, we allowed ourselves to be thrown up on the beach. But here another small problem arose—the sand was too hot to tread barefoot, nor was there any shade right down at the sea line. Moreover it was obvious that we would have to dispute our lunch with some large golden hornets which had smelt the fruit and wine. However, the petrified forest came down almost to the water's edge, and one or two of the few stone trees left upright promised us a small pool of shade which we lost no time accepting. Here it was deliciously cool, for a light fresh breeze crept down from the dunes. We unpacked our victuals and suddenly realised how very hungry we were; ravenously we attacked the sandwiches of cold goose and turkey. Thirstily we drank the wine and the iced water in its thermos flasks. Then at last we settled back, replete with food and physical well-being, to hear Akkad out; it was a strange spot, this forest of dark petrifacts, this grove of ankylosed trees. From time to time there would be a small crack and a brittle piece of a stone branch would break off in the heat and fall to the ground. We leaned our backs against the dead stone and listened while Akkad, now with an air of peculiar intensity, holding the edges of his bathing wrap together and looking somewhat like a large praying mantis, began the homily which was our first detailed introduction to the gnostic canon.

How to summarise what he had to tell us I do not

know; for my own part the whole long speech passed through my consciousness like a rainbow silk of different colours. It was an exposition at once allusively poetical and factual, but knitted together with persuasive coherence, and formally, intellectually, quite watertight. I think I have never listened to anything with quite the same careful intensity as I brought to this first sermon by Akkad in the petrified forest. It was I suppose because I knew that he was going to explain things which up until then had seemed to me inexplicable. Best of all, he was going to provide some explanation of the drug-vision we had all experienced. So I closed my eyes and listened to that quiet seductive voice expounding the grand outlines of the gnostic scheme.

What did he say? I can remember even after so long. He began by speaking about the sense of inner estrangement and alienation from the so-called real world which was the mark of the religious nature when once it awakes from its sleep in the world. Sometimes it awoke spontaneously, of its own accord, sometimes in response to a vision or human experience of particular intensity, or by mere accident. When it woke it quested for a metaphysical frame to contain it, to nourish it like a plant, to make it fruitful. It sought a humus in which it could flower. Of all the religions in the world, and they were as numerous as the sands of the sea, there was nothing quite like this group of gnostic systems, shattered fragments of which were all we had available today in various tongues—so well had the organised religions of the so-called perfect Good done their work of extirpation. Their adherents could not bring themselves to face the bitter central truths of the gnostics: the horrifying realisation that the world of the Good God was a dead one, and that He had been replaced by a usurper—a God of Evil. Perhaps this sounded exaggerated to us, he said, but it was the heart of the belief, and the distress and alienation of the believers was due to the deeply implanted conviction that only a miracle would ever dethrone this great Demon of Darkness, who had waited his turn so patiently and who now sat in the judgement seat over all. It was the deep realisation of this truth, and its proclamation, that had caused the gnostics to be suppressed, censored, destroyed. Humanity is too frail to face the truth about things—but to anyone who confronts the reality of nature and of process with a clear mind, the answer is completely inescapable: Evil rules the day.

What sort of God, the gnostic asks himself, could have organised things the way they are—this munching world of death and dissolution which pretends to have a Saviour, and a fountain of good at its base? What sort of God could have built this malefic machine of destruction, of self-immolation? Only the very spirit of nothingness and auto-annihilation. A world in which we are each other's food, each other's prey.

Swiftly Akkad sketched in two or three of these despairing systems, each bearing the impress of its inventor's personality in divergences of detail: but all united in this central despair about the metaphysical *status quo*. Slowly, in his quiet voice, with its flavours of an ever mounting disenchantment, he sketched in the terrible fresco of the present world, often in the form of a long quotation which attested as always to the formidable memory of this strange man. "The praying mantis which devours its mate even while it is fecundating her, the spider trapping the fly, and the *pompile* which stabs the spider to death, the *ceceris* which with a triple stroke of its sword scientifically destroys the three centres of the *bupreste's* nervous system: and carries it off so that its larvae will be able to eat it still living, choosing their mouthfuls with skill, preserving the vital parts with a terrible science, unto the very last mouthful of the victim's flesh. Then the *leucopis,* the *anthrax,* the worm of which simply applies itself to the flank of the *chalicodome,* and sucks it dry through the skin, ingests, pumps out this living broth which is the young larvae, and then dries it cunningly, in order to keep it also fresh, living, until the last mouthful. . . . The *philante,* the bee-killer, before even carrying off its victim presses out the crop to make it disgorge its honey, and sucks the tongue of the wretched dying insect as it sticks out of its mouth. . . ." He went on then in French, stumbling over the scientific words for which he could not find an immediate translation in English, "Quel tableau que la Création! Un massacre général! Les lois les plus féroces, les plus barbares, les plus horriblement inhumaines: luttent pour la Vie, l'élimination des faibles, l'être mangeant l'être et mangé par l'être . . . Si dieu existe il ne peut être qu'une intelligence sans coeur. . . ." He paused for a moment and then said, almost under his breath: "What implacable logic." Silence. A long silence. A very long silence.

"Then is there another kind of sense which is not just nonsense?" asked Piers, but the question seemed more addressed to himself than to Akkad, and his only answer was a look which hovered on the edge of ironic amusement. It seemed to say: "You know the answer to that question—why ask it?" I realised then that the gnostic refusal to accept the state of things constituted a particular kind of bravery without vainglory, a despair without tarnish. Sylvie lay beside me, her head on my arm, breathing slowly and evenly, as if she were sleeping; but I could see from the set of her features that she was awake, and following. And now she said in a small musing voice: "But if one believes that, what would it do to love?" Only a woman could have asked that.

The question seemed to hang there, dangling like a

spider on the end of a long thread woven from its own entrails. Akkad said: "If you had seen nothing last night, or just a pretty snake, I would have been wrong in my feelings about you. But the fact that you saw something—which you cannot yet interpret, never mind—proves the contrary. In other words you are on a slope, you are sliding. There is no point in making provisos, clutching at branches one either side, asking questions, trying to pretend that you have accepted this pure experience on probation. *This is it!* It has happened to everything including this love of yours which you find strange but which for us forms a sort of disembodied illustration of the precepts of the gnostic incarnation after many old texts. Old Hippolytus has spoken of you in his tract on the refutation of all heresies. The Myth is as follows: There were three unbegotten principles of the universe, two male and one female. One male principle is called Good, who takes forethought for the course of things; the other male is called Father of the Begotten, but he is without foreknowledge and invisible. The female is without foreknowledge, wrathful, double-minded, double-bodied, a virgin above and a viper below. She is called Eden, she is called Israel. These are the principles of the universe, the roots and springs from which everything came. There was nothing else."

Sylvie had begun to tremble a little; she placed her small hand upon my thigh, as if to seek solace or companionship. Then she said something which had independently entered the minds of us all. "You are speaking of suicide, then?" Only a woman could have asked that.

"For the elect it was always so," said Akkad dryly, after a pause. "The poets have shown us the way. For those, in every age, who feel the deeply humiliating condition of man and nourish any hope, I won't say of ever changing it, but even ameliorating it . . .

143

they sense the great refusal as necessary. The refusal to conform to the laws of this inferior demon leads insensibly on towards death. But then death . . . What is it after all? It is nothing. It is not enough! We will all die. Yet to the pure gnostic soul the open gesture of refusal is necessary, is the only poetic act. As the Sufi poet says: 'Close thy lips so that the tongue may taste the sweetness of the mouth.' All those emblems of a hunger which engenders self-destruction, which pushes things to the very limit of the sensibility, those belong to us; and they must be strictly differentiated from the privations and prohibitions which spring from the tenets of any branch of Judaeo-Christianity. Their laws are different and based on violent repressions; ours are absolute but personal. Refuse, refute, renounce—all religions carry in them a counter theology. But only ours is based squarely on the sad fact that the spirit of evil has usurped the universe. Yet ordinary suicide, banal self-destruction, that is forbidden to us."

"Was it not always so?"

"No. You have seen the likenesses of pre-Adamic man and the pictures of Eden which are found in ancient texts and in ancient poets. Recorded history is too long for us to be exact about it, the mist closes in and the tracks begin to blur. But we can speak of our own age, the civilisation which is ours and in which the gnostic role has been permanently derided, attacked, even physically obliterated, whether we think of the cathars of Provence or of the gnostics of Egypt who have been forced to live under cover, in hiding. Or else to scatter and take refuge in foreign lands like the Bogomils and Bosnians. It would be wearisome to follow out this theme in detail, coming at last to the prophecies of the Tarot, but I can give you the rough outline of what we believe as true for this time. The presiding demon is the spirit of matter, and he springs fully armed from the head of classical Judaism of which all European religions are tributaries. The Prince is usury, the spirit of gain, the enigmatic power of capital value embodied in the poetry of gold, or specie, or scrip. When Christ flogged the money-changers, poor harmless men, he was not behaving in an irrational and neurotic manner. No, he had seen the Prince seated among them, smirking and rubbing his hands. He had recognised suddenly the dark glitter in the fiend's eye; for the Prince knew full well what the fate of Jesus would be, just as Jesus himself knew. Our proto-gnostic had allowed himself to be trapped, deliberately. It was his masterly refusal to save himself which stamps him as one of us. But the moment of fury marks him also as very human. At least to give the demon a real thrashing in the flesh for once, in the flesh. The Bible does not say if it smarted, the beating. One hopes that it did—though of course this is childish, for it changes nothing in our blind fate, the unrolling of which is quite predictable—a dead certainty in fact. How pleasant the English phrases are, and how pregnant, when you stop to think. What could be blinder than fate, what could be deader than certainty?

"So Jesus went to his foolish personal fate, dragging humanity with him, and not even leaving behind a coherently formed system of beliefs which would distinguish him once and for all as no Jew of the Temple but a renegade Jew and a gnostic. Jesus, like so many Jews, belongs to our persuasion. We can infer this from his behaviour and his fate. His end was poetic and not theological; the cosmogony from which his spirit issued was not one of the four Ms—which characterise our own age with such a great depth of focus. I mean Monotheism, Messianism, Monogamy, and Materialism. But you can illustrate this simple thesis at every level—whether you take Marx's great analysis of our culture or the Freudian analysis of absolute value as based upon infantile attitudes to excrement. Gold and excrement, that is poetic indeed! The cornerstone of culture then is another M—*merde*. The gold bar is the apotheosis of the human turd. You will see from this how radically we poets of gnosticism part company from these Judaic thinkers. Every age has its metaphysic, and every calculus is built up upon a first term, a bedrock. Possession for Marx and possession for Freud have dictated excrement as the basic term upon which the calculus of our philosophy raises itself.

"But we have substituted another term, we have let sperm stand in place of excrement, for our world is a world not of repression and original sin but of creation and relaxation, of love and not doubt. This is what sets us apart from the others who today rule everything in the name of death. I do not need to mention other great Judaic creations of the day. They rule the hearts and minds and presumably will do so until our age comes to an end in one form or another. But one cannot wait around, one must engage one's forces, one must believe something. Self-realisation is an imperative. But how truthful dare we be? How truthful will we be allowed to be? The answer is not far to seek; we are still regarded as the enemies of the *status quo*, the vested interest which the Prince has in keeping us quiet. There is only one thing, one weapon which we hold. He is terrified by the idea of the gnostic suicide by attrition, by a steady denial of the world as it is. He is only troubled when a poet gives him the lie. Then for a moment he feels himself shrivelling in the flames. Apprehension fills his soul; but then he recalls that we are not numerous, and for the rest of the world seem to be simply a small band of wrongheaded fanatics who refuse to admit the sovereignty of darkness, who refuse to be ruled. We are not hard to crucify, and the death is an elegant one in its sad way. He can wash his hands of it before the people and the majority will accept his excuses with a bonus and a rise in pay. As far as death is concerned one must develop a certain discretion about choosing one sort from another. All questions of sorrow, fear, illness, for example, must be drained away until only the pure precipitate, like calx, of the gnostic death remains. This style of mind once achieved redeems all nature for a second or two, re-establishes that self-perpetuating cycle of joy which was the bliss of yesterday—the ancient mode of yesterday.

"Yet when we say nature we really mean rhythm, and the basic rhythm is oestrus, the beating egg in its primal pouch. Naturally having lost the marvellous amnesia of sexual periodicity we live by a time-pining, time-bound, chronology. And we never forget that death sets in with conception. This alters everything, even an element like love. We are making the orgasm more and more conscious. Yet to have loved capably and methodically, to have loved with a sufficiency of attention for the fragility of the thought and the transitoriness of the act—that will teach anyone the truth of what I say about death. Ah, but once your words start to make super-sense you must either stop talking or become a poet. Choose!

"We believe also that every thoughtless or inconsequential act vibrates through the whole universe. And all the time thoughts pass through us in floods, there is no time to touch them with the wand of consciousness, to magnetise them, to redeem them, so to speak. Fish in their shoals pass not more thickly. Yet each one has ideally to be realised separately. How is this possible? Yes, there is a way, we are sure of it. There is a type of realisation which makes this possible. Ah! but the new universe has got cancer, it is evil, that is to say mediocre, to the very marrow, in the biological not the moralistic sense. It is, poor thing, twisted and luckless and out of kilter, foredoomed and star-crossed. Inferior demons have painted it in their likeness. Our hopes of stepping outside this sepulchre are very faint, but they are there. There is a way to comprehend the gnostic's giant onion of a world, the concentric circles, with the Pleroma beckoning there, the white heart of light, the source of that primal vision which for a second or two can recapture paradise. We can make amends by loving correctly.

"Thank goodness, nature's machinery is vast and intricate and completely comprehensive. There is no norm, no absolute. Every deviation is allowed for. Yet total freedom is the key we must dare to turn in order to repose her. It was not always thus, and sometimes when we are asleep we dream that it will not always be so. Our intitution gives the lie to so many of the prime notions like *omne animal post coitum triste* and *inter faesces et urinam nascrimur*. These ideas belong to the impoverished world of our modern demonology."

"But how to realise?" It was Piers' sad voice now that interrogated the sea-hushed silence and Akkad sighed, though he remained smiling still. He said: "A rather cruel paradox centres about the two notions which we express by the words 'knowing' and 'realising.' You can know something and yet not realise it, not having lived it, as we say, for in our inarticulate way we are aware of the distinction. Realisation is a real sigil conferred upon an experience—like a food product which the system has passed without assimilating. And the head knowledge, the conscious product, often vitiates it by coming first, so that even if you realise it and live it, later on it has somehow lost its kinetic value as a motive force which shapes the psyche. Powerful imaginations can be dangerous; they live ideas out so powerfully that when the time comes to 'realise' them, to perform with a real woman, say, a Muse, they are either impotent or else experience the taste of ashes. Poor desperate descendant of protoman tries to still his fears by classifying them, by making an index of them. He hopes to delimit them thus, but they extend on all sides of him to infinity. So he spends his time, turning in the trap. Then he decides that there is no way out. But there is, in fact, a secret way of transcending them, of turning them to account. One must begin by pretending in order to end by realising. Pretend that you do not fear by acting fearlessly, at whatever cost. Habit is very powerful. One day you will become what you mime. The parody of goodness can make you really good."

"And what about suicide?" It was Piers' voice again, pitched on a humble and trusting note, but again as if addressed to himself.

"You are forbidden to undertake an act of conscious self-destruction. Suicide in the active sense, a bullet in the mouth, that is not what is meant. Everything lies in the act of acceptance, to join finally the spiritual trust of the mature who have tasted the world to the full and wish to be purged of the physical envelope. They join the inner circle and make an act of acceptance—that is what constitutes the gnostic suicide. They accept, then, their own execution, but it is not their own hand that is raised against them. They never know how it is carried out, the sentence, though they are told when; they receive two warnings when their time is running out, and this gives them a chance to put their affairs in order. Then, after a certain time, it can come about at any moment. An executioner and a method has been chosen, as well as a time, but not by themselves. The person who is the instrument is chosen by lot, and is always one who himself has joined the inner circle of the faithful and renounced temporal life. The procedure is one of impeccable order. In the end we imitate process and there is nothing disorderly about process, however much it may seem so. The very concept of order in nature is homemade, the product of our finite minds. In the theology of process, the queen of the sciences, coincidence and contingency rule, but never fortuitously. Never. I know it sounds nonsense, but it is so."

Suddenly Sylvie cried out: "Akkad, don't encourage Piers to take all this too seriously. He mustn't. He is far too quixotic, far too extreme. It would be very dangerous for somebody with his type of temperament." Akkad looked at her gravely and said nothing; but now it was Piers who was angry with his sister, his eyes shining. "For God's sake, Sylvie. You want me to take all this lightly? Akkad is describing my own interior mind, my own character and temperament, and you wish me to regard it as simply a sort of intellectual novelty. I feel I would go to the stake for this." Sylvie turned to embrace him apologetically but to me she said: "You see? I feared as much." In a sense this episode marked the point of divergence in all our attitudes to Akkad and his sect; Piers was determined to go on towards deeper knowledge, profounder identification with the gnostics; while I did not wish to advance further than the portals, so to speak, of their system. I felt suddenly detached and indeed a little sad as I watched the brother and sister exchange embraces to put away the memory of this little but deep disagreement. How remote it all seemed, the rest of life as we had been living it! I felt all at once like Robinson Cursoe alone on his island; below us was the drumming sea, all around us were the petrified trees and the melancholy dunes. Somewhere far away was the Alexandria of our memory, with its comfortable flats and shady villas waiting for us. We had become ghosts, uneasily haunting this strip of desert, exchanging momentous fictions about

God. It was presumptuous. I lit a cigarette and smoked it thoughtfully, pondering on what Akkad had told us. There were other initiations, he had said, of various degrees of knowledge; but I felt that my own limitations of sensibility were such that I would never advance much further than this first impressive step, which had without any doubt marked my whole future outlook on life. I knew then that Piers would go on, stage by obstinate stage, towards the deepest knowledge; his whole attitude and disposition suggested it. As for Sylvie I did not know.

It was almost dusk when we packed up and set off once more across the desert for Macabru. On the return journey, not a word was spoken. It was as if Akkad had exhausted all the possibilities of language. We had been pumped dry and emptied even of coherent thought. Akkad seemed moody and withdrawn, and of course by now the fatigue of these long rides had begun to tell on us all. It was night when at last the oasis came in sight again, and we were grateful to surrender the fagged horses. Many of the guests had already gone, and the fair was in the process of packing up, of dismantling itself. By tomorrow the old silence would return to Macabru, everything would have disappeared as if by magic. That night we made plans to return to the city on the morrow, ferried by the little aircraft of our host. We ate a leisurely dinner, and took a walk in the little melting township as a gesture of farewell. Something memorable had happened here, which had tugged at our sensibilities. That much we knew.

When we finally returned to the city there was work to be done, people to be met, so that for a week or so we were not able to join forces for more than a few moments in the evening. Then came a long autumn during which Piers launched himself into a course of detailed reading and study in the old Patriarchal Library with its warped wooden floors and leaning landings crammed with Byzantine trophies and manuscripts. Akkad had obtained permission for him to use the great library from the Patriarch himself, whose chief secretary spoke several languages and was himself a scholar capable of steering my friend among the shoals and quicksands of the desert fathers, with their hysterical condemnations of the gnostics, and the fragments of this forgotten faith as outlined by ghostly and enigmatic shapes like Carpocrates and Valentinus. Sylvie and I followed all this as well as we could, but without the candent enthusiasm of her brother, who immersed himself wholly in these studies —to a degree that made his absent-mindedness something of a joke among his colleagues in Chancery.

He was also capable of downright absurdities like telephoning me in the middle of an economic press conference to say: "I think I have rediscovered the force of prayer; the thing is *prayer to what?* Remind me to go into this matter tonight." It *was* rather a problem—prayer to the god of process I presumed? It was hard to keep one's mind centred on the universe as a giant maggotry when the landscapes and humours of Egypt were so beautiful, and its passing days so enticing; moreover when one was loved. I put down the telephone and turned drowsily on my side towards Sylvie, whose sleeping nakedness lay close by me, echoing the curves of my body with her own pliant limbs. Sleeping, but only in that siesta of exhausted half-sleep which is imposed by the languid Egyptian afternoons with their tepid sea breezes and long calms broken only by the crazy hiccoughs of a tethered ass somewhere. When I closed my eyes the darkness throbbed around us and once more I returned to relive, re-experience the soft scroll of her tongue which pressed back mine and probed steadily downwards across chest and stomach to settle at last, throbbing like a hummingbird, on my sex. I held that beautiful head between my palms like something disembodied, and rememorised the dark hair cropped down, and then spurred up into its chignon, the crumpled ears of a new-born lamb, the white teeth and lips upon which I would soon slowly and deliberately graft back my happy kisses. It was hard to come back mentally to the old creaking library with fleas jumping from the cracks in the floor, the manuscripts crackling, and my friend working over those huge parchment tomes, lost in the nonworld of Carpocrates—the negative of the printed world we had thought we knew well, but which now seemed a delusion, and all the more dangerous because it was so enticing. "Kiss me. Again. Once more." Commands to be obeyed when issued by a woman. There was nothing derived about these pristine acts—everything was newly minted.

Before the winter finally closed in on us Piers managed to implement a scheme he had had in mind for quite a while; he borrowed the French Embassy's felucca, and on the pretext of an official journey into Upper Egypt got it set to rights. His mission being a small one and his Ambassador an amiable man he was able to combine freedom with pleasure to a degree not usually granted to young diplomats *en poste*. I do not quite know how he justified extending an invitation to me to join the party—but the result was that the three of us found ourselves in cool weather just upriver from Bulaq, outside Cairo, preparing for a journey of two weeks and perhaps more in this handsome craft. The felucca *Nasr* was some forty feet long with two masts and a couple of cabins, and manned by a crew of seven. During a long period of relative neglect by the French it had been used to ferry fruit and wood upriver and had thus become infested with vermin. However for Nile boats no remedy could be easier than to sink it in the shallows for a while, after which it could be pumped out and scrubbed clean with sand and pumice. After a day or so it was dry and ready to load. Piers entered into all the details of the journey with the *élan* of the born romantic—you would have thought we were mounting an expedition to Polynesia to judge by the quantity of the stores which he ordered—macaroni, rice, oil, tinned foods, fruit, dried vegetables, wines. It made us feel rather ashamed later to see on what short commons the Arab crew lived—but they did not appear to grudge us our rich fare, and probably equalised things up by the amount that they pilfered from us daily and quite shamelessly. But as they were both efficient and kindly we closed an eye to their depredations, only locking up ammunition, tobacco, and such expensive frivolities as cameras and medicines. All in all, it was extremely exciting, this manner of setting out on a journey by water, and despite my ironic amusement at Piers' enthusiasm I secretly envied him and shared a good deal of it. I was elected to be responsible for the medicine cabinet and the armoury—for we intended to do a bit of spot-shooting along the river banks at the end of each day; shooting for the pot so to speak.

One of the cabins was well appointed with a long divan and a heavy central work table, and was spacious enough to offer headroom and a place to put our trunks of provisions. The other had precious locker space as well as long bunks running round the outside wall. Here we elected to sleep. There was a kind of glassed-in hatch like a conning-tower which we made mosquito-proof against the long Nile evenings. All reservations made, she was an elegant and roomy vessel, and the crew were delighted by the novelty of taking aboard foreign passengers—with so many goods to be pilfered. The captain and the mate both lacked an eye, and quarrelled dreadfully; and during these quarrels they exchanged ferocious glances of a macabre kind with their single good eyes.

These cabins were to prove a godsend, for we were able at times to work over our books, maps and papers, and barricade ourselves against the talkative importunities of the Arab crew, who seemed to be dying of boredom. So it was that on a late afternoon we said goodbye to Bulaq, the port of Cairo. There was not a breath of wind stirring so that the Arabs were compelled to resort to their oars at once to fetch us into mid-channel and to clear all other shipping. This they did with great cheerfulness (it is always thus at the beginning of a voyage), accompanying their energies with loud songs. We skimmed along the surface of the river, elegant as a flying fish, the spray flying under the oars. Our course lay through the narrow channel between the island of Rhoda and the mainland. On both sides of us the banks were covered in the most luxurious vegetation; while here and there as we passed we glimpsed, through narrow openings, vistas of magnificent gardens and palaces whose grounds ran down to the water. From one such palace came the strains of music and song, obviously from the harem, and our boatmen were silenced. They listened with rapture. It was, they said, the palace of the great pasha called Halim Bey, and they were most impressed when Piers said that he knew the great man, and had actually dined at his table—a statement which was not strictly accurate, though useful.

It was not long before we had passed the points of the Nilometer—and then the broad hauntingly beautiful river opened its reaches to us like arms and we found ourselves gliding across a floor of dark glass which the evening light was turning to gold. Clouds floated in this mirror with their customary languor. Our crew resumed their singing as we sped on into the darkling horizon, while we sat on the forward

hatch and gazed at the intoxicating play of light and
darkness over the cool bosom of the ancient river.
There was no doubt that this was to be another memorable journey which would bring to an end the first
year of our stay in this beautiful land. No one respon-
sive to colour and landscape could remain the same—
and when this was combined with the companionship
of Akkad, and all the exciting intellectual enigmas of
the place . . . Egypt as an experience had separated
the old life as we were used to living it from the new
which was as yet unborn, undefined, as yet only a
whispering gallery of premonitions. Piers cleaned his
gun thoughtfully that evening, tilting the barrels to the
light and polishing them until they glittered. "How
will we ever get away from this country?" he asked in
despair, almost as if he had followed the direction of
my own thoughts. "We'll have to I suppose, one day."
But what he meant, I knew, was that we would never
be able to go "back" to the old life—something new
would have to be offered us in its place. After Macabru the old life in Provence seemed somehow so moribund and finished. We ached for the infant new to be
born.

We drove on thus at breakneck speed towards the
sunset afterglow, trying to clear the nearest waters of
the river before we anchored for the first night to take
stock of ourselves and the dispositions of our kit.
Things looked fair enough for a light breeze on the
morrow so that we might use our blunt lateen-sail as
a jib. It was powerful enough both to steady us and
make a little way in the veritable lakes which the Nile
had carved out of the river banks in the course of its
descent; for the rest we would depend on the two-
rope—from time immemorial ships on the Nile, as
on the Rhône, have been man-hauled when heading
upstream. But we were lucky in an unusual disposition of winds and countercurrents to be able to make

quite a distance upriver before the darkness threatened to close in and our crew found it necessary to seek a landfall, which they did at last after a number of violent disagreements about the choice of the place. The two one-eyed men yelled and gesticulated, and exchanged fuliginous stares. But at last they found a place to moor on the western bank.

As soon as the boat was made fast to the land by a short pole driven into the soft earth, the boat's crew kindled their dinner fire in little portable ovens on deck and began their cooking operations; as did also our body servant under the directions of Piers, who spoke by far the best Arabic. We noticed that the standard fare of the Arab crew was lentil soup and bread, with perhaps a few onions—meat was a luxury undreamt-of because of its price. Their usual drink was Nile water. Yet constitutionally they seemed pretty robust. On this first evening, however, as if to prepare themselves for the journey, they turned in early with none of the usual evening songs or dances to which we later became accustomed. A heavy damp came off the river, and a dense ground-mist blurred all clear outlines. We ourselves ate soberly enough in the cabin, and were glad of a small charcoal brazier over which to warm our fingers. It was the first breath of autumn cold, and the days were to be continually deceptive at this season—as if they kept forgetting and reverting back to the summer we had left behind. Some nights for example were damp and cold, and some warm and fruity and humming with mosquitoes. No two were quite alike.

But on this first evening we tasted for the first time the feeling of spaciousness that the Nile always conveys, for its levels are never stable, they are always falling and rising; and its banks and boundaries shift and alter, appear and disappear under one's very eyes. Islands emerge and fade, swallowed by the rising tide,

or else sprout up again with fully grown trees on them
by some freak of level—as if fresh from the potter's
wheel. All this was to come; but for this first evening
we ate soberly, drank a brandy with our coffee and
then set our books and maps to rights. Finally I
turned in, and so did Sylvie, leaving Piers with his
diary which he was determined to fill with news of our
doings. I took one brief walk on deck before turning
in. The Arabs lay everywhere like fallen skittles,
muffled into bundles against the damp; some of them
had clenched themselves up in their rags until they
looked more like hedgehogs than anything else. A
lone river wind sighed in the cordage of the ship.
Then, after a long hesitation, a harvest moon came
bobbing up, turning from bronze to white as it rose.
It was of such a startling brightness, and penetrating
all the chinks in our cabin with such a piercing glare,
that Piers was roused from his book to find that the
yellow oil-lamp could hardly hold its own with this
moon which gave such a wild and strange colouring
to the place—the books and maps, the pots and pans.
Somewhere a jackal sounded, its doleful howling min-
gling with the distant barking of dogs. Nearer at hand
on the brilliant river came the croak of some night-
bird stirring. I fixed my bunk to my liking and said:
"Piers, don't stay up too late; tomorrow will be
a heavy day." He shook his head. "I won't," he said.
Later as I drowsed off I heard him close his diary,
blow out the lamp, and then make his way to his own
bunk. He set a pistol by his bed with a small torch,
while under his pillow he placed the precious wallet
which held all our passports and money and papers.
I lay for a long while suspended between waking and
the sweet unreason of dreams; I heard a boatman
talking in his sleep, and the scatter of drops along our
prow as a freshet of wind struck us. Then oblivion
came and I felt my mind stretching out towards the

frontiers of love and childhood, so that when I turned, and when a hand came out of the darkness to rest its fingers on my wrist, I did not know whose it was.

From that point forward day merged with day and night with night to such an extent that time became fluid, distances illusory; we were moving from one dream to another, merging from one truth into another in a way that gave the lie to the banal chronology of Piers' diary, which tried to segment our lives in so untruthful a fashion. When one is fully extended by day and exhausted every evening one lives differently, without the weight of yesterday or tomorrow on one's shoulders. I stored up simply a constellation of moments, a firework displays of small but brilliant incidents which were like a set of coloured engravings of this great river with its moods and silences, its strange caprices and impulses. It was never still, and it compelled the imagination to follow its flight across the ancient land, as if it had been some marvellous steed running wild in the exuberance of youthful beauty. But it was sinister, too, and ruthless. Ask the huge crocodiles in the upper reaches! Here and there the hurrying water had carved up the soft banks, intruding on a nest of cobras and carrying them off, or else had invaded the shallow grave of a boatman buried, as they always were, on the tow-path they had so often trodden. A corpse whirling down the river, trailing its wrappings, as ancient as any mummy of the Pharaohs. Or else walking in the calm evening through a forest of tall supple date palms to a village where a quaint old lady sold us milk by the tin cup and where we took the early evening flights of turtle-dove which tried desperately to rise steeply enough to avoid our guns, but were pressed down low by a river wind. These little birds would be feathered in the evening by the Arabs and then cooked by Piers. I can recall so much, but cannot give the memories order and shape, so completely had the days fused together. It did not take us long to feel the imprint of this wild life without cares and preoccupations.

We let our beards grow. We did not change our clothes despite the well-meant offers to wash them on the part of our servants, who were somewhat shocked at our unkemptness. Nothing mattered but this succession of marvellous days that flew by, bearing us on their backs, as the river water bore the *Nasr*. One day in the upper reaches we came upon immense flights of pelicans which lay in—droves, shoals, what shall I say?—upon the surface of the water and showed no alarm; only when we approached quite close they did get up, or half get up, screaming harshly and beating the water with their vast wings. To Piers' utter fury and humiliation the Arab captain, without asking his permission, took up his charged gun which was lying, broken but loaded, on the hatch, and discharged it into the mass of birds, killing one outright. It upset us terribly—as if it had been an albatross; but the crew could not understand our shame and fury, and cheerfully tumbled overboard to retrieve it, the water being shallow and the day windless. It was quite an effort to get it aboard, and now the deed had been done I swallowed my anger and allowed my curiosity to get the better of me. It must have weighed about forty pounds, this opulent bird. The thick soft delicate plumage of the breast was milk-white at the roots, but if you blew on it you found the top part tinged with pink or rose colour. This shows up most beautifully when the bird rises on the wind and turns its breast slowly into the sun. It had a touching, ungainly beauty which made us regret even more the shot which had cost its life.

Before the Arabs should feather it—for they showed every sign of being prepared to eat it for dinner —Sylvie had it laid upon the hatch in the evening sunshine while she sketched it. But when the dusk came it was surrendered to the cooks, and here Piers was sufficiently French to take an interest in their manner of dressing it. The meat was distressingly coarse and fibrous like old beef; but worst of all, it had an oily fishy flavour which made it most unpalatable, so we abandoned all hope of sharing in the repast. It must be said that the crew themselves showed every sign of enjoying it, greasy and fishy as the taste was. They made some attempt to burn out the fish smell by filling its stomach with live coals, but as far as I could see, without achieving anything very remarkable. But eat it they did, unto the last morsel. The Arabs, according to Piers, called this bird Gamal El Bahr, which means River Camel—perhaps some vague association stirring between the hump of the camel as a place where water is stored and the pelican's enormous shutter of a beak? Who can say?

Daily the Nile seemed to increase in grandeur and magnitude, and for a whole series of days we found our path running across something like an inland sea or delta, full of lovely tufted islands, some sinking and some emerging under the vibration of the waters. They had the lonely fragility of dreams in which one could only half believe. I could see now how it must be on the other great rivers of the world, the Yangtse or the Ganges or old Amazon. A whole world passing by in a kaleidoscope of colour, yet always changing, always impermanent. All day long this feast of colour, and then at night the heavens thick with brilliant stars like the loaded boughs of an almond in blossom. Standing on deck at night, listening to far-off hyenas barking and following some spot of light from a village, one drank in an immense peace and calm, feeling the old river stealing by beneath one, licking the prow of the ship, sliding beneath the dreams of the humble Arabs like a floor of glass.

So we came to the region which throws up a few riverside mountains, so pitted and hollowed by wind and sand that they have become the home of millions of birds. Here the number of cormorants and black Damietta duck was prodigious and beggared all description; every morning at dawn, with a tremendous hurrying of wings, they arrived in huge flights from the direction of the desert. They sounded like an approaching storm; then they settled with a thunderous clamour upon the mountain scalps from which they came down from time to time to dive for fish. Pigeons, hawks and swallows also abounded here. And here too we struck relatively low-flying geese with hides so thick that it seemed quite impossible to hole them or bring them down. You could hear the smack of the shot like a drum on their feathers, but they did not even deign to break formation. I tried some ball on them, but always missed owing to the height and the lack of a choked duck-gun.

And then at night, anchored under these unusual cliffs with their sleeping bird populations, to see the white moonlight falling upon a wilderness of jewelled crags, touched in with ink-dark shadows of grottoes, chasms, caves. How small and frail was our light on the sleeping ship.

I must leave to Piers the account of the journey in all its details; for somewhere among his affairs the old diary must still be knocking about with its long list of temples and towns, monuments and tombs. For my part I simply engulfed everything wolfishly, never even pausing to ask the name or the history of a site. I knew that we could look it all up later on if necessary. For me the raw experience was enough. Later of course I rather regretted my lack of documentation, for my memory was far from infallible and I tended to mix up places and times without discrimination. But Piers was indefatigable and spent a fair while every evening bringing his little book up to date while Sylvie slept with her arm thrown over her face to ward off the moonlight and I cleaned the guns or did our accounts.

When at long last we turned back for home we enjoyed a period of very favourable weather characterised by fair soft breezes and long calms, which enabled the sailors virtually to leave the *Nasr* to make her own way downstream with the current while they told stories and smoked all day. One of them, the eldest, was a sort of merry andrew and was not above dressing the part with a weird cap of jackal's skin with many hanging tails and tassels. This individual seized hold, tambourinewise, of an earthenware vessel covered at one end with a tightly stretched skin, and started to beat and thump on it like a drum. His fingers syncopated deftly while he launched into a monotonous air, a song at once repetitive and strangely rhythmical. At times another musician in the crew came to accompany him on a double flute, made of two long reeds, which uttered a sharp and plaintive note like a river bird. With this he improvised a lingering wavering cadenza to the original song, the audience meanwhile beating out the time with their palms and showing every mark of joy. One night, too, from a village quite near the point of our landing for the night, the peasants were drawn by the sound of our water-music and the women came down to the river's edge to dance for us—a magical, unforgettable sight under the moon.

So at last it came to an end, this timeless journey into ancient Egypt; and one afternoon, listless as the calm itself, we drifted into Bulaq once more with only the current, steering our way through the various craft towards our berth where the stately Embassy kavasses waited in their regal uniforms like great ventripotent pashas for us to land. It was a tearful business saying goodbye to the Arab crew for we had become fast friends and hated to part from them. But there were papers to be filled in and signed, a manifest to initial, and various other small duties such as present-giving and tipping. All this to complete before we finally handed over the boat to the French Embassy again! But all formalities were complete by dusk and the three of us, silent and rather melancholy, climbed into Piers' duty car and told the driver to take us out on the road to Alexandria.

The night was cold, and the stars were brilliant. Winter was on the way, and my thoughts turned towards the year's end, for we had been granted a long leave for Christmas by our respective missions, and we had great hopes of spending it at Verfeuille together. I watched the glittering desert wheel past us as we sped on towards the sea; Sylvie drowsed in the crook of my arm while Piers sat beside the chauffeur in front in a somewhat Napoleonic attitude, head on his breast, dozing between military engagements, so to speak. Our headlights cut a long yellow path of light upon the dark macadam which here and there had been invaded by desert sand-drifts. We were so replete with this enriching adventure on the river! It had left us speechless with joyful fatigue.

The evening life of the summer capital was in full swing when we threaded our way into it, though by now the gay summer awnings and street cafés had vanished at the first hint of autumn freshness. Piers had me dropped off at the Embassy where I lived in a small flat, and the chauffeur helped me carry my things up to my quarters. I had promised to join them later for dinner, though it was going to be somewhat late. I poked my head into the Chancery but everybody had gone home except Rycroft the messenger, who was chaining up a bag for London. In the dispensary I found a note telling me about a patient of mine whose child was ill with measles, also a dinner plan left by the social secretary. H.E. was giving a dinner party in honour of a visiting dignitary from London and I was bidden to hold the leg of the table as part of my social duties. The bachelors and the third secretaries in a small mission get most of these corvées. However, that was not for a couple of days, and the measles could wait. I bathed and changed, and took the lift down to the garage in search of my own car. It bore me across town to the apartment of Piers—a sumptuous enough place to suit a career diplomat who had a fair amount of entertaining to do. Needless to say it was seldom very tidy in spite of his domestics; books and paintings lay about everywhere, and latterly even old missals and Byzantine parchments which he had borrowed from the Patriarchal Library with the consent of the secretary. It was into these tantalising works that my friend had plunged after his shower and a change of clothes. Dinner would be a little late, so after some hesitation I accepted a whisky and a cigarette with a grain of hashish loaded into its body by pinpoint. It was not enough to do more than soothe my weariness and bring me a quiet sedation which would stand me in good stead when at last I got to bed.

"Piers, where are you now with Akkad's little initiation? I feel I have learned all I will ever learn."

"It's hard to disentangle," he admitted softly, "but only because the traces have been covered over by the wicked invective and progaganda of the Church Fathers, who had every interest in representing the gnostics as fostering obscene rites in their religious ceremonies. But this belief throws into relief every form of heresy, every form of chivalrous dissent from the great lie which the Church would have us live by. You will find little fragments of this basic refusal to sign the confession (to use modern Russian terms) in so many places that it is quite bewildering—sometimes in quarters not specifically devoted to gnostic beliefs. At home in Provence of course the cathars have always been self-elected and self-created gnostics. But what about the Courts of Love and their gradual extinction? The love the troubadours extolled made orthodoxy very thoughtful—in particular because it posited a new freedom for the woman, and a new role as Muse and refiner of the coarser male spirit. This was not to be relished by people who felt happier within the iron truss of the Inquisition . . . O I can't tell you how my eyes have been opened, and how grateful I am to Akkad. I've hit bedrock with this system, and I feel I shall go to the end of it, I feel it."

"Tomorrow I am going to the scent bazaar," said Sylvie in order to shut him up and change the subject, which was for her both boring and somewhat frightening. She knew that her brother was capable of any quixotry, any excess.

There matters stood. The season dragged on, deepening towards the winter and our departure, which lent an air of pleasant expectation to things. The diplomatic winter season of balls and dinner parties became almost pleasurable with the knowledge that soon we should be free of them for several weeks, and back once more in France. Toby had already gone back to Oxford for a term and Sabine had characteristically disappeared again. Then there came a completely unexpected blow for Piers in connection with our gnostic enterprise. It fell out like this. It was our habit about twice a week to stroll down the Hellenic end of the town to where the barber of Akkad had his gorgeous emporium—where ladies and gentlemen alike were barbered and scented. Here one was rather coddled and made much of, coffee and pipes were provided, and such newspapers as had arrived from Europe by

seamail. At a pinch one could devour a cake while
one was being expertly barbered. At any rate Piers
was a frequent visitor. One day he picked up an old
magazine in the shop and propped it on his knee to
read while his hair was being trimmed. He came upon
an article about hoaxes and frauds and sharp practice
in general in Egypt, and among the various types of
criminals of this kind—card sharpers, forgers, white-
slavers and so on—he was surprised and chilled to
find described in great detail the practice of supposed
religious initiations which had been mounted by criminals wishing to take advantage of gullible tourists.
The various steps were carefully described, beginning
with the partnership in a secret society, of which there
were many hundreds in Egypt (all false according to
the journalist); then the attendance at a ceremony of
initiation: finally . . . but Piers read no further. His
heart beat so fast that he felt almost suffocated. The
astonished barber had to surrender his client half-
shaved.

Piers took up the phone to ring Akkad's office only
to find out that he was away for a few days and would
not be available until the weekend. It would not be
possible to describe the state of confusion and distress
into which the article pushed him. To make matters
worse, among the illustrations was a picture of the
ceremony (identical to the one we had attended) in
the Abu Manouf mosque, over which Akkad was presiding with an air of manifest deceit and yet imper-
turbably—or so it seemed to the distracted eye of
Piers. He did not know what to do, where to turn. His
whole world seemed to have turned turtle. He took
the details of the publication and placed an order for
a copy with his newsagent on the way home. His brain
was really spinning, and he felt on the point of collapse—so deep had been his investment in this whole

business of Akkad's, so blind his belief in what he had been told. Could it all have been a fake?

I came into the flat after lunch to find him lying spread-eagled on the sofa with his face in his arms, silent and pale. He looked like a man with a high temperature, and I irritated him by trying to take his pulse. But he was wounded and distraught and accepted a whisky, which he drank with a trembling hand and a vague and absent-minded state—his whole thought was fixed upon this momentous, and to him terrible, story which threw into doubt the honesty of Akkad's actions and the *bona fides* of the sect. My alarm was so marked that at last he stirred himself to stand up and tell me the story, holding out the offending magazine in order to let me see the telltale illustrations. "I've ordered my own copy," he said sadly. "I intend to face Akkad with it. I'll have to give this one back to Fahem."

He groaned and slumped forward on the couch, cupping his chin in his hands. I read the article through thoughtfully. It went as far as suggesting that this form of cheat had originally been organised for the American tourist industry, but that the original organisers had found that not only the Americans were superstitious: from all over the Middle Orient believers came to be "initiated" as well as from Egypt itself. . . . It is difficult to describe the mixture of feelings I experienced as I read all this; in part amusement, in part relief, and in part a base desire to say "I told you so," though of course I had said nothing at all, nor cast any doubt upon the proceedings. In fact I had been as deeply disturbed and fructified by them as had been the others. And now the whole thing was called into question. . . . Piers had tears in his eyes as he said: "What do you make of it?" I shrugged my shoulders and sat down soberly. "We have been hoaxed, that's all. At least Akkad did not charge us anything for the experience."

"I suppose he thought it was funny," said Piers angrily, striking his knee with his clenched fist. "I have a good mind to challenge him to a duel—to send him my seconds."

"You haven't any: and duelling is out of fashion. Besides what would your mission say? And if you killed him, what?"

Piers walked up and down like a caged tiger glittering with a theatrical malevolence. "One's friends!" he said bitterly as if to the paintings on the wall. "One's friends!" I caught the inexpressible contempt of his tone and said, "Piers, sit down for a moment and just think. What has this news done to our whole belief? It has simply torpedoed it, that is all. But how salutary! I wouldn't want to go on believing something false, would you?"

"But how I needed it," he said wistfully, like a child. "How it seemed to fulfill my sentiments, my ideas. Oh it can't be a hoax, it really can't be. Akkad couldn't do such a thing!"

He looked as if he were going to give way to tears.

There was nothing to be done about the news except to bear it bravely, like the death of a friend or the failure of some great project on which we had set high hopes. That afternoon I took Fahem back his magazine on my way to the infirmary, hoping that the whole business would gradually die down and that Piers would find some other field of study, some other philosophy to absorb his passionate beliefs. But I must confess that it did not seem likely, and I waited for the return of Akkad with some inquietude; I did not want there to be a falling out among such good friends as we had all become, for Akkad was as much Egypt to us as the country's grand landscapes—their poetry seemed resumed in him, in his gentle and poetic mind.

Two days of intense despair passed on the part of Piers, who went about as if in mourning for the death of his mother; he was sufficiently upset to sleep badly and I had to prescribe a sleeping draught. Then the newsagent delivered another copy of the magazine, which he propped up on the window-sill to await the moment of Akkad's arrival. It was to be somewhat unexpected. Akkad appeared instead of giving a telephone call as he usually did, and just before lunch, too, an unusual time for a visit. He stood modestly, kindly, with his green Scotch hat in his hand, on the doorstep of the flat, asking to be let in. Piers leaped up and confronted him with a kind of affectionate fury.

"Akkad," he cried, "why did you do it to us?" Akkad blinked mildly from one to the other of us, looking puzzled. "Macabru," went on Piers. "The whole thing a bloody fake—why did you do it?" He thrust out his arms half pleadingly, half aggressively. Akkad put out his hand and said: "How did you know? When did you find out?" In answer Piers snatched up the magazine and pushed it at him, pushed it almost in his face. "This," he said. "This article, Akkad!" Our friend continued to look bemused so I took a hand in the conversation and tried to find the article. Would you credit it? It was not there! I leafed grimly through the magazine page by page without finding it. This caused a somewhat dismayed halt on the part of Piers during which Akkad sat himself down by the fireplace and looked from one to the other of us with a curious expression, a sort of frail affectionate happiness as if somewhere in the heart of this situation something joyful was fermenting. I felt rather vexed with Piers, he cut such a silly figure in his childish chagrin and excitement. "Well, have you found it?" he cried impetuously, and Akkad looked on quietly with a grave face and those pursed lips. I hunted leaf by leaf through the magazine in a most exasperated way without finding the article; then I went through the table of contents most carefully. It was not there either. Piers gave a cry of rage and snatched the magazine from me to repeat the pantomime. It was no good. The article had disappeared. He sat down with grim face in an armchair and, cupping his chin in his hands, stared malevolently at our friend, who gazed back with a kind of innocent resignation, yet offered no explanation of this strange occurrence. "It was there and you know it," said Piers at last in a choked voice; and Akkad, as if to spare him further pain, nodded and said: "Yes, my dear Piers. It *was* there. I know it was there. I put it there, you see; and I put it there specially. Some time ago I asked Sutcliffe to write it for me for use on such an occasion. And I left the magazine with Fahem, who produces it for clients when I tell him to. There! Now are you satisfied?"

Piers listened to this with his mouth open; his cheeks flushed with vexation and pleasure. As Akkad ended he stood up and cried out jubilantly: "I knew it. I knew it all along." Never have I heard such a ring of convincing triumph in his voice. No wonder the collapse of all his beliefs had made him suffer so acutely. But what a crazy thing to have done; I myself felt annoyed with Akkad for playing with my friend's beliefs like this. "But why, in the name of heaven, did you do it?" I asked him, and he gazed smilingly at me and replied with the utmost satisfaction: "I am so glad the little plot worked out all right. You see, it was very important, Piers, a most important test. Do you realise, my dear friend, that you were able to go on believing something which you *knew* to be untrue? Your belief was not shaken, was it?"

"No," said Piers.

171

"It was not a matter of faith, but of a dead certainty, scientific certainty, we might say. I did not doubt that you were one of us, but I wanted to be reassured. So I take every opportunity to create doubt. Now, if I went further and told you that the article was not a fake but *true*. . ." But now Piers burst out laughing and turned away in mock-exasperation. "You have made a fool of me," he said, "and perhaps I deserved it. But I hope from now on you'll take me at my face value, and not repeat this kind of hoax."

Akkad said: "I won't, but only if you promise to realise that we are treading a very narrow path between reality and illusion in this view of things. It is surprising only to those of us who have been conditioned by other patterns of thinking."

"No it is not surprising," said Piers, almost as if to himself. He picked up a letter he had started writing from the writing desk, and, switching on the lamp, read out a few lines. "Man is in a trap, according to Akkad, and goodness avails him nothing in the new dispensation. There is nobody now to care one way or the other. Good and evil, pessimism and optimism—are a question of blood group, not angelic disposition. Whoever it was that used to heed us and care for us, who had concern for our fate and the world's, has been replaced by another who glories in our servitude to matter, and to the basest part of our own natures." He broke off and looked enquiringly at Akkad, who nodded and lit a yellow cigarette. "Shall I go on?" asked Piers, and without waiting for an answer concluded with: "As for man—we are protected from the full consciousness of our own natures—and consequently from that of the real world—by a hard scaly integument, a sort of cataract, a lamination covering the actual soul. It is a coating of rubberoid hardness, difficult if not impossible to pierce. It insulates us against reality, this skin. Hence unless we make a special effort we can only see the truth indistinctly—as we see the sun, through smoked glass."

It was part of a letter to Sylvie; the two of them often wrote to each other like this. Piers put the letter in an envelope and slipped it into a green morocco-covered volume on the window seat—his sister's diary. "So far it will have to do, Akkad."

Akkad was happy now, radiant. "We cannot have it said too often, defined too often; it is such a delicate matter to slip a noose around, that every attempt is a help to us all. We need purer and purer definitions to keep us from being coarsened by the values which the world imposes on us, and which we must try our best to refuse. I think you have grasped the matter more clearly than most—perhaps your French education has helped? You see quite clearly that the stability of the gnostic universe is quite inadvertent; the conformity of matter to models or modes is very precarious and not subject to causality as they imagine. Once this dawns on you the notion of death is born and gathers force so that you start, not to live according to a prearranged plan or model, but to *improvise*. It is another sort of existence, at once extremely precarious, vertiginous, hesitant—but truthful in a way that you never thought you could be. . . ." They embraced laughingly, and all at random, as if completely carried away by the identity of their thoughts, their ideas. The good humour of Piers was now completely re-established, and he made no attempt to disguise the fact that relief played a great part in it. "What a relief," he repeated, pouring himself out a drink and signalling us to do the same. "And yet, Akkad, suppose that I had been left without a chance of learning the truth—namely that the article was a fake . . ." Akkad gazed at him beatifically and said: "This is really what I should have arranged, only I had mercy on you; ideally I should have left you to struggle with the matter, with doubt fermenting all the time and poisoning your inner certainty. But I am a softhearted man who does not like to see his friends suffer, so I decided to tell you the truth of the matter. But if you wish, I could now go on and point to a number of senses in which the fake article is true. I mean, you could question many things about our group and we would be unable to provide convincing explanations to rebut you. Some have for example questioned the little bit of folklore with the mummia—real mummia I hasten to add. What does it do? The ceremony is buried so deep in our history that nobody could explain it—we blindly follow it; but as for its origins, they must stretch back beyond the beginnings of Anno Domini. And we procure and prepare it with great fidelity, after the ancient practices which have been handed down to the embalmers of Upper Egypt. Intriguingly enough the reference in Shakespeare's *Othello* is quite accurate—where he speaks of 'mummy which the skilful conserved of maidens' hearts.' But if you questioned that as a bit of sympathetic magic or harmless folklore I should be hard put to it to find a way of contradicting you."

Akkad sat down once more, and this time as if he were entrenching himself, which indeed he was, for what followed was a kind of marathon intellectual orgy which went on all afternoon until ten o'clock at night. It was as if for the first time the two friends had met after a separation of a hundred years. The servants kept announcing lunch and retiring again with reproachful looks. Lunch was ignored until poor Ahmed's soufflé had gasped its last. Then the meal was eaten in perfunctory fashion between disquisitions, arguments, agreements and a certain amount of wild laughter. Sylvie had gone out for the afternoon to ride

so that the three of us were alone, and I must say that
this time I followed Akkad's ideas with greater ease,
and I also found him both charming and beguiling as
a companion even though there was a certain monotony of exposition in what he had to say about the sect
and its beliefs. It is not possible to reconstruct more
than a part of it—inevitably the part which most in-
terested me. "You speak about society, Piers," he said,
"but your view of it will fundamentally depend on
what view you take of the human psyche which has
formed it, of which it is a reflection. For us the equation matter-spoil-loot-capital value-usury-alienation
. . . seems to sum up the present state of things. It
runs counter to nature, that ideal nature the direction
of which we believe has been usurped by an inferior
demon, the Fly. Of course if you are a Marxist you
will see it in the terms of economic values, labour
costing and so on. If you are a Freudian in terms of
an impulse-inhibition machine, excrement-oriented
and for the most part hardly educated beyond the
anal stage."

"And we?" said Piers. "How do we see it? The
group I mean?"

"Something like the view of society that Arthur had;
the Knights of the Round Table, a society of guilds at
its best. That is probably what you smell and what
attracts you to us, for you are clearly of that Arthu-
rian stock, at least by birth."

Piers burst out laughing and shook his head.
"Alas!" he said, gazing at us both and shaking
his head. "Alas!"

"Why?" asked Akkad.

"Because," said Piers, "de Nogaret was a traitor,
the original and famous one, my ancestor. He was the
King's secret agent sent to spy on the Templars. He
joined them under false pretences, in order to betray

them, which he successfully did. He played the role of Judas in the whole affair. Some say that his grandparents (who had been cathars) had been condemned and burnt at the stake, and that this was his way of revenge. I would very much like an excuse of that kind to hide behind. But the fact remains that he was paid so richly in lands, manors, rivers and farms by Philippe Le Bel, that I can only think that the traditional thirty pieces of silver must have been the stake. So perhaps did he, for he went grievously and publicly out of his mind in the end. And then my family, his descendants, by poetic justice lost all he had gained by this act of betrayal—everything except the old château of Verfeuille which becomes more of a financial burden every year." He fell silent, and sat staring down at the table-cloth as if he were seeing in his mind's eye these scenes of his family's ancient history being enacted. I knew that these facts hurt him deeply; he could never speak of them without being upset. Even when he was helping Toby with his research into the Templars these true revelations cost him an effort to make. It was brave too, for he could easily have destroyed all the documents which were there in the muniments room at Verfeuille and so left the whole thing as the mystery it has always been. "I am a descendant of Judas," he said quietly, as he turned to Akkad, "and I don't know how that will fit into a society which . . ."

"The Round Table also had its Judas," said Akkad, and smiled at Piers' obvious sorrow. "Come, take heart. You would have a harder task if you were the son and heir of Arthur. You know, we say that the gods are simply dogs who spell their names backwards."

It was almost dusk when Sylvie walked into the flat with her purchases and an air of subtly disquieting

176

stillness which at once alerted the concern of her brother, who rose to greet her and take her parcels from her. "Have you seen the paper?" she said, turning to Akkad. "I bought one, and look at the front page."

The face of Casimir Ava the actor was unmistakable—the professional photo showed him in the costume of Hamlet, dagger in hand. But the headline spoke of his death in a car accident on the main Cairo highway. His petrol tank exploded, no doubt from the heat, though this was rather unusual, and he had not been able to free himself and escape the sudden blaze which swept the vehicle. Piers read out the news aloud to us, his brow wrinkled with sad amazement, for he had had a particular fondness for Ava—despite the fact that his sister could not bear the sight of him. I glanced at Akkad's composed face and thought I saw a kind of resigned expression, either of foreknowledge or of already being in possession of the facts. Had he known? Of course such an item of news would excite the whole city, and the telephone could have carried it all over the place; yes, he could easily have known. And yet . . .

The singular thing was that there was a witness to the accident—no less than Jean Makaro, who was chief of police in the city; he had been following behind Ava's green Lagonda and had seen the whole thing. It did also strike me as unusual that both men were part of the Abu Manouf group, and I was about to make some sort of remark about the fact when Akkad, fixing a candid and calm eye on Piers, uttered a strange remark. "Now do you see that we are not joking?" he said, and rose to put out his cigarette and take up his hat.

How long ago all this was—and yet how perennially fresh it is, like everything else in the context of

Egypt, with its mirages we have carried about everywhere in our memories for so many years.

It would be a charity to find one's way through this labyrinth of concealed motives, and doubtless this is what Sutcliffe's unfinished book first set out to do; but either the material proved too prolix and too contradictory for him, or the simple defection of Pia robbed him of the necessary emotional strength to create. The greater the artist the greater the emotional weakling, the greater the infantile dependence on love. Of course I am only paraphrasing in my own words what he himself has written over and over again. And now he has gone, leaving behind the Venetian notebooks and a hamper full of letters, both received and sent; for he always wrote in longhand, and always took copies of his own letters. That is how I know so much about his relationship with Pia. He kept all her shy, hesitant and accidentally brutal letters in a velvet folder of bright green colour.

"In our age it is best to work from documents," he used to say.

It has done me good to put so much down on paper, though I notice that in the very act of recording things one makes them submit to a kind of ordering which may be false, proceeding as if causality was the real culprit. Yet the element of chance, of accident, had so much to do with what became of us that it seems impossible to search out first causes—which is perhaps what led to the defeat of Rob in his fight with his last book. He was overwhelmed, he says, by realising to what degree accident had determined his life and actions. If he had never met Toby, he would never have heard of us, while it was an even stranger acci-

dent in Venice which led him to make the acquaintance of Akkad.

Meanwhile (I am quoting him) he had lost his
"tone of voice" in writing, which he compared to the
sudden loss of a higher register by a concert soprano.
His voice had broken. This must have been after the
failure of Pia's analysis, and her defection with the
negress. The great Sutcliffe found himself at last on
his own with only his art for company, clanking across
the Lombard Plain in the direction of Venice—all the
nervous sadness of the violet rotting city. It had become clear to him that the salt had gone out of everything, but in order to stop the fountain of tears which
burst like a whole Rome in his heart, he had to adopt
a bristling flippancy, a note of Higher Unconcern,
which gave literature one of the novels still regarded
in the best circles as somewhat funny-peculiar; it was
self-immolating, that horrible laughter. Paradoxically
he could not help thinking that had Pia *died* things
would have been better for him, because clearer. But
simply to desert him for darling Trash, the Negress
. . . To be sexually betrayed is to be rendered ridiculous, and if one is famous and marvellous in one's
own conceit, Why it is only the sense of outrage which
keeps one going. Of course these are more the sentiments of a woman than a man, and if one probed them
one would reach the central chamber where the first
dispositions were taken, the first complexes stored up.
And how lovely Trash was with her deep-rosined fiddle
of a voice and her skin smelling of musk melons and
her little stilted pointed accent of the deepest south; a
lazy sensual toreador of the love-act, marvellously armoured against ideas like psychoanalysis or Romantic
Love by the fact of falling asleep when one uttered
a word of more than one syllable. "My, my," she
would croon, turning over lazily on her side and falling into a coma, "you slay me, honey." To think that

Sutcliffe never guessed, that it had been going on even before he had met Pia. It was infuriating. "I guess Robin's sad to death, honey."

Yes, Robin was sad to death all right, sitting bolt upright in his first-class compartment, writing another long whining letter to the pale girl—who to do her justice was suffering just as much as he was. *Pia loves Rob,* she had written it with her lipstick on the walls of the *vespasienne* in the Rue Colombe, waiting for him to finish, holding her pampered borzoi on the leash. Trash was taking an English lesson with a French whore who had the longest tongue in Christendom. What happiness he knew, in all his innocence, what pride in this girl with the slit of a mouth—so spoiled and gracile a slender body. Trash was simply a cultivated American friend from the University of I forget, who knew how to massage rheumatisms away, stiff neck, and all that. After he knew, he developed a pain in the lumbar region worthy of a lumberjack, but there was no Trash to help him with long coffee-coloured fingers so apt for ragtime on a piano late at night.

Thus Sutcliffe writing about himself; out of the inexplicable confusion of the Venice notebooks some sort of self-portrait does emerge; but he tried out several tones of voice and found none to fit his mood and theme. He was proposing to write about himself, to make himself the central character of his own book, but never quite found out how to situate the Sutcliffe of his invention squarely in the realm which his creator inhabited. The resulting manuscript is indeed something of a puzzle, for almost before he could get the book started his "characters," that is to say Piers, Toby, Sylvie and myself, started to look over his shoulder, so to speak, and talk from themselves. He felt at once elated by the thought that he had discovered a possible impressionistic form for his book, and depressed by the incoherence in which his subjects existed. They were not articulate about anything —and specially about love, the subject which occupied him most. As for our own trinity, he was disposed to regard it as a misfortune which, with a little forethought, we might have avoided. But then, on reflection, he remembered that for years now he himself had formed (without knowing it) the third in a trinity just as ill-starred, with Pia and pretty Trash as the other partners. How should he go about the book, then? How much latitude had he to alter facts? Perhaps like this? After much hesitation . . .

"Sutcliffe—there was no limit to his greatness—became celebrated and tolerably affluent the year his wife died, and immediately set about reorganizing a life which had become staled with worry and illnesses. From now on, he thought, he would set off every spring on a visit to Venice. His best friend was a raffish Oxford don called Toby Goddard, who was working on the Crusades in a château near Avignon. After Venice he would join his friend there for the summer. That was the plan. It was indeed not merely the plan for this year, but the master-plan for the rest of his life. Why Venice? It was rather a vulgar choice—the mud smelt so strong, the water squirmed with rats. One dares to suppose that he was merely a romantic of the trashy kind. But no, his books attest to a greatness beyond question. Hurrah! Robin and Toby were both large shapeless men, according to their friends, who were known as Gog and Magog. (Sutcliffe had genius perhaps, but was no beauty.) They both dressed rather alike, in untidy tweeds, and were both tow-haired with blond eyelashes. They also shared a fearful myopia of identical dioptry, were apt to bump into inanimate objects, sit down on invisible chairs, or bounce off each other as they shambled about talking and gesticulating. Both could walk on their hands and once had a race round Saint Peter's in this way which Toby won by a short head. Venice, then, and genius . . . what more does one need? He proposed to rationalise these rather expensive journeys by telling himself that a writer needs more than a cork-lined room in which to work. Needs space, elegance and the compacted nostalgias of an ideal past expressed in stone and metal. And to hell with Ruskin. So the huge man, wrapped in his tweed overcoat which smelt like a wet animal, set forth in the year 19——to welcome a late spring on those legendary canals. Gog parted from Magog in Paris with many unsteady protestations of esteem and regret; soon this incomparable couple would be reunited in the south. In Avignon.

"He always carried about with him a black leather despatch-case full of water paints, pens, and bottles of Chinese inks and Japanese sepia blocks. So it was that the pages of his lonely letters were brilliantly got up with drawings in mauve, scarlet, yellow, green. . . . It was his way of cheating a professional neurasthenia to sit on a balcony over the loop of a canal and write these letters which were afterwards illustrated in crayon or gouache.

"Letters to whom, we may ask? Why, letters to the few friends he had in the world, like the brother of his wife who was rather a slowcoach of a doctor, distressingly sincere. He resembled his sister in nothing save the shape of his hands, which were slender and delicate—but what was that to Sutcliffe? He wrote to his wife still—long chatty letters to keep her up to date with his sentiments and movements. These efforts he either destroyed by posting them down the lavatory or —if they contained fragments of marvellous writing, poignant and regrettable incidents remembered—he sent them to Toby, or to Pia's brother, with instruc-

tions that they should be spared and put somewhere
safe. One day, he thought, he would fish out all this
disorderly material and light a bonfire among the
olives in order to say a final *Ave* to this writing life so
rich in promises and so fertile in disenchantments.
Yes, one day he would be an old hack, gone in the
tooth, broken of nerve and talentless—dried up like a
river bed. What then? Why, then, the Far East perhaps, some little monastery in the Thai hills, a bald
dome, silence. Or the Trappe at Marseille where he
would sit all day wearing an air of petulance like a
latter-day Huysmans. Sutcliffe didn't see this part very
clearly; one doesn't as a rule. Like all narcissists he
was convinced that old age and death were things
which happened to others—and he made inadequate
provision for them, though his mirror warned him repeatedly. His teeth were getting fewer and would soon
have to take on reinforcements if he was to continue
eating well. His sexual needs were sharper and yet far
too quick, *O ejaculatio!* He couldn't stand brothels and
so was at the mercy of passing sentiments which did
not often come his way. He rather saw himself as *Sutcliffe accoucheur des dames, accoucheur d'âmes*. The
ideal prostitute he dreamed of merely, seeing her as
a postulant discharging her obligations to a god—
through fornication the human shadow drinks, the eidolon of man or woman. No use asking him what that
last phrase meant. Sometimes his wife suffocated under his clumsy tenderness and felt like a conscript. If
you want to know how she died read on from here. In
another country, among olive trees of steel grey. In
some ways for a writer whose imaginary wife has just
died, death has about as much reality as a painted
dog. Sutcliffe thought to himself: life is only once, old
boy. All that we think and write about death is fictitious. Theology is very old ice cream, very tame sau-

sage. Best go on hoping *pour l'amour à quatre pattes*
—love on all fours.

"Affectivity, then, worn down like an old dog's molars. What you have bitten off as reality you will be
forced to spit out. Here in Venice, these thoughts
hardly belong to a place which so confidingly trusted
in the idea of civilisation. One was forced to reconsider
the idea against one's will. Sutcliffe tended to see it as
some poor Penelope, trying to weave up the original
couple on her loom, while she waited patiently for the
return of you know who. But in this age the hero never
comes, and now we know that he will never come. We
must be content with *L'amour vache* and *L'amour
artichaut,* he loves me, she loves me not. . . . . In default of a god we must be content with that. Maybe it
is all to the good. When god existed such was the terrible radiance of the thing that the ancients only dared
to gaze at his behind, fearing for their eyesight and
perhaps for their reason. According to Freud this led
later to an irrational fear of sausages, or of being run
over from behind, or impaled by father. What else to
record? Yes, Sutcliffe one day fell among cannibals
and was masterfully abbreviated; later at Athos he
was much troubled by the indiscriminate farting from
the monks' cells—love-calls of old Byzantium he supposed. . . ."

What a mysterious business.
Wound up one day like a clockwork toy
Set down upon the dusty road
I have walked ticking for so many years.
While with the same sort of gait
And fully wound up like me
At times I meet other toys
With the same sort of idea of being.
Tick tock, we nod stiffly as we pass.

They do not seem as real to me as I do;
We do not believe that one day it will end
Somewhere on a mountain of rusting
Automobiles in a rusty siding far from life.
Pitted with age like a colander
Part of the iron vegetation of tomorrow.

Sutcliffe, the Venetian Documents

Arrived, the great man dumped his luggage at the hotel and putting on blue-tinted glasses set out to have a little walk and smell, deambulating with caution however because somewhere in this fateful town was Bloshford, the writer he hated most in the world because he was so rich, his books sold like pies; Sutcliffe's superior product sold well enough, but Bloshford carried all before him, and had managed to buy a couple of Rollses! It was vexing that he too spent most of his time in Venice—it was the site of many of his infernal novels. If ever the great Sutcliffe was in a bad temper his thoughts turned to Bloshford and the oaths mounted to his lips. Ah that bald pear-shaped conundrum of a best-seller—that apotheosis of the British artist, the animated tea-cosy! "You just wait Bloshford!" he might murmur aloud. A man who seemed to be held up by the bags under his eyes—every time he saw a bank-statement he breathed in and they inflated. A man who didn't drink and couldn't think. A man who could not plant a corkscrew straight. A heavy-arsed archimandrite of British prose. . . . When the man approached you with his bone-setter's grin you had to bite hard on the bullet.

Thus Sutcliffe taking an evening prowl among the hump-backed bridges and curvilinear statuary, a bit soothed by the breathing beauty of so much lonely water. What would Bloshford be doing now? At the flea market probably, buying a clockwork pisspot that played "Auld Lang Syne." Doubtless he had begun a new novel . . . *La merde, la merde toujours recommencée* as Valéry remarked, probably thinking of Bloshford. Enough of this.

He bought some fruit from a stall, and furtively ate it as he walked. The other half of his mind dwelt in Angkor Wat.

All that colossal winter breakdown, the nightmares, the sedatives. After nearly a decade of marriage you expect something to wear out, to blow a fuse. In this case he saw himself sitting beside the breathing slender figure of Pia like someone in an old engraving—a beastly old Rembrandt exhaling the perfervid gloom of Protestantism and a diet of turnips. He could think of nothing except her condition, and how she had got that way so suddenly. Of course, he knew it was something that had been held back, festering, and had suddenly exploded. But what? Neurology at that epoch was medieval except for its chemistry. So we were sent to a feast of psychiatry at Vienna where darling old Freud put his magnifying glass over their lives, their dreams, our hopes. It was a momentous meeting for Sutcliffe the husband, but even more so for the writer, for here was an old humble man who had given birth to an infant science. To see through his eyes was an experience like no other on earth. The writer rejoiced, for the old doctor treated all human behaviour as a symptom—the intellectual daring of this feat changed his whole life. Lucky, too, that the suicide of Pia had misfired, for thanks to this endearing old Jewish gentlemen with his pocketful of dreams, the true nature of her breakdown was varnished and framed. He had not guessed that a bad attack of conscience could lead to a complete mental overthrow. This was the case, and the doctor insisted that she tell him the truth about Trash and herself. The crisis had been precipitated by Trash's threat to leave her and set up house with another girl. But this wasn't all. Standing pale before me in our hotel room, and wringing her white hands very slowly as if wringing out wet linen, she said: "This is a terrifying predicament, to realise the truth about inversion, because I really have come to love you, Rob. With all my heart and as much of my sex as I humanely can. Really love."

The great writer had to put that in his pipe and smoke it—there was nothing else to be done about the matter.

A winter of walking about in the rain down snowlit streets; overheated hotel-rooms with the smell of furry moquette; and money pouring away down the drain, down the sink, down . . . dull opiates which offered no Lethe. It was the turn of Sutcliffe to become neurotic, sleepless. But instead of losing weight he put it on, for the same reasons; he could not resist the Vienna cafés with their extraordinary range of pastry. He began to look tearfully like the fat boy in *Pickwick,* and his eyes began to give trouble. But in order to play his part he had to turn priest and listen to the whole confession of the only woman he had really wholeheartedly loved; and in her brave tearful stammering realise that really, for the first time in his life, he was truly loved. It was only this malefic predicament that had unseated them. "Robin sure is sicker than a cat, honey." Yes, Robin sure was sicker than a cat!

I only saw the old man-in-the-moon a couple of times to talk about Pia. It was enough. He was full of endearing quirks of a strongly Jewish cast—after all, who else could rename love "an investment of libido"? It was marvellous. It kicked in the rear poor little Narcissus gaping into the stream. It was intellectually the most electrifying experience that Sutcliffe the writer had ever enjoyed. Reading up a bit of this extraordinary lore he began to see some of the reasons behind his own choice of an investment in Pia—the shadow of another comparable inversion. What he had admired sexually in her was that she looked so boyish. Abrupt gestures and hair tossed out of eyes. For all her daffodil fragility she was a boy. Then he remembered once that after a fancy-dress ball when she was dressed as a soldier she came to bed still in her military tunic and the result had been more than somewhat outstanding. Never had he been so excited! But this type of predisposition could not be cured by rushing out to a brothel and ordering a friend of Baron Corvo. It wasn't sufficiently enracinated, sufficiently powerful, the strain; not as powerful as the corresponding strain in Pia. Meanwhile the great attachment had clarified itself as the genuine article . . . ahem, he coughed behind his hand, as Love.

There was plenty of time in this Venetian spring to go over all these scenes in his mind for the umpteenth time, his lips moving as he re-enacted them, as if he were reading the score of some strange symphony, as indeed he was. In the intervals he wrote a line to his ungovernable friend Toby—the accident-prone don —to cheer himself up with harmless sallies. Listen to the puttle of the vaporettos, finger that fine glass full of smoky grappa or sugary Strega with a meniscus left by the dying sunlight on the lagoon's horizon. Sutcliffe, pull yourself together, man. What do you propose to do with the rest of your life? Surely somewhere there was a dusky Annamite girl to be found, softer than promises or cobwebs?

Stirring his cold toes in his huge lace-up old-fashioned boots he admitted that he was lonely, that he really hated Venice on that first evening. He wondered whether he should not take the train south right away down to Provence, which though less rhetorical and emphatic than Italy has its own lithe grace of a Mediterranean kind; as Toby used to say "something of Sicily mixed with something of Tuscany." But in the final analysis it was not landscape that irked him by its presence or absence. It was lack of company, it was lack of love. See the great man then staring into the water from a lonely table; his cigar extinguished, his book closed against the twilight. Nightfall.

But his real problem is to forget. The best way would be to let one passion cast out another. We see from this that he was rather disingenuous. He had come to Venice not only to cure his prose of words like "chrysoprase" and "amethystine" but also to cure his soul of its private hauntings. He had come here, in the last analysis, for peace of mind. There were still memories that made him moan in his sleep, or that when awake returned with such force that he dropped knife and fork and felt as if a ball of bloody rags was stuck in his throat. Such compulsive thoughts made the tweed-clad mandarin stand up abruptly and take a turn up and down the balcony, whispering curses under his breath.

To be more explicit still, it was here in Venice that she had elected to tell him everything, which explained the peculiar hold of the place. Those scenes had marked his mind as if with a branding iron. The old American duchess, for example, who entrained them into her circle. Pictorially alone the scene was extraordinary. Huge sides of oxen were delivered to the house in the Via Caravi, whole beefs split down the middle. In these bloody cradles they would lie and make love while the men in blood-stained aprons stood around and jeered. He could see the pale Pia like Venus Anadyomene in a thoroughly contemporary version of Botticelli lying pale and exhausted in a crucible of red flesh with the black glossy body of Trash looming over her. . . . Once there had been a little blood in her footprint on the wet bathroom floor, but this was her period, or so she said.

He was not to be blamed if therefore, for clinical reasons, he nursed some vague premonitory feelings about an adventure which might help him to forget a little. The image he had in mind was, as to flesh, something on the lines of Raphael—plenty of it, that is, and softer than cirrus. Vaguely he hoped for a cloud-shape but he wanted it more localised in association, more specially Venetian as to colouring. He pictured thick lustrous auburn hair, a little brush-repellent, a little wayward, sweeping out at the nape into a veritable squirrel's tail which one could not resist stroking. Then also a pure intellectual beauty, work of an ancient master, which would make the saliva start to the mouth. These, then, were some of the trusting demands he made upon life in that slow Venetian spring—but they were provisional and not final. At the end one finds that one has to take what one is given or go without altogether. Sutcliffe did not give up easily, but he was prepared to bow, to face reality, to accept surprises at face value. If only to get away from the poisonous nagging of his thoughts. He reflected often on one such strange adventure which befell him one year in Stresa, with a fair girl from Périgord whose kitten-clear eyes were full of the symmetrical renown of her inner mischeif. Phew! Vega burned bright for a summer, blue star of the unprepared heart. Well, he had some of these countermemories in hand that first evening as he smiled into his shaving mirror, remembering that she had said: "You have very nice teeth and a most intelligent smile." He smiled at himself "intelligently" in order to savour the lady's approbation, which in his present gloom he found comforting. It was a pity that he had to hoist his spectacles in order to see himself at all. But there! It was springtime, and soon it would be warmish, a time for fleshly desire. Ah Pia!

See him stalking, then, with his rather dispossessed air among the fountains and marble lions fancifully upon the Lido. He was wondering how long he would stand it, this intermittently chilly Venice, when some spring chemistry came to his assistance in the person of a young girl who passed and repassed him, walking at a much swifter pace. She was a mature enough looking person, dressed in smart black velveteen with a bright green silk shirt, plus an eye-enhancing turquoise hanky at her throat. Arresting rather than beautiful. And no wonder that her eyes had turned lime-green in a very sunburned face. It was a heavy and rather solemn prow she bore with a strongly uplifted throat—an Inca face with a heavy root to the nose and widely arched eye. She was well fleshed, well haunched in pleasant roundels, soft as a primitive landscape, promising soft rain to a parched world. Mind you, all this would be intractable bum at fifty, but she was nearer half that age. She had a clear and masterful walk—in youth one knows what one is doing, or at any rate thinks one does.

The most discouraging thing about her was that she carried a book—no, not one of his books, though he swore that if ever he wrote about her he would say it was. The second time she passed his blood chilled for a moment because the name of the author on the dust-jacket began with a B—could she be reading a shoddy Bloshford? But then . . . relief! For by the foreskin of the Risen Lord, it was Bergson. At the end of the promenade he came upon her sitting on a marble bench in a sunny corner, covering the margins of the old boy with figures. A shopping list? He could not help wondering. He swerved about with what he hoped was an unconcerned expression and craned for another look. A tourist doing summary accounts, having overspent? He was not inquisitive by nature. Finally after wheeling about rather in the manner of a waiting vulture (he couldn't help feeling) he sat down beside her. She moved up to make room, smiling at him equably, calmly, composedly. A woman sure of herself. Later on he was to find with horror that all this math was to do with velocity and mass, with inertia and structure, and that he had to do with a pupil of Minkowski who had grave reservations about Bergson because he knew no maths. At the time Sutcliffe didn't know that Minkowski was the trailblazer for Einstein, but he pretended to in order to cause her delight and weaken her defences. But he didn't really want all this cultural stuff, no. On the other hand he liked women who could read and write, so why complain?

He began on a very high note with a remark about Aristotle, whereupon she loosed off about Bergson, saying something like: "It's just as if you had to have a physical model for everything before you could understand it when the thing can be stated by an algebraic equation. He has to use words which makes him as out of date as Aristotle." He was tempted to let out a shout, as if to stop a runaway horse, but he reined himself in. Classy stuff, all this; he wondered if she talked like this in bed. If so he would leave for Avignon at once. The idea came to him to ask her and she laughed a most enchanting laugh and said no, she didn't, adding: "Besides it is your fault, you started. Besides I am delighted to find someone who can talk about these things." Was she alone in Venice he asked, and she said that she was with her father, but added, because he looked so crestfallen, "But I am a perfectly free girl."

This was encouraging, in view of the fact that while he could swap a good deal of jargon, his hold on mathematics was flimsy in the extreme, and when he spoke of such matters her whole mood became dangerously intense. Sutcliffe beware!

Well, even the spring decided to play a part in this adventure, for the sun came out enthusiastically in a last evening burst. From the garden of Floriani behind us came a light bogus jazz and the ticking of Ping-Pong balls. The air was full of melody. She really was, if not classically beautiful, at least very striking with her merry clever Jewish face, its satirical smiling mouth, and so on. He coaxed her to a brilliant café where the dapples of yellow light played on her darkness like grains of gold—the sunlight firing at her through a screen of gold lamé. The motes dancing in her breath full of sunbeams. Intellectually she fired all her guns at him and he said to himself: yes, quite so, how clever, too true—but just wait till I get you to bed, my beauty. Sitting smiling at her over the friendly Cinzano winking at the brim, he told himself optimistically that it would be like sleeping with an electrical impulse, an ohm or a kilowatt. He would wrap the whole Field Theory in his arms and canoodle her into sharing the sleep of the whole universe. To hell with Bergson. As he thought about it, his feeling for romantic Venice came back: it would be quite unlike anything that could happen in poor degenerate England where football had replaced public hangings.

For a while she wouldn't tell him her name, preferring to remain anonymous, she said, for the mild drink and the sunshine had gone to her head, making her a bit blushful and youthful. When she excused herself and went to the ladies' room he instantly suspected the worst. He doubled round the corner and caught her as she was walking away from the back entrance of the café, with the clear intention of giving him the slip. She did not protest when he took her arm and shook it reprovingly. He asked her to explain this flight and she said: "Because I talk too much and I am angry with myself." The waiter came padding after them with the bill and he persuaded her, without undue difficulty, to resume her potations with him—he was prepared to hear all about electromagnetism and the speed of light if only he could go on looking at her and musing. It was the old Stendhalian crystallisation all right, and he thought back to all he had learned in Vienna about investing his bloody libido and indulging his narcissism. And all those awful silly case histories with their extraordinary language—phrases like "nocturnal pollutions," if you please. Why not "nocturnal benedictions," a natural relief from stress? "Why do you grin?" asked the girl and he found some sort of excuse for the rictus.

They talked on, weaving up a skein of bright thoughts, but all the time he realised that his conquest of her had become more and more improbable. Specially as it was now his turn to want to go to the lavatory, and he knew that as soon as his back was turned she would vanish, nameless, into the evening. Heavens, but she looked choice in her war-paint. So like a hero, like a philosopher, he decided to renounce her. He rose and excused himself, paying the bill as he did so; then he retired, gazing lingeringly at her the while and permitting himself a certain dark majesty as he withdrew, as befitted genius. She smiled at him, all warmth and affection, and he held that brown hand for a wee moment during which he recited the whole of *Paradise Lost* to himself. Then he was gone —and of course so was she.

He came back at last, but it was to face an empty

chair. There was nothing between him and his bloody
novel now, for when real life had nothing to offer him
he fell back on the dull brooding which one fine day
would squeeze out into a novel. They seemed for a
moment stale, the distractions of this quaint haunt-
box of a town. Old Venice glittering and liquefying
among her multiple reflections, wing of a thousand
peacocks fired up into a sun-cloudy evening sky.
Round and round the bloody novel like a blind horse
circling a well. His hero would be called something
like Oakshot, and he would be far from heroic. He is
seen standing all night in the Paris—Avignon express,
speeding southwards, summoned by the telegram
which told him of the death, suicide, disappearance,
or whatever of Pia. It had come from the brother who
was in the possession of private information which
might throw light on the matter. What sort? Well, let
that go for now. It would come to him later. A portrait of Trash with her lovely terracotta colouring, her
expansive gestures. Throwing wide her arms and crying: "Thank you, God," when she was pleased. Did
Trash perhaps fire a shot into her back while she
slept? No, Trash would be cruelly satirical—graduate
of Horrid College, Nebraska, who had taken a doc-
torate in Human Warmth and a diploma in manual
manipulation and morbid massage. Oh damn everything. The man standing in the lighted train . . .

"The southbound train from Paris was the one he
had always taken from time immemorial—the same
long slow-coach of a train stringing out its bluish lights
across the twilight landscapes like some super-
glowworm. It reached Provence at dawn, often by a
brindled moonlight which striped the countryside like
a tiger's hide."

What sort of chap was this Oakshot? Sutcliffe
yawned. Why not change his name to Rodney Persimmon and make him a homosexual publisher?

He was working off his petulance lingeringly, rather enjoying his suffering if one must be honest. He told himself that he would go to a brothel and hire some bloodless turnip of an octoroon clad in a straw mat and with a paper poppy behind each ear. That was it; but the mood did not last. Venice plucked at his sleeve —the fervent tension of flowers on stalls in the light wind, the flakes of apt sunlight, this huge museum of snowy architecture, the gallant spring, the amber women . . . in a little while he persuaded himself that he was cured, his heart was as light as a feather. He was prepared to spend the evening alone. Hurrah, yes, alone. To loiter and dine late under a striped awning over the water-wobbled, gondola-scratched canals. What would Oakshot like for dinner? Solid grumpy fare like whitebait. Not like Persimmon, who was all the time on the lookout for a dauntless boy. As for Sutcliffe, he was for seafood. He made some notes on his craft on the back of the menu and asked the waiter where he should dine that night. "Item. You must not yawn up your reader. Oakshot, if he resembles Bruce, will become a bore. A serious Toby, then? It is hard to chew." He smoked slowly and decided that he missed the young lady, yes he did; there was much that she had to say about determinism in science and the new attitude to causality which was apposite to his own intentions. . . . Be careful, for these notions sound cumbrous, and a novel must speak, not lecture. And Oakshot? Fuck Oakshot. If he closed his eyes he saw a gloomy tweed-clad figure eating a sandwich and swaying in a swaying train. What sort of man was he? He supposed that she had found him a trifle insincere and so disappointing. But had he enacted a really mammoth insincerity she might have loved him forever. In science the notion of scale . . . Never mind. His attention shifted to a young English girl who was eating scampi with her

fingers and saying: "What rotters the Italians are—
how perfectly septic." She had had her bottom pinched
in a vaporetto. Good. Good.

It was largely to drown this banal recitative that he
fell to scheming up a chapter or two of his book once
more. He was going to call it: *Tu Quoque*—O God,
he could hear the wails of his publisher already. Why
can't you give it a nice rational *terre à terre* title like
Cruise of the Beagle? Bloshford would have chris-
tened it *Oakshot Rides Again* and left it at that. It
was reckless, but with all the sumptuousness of the
city around him he felt feather-headed and irresponsible. He would indulge in modish prose musings and
if Persimmon didn't like it he could put the manuscript where it would do most good. By the bleeding
piles of Luther, the *molimina excretoria,* he would
stand his ground!

That reminded him—he had forgotten to take, as
always, a few sheets of lavatory paper in his inside
pockets, against accidents or paperless café lavatories.
Never mind, the hotel was not far away.

There was a barrel-organ with a nice monkey atop
dressed in a coloured cap with tassels, which beat
time perfectly to a plaintive little version of "Solo Per
Te." He sang a bit himself, huskily, nostalgically,
thinking of the unknown mathematician, beating time
with his fork. The long kaleidoscope of fish on the
stalls were full of frenzied glittering life, winking at
him: shellfish, molluscs, winkles and whales—all of
them throbbing and winking away for dear life among
the spattered reflections of the smelly lagoons. An old
man stood there, leaning negligently on a stall and
looking criminally like a Michelangelo cartoon. But if
you shut your eyes you could turn him into a little
coloured mandarin, block-printed by a slavish Jap.
Her dark throat with the sequins floating across it like

a shoal of tropical fish. Damn, why had she dumped him?

Forking up mouthfuls of fish he said: Now about this *Tu Quoque* book, and about Oakshot; let us suppose a man world-weary and world-travelled, who has spent a lifetime hunting for a philosophy and a woman to match. . . . Hum. The woman is dead. But he, who has walked the Middle East, has been marked by an encounter with a tribe of Druse-Benawhis. They feed him on lotus or whatever and induct him into the beliefs of the tribe—a kind of pessimism of an extreme cast. Actually the word is a misnomer, for truth cannot be either pessimist or optimist when you reach bedrock. These ideas had come to him after an encounter with a young Alexandrian in Paris, who spoke a beguiling and negligent French, and who appeared to be in possession of a number of far-fetched and recondite beliefs of a gnostic cast. He was a member of the saddest profession on earth —a banker and man of affairs. Between ulcers, which he came to Paris to have darned, he lived in opulence in Alexandria, where Oakshot had been invited to visit him. Akkad, the name. "I am not really a banker so much as a student of cosmic malevolence." The propositions of this languid fellow with the enormous soft doelike eyes much beguiled Oakshot. Sutcliffe. "What happens after that? I don't know."

He clung obstinately to the image of the man in the train eating a sandwich as it raced through the night. At the station his wife's brother, the doctor, would be waiting, with some privileged information about the death. Or perhaps Trash would be waiting in a white sports car. "Robin, honey, I jest had to do it to her." He shied away from Bruce a bit because he judged him to be a dull fellow and incapable of anything really dramatic as a role. He was a good chap and all that, but pretty humdrum. Nevertheless Pia had loved him and some of her pollen had come off on him, so that he himself felt a certain affection of kinship for him. But he was a dull dog on the whole, and inspired no fiction.

Akkad insisted that the whole of man's universe of sorrow was the result of a cosmic lapsus—something small in scale but absolutely critical in effect. Something as small as a slip of the tongue, or a moment's inattention—on the part of God, that is—which reverberated throughout the whole cobweb. A slip of memory, the bicycle-chain of recollection, which threw all the gears out of true, altered the notions of time and place. Thus human reality was a limbo now peopled with ghosts, and the world was embarked on a collision course with the spirit of default, of evil, at the helm, guided to destruction by inferior demons. That is how cosmic justice works—one little slip and the Pit yawns open. Man becomes an *être-appareil*, and *être-gnome*. He dare not face this reality. But the gnostic boys say that if you do face it you start to live a counterlife. (Oakshot grunted in a philistine manner and decided that people who talked like this deserved to have their hands cut off above the ankles.) Alternatively, Oakshot was profoundly marked by this little discourse and felt that he had tumbled upon something which related quite distinctly to his own life, the sad marriage that he carried about inside him like a dead foetus. Another kind of life beckoned to him; these beliefs did not promise happiness, there was nothing cosy about them. But they promised truth. Oakshot sighed and lit a pipe.

Leaving Oakshot to smoke his coarse shag Sutcliffe abandoned ship, so to speak, and pushed off for a stroll. All these ideas rattled around in his noodle like nutmegs in a tin, and he made no attempt to sort them out. He promised himself instead several days of gallery-going, to bathe his wits in colour, wash out his soul in rainbows. Memory dawdled him along diverse canals in a delighted trance of architectural circumlocution to where at last, in his little shop, Gabrielli hovered like a most ancient moth, among his exquisite vellums and moroccos. He was finishing the little Tasso which had taken him so many years—and had been destined as an anniversary of marriage present for Pia. It was at last done, and he had been about to send it to Sutcliffe, who made no mention of Pia, simply saying how very pleased she would be. All of a sudden he had the impulse to lift that withered old craftsman's hand to his lips, to kiss it with reverence. Looking into the glaucous old eyes he thought: we are the vestiges of a civilisation gone dead as dead mastoid. No doubt those desert boys were right—evil was at the helm and the pace was increasing. One could hear the distant thunder of the falls towards which we were sliding—the distant cannonade of doom. Meanwhile here was this little old man who had lived to see so much, frail as a leaf, still quietly working among his colour blocks and gold leaf. The little book glowed in his hand like a fire opal. Her name in gold upon the spine. Gabrielli was at peace because he was the master of his method. This was the key of all happiness. Why couldn't he feel that way about writing books? Oakshot hated books in which everything was carefully described and all conversations woodenly recorded. So did Sutcliffe as a matter of fact.

Back on the canals he suddenly found that he no longer cared whether God existed or not—so fantastic was the sunset that it all but sponged away his consciousness. You could have proved anything from such a display—about God he meant. So incredibly and painstakingly worked out and executed. Imagine the Venetians subjected to this on every evening of their lives. . . . It was too much. Only a blessed colour-blindness could save them from becoming madmen or at least ecstatics. "Look!" he cried to the gondolier who was slithering him back to his hotel along the darkening canals, dipping like a bat. *"Che Bello!"* Pointing like a demented Ruskin to the western quarter where already the dying sun . . . (space for ten lines of description full of sound and fury) *"Che Bello,* you bloody mole." The man stared dazedly along the parabola described by Sutcliffe's cane, shrugged and grunted, finally admitting, *"È bello, signore."* The great man registered impatience at this lack of spirit. "I knew it," he said. "Colour-blind."

He went up to his room at the Torquato Tasso to brush his teeth. There was a letter from his agent with a press cutting about his last book, faintly damning it in a supercilious way. He stalked to the bathroom again and with gravity dabbed out the bags under his eyes with vanishing cream. He was afraid of getting to look like Bloshford. As a matter of fact Oakshot had a steely bluish gaze, and hardly ever blinked, which made people uncomfortable at what they felt might be an implied reproach. People who blink too much are inevitably stupid, and Oakshot was not stupid. A little emotionally retarded perhaps from lack of sexual experience. Ever since he had climbed Everest with Tufton . . . At night one found sherpas in one's sleeping-bag and could do nothing. They suffered so from cold. Oakshot lost his trigger finger to frost-bite and had to give up lion safaris. To hell with him.

But it was still going on, the day; up at this level there was still a last splash of sunlight. He thrust open his shutters and stepped out onto his balcony. At the same moment the occupant of the room directly facing his over the narrow street did the same. They came face to face, nose to nose, so close that they could have shaken hands with each other. The little street was gay with hanging washing of all shapes and colours. He stared at the girl and she stared back at him. They laughed and sketched out gestures of helplessness. His posture said: "What is to be done? Fate is stronger than either of us. Clearly we were doomed to meet, perhaps doomed never to part."

"So it would seem," said the young lady. And emboldened by this hopeful departure of fate he permitted himself to look reproachful and ask her why she had abandoned him to his fate in that paltry fashion, condemning him to a solitary and far too early dinner.

She looked somewhat constrained and after a long hesitation said: "I knew your wife," and was suddenly silent. Sutcliffe fell out of breath with surprise. The girl added: "Not very well, but I knew her, and consequently I knew who you were, and thought that sooner or later the subject might come up and be distasteful to you. So I ran."

"You knew my wife," he said, almost as much to himself as to her. It had cast a strange kind of shadow over this incipient flirtation of minds. "I never met you, but I saw her in Avignon one summer, with her brother. I live quite near the place at Verfeuille."

Sutcliffe sat down on a chair and lit a cigarette. The girl said: "I saw your picture in the paper once." Instantly it was like a bruise which suddenly decided to ache again for no known reason. The girl facing him turned to hang up some small clothes she had washed, on the window-sill adjacent. "You need not have been unduly afraid," he said gravely. "I would have welcomed a talk about her—from anybody who knew her."

Actually this balcony meeting would be quite a good thing to happen to Oakshot; the girl would be different, a ragamuffin he had found in the stews.

They spent all night in a gondola heading for the sea. Wrapped in a cloak, listening to the heart-breaking serenades of a Goldoni gondolier.

He would have to change Akkad's name of course, perhaps he might call him Barnabas or Porphyrius? You could have him saying to Oakshot in despair what he once said to me—I mean to Sutcliffe: "You are the worst kind of man to whom to express these ideas because your interest in religion is purely aesthetic—that is the real sin against the Holy Ghost." Oakshot puzzling over the grand strategy of the gnostic, the fateful grammar of dissent which . . . and of course Oakshot would consider all logical development of such ideas in the direction of suicide or refusal to propagate in cathar fashion as damnably unhealthy.

The girl had turned back towards him and her attitude had changed; she seemed confused now and sad, as if she felt guilty of an indiscretion or a gaffe. "When you knew Pia where was I?" he asked and she replied that he was in Paris and expected daily to appear in Avignon. That more or less situated the date—it was while the great nervous breakdown of Pia was cooking. His own behaviour at that epoch hadn't helped either—drink and gipsy brothels and a dose of clap. He felt guilty not to have been more responsible at a time when she needed his help. The girl stared at him wistfully, almost commiseratingly, as though repenting for having broached the subject. Sutcliffe pondered. Then she said: "Would you care to come and have coffee with me? My father has gone to the opera and I am alone." His heart leaped up when he beheld . . . He stood up and decreased his trousers with his fingers, saying: "I would of course love to, but only on condition that you don't feel sorry for me, or vexed at yourself. Otherwise you will bore me and you haven't done so yet."

She nodded and gave him the number of her room.

So lightly and albeit sadly (Pia's frail shadow) he crossed the little square and found her hotel, the Lutece; curiosity prompting him to consult the register in order to discover her name. It was Banquo, and he wondered for a moment if she was not a member of the famous banking family of that name. Yes, her father must be the famous man he had heard of. "He describes himself as a famous ghost," she said later when he asked her.

She was sitting in an old-fashioned cretonne-covered armchair, clad in a green silk kimono with dashing chrysanthemums stitched all over it. In the rosy light shining from the standard lamp in its scarlet velvet hood her throat and hands were gipsy brown. Her toes with their lacquered nails were now shod lightly in Athenian thonged sandals. Well, there she was, calmly composed and amused, and very much mistress of the situation and of herself. Her confidence had come back, together with a new sympathy, and she appraised him with a serious and sweet arrogance which seemed to say: "Sir, for me man is a mere epiphenomenon." It was clear to Sutcliffe that she was a darling, a heart-gripping creature, at once brilliant and disdainful and a little sad. And she was so brown, so musky. They would make brown love, musky love, full of the sapience and wisdom of disenchantment, full of the sadness of fortuitousness, wishing it might last forever. Yes, safe in each other's arms they would watch the rest of the contemptible world as if from a high observatory. Her warm and capable hands touched his. Somewhere in the romantic and water-wobbled city bells rang out, the tongues of memory, and the faint engraving of human voices scribbled the night with song. They both sat quite quiet, just breathing and looking at each other quietly, with the innocent eyes of the mind. It was the right moment to speak about Pia for what she knew was of the first

importance both to the husband and the novelist Sutcliffe. There was one conversation in which Pia described how she suddenly woke up and realised that
she loved this loutish tousled man. And by one of
those extraordinary paradoxes in which life delights,
the blow of realisation came just when he was at his
most odious and had been behaving abominably. (In
the morning he wrote down the whole scene just as
the girl told it, on the back of a menu.)

With the inevitable distortion caused by too much
art it would read something like this: "She had been
planning to leave him for several weeks because of
his scandalous behaviour, his insulting thoughtlessness,
his vulgarity: when all of a sudden it was as if a
bandage had been ripped from her eyes. Suddenly in
this gross overfed disagreeable man she saw the artist,
divined the fragility and dignity of the enterprise
which had driven him to destroy himself as a husband,
lover, bank clerk, priest. Even as a man. She was
impelled to walk out into the street in a state of pitiful bemusement, scuppers awash with a host of new
and singular impressions. So this at last was love, she
told herself; and just at the wrong time, and with the
wrong man. She could have howled out loud like a
dog with the vexation of it. She had done nothing to
deserve this. She must never tell him. She walked up
and down the dark pavements of Avignon until the
number of men accosting her drove her back to the
café where he had just been slapped by a waiter. A
mass of spilled change jingled on the floor. His cane
had been impounded and was raised against him by
the barman. They were phoning the police while he
sat there, white as a sheet, like some frightened stupid
animal, like a wart-hog, refusing to leave the place
without an apology. This could only go from bad to
worse. 'Come with me, quick.' And she jerked his
sleeve, hoisted him ungainly up. He shambled into the

street with her and was at once sick against a wall. A hoarse sob doubled him. He said: 'I finish the book tomorrow.' She wept now as she hoisted him along, the silent tears of horror flowed down her pale cheeks. All was over with her. So this is what they meant by the phrase 'till death us do part.' "

Somewhere, thousands of miles away, Akkad was writing: "They refuse to accept the findings of direct intuition. They want what they call proof. What is that but a slavish belief in causality and determinism, which in our new age we regard as provisional and subject to scale." And in another corner of Europe Freud was formulating the disposition of the artist as a hopeless narcissist, incapable of love, of investment. The old bastard, who saw so clearly the pathology of the artistic situation. "People who have violent emotions but no feelings are a danger to us all," he said to Sutcliffe once. Ah but in that ideal world where everyone would be forced to do what they most wanted to—an intolerable situation would be created!

At some point in time, much later on, with a new sympathy and kindness this girl closed her eyes and put her hands on his shoulders, smiling a little rueful smile of complicity. It was marvellous to feel liked, desirable. The great man felt quite tearful with gratitude when he thought of the beauty of this youthful person. He felt the thought in all honesty to inform her that he was heartwhole, and well armoured against her after all that he had learned in Vienna, first from Stekel (shaped like a pipette) and then those findings of the momentous old gent called Joy. What a fool he was to ask himself if it was quite fair to make love to her on these terms. He succumbed like a sleep-walker. How marvellous to love her and yet . . . once below the photic zone where the great fishes gawped, their eyes on stalks, like untrained neuroses: somewhere in that domain comes the clickety-click, the classical *déclic,* of the cash-register consciousness, of the obdurate thinking soul. He knew it only too well, but closing his eyes he bored into her with his mind, trying to lose himself. He had forgotten everything now, even Oakshot. He was flirting with the truth of things now; he knew that all meetings are predetermined even though (perhaps because) one hunts for the person one is anyway doomed to meet. Someone with whom one could make models of one's anxieties and set them free to float, then catch and exorcise them.

Predators, within each other's eyes lay a hundred mirror-marriages. She watched him out of the corner of her eye like an investment—the *mot juste* of Uncle Joy. What a marvellous prison, then, these self-declaring kisses, spent at random as soon as ripe, self-seeding like cypresses. He had done the mental trick that he had learned from his Yoga teacher long ago. To elicit a sexual sympathy strong enough to seduce, you start by copying the breath, breathing in chime with the girl, feeling your way into her rhythm. Closed eyes. Concentrate devoutly, piously. Then mentally polarise your sexual organs and enter her very softly going up and down rhythmically until she feels your sensual drive and accepts it. Touch her breasts softly, her flanks, her nipples until the gravy starts and she starts to breathe quickly, turns pale and opens her eyes. Talk to her softly, lovingly. . . . In this whole transaction there was no vulgar forcing. The girl was paramount, her yes or no decided everything. But plead one could and with the power of thought and words one could excite and rough her up. O yes!

Sutcliffe was in luck; for this is precisely what the girl was doing to him. The result was that they met in a head-on collision of passions which rather scared them both. Ah this knowledgeable genius of a man, what didn't he know?

Come, tax that pretty strength
And try the thing again
From pain to gather pleasure
From pleasure gather pain.

She was lovely beyond all others, this Jewish dervish, with her sense of space and history, her echo-box of racial memories, her gallant hypomania. How deeply the night seemed perfumed by her and the silences after her deep soft voice had fallen still. That voice, O barracuda-music to the Gentile heart. A pensive cocoon of a sleeping girl with a pleasant tilt to the East. Sabine was surely her name, Sabine Banquo. Ah love with such a girl was like eating a cannibal's ear. She perfectly understood that man and woman were a single animal tragically divided by Plato; that it was a notion of the Muses. A deep friendship flared up between them between two and three-thirty in the morning—something irreplaceable and unrepeatable. And he was not even drunk. It was absolutely essential to behave as if nothing out of the ordinary had taken place. Anyway this was not love; for that is irrational. This had all the pith of an equation. "You don't want to ruin your lives?" said Sutcliffe, admonishing them both from the depths of his profound experience.

Then sleep came—we were entering the countries of sadness, deep below the photic zone with its huge gogglefish, where in the darkness the real task outlines itself like a sort of flare-path, namely how to make sense of oneself. You do not have to be an artist to recognise the imperative which is every man's. Yes but how? In this domain right sex is capital, it flenses the feelings of all the poisonous artifices brought in by the think-box in the guise of clever ideas. It is a conversion of the revoking mind into irresponsible cloud-soft laughter and smiling passion. With what a sag of misery did the genius reflect on the matter of capturing this experience in words. . . . Writers, those prune-shaped hacks in hairpieces sitting down to make a few lame pages hobble out of their typewriters—what would they see in all this? Custom-built Jewesses with desultory undercarriages made over by the divining heart into the dark hovering bird presences of history?

He had no idea what time it was when her father came in, softly opening the door with a small asthmatic wheeze. It woke her and she pulled the cover over his head. The old man said "Asleep?" in a discreet whisper. She replied: "Almost," on a pleasant loving note.

There was late moonlight thrown back from the mirror. The old man was in full fig, with his opera cloak on, decorations blinking on his breast, and a flap-gibus in hand. He crossed the room softly, almost precariously, to place himself in front of the mirror which was full of white moonlight and the reflection from the watery streets of the city. It was not as if he were drunk, no, but rather as if he were afraid of stepping on a loose board and so making a noise. He stood there, happily but sheepisly, gazing at his own reflection and saying nothing. He stared and stared at himself as if hunting for the least defect in his appearance. Alone, he nevertheless seemed deeply and serenely aware of her sleepy presence. "How was the music?" she asked at last in French and he replied, with a deep sigh: "Mortelle, ma fille." He leaned forward to touch the reflection of his right ear and then drew himself sharply upright, giving a reproving shake of his head. "I am staying on a few days," he said. "I have to raise a loan for the City of London."

Sutcliffe suddenly wanted to sneeze. He tried very hard to remember which musical comedy he had decided to be influenced by on the spur of the moment—or a Sacha Guitry play—and then pressed his nose between her warm breasts until the impulse left him. The man in the mirror said: "It is not enough just to keep softly breathing in and out as the years pass. One should try to achieve something."

"Yes, father," she said obediently and yawned.

"I wasn't thinking of you," said the old man.

He turned, as quietly as ever, and passed through the open door into the lighted corridor with a soft velvet good-night. He closed it softly and she lay back with a contented sigh. Sutcliffe, replete with her caresses and disarmed by the old man's extraordinary air—for he looked like Disraeli—snuggled back into his niche and sought the deeper reaches of sleep, while she lay awake, but happily so, at his side. What was she thinking of? He could not guess.

It was almost dawn when, because she could not sleep, she switched on the subdued light at her bedside and from the drawer of the night-table took a pack of cards. She spread them out, fanned them out in a prearranged pattern on the counterpane and began to ask them questions. Suddenly she stiffened and the timbre of her curiosity had the effect of awakening him. "Do you see what they say?" she asked, smiling. "That you killed someone very close to you. I think your wife." Naturally he was by now wide-awake. What a marvellous thing to happen to Oakshot, and all the more beguiling as this lady gave herself out to be a rationalist, and then started to behave just like Newton on Sunday! "Deliberately or just by accident?" he asked, curious to judge the effect of this information on his hero.

"Deliberately."

"Tell me more," he said, aware that all this kind of fortune-telling was bogus. But to his surprise he found that she was outlining, with tolerable accuracy, the plot of the book in which he had actually managed to do away with Pia, albeit in a semi-accidental fashion. She was in fact "reading" a version of a book which had enabled him to exculpate himself from his feelings of deep aggression against Pia—his desire to murder her. He asked her if she had read the novel in question but she had not. Yet in her slow and thoughtful description it was all there: the whole Indian Ocean around the couple, the calm night sea, the tropical moon like some ghastly mango sailing in clouds. The lady in her evening gown; tippet sleeves and sequins, every other inch a memsahib. Which of the many versions, all disastrous?

Sabine laughed suddenly and said: "I cannot guarantee any of this. I have only recently started playing with it as a system. The Tarot."

System! In the book they went onto the boat deck after dinner to take the air—the still ambient sterile air. Their quarrel had been a momentous one—they had each said wounding, unforgettable things, things which could never be sponged away, excused, taken back. They were buried deep in the ruins of this collapsed edifice of their marriage, their love. How pale she was! They went slowly aft and stared down at the throbbing white wake which stretched away under the moon to a dark horizon. He tried desperately to think of something clever and healing to say but nothing came to his lips except curses. "I see it all now," she said in a low voice, and with an inexpressible bitterness. Then with a kind of effortless gesture, gravely as a dancer leaning into her opening steps in time to music, she vaulted the rail, fell, and disappeared. He had made no effort to stop her.

An alarm bell sounded and for hours now the ship turned, the waters were sprayed by searchlights. Boats were lowered clumsily, accidental manoeuvres of the oars, heads nearly banged, etc. Floats and lifebelts spattered the calm sea, voices crackled and boomed from radio and loud hailer. Nothing came of it all. Yet she had been an excellent swimmer and had won many cups and medals. In the first-class bar where he at last shambled to drink an exhausted Cognac the gramophone, albeit tactfully lowered, played "Bye-Bye Blackbird." To his surprise the whole thing only irritated him; he was ashamed not to feel Pia's sudden death more acutely. In the book he had called himself Hardbane, an Anglican clergyman.

Sutcliffe dozed off at last in a mild amazement, to awake much later and find that dawn's left hand was in the sky. No; he had not pushed Pia, though in the novel someone distressed him by hinting at it. Their quarrels had been overheard. Sabine had thrown the cards down now and was talking in a low voice about travelling through central Europe with the gipsies in order to learn their language. Despite her warmth and cherish he dragged himself awake and betook himself to the bathroom to dress. He embraced her tenderly and extracted a promise to meet him in the afternoon at their first café by the water. And so with confident tread back to his own hotel, tipping the sleeping nightporter royally.

Once back in his den he pushed open the balcony doors in order to feel nearer to her and crawled sweetly into bed as if into the arms of his mother. What could be more divine than to sleep one's way forward into a sunlit day on a Venetian canal? He would wake for a stroll and a late breakfast among these stone galleries now made doubly beautiful by the experience she had offered him. But his own sense of prediction was not as acute as hers for that afternoon in the sunny café the waiter handed him a message. A premonition of the envelope's contents flashed into his mind. Yes, it was so. She was leaving Venice with her father. (Had she forgotten what he had said to the mirror?) Vaguely she expressed the hope that they might meet again one day, but added, on a minatory note: "I try never to let anyone become indispensable."

If anyone had asked him why he laughed so ruefully and struck his knee with his hat he would have replied by quoting Flaubert: *"Je ris tout seul comme une compagnie de vagins altérés devant un régiment de phallus."*

He determined there and then that the whole city lay in ruins about him, and that it would be as well to depart for Avignon at once. To reinforce the decision he sent Toby a telegram and set out to locate a little car to rent for the journey.

In his little red notebook the following random thoughts formed and were jotted down, like the slow interior overflow of a stanchless music. Often they made no sense at all when he looked them over, but he believed firmly that one should have the courage to write down even what one did not fully understand. Somewhere it was "understood."

As follows:

An excellent lesson in generosity. It was clear that there was no future in an affair for her—I am too old. Steatopygous novelist.

Trash's voice echoing all the gluttony of fiddles, so deeply rosined. Coughed on her cigarette smoke like a tuba. The moon glow of her warmth, an emphysema of cordiality. Said: "Robin has enough sympathy to float a ship, honey child." Alas.

Sitting at Quartila's on the canal with Sabine watching the stars flowing by—our loving minds simultaneously ignited by a falling star. "Look!"

As in death, so in dreams, people age at different speeds, and their mathematical position *vis-à-vis* death at any given moment is not easy to calculate. One

214

swings towards and away from, if one is an artist. Only race I know.

Her laughter was always hurt in the sound, and the subject had to be choice (Pia).

Skin smelling of musk melon and small sightless eyes with cataracts (gipsy whore) like a chapel with windows of mother of pearl or (Cairo) coloured and oiled paper.

Underprivileged hearts lodged in bodies borrowed from nymphs fashioned in gold dust.

Was told of a blind woman who was set upon by a gang of children and beaten to death in a game of blind man's buff. My informant was a doctor and when I asked eagerly for details (he had been called) he said: "She was of massive stature and she had the *cor bovinum* which one always associates with sudden heart failure."

Epistolary alpha beta theta . . . the sweet compaction of biting foreign lips.

> *Trash for President!*
> *Robin for Wingless Victory!*
> *Pia for Pope Joan*

The stifling love of the two women drove him mad with envy. He was starved, nay, mutilated in his powers of projection. He was terrified that he would be forced to fall back on the great weapon of illness.

Bad gash in a waiter's hand from a tin-opener—dark arterial blood dries violet like the ink of emperors and popes.

Two days later the little car went droning and banging and humming and snoring across the Lombard Plain in the direction of Provence with the amazing man at the wheel. Amazing because still alive and smiling. Amazing because so limitlessly great!

AN ASTONISHING LETTER

What a divine journey in the little bull-nosed Morris. We left a plume of white fragrant dust brushing the olives right from Lombardy to Provence, with many fertile breakdowns, many desultory conversations with grease-beclobbered mechanics, the new masters of our civilization. That is the way Sutcliffe went . . .

Cloven by dimples . . .
Carried off by an effulgence . . .
Disseminated by rumour . . .
Embalmed by inadvertence . . .
Hung drawn and quartered by Common
Consent . . .
That was the way poor Sutcliffe went.

Yes, it is the conversation of spiritually mature mechanics which invests the petrol engine with awesome mystery. And the fragrance of petrol along the dusty roads leading me to Verfeuille where I hoped, by meeting the young brother, to renew some of the sentiments which attached me to the elder sister he so much worshipped. (Honey, Robin is sad as a cat.) What greater joy than to lie under a car with a man who can explain the motions and functions of fly-wheels?

The happy filth of garages
Where men who love their mothers toil
Like babies who their napkins soil
The fruit of mirthless marriages.
What odours rise from grease and oil
The child being father to the man

That nobody disparages
Toiling on horseless carriages.

In my new book I must put in something in praise
of the engine. "Huddled in dirt the reasoning engine
lies," exclaims Rochester. "As this machine is to him
Hamlet," cries Hamlet to Ophelia in the mysterious
First Quarto. . . . No literary allusions, please.

I have been here several days now, a little sad and
disappointed to find a certain constraint between myself and young Bruce; nothing lacks in courtesy and
warmth, but there is a lean shadow of constraint which
makes me feel how much older I am than these three
young people. Nobody has mentioned Pia. Young
Tobias is however in full form and gives me life and
hope. But the three others—I don't know what it is—
seem awkward and preoccupied by their situation
which sounds so superficially romantic and is in fact
extremely complicated in the jumbling of their feelings. I would not propose to write about them for fear
of not being able easily to rationalise a situation which
even to themselves seems weird, equivocal, anoma-
lous. In the heart of the matter too, I seem to detect
a romantic fraud—for can love exist in any dimension
without jealousy? I don't believe it. Yet in the long explanations that Toby has extracted from them, and re-
tailed to me, that seems to be their case. But the
brother and sister . . . what beauty and vehemence!
Bruce is a solid boy in his blond way but nothing like
as striking as the other two. They have come from the
pages of old Laforgue.

For the rest I spend all morning on this high balcony overlooking a sweep of olive grove, the young
man Piers I can see sitting in the lotus pose in front
of the little wooden pavilion smothered in roses. He
does a stint of Indian meditation every morning, and
speaks of it with endearing solemnity. So does the girl.

At times the Midi, when first one knows it, seems slightly spurious in terms of its folklore, but a very brief acquaintance with its inhabitants cures this impression. One realises how old and withdrawn and intact Provence really is, and how little it is part of France. It is, rather, a separate Mediterranean nation —perhaps the impression is conveyed by the fact that it is unashamedly pagan in attitude, and a product of an olive culture. It is leaner and thirstier than the north; indeed after Valence where the olives begin the cuisine replaces cream and butter with olive oil, which gives the characteristic tonality of the Mediterranean. And as if to confirm these sudden impressions the inhabitants smile, offer one old-fashioned courtesies and appear never to hurry. They have all the time in the world because Provençal time is not clock time as we live it in the north.

Avignon itself is somewhat dirty and dilapidated with its cracked pavements, scavenging cats and chewed walls—in some places the bastions have been worn down by time to stumps like ancient molars. Here and there a higgledy-piggledy mass of twigs on a rooftop marks the site of a raven's nest, which increases the impression of dishevelled carelessness. Moreover for a place with such a tolling name it is a mere village, and under some aspects of weather and moonlight reminds one of some lost village on the Steppes. I am quoting Toby a little here, after he described to me a winter spent here with the tinkling river full of ice. Yes, it is a long time since the Popes had everything in hand. Their riches and their profligacy created a factitious life which fattened the reputation of this queer town. Vice and crime flourished with the counter trade in silk and bells. Day after day the long silk processions threaded their way through the monuments. Church bells and saluting guns predominated—the boom and the wingbeats went throbbing over the waters with their famous bridge. It has all vanished, and the innate vulgarity and pretentiousness of the architecture can be seen, for it is no longer decorated by silk gonfalons and mountains of blazing candles.

How long since Petrarch sighed and sobbed his way into old age, verse after dry verse like the beat of a metronome in the shrinking skull. And yet I believe in great attachments, in the stabbing recognition that assailed him as it assailed Dante. Freud can keep his mouth shut firmly on his cigar. The good poet needs an unripe girl as a Muse. And yet, from one point of view to suffer because of a hollow passion for a middle-class *allumeuse*—what a tragic fate! Suppose he had won her in marriage only to find that it was like sitting about in wet shoes? A real novelist would find the theme worthy of him.

No, walking about here in the woods with young Tobias I have been charmed, as indeed everywhere in this country, by the way that the vegetation had invaded everything, colonised it. Summer-houses completely brambled in by roses and honeysuckle, statues covered in green ivy with only one free ankle left to view, walls where every cranny was a nest and the coming and going of the birds made one feel one was in the heart of virgin jungle. Nightingales—but dozens at a time—chanting in moist woods whose green mosses were bisected by splashing rivulets from the overflow of pure springs. The calm happiness and bounty conferred by tutelary water nymphs or river gods—and indeed the Rhône was once such a god. Then the silky air, the ambient cool air. The quiet folded-away quality of the chalk and limestone valleys with their sectors of violet dust and red—the signs of a soil rich in bauxite some wiseacre tells me. All prospects lightly powdered with the flowing dust of clay which the hot sun had rendered friable. And the tall bowed skies, so reminiscent of Attic scenes, fill and empty like great sails with the breath of the rogue wind known as mistral which scatters the olives into screens of silver-grey, supples out cypresses like fur, and rushes to explode the spring blossom of almond and plum like a discharge of artillery. The walls of the crooked studio where I have been lodged (in case I need to be alone and write) have prompted me with their yellow photographs to indulge myself with this brief discourse on landscape—it is more or less what I can see from my high window as I glance sideways down across the park towards the Alphilles in one direction: and towards the cross-hatched red-tiled roofs of Avignon in another. These broken planes of red and brown terracotta fan slowly down towards a white scar of river. It is brilliantly sunny, and not in the least cold. Work? We sit for the most part before the great fireplace and eat chestnuts, Toby and I and Bruce. The constraint which I noted yesterday has begun to thaw out; the temper of my relief has shown me that I really came here because I was lonely. These are the penalties of a paper life; my best friends are all correspondents, people I deeply cherish because I seldom or never see them. The old divine duchess of Tu, for example, writes me voluminous letters almost every week in which she has distilled the essence of her kindly and amoral philosophy of disenchantment. She smokes long green cigars, and once played the banjo in a diplomatic jazz-band. What is intriguing about these letters is the absent-minded tone—for the old darling is trying to write her memoirs in halting and hesitant fashion; sometimes when the flow gets dammed up she turns the next few pages into a letter to me. In this way I can see the gradual shape of a book emerging, and also be amused by her stories of a long life of travel and misadventure. She is the only old lady I know who relentlessly summers at the little town of Cz and this in memory of a love affair which endured for a decade, only to be cut short by death. Cz! The nightingales in the woods and that weird inflected language.

I wrote to her a great deal while I was in Vienna, and impressed her very much by retailing many of the more comical elements in psychoanalysis; for example that all bodily openings in the dream are equal to one another. In German the vagina has been called the ear between the legs, and in some circles girls are encouraged to listen with the clitoris! The old dear has never forgotten.

This to explain myself a bit to myself—for who else is listening? Perhaps that other self who should figure somewhere in the list of viable selves; the self I had somehow hoped to "invest" in my pale and pretty Pia. What a folly to invest in anything! Old Joy invested me with a characteristic Jewish pessimism and monomania. We are dealing with a falling market, our poor little investments become year by year less valuable; I am tempted to launch myself into the rhetoric of the stock market which describes stock as being "mature" or "bearing," just like fruit trees. But the problem of a private diary, whose only function is (like the scales of a violinist) to keep a writer's hand in, is to determine who is going to be amused by it. In another life poor Sutcliffe will no doubt chortle over these lonely sallies. For the moment they filled in the space before lunch: the days before death.

Of the inhabitants of Verfeuille the most striking are the two who own it, the brother and sister. They have a frail nobility of aspect and address—there is always something futile, defenceless and endearing about aristocrats. Nothing can be done for them, one feels, except to feel happy about their existence; and this is difficult, for they are often such hell on earth.

Toby has told me about them, and of course in this rather strait-laced epoch their situation is unusual.

221

There is something unfinished and undefined about them. The word "lovers" always alarms me and fills me with distrust. In my last book a couple not unlike them both began to form and I was forced to remove them because they began to sound implausible. Why, I wonder? Piers and Sylvie have a little the air of people who have played safe from selfishness, remaining deliberately childless. They are a little like babes in the woods, somewhat lost in this rambling house and straggling grounds of a property which they neglect owing to an ignorance of country strategies. The third babe is Bruce, and this adds singularity to the scene, though the whole matter is treated with a completely natural unselfconsciousness which makes it seem as simple as a prism. I reflect on Bruce and Pia alternately: the image of their inversion dwells in my mind and provokes the slow burning fuse of jealousy, for they have achieved happiness thereby. And yet . . . I cannot doubt the pain of Pia's fragmented love for yours truly. I watch the young medical student smoking his slow pipe as he plays chess with Piers, who by rights should have been his rival. The girl wanders and reads, swims in the river, or plays the grand piano. The old château is full of the shadows of another kind of discontent, however; I gather that grave money troubles lie ahead and that there is a prospect of sudden separation to be faced. Piers may have to work, and the thought makes him sad and preoccupied. He is a small-boned and finely built boy, very French in temper. He is "nervous" in the sense of a thoroughbred horse. Ardent in all things, including friendship. I have wanted for nothing since I arrived. I am at ease with them both for they do not know Pia except by name. Describing their attachment to Toby, Bruce produced rather an interesting simile—likening it to the sexless camaraderie of explorers or mountain climbers, travellers bound by a common voyage.

Well but . . .

We sit down to a patriarchal dinner in the great central hall every evening, about thirty strong. The long central tables are joined together in refectory style, giving the room a monkish touch. Our end made a cruciform shape; but while we start off thus with workers below the salt and dons or bosses at high table the conversations and the good wines prompted a good deal of movement in both directions. Bruce went and sat by an old lady who seemed to play the role of chief housekeeper, while the shaggy old gamekeeper slipped into the vacant seat beside Sylvie and talked to her in an animated register about pheasants. Children swarmed about as if in a Neapolitan cathedral, while on the rush-strewn floor the hounds scratched and the odd flea jumped.

Uninhibited were the voices flying about like doves. They speak with a fine twang and brio down here and my own rather precise version of a French accent sounds affected. I practise their way every morning while I shave—repeating the phrase *"une sauce blanche"* as if every word in it had two syllables. This latinised twang goes trailing off through the nymph-begotten groves which echo Italy and Spain. Of course the Midi has its own proud lore and a lot of elementary nature poetry of the ding-dong-bell-pussy's-in-the-well sort, which appears to contain no abstract words, which makes Valéry's existence such a mystery to ponder over. For the rest the place engulfs one and its habits and superstitions make one feel the pagan roots of the marvellous inland sea which colours our lives.

One feels (unlike Italy) far from a Catholic priest here, and to do them justice those one runs into in Avignon have a somewhat hangdog air, as if they felt vaguely apologetic for existing among the olives. So many things, however, are a genuine heartbalm, like the prickles of the Pleiades rising on the night.

Piers tells me that the local patois image for stars in their first state (like an etching) is "flour sprinklings." In the long evenings we play a stately game of bowls on the greensward before the front portals of the château in which the old gamekeeper and the steward take a thoughtful part. In the middle of the night, but late, perhaps near dawn, the unearthly shrieking of peahens in the woods. At dawn the dark girl with the gun goes stepping softly through the misty brakes, while in the nether mist moves an invisible swarm of clonking lambs. Why is it that all country ways are reassuring, touch the roots of feeling—for I myself was brought up in a town? Toby has his hair ceremoniously washed in the yard, seated on a milking stool, and draped in a white sheet. The strapping milkmaid hisses as she washes his head as if she were currying a horse. She uses *savon de Sauveterre,* the same honey-coloured cakes that are used to wash clothes. Then comes a vinegar drench which makes his hair so light and fluffy that he is aureoled like an angel and has to hold everything down with a beret borrowed from Piers.

For insomnia, for stomach pains, even for red noses, there are herbal teas of the most astonishing virtue, though it is not these which young Toby has been sampling, for after a night in Avignon he looks rather as if autumn had o'er brimmed his clammy cells. He has found a gipsy brothel, however, of the utmost charm, with music and raven-black ladies. And this is where he proposes to lead me to lighten the pains of long continence.

The old costume of Arles is going out very rapidly but the elderly folk are still proud to wear it—the high piled coif of snowy linen, with its high crown like Cretan queens, the hair twisted into a million rats-tails and spangled with coins. Dark skirts and snowy aprons. The bright lace—the *fichu*—is still there. (I am making a portrait of the housekeeper from the life.)

To love, then, to conjugate the great slow verb . . . Some people have all the luck. It would have been a pleasant thing to enjoy the artistic privileges of a troubadour, who was fully entitled to love the queen, and probably spent the days in disreputable ways while her lord was absent. *Droit du jongleur*—it is roughly what Bruce must enjoy in his quiet relationship with Piers and Sylvie. But this is not how he sees it himself. In further meditations upon the unholy trinity they form, I had a sudden small gleam of light. I suddenly saw the underlying unity of the three children as a total *self,* or the symbol of such an abstraction. Against the traditional duality-figure of our cosmology I placed a triune self, composed of two male and one female partner—a gnostic notion, if I remembered correctly. "To romantic people only the romantic can happen." This led me back to the dissatisfaction with my own rather carefully landscaped novels with their love-motivated actors. I supposed that I was not really ripe to write about the Other Thing, which I had vaguely situated in or around the region demarcated off by the word "God." That is perhaps why I caught an echo here and there of Akkad's notion of a still-born God, an abortion. I have always ferried about with me a weight in that part of me which I always symbolise as a sort of marsupial's pouch—my womb, in fact. There is something dead in there, or unrealised, soggy as a Christmas dinner. It won't get born. I have tried every kind of ergotic mixture to provoke the necessary contractions of the pouch—for even a still birth would be better than no birth at all. But no, it swings in me as I walk, all this undigested Christmas pudding, with its sixpences and holly and little British flags. Our Lutheran gut-culture, so to speak, our inner piggy bank with our paltry savings.

225

It is late and the strong Marc we drank after dinner has set me thinking furiously. The sharp differentiation of the sexes in our culture was shaped most probably by monogamy and monosexuality and their taboos. It was an abuse of nature. Thus the typological couple which has come to dominate our style of psyche was the baby-founding duo, husband and wife, city founders. But now comes the great revolution—praise be to Marie Stopes who has freed the woman from sexual bondage by the discovery of contraception and restored both her self-respect and her freedom. That is why the sharp distinction between the sexes has begun to blur, with man becoming more feminine and vice versa. In this context my trio of lovers must present the prototype of a new biological relationship, foreshadowing a different sort of society based on a free woman. A matriarchy, then?

I wonder.

I wonder.

The fact of the matter is that they are irritating me profoundly by posing questions of capital interest to a novelist: namely how to render them plausible, real, for the purposes of a fiction. It wouldn't work. One would be defeated by the romantic content, if only because they are what they are—young and handsome. In order to seem plausible to a reader they would have to seem real to me—and they baffle me. If I changed their characters, however, it is possible that I could render the whole thing more convincing. Supposing Piers was a pursy fat little peasant with perpetually moist lips and the drunkard's unfocused eyes. Supposing Sylvie was beautiful but totally deaf, trailing a withered leg? As for Bruce, the village doctor—he might have a lupus strain spread like a purple caul over his face and neck. . . . Yes, that might work. Nearer to Zola, alas.

This evening Sylvie played two-handed piano with

Piers while Bruce stared into the fire, a little saddened by a reference made at dinner by Piers about an impending crisis which might spell a new order, a possible separation. I could not help envying them Verfeuille—there was nothing else in life they seemed to need or want. The Philosopher's Stone was theirs. Or was it simply their youth that I envied?

All day we had been pelted by a freak rainstorm which sent the temperature down and justified a deep fire of furze in the hall fireplace. It was here that I read them what Piers always referred to as "the astonishing letter from Alexandria." It came, as may be imagined, from my friend Akkad and was full of what I regarded as special pleading for his gnostic cause—though why he should have urged these things on me I cannot say. He knew me for an ironist and a sceptic, unlikely at any rate to fall into the toils of some grubby little Middle Eastern schisms. I think Piers was a little shocked when I said as much. For the letter ignited him into a frenzy of appreciation; it seemed to him that Akkad's insight matched his own. Well, the letter described a sort of nougat-land before the Fall, so to speak, before the Flood: before the fatal death-drift started which was to become the reality of our time. Akkad wrote: "Yes there was a definite time, a definite moment, which one can visualise in a manner which makes it as actual as tomorrow will be. There came a radical shift of emphasis, as marked as any historic moment like Copernicus or the Fall of Constantinople, which pushed the balance over from the domain of spirit into matter. Hints of this can be traced in the old mythologies. The whole axis of the human sensibility was altered—as if somewhere out of sight an Ice Cap had melted. The ancient vegetation gave place to our new steel vegetation, flowering in bronze, then iron, then steel—a progressive hardening of the arteries. The table of the essences gave place to the table of the elements. The Philosopher's Stone, the Holy Grail of the ancient consciousness, gave place to the usurping values of the gold bar; it was the new ruler of the soul, and now the slave, deeming himself free, measured his potency against coin, against capital value, the wholly saturnian element in his nature. The dark sweet radiance of usury was born. And freedom, which is simply the power of spending—its prototype the orgasm—was shackled in the mind and later in the body. The faculty of accumulation, the usury, embedded itself in the very sperm sac of man, who began to found cultures based on key repressions—the faculty of storing, holding back, accumulating. Then came periodic blood-lettings in the shape of wars with their symbolic cutlery of steel weapons—the penis and the vagina are plain to the view as well as the lathe-turned egg of death. This death-desiring culture could only be consummated and realised by suicide. The new sacrament was to spill blood, not to spill sperm, and impregnate the universe. To hoard gold and to spill blood were now the imperative, and this is the order against which our small communion of gnostics is opposed; we are quietly opting out, and in some places and times, pushing the issues as far as death. Sperm against specie.

"This basic shift of emphasis has many other, and sometimes dire, repercussions. For example duality became the key not only to philosophic thought but also to language itself whose basic brick, the word, features this central dichotomy. With everything changing scale and relationship like this, death became obligatory, mandatory, instead of being a choice, arbitrary, and under the psyche's control. Before this time you could have your cake and eat it, so to speak. You were not obliged to die if you knew how to go on living without wearing out—you could cross the time barrier into the deep hibernation of selflessness, such as the wise men of the East still know in fragmentary form, for it falls just short of immortality. But what I speak of was not the fruit of effort or meditation or the fruit of exceptional minds. It was as ubiquitous as it was optional. The sense of freedom conveyed by this state of affairs can hardly be imagined by spirits like ours, so bent and bowed are they under our perverted system of values. I can hear Monsieur Le Prince chuckle in Machiavellian fashion as he reads this over my shoulder. You will say that we only imagine him this depressing locum tenens: that he is a sort of carnival head, a totem head like the ones the Templars are supposed to have set up to replace the cross. Nevertheless what is imagined with enough intensity has a claim to be real enough. It is always useful to have a point of focus for the wandering and promiscuous mind—hence ikons and altars and shrines and herms. So, my dear Rob, if you meet an angel on the street be polite and raise your hat like Swedenborg; and if it descends like a dove on your unbeliever's head then remember that it is a Blakeian or Rilkean angel and must be fed on poetry, which is the manna of the old initiates. Yes, that other world, Rob! One sometimes sees it so clearly. Those who surrendered their lives while living in it did so with the quiet relief of a helmsman surrendering his great wheel in a heavy swell, happy to go off watch, to go below into the underworld. In other words the key to the whole stance was the redeeming of death, which is always present in the psyche and can be realised and used up like an electric charge, like a philosophic power. Failure to do this thing withers one. Today death is a limbo peopled by the living.

"So it is that we believe that this world, so much misused in its powers which are wholly beneficent, and although worn to a shadow of its former seraphic self, is still accessible on the old terms to a happy few, a

minority whose duty is to hold the pass, to fight
a Thermopylae of the psyche until perhaps by some
lucky switch the emphasis changes again and we can
hope that man will no longer be turned to a pillar of
salt for turning aside to gaze upon the truth. Is truth
redeemable by the direct vision? Yes; we believe it is.
Across the abyss of our present despair and darkness
the frail light is still there, though it seems always to
be flickering out. Of the two forces in play in the world
the black is winning, and may win completely. When I
am depressed it seeems most likely. What can be done
to reverse the situation? Nothing, you will say. But
there is a kind of nothing which we can do creatively,
which will add oxygen instead of diminishing it, which
is more fruitful than fruitless. But we can't do this
without facing the basic truth courageously—namely
the death or banishment of God and the ascendancy
of a usurping power of evil. There we stand."

The enthusiasm of Piers for this pie-in-the-sky
idealism was endearing, but he read into it more than
I myself could see. Perhaps I am blinkered by my
mental sloth and my curiosity? At any rate these formulations make me quite impatient. I remember Pia
saying once: "If one really deeply believes something
one shuts up and never dares to speak of it."

Yesterday, today, tomorrow—the chrysalis of time re-
solving itself into the butterfly of process and death.
In dreams the links seem much more clear than in
waking. This week I wrote a long letter to Pia and
posted it to the notice-board for messages at the Café
Dôme in Montparnasse. You never know. I dreamed
of her in two or three old situations and tried laboriously to analyse them when I awoke. As a matter of
fact like many women she remained extremely child-
like in her feeling-range. A sort of child-wife in many

respects. Sometimes there is an organic foundation which stamps such girls as half-developed, and which their psyches echo. The uterus is small, narrow and elastic like that of a child. The breasts are beautifully formed but small also—mere sketches for motherhood. The hips are transversally narrow, the limbs most gracile, the face and often the posture decidedly infantile. Many perverse trends are hidden in all this innocence —one detects a hidden criminality because of the great interest in crime stóries and so on. . . .

Among other things I sketched out the story of the great theatrical hamper we carried about with us for so many years. I was always forbidden a glimpse of the contents, and was indeed implored not even to mention its existence. Pia blushed and paled in turns if ever, in a fit of exasperation, I inveighed against its cumbrousness and weight—as when we travelled by sea. It had to go with us. The label said "linen." I followed my instructions and never asked about it, never spied on her. The soul of honour was I. Then during the period before the crack when she had become progressively more anaesthetic to mé sexually (I did not know that she had met Trash already) the singular old wicker hamper came into its own. What do you think it contained?

Mind you, whenever I had to go away for a while, I had a feeling that she opened it, for she moved it into the centre of the bedroom floor wherever we might happen to be. Well, I said to myself, if it keeps her happy to gloat over a lot of linen what business was it of mine? After one flaming row I left the house, however, saying that I was going away for the weekend. Inevitably at the station I repented and took a taxi back to the house intending to make peace with this dear torment of mine. Guess what I found?

She was seated on the floor before a blazing fire. The hamper stood beside her, It was wide open now, the lid thrown back. All around her, sitting on velvet cushions of different brilliant colours, were dolls of all sizes and nationalities in bright costumes. A beautiful miniature tea-set on the floor before the fire contained real Chinese tea. My dramatic entry—I was moist with regret and a heartfelt adoration—caught her in a fearful state of disarray—speechless and pale. But when I saw the dolls I seemed at once to recognise my real rivals and an overwhelming rage seized hold of me. "So that is how it is," I said, and all the bile of old sterile disputes rose in my throat. I did not clearly know precisely what I had divined in this infantile display, but I knew with certainty that these little homunculi must be put out of the way. They constituted an obstacle to our relationship. I seized one, and then another, and tossed them into the flames. I caught a glimpse of myself in the mirror, grim-faced as a German professor. Pia let out a shriek and fainted, while I continued the pillage of her dolls, which I now realise must have represented a whole lifetime of memory, of childhood. It was worse than murder. But I acted like a maniac in a trance, unaware of the meaning of my acts, aware only of blasting jealousy. It was like the sack of a town. The poor woman looked with horror-widened eyes at the ogre who was tearing her memories limb from limb and hurling them into the fire: then broke. I had profaned the inner reality of her far childhood.

She lay in this sort of catatonia all night long, and when she did awake in the morning it was with an extravagant fever which set the local doctor talking of typhoid and meningitis. I sat beside her bed, pale, soaping my hands and pleading for forgiveness. But she ignored me, closing her eyes, to sink ever deeper into the sheltering fever which cradled her and which might, if her heart went on beating as it did now, manage to carry her away into the super-silence. So it was that I played my part in provoking her illness—perhaps the greatest part. Clumsy, lumbering Sutcliffe, myself, he, I.

The change in her when she did come round was marked. She had become languid, slow-witted, and protested that she was old and finished. Indeed she looked ten years older. The new crop of worry lines around her eyes I attributed to the calming drugs they gave her. But the tone of her whole spirit had changed. Partly it was revenge, and partly it was that she was in mourning for the destroyed selves, her toys. This mood endured for a good long time, and her skin became greasy and her fine blond hair lank and toneless. Then the attacks of kleptomania began which precipitated more medical intervention and set us on the road to Vienna where (God be praised!) we learned a very great deal, though not enough to save the wreck of a marriage which had been perhaps imperilled from the beginning by the genetic distribution of the good fairy who divides things into male and female. . . . I was suddenly alone, and now I knew it. And then the return of the native—which was no return at all. It was obvious that things could never again be resumed on the old basis. And in the intervening time I had become aware of so many little tics of character which I had never noticed before. My new scale of judgement, thanks to Joy, was of some help. For example Pia could never spend the whole night in bed with a man; she must get up and go away to another bed after making love. These small and indeed insignificant things only began to become significant for me after the whole Vienna period which was at the same time inspiriting and depressing. I think because I realised that the whole system of Dr. Joy was limited and narrow in operation, though absolutely marvellous within very small limits. But it could or would never arrive at formulating something like a philosophy by which one could live. It was a lever, and as brilliant an invention of our epoch as is the petrol engine. Anyway.

The lady in the painting, do you recognise her, under so many layers of childhood, coat after coat of whitewash? It takes a lifetime to learn to die with all you have learned, or else to live with it.

Yes, there we were with our sackload of misfortunes, and there was old Doc Joy with his grave and beautiful formulations—he refused himself every ignoble consolation when thinking about man. We learned, hand over fist, but the more we learned the less hope we had, the deeper the division seemed to go. It exasperated me when Pia told me that she only loved me because I smelt like her father. I suddenly remembered how she used to take up a sweat-shirt (I was a rowing man and still like to take a boat out for a skim): pressing it to her nose, closing her eyes in an absurd rapture. It was no compliment. Her old father, the retired Ambassador, lived on forever in Tangier, stone deaf; going for a drive in his car sometimes, or else passing away a long retirement full of boredom by playing gin rummy or bridge. A sort of benign cyst of diplomacy who had risen by gravitation and sleek kindnesses. Poor Pia! Other smaller and more touching things. When I had reproached her for something which hung heavy on her conscience she would stand against the wall and cry into the wallpaper, throwing behind her arm over those poor eyes. And I suddenly saw stretching behind her a long chain of infant misdemeanours expiated by this standing against a wall. In the other life, in the old days, our nurses and our parents punished us in this fashion; and feeling reproved by my cruel words, she instantly accepted the blame and expiated the rebuke in this way. It gave me a lump in the throat when she did it.

It was in a way to placate the gods and assuage a

guilty conscience that I recounted all this to the old duchess last week. Afterwards I was annoyed, at so obviously trying to claim sympathy. She was wise to write back about other things, about how the duke made her take banjo lessons; also about his terrible fear of being bored. He had come to the conclusion that idle conversation was a sin. Whenever people called he retreated to the end of the garden and sent word that he was praying. As he was supposed to be a devout Catholic. . . .

Another form of expiation was to take up Toby's invitation to visit the gipsies whose ragged and sordid encampments ring the walls of Avignon—they have been forbidden the interior. Here lying on some filthy straw pallet in the arms of a gipsy girl I can formulate more clearly my explanations of past events—reminded by a gipsy doll pinned to a pillow, as if for an act of sorcery. The doll sent me back to Pia, and then to odd thoughts of association which had been stirred up by the patient mage, Joy. In the layer beneath the dollies (as in a box of chocolates) were stored all sorts of necrophiliac thoughts and tendencies which lead to an exaggerated dread of graves, corpses, etc. These fears are sublimated into love for statues, waxworks, effigies, all dead objects. The reason for the fascination is the appeal of defencelessness. The corpse cannot defend itself. "Listen to that," I cry to the sleeping gipsy. "The corpse cannot defend itself, nor can the sleeper."

All round they are cooking over wood fires. The encampments hug the walls, and have been here so long they seem to have grown right into the ramparts. Here they live a sort of raffish troglodytic cave life, these birds of prey who dress like birds of paradise, and scorn to learn a word of French—or just enough to tell fortunes under the bridge, though their real relish is quick and pleasant whoring.

Well, then, here I am in Avignon; the falling of the grey municipal night over the dusty recreation grounds trampled by the ghosts of public children. . . . I walk among the empty benches and the loops of twisted wire which try in vain to encourage roses. These gardens are unlike the opulent ones on the headland with their marvellous views and splendidly tended greenery. They are more in my mood however, more contemporary.

The centurion walls girdle the sable roofs whose sliding planes take the light at different angles, turning terracotta, tobacco, violet: at times the city looks very much like a brown piecrust cooking away in its stone dish. But now twilight has its own degrees of brown dark, sprinkled in patches of shade on grass or freckling the lemon-tinted bark of the tranquil planes. And everything held superbly in frame by the headlong river which cuts its sinuous path towards the necropolis of Arles. Once, says my historian, Toby, corpses were confined and tipped into the swift river together with the burial fee; they were fished out at the Alyscamps and decently interred. Along the banks of the Rhône where I have been walking stretch the tents and booths of itinerant vendors of toys, coloured ribbons, sugar plums, straw hats and shawls; as well as wares which address themselves to the taste and judgement of agriculturalists—rope, sheep bells, sieves, harness, pitchforks, chemical sprays and fertilisers, ploughs. The garment stalls carried the traditional blue vine-dressers' outfits, sunhats, and the great willow pitchforks grown in *espalier* at villages like Sauve. Inevitably the gipsies blend into all this, flickering here and there in their bright rags and jingling jewelry to catch unwary clients superstitious enough to cross their dirty palms: or thieving: or whoring openly in the shadow of the bushes which fringe the river. Though here we are relatively far from the sea the advent of the car and the train has brought fish to our doors and in Avignon one can eat the best fresh fish of the Mediterranean. Of course the primitive and dusty old coach roads discourage modern traffic so that in contrast to the tamer country round Nice and Monte we must seem more backward and dusty here. No matter. Things feel more authentic; everything has bone-structure and style. And the land is all the more delightful for being a little unbarbered, unshaven.

Under the famous broken bridge which the inhabitants of Verfeuille have always regarded as a highly symbolic structure, there are sometimes real dancers, during the frequent fêtes and holidays. There is also the famous cockade-snatching fight such as someone has just rediscovered on the vases of Crete. It is kinder than the Spanish fight for it does not slay the bull: it is the white-clad man who is in danger. The bullring is easily and hastily improvised by placing the carts in a ring to form an arena. The audience is mounted on the carts. Here we have snuffed enough red dust to see the summer out, and drunk enough red wine to float a gunboat. And from time to time, in a trick of slanting light, one is reminded that the Middle Ages are not so very far behind us—as a reality rather than as an abstraction. Machicolated walls grin with the gap-toothed, helot-dwarf expression of the louts in Breughel. Up against the night sky the massive and ugly factories of God loom like broken fret-saws. In the green waters of the great fountain of V., which throbs on with the heartbeat of Petrarch's verse, the polished trout swim and swarm and render themselves in all placidity to the gaff of idle boys. Darkness is falling. I am hunting among all these booths for young Toby, whose potations never cease to amaze me, and whom I will doubtless find at one of the wine stalls which offer free drinks as a kind of advertisement for country wines on direct sale at the fair. Sure enough. He stands in a clumsy and dogged way with a glass in his paw. Under his arm the latest Pursewarden much battered and full of river sand (we bathed this morning). Vainglorious though I am I do not hold this against him for P. is the only endurable writer in England at the moment, and I gladly cede the palm to him as the saying goes. Toby has hiccups and is trying to cure them in the only way he knows. By drinking from the wrong end of a glass.

It only takes one match to ignite a haystack, or one remark to fire a mind. Piers is determined to meet Akkad on his next visit and to plumb all the mysteries of the sect; and by the same token Toby has suddenly seen the way into the centre of his own work. The little that I was able to tell him of the gnostic predispositions suggested a possible solution to the nagging old problem of the Templars—wherein had they sinned, why did they collapse? The suggestion that the central heresy might have been gnosticism suddenly blazed up in his mind and gave substance and form to all the dispersed material he had been wrestling with in the muniments room of the château. The mere possibility that he had a theory which might be fitted into a thesis to be offered for a Ph. D. produced such a wild fit of exhilaration that it led to a three-day drunk of notable proportions. We kept meeting him and losing him in the town. At each encounter he seemed drunker, slower, more elaborate. And when Toby drank too much one was never sure what he might say or do. For example take the only taxi and cry: "Follow that neurosis!" Or recite nonsense verse: "The apple of my gender aches, I seek an Eve for all our sakes." And then of course Byron

—for he sees himself as Byron and is continually addressing an imaginary Fletcher—but this happens mostly in bed.

"Fletcher!"
"Yes, my Lord?"
"Abnegate."
"Very good, my Lord."
"Fletcher!"
"Yes, my Lord?"
"Convey my finest instincts to the Duchess."
"Very well, sir."

In the incoherent maze of his rocking mind all sorts of diverging ideas and thoughts bounced off one another. "I see little point in being myself, O sage," he might intone. Adding: "Sutcliffe, that huge platform of British flesh and gristle ought to be in a dog-collar. He is criminally drunk and has joined the engineers of sin. A murrain on his buttocky walk and chapped hands. Free will is an illusion, honey, so is the discrete ego, say the Templars. Who impregnated them with this folly? The wrath of the nymphs was hidden from them until the last moment."

Or simply fall down on a bench and go to sleep like any tramp using Pursewarden's *Essays* as a scant pillow. Only the cold and dewy dawn would awake the unshaven sinner and drive him down to the Princes hotel, or back to the château.

"My advice to Robin Sutcliffe is as follows," he might add, and recite aloud while his finger marked the bars:

> Always shoot the sitting duck
> Pass up the poem for the fuck
> At worst the penalty may be
> A charge on poor posterity.

"Fletcher!"
"Yes, sir."

"By the navel string of the Risen Lord, bring me some bicarbonate of soda tablets."

"Immediately, my Lord."

Somewhere, under a bamboo ceiling, hidden in a coloured transfer of tropical birds, there where the great philologists keep holiday, she may still be waiting for me. "Darling," the letter said, "Burma was such a trap. I feel I am going mad."

Wandering in the older part of the town, near the market, I found a few barrowloads of books for sale; among them a very old life of Petrarch (MDCCLXXXII) which I riffled and browsed through in the public gardens of Doms. It would make the ideal going-away present for Sylvie. I was not so hardhearted as not to feel a quickening of sympathy at the words of the old anonymous biographer of the poet.

J'ai cru d'ailleurs que dans un temps où les femmes ont l'air de ne plus se croire dignes d'être aimées; où elles avertissent les hommes de ne pas les respecter; où se forment tant de liaisons d'un jour et si peu d'attachements durables; où l'on court après le plaisir pour ne trouver que la honte et les regrets, on pourrait peut-être rendre quelque service aux Moeurs, et rapeller un Sexe aimable a l'estime qu'il se doit si l'on offrait à ses yeux, d'après l'histoire, le modèle d'un amour délicat, qui se suffit à lui-même et qui se nourrit pendant vingt ans de sentiment, de vertus et de gloire.

Alas poor Pia! My mind went instantly back to the lakeside of Geneva where I had the first glimpse of the slender pale girl buttoned into white gloves. Parasol, pointed shoes, light straw hat. They had sent her

to a finishing school and on Sundays the girls strolled
by couples along the lakeside. She was on the pale
side, and a little too slender, too much waist to her
severely tailored suit. I had a rendezvous with someone else, and was waiting in a little café among the
gardens when she passed by, smiling at something her
friend said, and left that little ripple of complicity in
her kindly glance which provoked my interest—an
interest which deepened as I watched her eating an
ice, dainty as a cat. Nothing I learned about her afterwards surprised me—it was as if I had always
known about that sad and solitary life among the
great embassies, always taught by governesses and
tutors, always forbidden the company of other children of the same age. The little brother was too young
to be a companion for her. So that even the strict
Geneva finishing school seemed a marvellous escape
from her former life. The degree of freedom permitted
the girls seemed to her to border on the dangerous. I
followed her, and from a chance remark learned
which church they worshipped at on Sundays. The
next Sunday I made a point of joining them in these
obligatory pieties. On the second Sunday I passed her
a note asking her to dine with me and telling her the
name of my hotel. I added that I was taking Holy
Orders very soon. I did not believe for an instant that
Pia would accept. But even staid and gloomy Geneva
seemed to her, after what she had lived through, a
carnival of freedom. For once in her life she showed
a wild courage, an almost desperate courage—I mean,
to use a back door and scale a low fence . . . I
couldn't believe my eyes. I was completely knocked
off my plate in a similar manner to old Petrarch.

*Le Lundi de la Semaine Sainte, à six heures du
matin, Pétrarque vit à Avignon, dans l'église des
Réligieuses de Saint-Claire une jeune femme dont la*

robe verte était parsemée de violettes. Sa beauté le frappa. C'était Laure.

How simple, how ineluctable these experiences seem when they come one's way. How calamitously they turn out. Perhaps not for the lucky, though. Nor for them.

The old doctor in Cz once told the duchess: "I have always felt that I was a spare child, a spare part, a spare tyre. People only turn to me in distress. Nobody wants to share their happiness with a doctor."

"Fletcher?"

"Yes, my Lord."

"Hand me my lyre."

"Very good, my Lord."

"And also some purple therapy. I am a bit cast down by my hypogloomia or common hangover. Some methylated spirits, please."

"At once, my Lord."

> Smoking living salmon
> Stuffing living geese.
> I'm a little Christian,
> Jesus brings me peace.

(A spontaneous lyric outburst by Toby as he stood face to face with the Palace of the Popes.)

To feast on loneliness—it is too rich a diet for a man like me. Yet I have had to put up with it. Piers said: "People who can no longer fall in love can simply pine away, go into a decline, and select unconsciously a disease which will do the work of a pistol." He is not wrong. Despite the new-found freedoms the area of misunderstandings about love remains about the same. The act is a psychic one; the flesh simply obeys with its convulsion-therapy and amnesia. Yes, but now that the young have at last, thanks to Marie Stopes, found the key to the larder, it will be apple tart and cream for breakfast every day, and cakes and ale all night. Why should I make such extraordinary claims upon life when I have all the gipsies of Avignon to choose from? Because I am a fool. I remember that I wanted to bleat out: "I love you," but she put her hand over my mouth and all I felt was her breath in my fingers.

In the evenings I take a long slow bath by firelight in my room; a large hip-bath does service for something more modern. A big sponge with dilatory squeezings warms my body. Then to wander the lamplit maze of the old house, taking always the direction pointed out by the distant piano. Lights blaze upon the wine glasses. How much longer will this life go on for them—living in the quiet parentheses of Verfeuille's pulse-beat? After dinner to play a round of cards or drowse over a book. I feel all the magnet's deep slumbering passivity, the bare weight of inertia. Toby accuses me of being selfish because I pay no heed to social problems, but there is no social answer to private pain, to loneliness, alienation, the need for love. Once a French girl, grubby and unwashed, lips hewn apart with yawns, smelling like the métro in summer, completely absorbed my affections for two months. Her reactions had been slowed down by a youthful meningitis—it had slurred up her speech, and the stiffening of the muscles on one side of her mouth gave her great beauty and stealth. A committee cannot love, a society still less. She brought me an unusual happiness, which is only the sense of wonder suddenly revived. I told Pia all about her and she listened with her patience coiled up in her like a cat saying nothing at all. I snatched off her fresh straw hat and kissed all those sunpilfered freckles with gratitude. In those days I was lighthearted and used to sign all my letters: "Well cheerio, best agonies, Rob." I little knew!

"My whole philosophy is this: that people who give one too much trouble should be arrested and turned into soap." (Toby. The last words roared out and punctuated by a bang on the table with fatuous fist.)

As for Trash, her terracotta beauty was proof of the pudding; the plum-tones softly dusted by her powder—a Greek vase dusted with bonemeal. In the morning, naked, she did what she called her personal Intonement. The text went as follows, rising on toes, hands and arms spread out to heaven:

> Who's the Bestest?
> Who's the Mostest?
> Who's the particularly particular?
> Who's the specially special?
> All together: "Why, Trash of course!"

The little lap-dog with its coat of scarlet velvet was named after Pia. It walked on its hind legs with enthusiasm. When she showed it the whip it immediately got an erection. Afterwards when it died they buried it by moonlight, in tears, with loosened sphincters. Ah, the sweet mooncraft of the dark lady of the soblets!

Trying to explain to Piers that the stream of consciousness is composed of all too painfully conscious bits with the links suppressed; free association does the hop skip and jump along these points, behaving like quanta. He will not believe that the art form of the age is not the diary any more but the case history. Anyway stream of consciousness is a misnomer, suggesting something flowing between banks. Milky Way would be more accurate. Consciousness is a smear. Come, Trash my love, throw them coal-black haunches over the moon! Pia's love will do you good, it will cure both your pretty dimples.

At night poor Robin's slanguage fails;
He feels his mind go off the rails.

Out there on the plateaus of his loneliness he feels
the freezing pelagic spray drying on his cheeks. He
stares and stares into the eye of the blizzard but all
is wiped away by the softly falling snow. "Toby, the
minute you start to have opinions about day-to-day
matters you cease to be an artist and start to be a
citizen. Choose." But I was angry with myself for getting lost in the shallow meshes of such an argument.
One should never explain, merely hint. Bruce said:
"When we were younger we were actually and physically moved by books. *Seraphita* so disturbed Piers
that he threw it aside and rushed into the open air;
feeling suffocated at being found out. He writhed on
the grass like a dog to drive away the vision it raised
of a perfected love between himself and his sister."
Yes, when one was young—poetry with the requisite
built-in shiver. Then later one finds oneself facing love
affairs as full of bones as any fish—beauty bold and
sweet or full of peace and weariness like Pia,

> *en pente douce*
> *au bout portant*
> *glisse glisse chérie pourtant*
> *vers bonheur béchamel*
> *love, the surprise parcel*
> *will never treat you well.*

A kiss like an interval between points in mathematics, like a cigarette-end burning in the dark. I
asked her once when we had been drinking a very
human wine to tell me what it felt like with Trash.
She coloured deeply and was silent for a long while,
her eyes all the time fixed truthfully on my own, a
little wrinkle of thought on her brow. Then: "Trash's
body smells of wedding-cake."

Life with Toby

Without the company of Toby I should never have had the courage to return to the château; and the fact that he began so earnestly to work gave a high seriousness to our new life there. While he laboured in the old muniments room on the medieval deposits of several generations of Nogarets, I sifted softly through the archives of a more recent time—Sutcliffe's papers, his letters from Pia; from the duchess, and from other people in his life. I occupied Piers' old studio and Toby the three guest rooms—this purely for company. So, like a couple of retired bachelors, we put up a common front against the gnawings of solitude. Once or twice the lawyer came up to Verfeuille on some business connected with Piers' affairs, and once I glimpsed the Abbé in the grounds though he did not greet me, and did not actually enter the château. He had a long talk with one of the older servants and then sent to demand permission to visit the vaults where the family had for generations buried its dead. This was at once granted. He disappeared into the wood for an hour or two and then returned, once more to the servants' quarters, to give back the keys. Summer came and we went for long walks in the heat, in the perfumed dust of the Provençal countryside.

Toby's great study, entitled *The Secret of the Templars,* was well on the way to being finished; it had taken him a number of years as far as the execution was concerned, but of course many more if one counted the length of time he had actually spent reflecting upon the subject and reading round it. It was a lifework, and his reputation as a historian would stand or fall by it. It was a strange period for me. We spoke little about the tragedy of Piers, and once a week we rode down to Montfavet to spend a few quiet hours with Sylvie. But for the most part it was long walks and early rising. I felt less of an orphan.

It was during this period that Toby decided to read me a few of the opening passages from his book in a suitable décor for it—a deserted Templar fortress which stood on the dry flanks of the steep ravines beyond the Pont du Gard—that bronze masterpiece of Roman plumbing, constructed apparently of a stone like honey-cake and set in its steep context of rock over the slow Gardon. We slept in the fort, and that night a bronze moon rose over it like an echo. The situation was suitably romantic for the reading of a work which was designed to surpass Gibbon in style and mellifluousness. . . . At least these were the pretensions of the author expressed for the most part when he was slightly flown with wine. Appropriate too was the great fire of thorns and furze which he had stacked against the walls of the inner bastion. This huge fire bristled and roared up into the calm sky, making the gloomy precincts as bright as noon—and enticing the lizards and snakes out of the rock to bask in the glare. Our blankets we had spread in a sheltered corner. Toby, placing his gold-rimmed spectacles on his nose, set our dinner to simmer and uncorked a demijohn of the old Verfeuille red which glowed in our glasses with the embers of old recollections of half-forgotten journeys and excursions of our youth by

the light of the moon. Then he seated himself on a
stone and took up the thick manuscript, a whole life.

"Even after six centuries of silence the name echoes
on, troubling and mysterious, vibrating in our memories with a kind of tragic uncertainty, tragic doubt.
The Templars! What was their sin, what caused their
sudden, almost inexplicable destruction? The dust lies
thick upon the manuscripts which should provide an
answer to such a query, but which in fact only seem
to accentuate the mystery by their extraordinary ambiguities, their improbabilities. The more one studies
the evidence the less convinced one becomes that the
truth has not been tampered with: that the secret has
been deliberately hidden, that the so-called facts lie,
that the existing evidence darkens judgement. Is there,
then, no answer to the secret of their strange fate—or
must we rest our case forever upon surmises and evidence as baffling as it is circumstantial?

"Across the whole of Europe and the Mediterranean Sea, from the fogs and rains of the north to the
sunshine and orange-lands of Syria, Portugal, Mo-
rocco, are spread the sad relics of this order—abandoned castles and keeps which still insist, by their
malefic silence and desuetude, that something momentous and tragic came to pass on that faraway Friday
the thirteenth in 1307. On that date one of the most
powerful religious orders the world has ever known
was struck down overnight, to founder and disinte-
grate without defence in the fires of the Inquisition at
the instigation of a weak Pope and a criminal French
King. Fantastic accusations were formulated which
stupefied the finest minds and hearts of this order, so
long renowned for its piety, self-abnegation, and devotion to duty. The Templars were the foremost fighting arm of the day, in terms of military strength quite

capable, one might have thought, of conquering the whole of Europe; moreover, from a political point of view, the knights were the bankers who handled the gold of the kings. . . .

"Yet at dawn on Friday the thirteenth in 1307, in conformity with the *lettres de cachet* sent out by King Philippe Le Bel to all the seneschals of France—orders they were forbidden to open and read before the twelfth of October—the 5,000 field officers of the Templar order, from the least important up to the Grand Master, Jacques de Molay, together with his personal bodyguard of sixty armed knights, were arrested at the instigation of the chancellor of France, Guillaume de Nogaret. They were taken up in one night like rabbits. There is no record of a protest of any kind nor of any resistance. The main attack was launched at the world headquarters of the order, the Paris Temple. Why?

"The accusations formulated against them seem, even in retrospect, astonishing in their extravagance; one has the impression that the knights themselves were dumbfounded by them, rendered incapable of reacting out of sheer astonishment. A religious order world-renowned for its frugality and chastity was suddenly accused of heresy, sodomy, secret practices, and religious beliefs hostile to the Christianity of the day. The suddenness of the blow, the perfect timing of the attack, and the devastating nature of the charges left no time for thought, no time to prepare a defence against such outrageous suppositions. It would not be an exaggeration to say that the whole of Europe was struck drumb also with surprise; and then became scared and uneasy about the gravity of the charges and the increasing flimsiness of the evidence brought against the knights. The long sad trials began which were to drag on and on into what must have seemed an infinity of cruelty. The less the Inquisitors found, the more summary their judgements, the higher burned the pyres on which the bodies of the Templars smoked. Nobody was convinced: yet everybody was silent.

"But the silence of bewilderment or outright disdain could do nothing to help the knights in their fearful religious dilemma. They wondered, they hesitated, they compromised. Could the King be serious? Or was this a vulgar attempt by a spendthrift always in need of cash to wrest the Templar riches from them? If so, what a dangerous way of achieving his ends—for the order had a fully armed fighting force of 15,000 knights in the field: perhaps the only fully equipped and mature military order then in Europe. They did nothing. The long dreary Inquisitions into their heresies, which today cover a mountain of parchment in Toulouse, Avignon and elsewhere, an extraordinarily disappointing in their lack of coherence, their ambiguities. Yet the basic fact remains that in one night, over an area of roughly 150,000 square miles a total of 15,000 persons were taken up by the authorities. There was no struggle recorded anywhere. What could have caused every single preceptory to surrender so completely? A consciousness of the innocence of the knights? A belief that an inquiry would vindicate the order? Surprise? Yet the Templars would seem to have held every trick in their hand had they wished to resist. Their chain of fortresses, like mastodons, was impregnable, their armies were crack fighting ones. Afterwards the King, Philippe, tried to shift the responsibility to the Inquisition, saying that he had acted on their advice. But this was not true, for they were informed after the event, though they were invited to join forces with him and handle the trials in the best religious style. Nogaret had sent twelve spies into the various chapters to collect evidence against the knights. It is worth remembering that his parents had been burned at the stake as cathars by the very Templars whom he helped destroy. At any rate he ignited the pyre, so to speak, at the instigation of the King. But though the flames burned high and long there remains something mysterious and unrealised about the whole business. The truth eludes one. For example, of all the thousands of Templar knights tortured and interrogated over a seven-year span, only three confessed to homosexual acts. . . .

"But the traditional view of the matter should be set out clearly since it is the view which holds the academic field today, and there is no inherent improbability about it. It runs as follows, and the chief proponent of it is Professor Basil Babcock of Oxford:

" 'The real sin of the Templars is far from mysterious—though it is never mentioned in the long list of 127 questions addressed to each of the knights by the Inquisition. The sin was the sin of usury, and the only rational explanation of their sudden and catastrophic fall turns upon it and upon nothing else. They were, we must remember, the most powerful and widely extended money-lenders and bankers of the Middle Ages, and their enormous wealth first grew from the fact that they financed the Crusades as well as taking an active part in the fighting in order to safeguard and watch over their investments. The Temple in Paris was the focus and centre of the world gold market. The Popes and the kings were encouraged to deposit their wealth with the Temples for safety—wealth which was not locked away in the vaults but reinvested under guarantees and at a lively percentage. In sixty years of studious banking backed up by the might of the sword and the chain of fortresses stretching across the civilised world the wealth of the Templars cast a shade over the riches of kings and Popes alike. It exercised a strange hold on the economic pattern of Europe's life. With riches comes cupidity, and with power insolence. So the stage was set for the downfall of the order.'

"It is the purpose of this detailed study to suggest that there was in fact a Templar heresy, contracted perhaps in the Orient, which, on religious grounds, and from the narrowest Christian viewpoint, justified their total destruction. While they were *outremer* in the service of the Cross they became contaminated with the secret gnostic beliefs which coloured their notions of good and evil and which qualified their allegiance to the Pope and Christendom. They became secret dissenters, and in the technical sense, or purely theological sense, supporters of the Antichrist of the day. At first sight this explanation of the mystery might seem somewhat bold and perhaps even rash. But there is enough evidence to support it, and we hope to show by a painstaking examination of available records that this is, in fact, what happened, though of course not all the knights were necessarily in the know. The order transformed itself from within and disseminated knowledge at different levels—a sort of freemasonry in structure grew up; and naturally enough, because just to think such things, which threw the whole of Christianity into question, was extremely dangerous. They lost their gamble, and were rooted out, extirpated to the last man. Issues may have become confused, evidence tangled and muddled. But reason there was, and the present writer hopes to show it."

Toby threw down his manuscript and tossed some more wood onto the fire. I was silent. Despite the rather heavy rhetorical flourishes it was not bad as an introduction to his book. It was at least a direct challenge to the prevailing authorities. I watched him pacing up and down, organising the dinner, with the light glinting on the gold rims of his spectacles. Memory seized me as I lay, sunk in a composed drowse, before the vast fire. Our shadows danced upon the walls and

I thought of Plato, and then of Akkad. I thought of
our lives, our travels, which now had diminished and
faded into a kind of limbo where we had nothing much
more to expect of the world. The fire burned, the
whole of Provence (our own land) slumbered around
us in the light of the dying moon. Toby was going grey
at the temples, so was I. And the dead? They slumbered peacefully, waiting for us to join them. We ate
in silence and happiness—the silence of deep thought:
for the threads of everything Toby had written led us
directly back to our own youth, and to Akkad and the
adventures of the deserts which ringed Alexandria. I
saw how the theme went now, and I could see that if
Toby handled his materials with circumspection he
would have a book which would not be easily superseded in its domain. He sat and riffled through it by
the fire, and began to talk and expound, no longer
content to read the prose in his somewhat stentorian
voice.

I lay and drowsed. Some of these things I knew, and
some not. I had entered, thanks to the wine, into a
state of warm bemusement hovering on the borders of
sleep. Yes, Avignon became Rome in 1309, just at the
time of the Templar trials; Toby said: "Of course all
of this I owe to that chance remark of Rob's, and the
letter from Akkad. Do you recall?" Drifting through
my mind came sadder fragments from the Sutcliffe papers which I had been trying to arrange in chronologi-
cal order. "Honey, Robin is all heaped up with sadness. His roses don't sing no more. He's all cased up
in sorrow, poor Robin. He's gone silent, he needs
subtitles, honey." Trash, with her "pretty hobbling
French" . . .

"To get to the bottom of the matter," Toby was saying as he scanned his huge typescript, "one must try
to see what was behind the questions posed by the Inquisition. For example, those concerned with sodomy.

For while sodomy was not more rare in the Middle
Ages than it is today, no stigma of effeminacy attached
to it. Many Crusaders must have been of that persuasion, and of course the popular revulsion to unnatural
practices went deep. Indeed the penalties were hard,
though almost never invoked. The charge was punish-
able by being burned alive or buried alive at this time.
But this was only what appeared on the statute books.
Yet the Jews, for example, were never charged with
sexual aberrations by their medieval persecutors. One
wonders why. Even the charge of ritual murder
seemed to lack any specifically sexual tinge. In the
case of the godless Moslems they were merely criti-
cised for a superlative incontinence. But—and here is
a fact of great significance—homosexuality was thoroughly identified with *religious dissent* of the gravest
kind—so much so that Bulgar, that is to say Bogomil,
remained always by connotation a religio-sexual
charge—whence later *bougre* and *bugger* evolved from
it. . . . You see?"

The firelight splashed upon his grave features as he
expounded; but now his exposition was punctuated by
yawns. We lay watching the climbing sparks spray
the night sky. The whole of this rich elucidation of the
gnostic sin—some of which I had heard or read before
—went drifting through my senses like a drug, illustrated as it were by a great gallery of coloured scenes
from our own history, our own encounter with the last
survivors of this ancient heresy. I saw the large opaque
eyes of Akkad gazing at us across the whorls of incense. The great snake, the Ophis of their beliefs, rose
hissing once more to the height of a man. Toby was
talking with regret of the shattered remnants of Gnosticism, of how the central faith had been shattered and
dispersed by the persecution of the orthodox; riddled
by schisms, weighed down under the sarcasm and hatred of the early Christians, they took to the deserts,

wandered into Syria where the mountains sheltered them, or followed the gipsy trails into Europe, gaining precarious footholds in places like Bulgaria which lent them such an unsavoury name. Meanwhile the Church Fathers saw to it that all accurate documentation on their lives and beliefs was destroyed or garbled. Can they have been as vile as the orthodox believed them to be? They were, after all, the real Christians. . . . I could hear the voice of Sutcliffe cry *"Libido scienti! The very albatross of unreason!"* The pitiful fragments remaining can only offer us a hint of those early systems which were grouped around the basic contention, the basic grammar of spiritual dissent. Early communists like the Adamites, for example, who proscribed marriage as sinful and declared all women common property. Sex played a leading role, if we are to believe their enemies. The first conventicles were in caves, and the religious services led to mass sexual congress. Carpocrates . . . ; Epiphanius speaks of a sect which during secret rites sacrificed a child, doing it to death with bronze pins, making an offering of its blood. They were accused of eating human flesh—and their fire-baptism is one of human flesh turned to ashes by fire. A child gotten upon a mortal woman by a demon—our old friend Monsieur in fact. The ashes were a religious viaticum, a sacrament at birth and death alike. . . .

Unsavoury?

"You know very well," says Toby, "that I have always been in love with Sabine. She has always exemplified this horrible faith to me. Rob was right to call it a grubby little suicide academy. It isn't even a pessimism of a philosophic kind for that would be the opposite of something. It's worse, a sort of ungraduated colourless hopelessness about the very fabric and structure of our thought, our universe. A silent anguish which rises from the depths of non-being. A flayed mind still attached to the tree, but which won't give in, stays upright under the lash. How could an ordinary healthy man like me go in for it? It revolted everything in me, and yet without it, Sabine would not be half as perfect as she is. Yet it is thanks to her that I know what I do about the provisions made by the central members to do away with each other, since individual suicide is forbidden to them. You and Slyvie never belonged to the inner club, neither did I. But Piers did and Sabine did."

"Is she dead then?" I was startled.

"No. I had a letter last week from her."

"Toby, are you making this up?"

"Upon my honour, no."

"Then where do the Templars come into the picture? Surely the chief charge against them was the setting up of a false God, an idol as focus for their black masses. Where does that fit in?"

He sat watching me with curiosity for a long moment and then said: "I have been thinking a great deal about what you told me. You know the mysterious idols they were supposed to set up to worship in their chapters—were they really human heads treated with natron after the Ancient Egyptian pattern—idols of Persian or Syrian provenance? I am waiting for an answer, and it must come either from Akkad himself or from Sabine. I simply dare not go any further than that for the moment. Because of Piers."

Of course I could see that in his mind he was thinking back to our conversation about the macabre funeral —it had shaken him as much as it had shaken me. "When they decide to join the fraternity in the full sense they agree that when their time comes, and lots are cast to determine it, they agree to be murdered by someone belonging to the chapter who will be designated for the task—but they will never know exactly who and exactly how the order will be executed. You understand, I took all this for an elaborate joke for a good while, until the facts convinced me. Those names on the so-called death-map of Piers—remember? But what he was actually trying to do with that map was to assess the probabilities, to try to guess who might have been told off to do the deed. Piers had received the little package with the straws which showed that the chapter had considered his destiny. He must have been warned that only a few months lay ahead of him—it was customary. But I suppose he was curious, excited, perhaps very much afraid. It is not agreeable to be informed that one's time is up —whether it is a doctor or a gnostic who brings the information."

"And the Templars?"

"Well you know, the setting up of idols and the gnostic baptism by fire—there were hints of all that; my thought is that they were of a degenerate valentinian order. The idols represented the eons, divine emanations, and their origin was probably ophite— about which we know a thing or two at first hand."

"I see. And what about the great aerolith at Paphos which they are supposed to have worshipped under the name of Bahomet? Have you any explanation?"

"The name could be either a corruption of the word Mahomet or come from *bàphe metéos,* the baptism of wisdom. Why not?"

"A gnostic hint?"

"Yes. You know, Bruce, the Templars' primitive role seems to have enjoined them to seek out and redeem excommunicated knights and admit them to the order after absolution by a bishop. Naturally at first they gathered up a rabble of rogues and masterless men, perjurers, robbers, committers of sacrilege, who streamed into the Holy Land in the wake of the armies in search of plunder and perhaps salvation. Unlike the Hospitallers it was a military order from its very inception. The pretensions towards chastity and spartan living were very clearly defined. Plain white was their colour, plain white wool, linen undershirts and drawers of sheepskin. Their standard was a piebald one. They offered hardship, poverty and danger as the only rewards for joining them. You see, they were not joking! They were inflexible moral puritans—just the kind that suddenly breaks under certain exotic influences. Now while they were on active service in the Middle Orient they came to grips with the Assassins, a sect based in Persia which performed ritual killings under the influence of *quat,* hashish. The leader of this sect was the Old Man of the Mountains—Hassan ibn as Sabbah, whom the Templars knew well. His Assassins were free-floating mercenaries who made common cause with Saracen or Druse, or any other group that took their fancy in Lebanon or Syria. But their transcendent aim was not so much the destruction of the infidel invader as that of the Orthodox Caliphate at Baghdad. But in their way they formed a sort of Moslem military order not unlike that of their Christian adversaries.

"There is an odd similarity in the hierarchy of the groups—it extends even to the costume: the fighting uniform with the red hood for example. The whole thing was really a momentous meeting of a grass culture (blue grass, hashish, *quat*) and a wine culture —the Christian wine doing service for the Redeemer's blood. Wine as a blood substitute held the Christian guilt partially in check, but not always. When it broke out, as in the siege of Jerusalem, one sees what a hecatomb these creatures could build of their fellow men. They wanted to drink blood, they could not disguise it. The Assassins killed frugally, imagining they were killing minds, dry as flies."

He was silent, thinking, with his sleepy head on his breast. Then he went on. "Grape and grass cultures suddenly meet and for a while do battle. Then one side wins with the sword and loses morally. One kills like an automaton, the other must drink the blood of the victim. The Templars started going astray right here."

He chuckled and placed the sacred typescript under his head to form a pillow. "Can you not *now* see the right true end of poor Babcock? His hair will fall out around the time of the menopause, he will wilt, he will lose all his mayonnaise, Bruce."

But my mind was far away from these common-room squabbles. "Tell me what Sabine had to say," I asked and a preoccupied silence overcame him. He said suddenly: "How difficult is it to remove a human head?" "Not very difficult," I said, "and it can be done quite neatly. Just clamp off the big arteries, section the cartilage with a butcher's saw and lift."

"I do not know what to think about Piers, and the letter Sabine wrote was full of ambiguities. One thing is sure, Piers had received his *laissez-passer* and was waiting for the blow to fall. He must have confided in Sylvie, hence her relapse, her conflict, for she would have wanted to go with him and at the same time stay with you. Her relapse was a compromise which absolved her of refusing to choose."

"And the head—are you suggesting that there is some disgusting secret society trying to resurrect Templar practices with the head of the last Nogaret?"

"We won't know the truth until Sabine comes and tells us. I can think of a number of different explanations of these facts, but none which covers all the possible contingencies. In every explanation there is an odd fact or two which won't. But usually the truth is quite simple. Suppose it was Sabine herself who had been elected to complete the task? Piers could hardly be suspicious of her. We know that she was among the last of his visitors, perhaps the very last."

"Yes, but how did he *die?*"

"Of course they found no trace of poison, but there are quite a lot of poisons which leave no trace. Fresh prussic acid for example among others . . . But of course none of these considerations would explain the removal of his head. Who took it off and why?"

"The death mask was made on the orders of Jourdain, but nothing so drastic as the removal of the head would be needed for that sort of operation."

"Of course. You know, Sabine once told me of a very clever murder which took place in Alexandria —it was on the pattern of Judith and Holofernes. To drive a nail without a head swiftly into the skull of a sleeping man . . . the hair would hide its existence. But of course in an X-ray one would see the shadow of a spike that stuck into the brain. . . ."

Far away, on the stony *garrigues* by the fading light of the harvest moon, one could hear the musical calling of wolves. Provence slumbered in the moist plentitude of harvest weather, the deep contented mists and damps of fruition. The dusty roads were furrowed by the wobbling wains and carts and tractors bearing their mountains of grapes to the vats. Blue grapes dusted with the pollen of ages. In the fields lines of harvesters moved with their pruning hooks and sickles; followed by clouds of birds.

"Toby!" I said, and he gave a grunt, hovering on the very borders of sleep. "Do you really believe that something like that happened?"

"I can't tell," he said at last, "but if anyone knows the truth it will be Sabine. I have a feeling she will turn up one of these days and then we shall get the whole truth from her. I have written to her everywhere." When she was wandering the world like this she had no address, not even a Poste Restante. The faint chance of reaching her was some celebrated café with a notice-board on which one posted letters, the Hawelka in Vienna, Molard in Geneva, Baudrot in Alexandria, Groppi in Cairo, the Dôme in Paris. . . . There was an outside chance of catching her on the wing in one of these places.

If one were lucky she would reply at once. But some sort of obstinate premonition seemed to tell me that we would not see Sabine again—she had hinted in a recent letter that she too had received her quittance, her message—and that all these brain-wrenching problems would remain unanswered, lie buried in the dusty future or the rotting palimpsests of the past. Provence is particularly rich in myths and symbols, and does not like to be interrogated by the idle forebrains of modern hominids. It was like the key— the great key which the Nogarets had handed down to Piers. The legend ran that it was the key to a Templar vault where a vast treasure had been buried out of reach of the King. But where to find the lock which would fit such a great pistol-key? Piers spent years travelling about all over the country in a vain attempt to find this perhaps mythical treasure. In vain! In vain. Now the key lay in the muniments room and was used by Toby as a paperweight. There too I felt that no issue to the mystery would ever be found. It was all part of the Provençal image, the story of a land which from ancient times had given itself up to dreaming, to fabulating, to tale-telling, with the firm belief that stories should have no ending.

Dawn was breaking and a heavy dew had settled on our blankets; we would be slightly stiff and perhaps a little rheumatic as we retraced our steps to the little inn by the Pont du Gard where we had left our horses.

THE GREEN NOTEBOOK
(Sutcliffe Papers)

Comedy or tragedy? Which side up, old boy? The truth is that one could make either out of our troubles. When, for example, I decided to take my "Homosexual component" (O! felicity of phrasing) for a romp I instantly got a clap. After all, Dr. Joy had assured me that my choice of a boyish sexual partner like Pia argued a heavy homosexual layer in myself. Curiosity got the better of me. But it was like sleeping with a graphic mule. It was ludicrous, it was tragic, it was funny. Pia was upset when I wrote her but Trash, in telling me so, added: "Honey Rob, I'm gonna tell you I jest laughed myself yellow when she read me your letter. You crazy great man you. I'd jest love to've been with you for the kicks." Things are what you make them and a salutary clap is where one might imagine it to be. Clowns weep where angels fear to tread. For quite a while I was out of action. Sat alone of an evening mulcting a piano of tunes: Poor Rob.

A few words passed between us that evening in the sunken rose garden where they had planted Chinese tearoses the colour of champagne. Perfumed, and yellow for Tao. I can still feel the weight of those words, like an oracle which brushes schizophrenia. Pia sat so still, hardly breathing.

At the beginning, afraid of losing her, he hit upon an idea of genius. "I must get really ill to make her love me." He did, it worked, now they are married—or were. I can show them to you if you wish.

Ah! Pia, aim always for the lowest uncommon denominator. Trash, you big out-of-date Thing, come here and put your shoes in my mouth and your puss on my hat. I'll fit you, my black giraffe, and teach you to solder those rubber lips to Pia's.

In the château at Verfeuille when an old chambermaid died in her bed, from "natural causes" as they say, they covered all the mirrors in the house with black crêpe until her funeral.

What does it matter? Every wish contains some grain of death. The mind has an idler switch, an automatic pilot. That is where the pretty inventions come from.

Talking of collective nouns with Toby, pride of lions, flock of sheep, etc., he suggested an "amazement" of women.

In the midst of life we are encircled by the great sea of death about which we know nothing. For the sage silence is a fuel; it whistles through the rigging of the nerves like a Force 8 gale. Time has it in for us, and we for time. I was aware of this all the time, with every single kiss. At Innsbruck the *föhn* was blowing enough to drive one mad. The old novelist confided his manuscript to a traveller in Malta who on arrival in Marseille was found to be suffering from the plague. They burnt all his belongings, and that is how the work disappeared. (Coleridge.)

Sylvie says that the word "love" is a blank domino. She is right. I am swallowing my pride. *Ame soeur, âne sûr.*

When loneliness goes gaunt, Pia, nourished on long absences, honey . . .

Régine had the air of a rather vulgar duchess playing a part. Had she been a real duchess like old Tu she would perhaps have been even more vulgar but much more natural.

Cloudy white wine of Aramon with a bluish meniscus hinting of ethyl.

Swollen tongue, cloudy urine, enuresis, spatula . . . Ugh! Dying of an obscure kidney condition. The old defeated priest. I felt sorry to be so anti-Christian when I saw him so nobly suffering.

Je souffre chérie, donc je suis bien portant, c'est à dire presque humain.

> *Je suis ni un refoulé*
> *Ni un cérébral*
> *Mais un vieu Epicurean*
> *Un peu ogival.*

Printer's ink from a proof gave him Scotland Yard hands. Ink lingering malingering.

The blood chirps and twitters, it is dateless;
Our ancestors send their dead tap-roots through us.
Her toes printed in baby powder
On a bathroom floor in Orta. Clean and pink as
    pigeons' toes.

Outside the window a catspaw of wind on the dark
   sifted lake.
One sail throbbing, trying to break loose.
On the balcony beauty takes you by the throat. Yield!

Munch the black flesh, Rob,
Thou gnostic stained with camel juice
As a woman she seemed to me
        une cherchesolitude
        une souffredouleur
        une fauchepistolet
        une polycombinable.

Ah God, for some simple mentholised concubine
whose primitive telephone is all ears.

    As dolls live on in children's sleep;
    So she in mine where angels come to weep.

    Love tamed by a tolling life
    Reason acclimatised by love
    As below, so above. A wife, a wife!
    My kingdom for a knife.

    Wanted: a tripod not a pulpit
           a poet not a parson
           prophecy not homily
           lux not lucubration.

Mon cher, parler c'est de manquer de tact.

Toby's Old Man of the Mountains
His assassins' balls were blue as fountains,
Their scrotums were deep umber
And their penises sweet lumber.

I often amuse myself by imagining a privileged communication about my case, if case it be, between Doctor Joy and Doctor Young. "This fellow Sutcliffe who is clinically suffering from an aggravated spleen due to the pangs of disprised love, much resembles the celebrated gentleman we find in Janet. Beset by a massive depression which induces listlessness, apathy, inactivity, he himself describes his state as a 'crisis of lifelessness.' He has tried everything to wrench himself free of this fearul *cafard*—for six months he kept himself drunk on alcohol or smoke. In vain. Nothing amused him, nothing beckoned. He decided at last to commit suicide, and strangely enough the moment he came to this decision he felt very much better, quite toned up in fact. The excitement engendered by the decision to die perked him right up; he had not felt so gay for ages. He smiled as he wrote all his friends touching letters of goodbye. It put him in a very good humour and he began to really enjoy life. He amused himself by firing at his reflection in a mirror, and then actually turned the weapon on himself. But he only caused himself a scratch. With disgust he noted that suicide was really too painful, and he set the thought aside for a while. Then like a blue fruit the melancholia started to grow again."

For a while he could see her very clearly when he closed his eyes. Tall lace-up boots of cream-coloured kid. A long closely buttoned coat like a guardsman's trench coat with copper buttons. White kid gloves.

266

A scarf of blue at her throat and a kind of Scotch bonnet on her brilliantly blond head. The eyes could go sea-grey to bright periwinkle-blue, gentian-blue or soft plumbago. She walks by the lake this tall pale girl with bowed head; she is reading Amiel, and the tears of sympathy come into her eyes. Hidden away on her shoulder is the tiny vaccination mark, prettier than any beauty spot, whch he had so often kissed.

The hair very fine and softly wavy, a kind of Circassian ash-blond. For a while they navigated by the eyes, those plant-bulbs of the head, which convey everything without a sound. Two intuitives find language an obstacle, a clumsy hurdle. The eyes understand wordlessly—for words conceal more than they reveal. How hard it must be to be blind and desperately in love!

In her sleep she grinds her teeth; waking at dawn a glance of pale fire, like a sodium lamp. Naked and un-cocooned I took the nymph in my arms, drawing a blank slip in the lottery of love. A doctor of literature with concrete eyes. The suave machinery of psycho-talk. I walk the public gardens like a scalded hare. Fat quibbling bottoms of mothers and prams. In the shop windows I gaze eagerly at my own beauty—but all I see is a big baggy man obviously suffering from piles, sunk into his overcoat like a canvas-backed duck. I heard of an old artist who mounted the skull of his mistress on a velvet cushion with jewels for eyes.

It is night now, deep night, and my skull is full of grey mutter.

How I have come to hate this town! Full of Negroes and fretful lepers with squints. Cold as a wife-swapper's embrace, and full of unverified girls. It is dead; lunatics never take holidays. "Smoked out by smoke like old beehives, the stinging vestiges of other lives."

One basic question whimpers and sobs on below all the others: where have we come from? Where are we going?

I feel terrible today, like a parenthesis between two cultures both of which I loathe. The reviews of the new book were all bad or grudging. A critic is a lug-worm in the liver of literature.

It was full winter I recall. My first in Geneva. I had stayed on because of her. I went one evening to collect her for the concert. Deep snow was falling and the wind was as keen as a razor; the frost hurt, and it was almost impossible to stand upright. They had filled the tramlines with sand as a brake to prevent the trams from skidding off in all directions like pebbles on ice. She was waiting for me in the hall of the gloomy aquarium-like apartment house where she had a flat. She was framed in all the splendour of her evening dress and the magnificent fur, against the lighted mirrors of the lift. And she was on *crutches*. In *furs*. She had broken an ankle while skiing. I stared speechlessly at so much beauty and surprise. I almost sobbed with lust.

Where would you imagine all this would end? Three guesses would not be enough. Pia had been impelled to take Trash to every one of the places we had visited together after our marriage. I suppose I had some foolish notion about educating her sensibility, a notion which perhaps she also shared *vis-à-vis* Trash. But what could one do with darling Trash? She screamed with laughter at Venice, the Acropolis

seemed to her insanitary and all broken up, Cairo made
her laugh even more because of the donkeys. . . .
Painstakingly Pia waded through the sum of the
world's culture, following in the footsteps of the Master. And so at last they came to Angkor Wat, but by
this time Trash was beginning to fall ill; the slow fever
was tenacious: was it malaria perhaps? Her teeth rattled in her black face. She had sudden fits of febrile
weeping, from pure fatigue. But relentlessly Pia
pressed on with her lover. I think that she knew that
Lokesvara held the secret to our lives—it was there,
curiously enough, that we had really loved each other.
You know the Chinese fancy that one has two birth-
places—one the real physical one, and one which is a
place of predilection, the place in which one was
psychically born. Our love was born in the upper terraces of the Bayon. Those huge mastodon faces carved
out of the bare rock, the colour of putty, cigar-ash,
graphite, exuding that tremendous calm—the boom
of the celestial surf on the shores of the mind. Here
she took my hand and held on to it like a terrified
child. Slanting stone eyes, thick stone lips, in which
the vision turned inwards upon the life of the mind
bathing itself in the glow of reality. One realised the
sheer fatigue of living in this temporal relativity, and
also that it wasn't necessary. There was a way, expressed by these stone clouds, of sidestepping the
time-chain. She said: "I'm terrified with joy, Rob."
And now poor darling she had for company the ob-
livious lover. The screams of laughter uttered by
Trash rang out among the statues. "It's just the dam-
nednest thing since Cecil B. de Mille," she must have
shouted. And Pia? Did she recapture the old silence
and think of me? I see her walking about, pale and
withdrawn, perhaps just whistling under her breath
as she often did.

The entrance to the Prah Khan stays the mind with

its calm surprises. A broad avenue peopled with a line of lifesized genii. On the left the daevas with their calm smiles, slant eyes, and long sweet ears pricked up to catch the music of inner silence. To the right the cold and serious asuras, round eyes, saddle noses and their mouths turned down sardonically. Both lines hold in their negligent hands a gigantic serpent, its seven-headed hood spread, its teeth and elaborate feathered crest alerted, to spread out in fan fashion before the leading figure. It is writhing, trying to escape, but they are calmly holding it to form a balustrade along which one walks, pacing up large grey flagstones. I remember the rustle of dried leaves under our shoes. Lizards like jewels rubbed their eyes and tapped the stone, curious to see strangers.

We did not look at each other because we felt shy. Immediately beyond this kind of snake balustrade the forest opens in all its prolixity; in ancient times there was a lake hereabouts but it has largely dried out, and its marshwater is so thickly covered with waterweed and lilies that it looks like an Irish meadow. You walk stiffly, indeed a trifle ceremoniously, up the long avenue of genii and through the last portal; and then you find yourself unexpectedly in a sort of labyrinth of courtyards, chambers, corridors and vestibules. An occasional shattered statue smiles out of its mutilation like a war hero. There is a troubling stench of rotting bat manure, rancid and heavy, and in the darker chambers comes the twitter and scutter of these twilight colonies hanging in the darkness, making a mewing noise like new-born babies in a clinic devoted to twilight sleep.

Then of course comes Angkor Wat itself, like a quiet but breath-snatching verification of what had gone before. The wide stone causeway stretching over a moat was empty of pilgrims. A feast of water flowers studded the water. Water upon water, trisected by these passages, and on either side green meadows alive with egrets and snowy pelicans. The five-coned towers form a quincunx, and their flanks are scooped into niches in each of which has been placed a smiling Buddha shaded by a nine-headed naga like a big palm fan. As you advance the bas-reliefs start contending for your attention with their writhing motifs. Elephants with their trunks locked in deadly combat and their riders hurling arrows: chariots full of gesticulating bowmen: an inextricable swarm of dead and dying, victorious and defeated in the last frenzy of war: bridled tigers: ships with dragon prows advancing methodically over mythological rivers thick with crocodiles and great fishes. This is the world, the real world, munching itself to death. Your world and mine.

But turn away from it and you will find an immediate reassurance in the other one. The tranquillity seeps into you as you watch the sun slanting down out of heaven to turn everything soft as ash, violet, mushroom. Yellow-robed monks come out of the monastery of an evening to spend a quiet breath of time sitting by the naga heads; their little ivory faces quite calm and expressionless. Fit descendants of those people on the war frescoes who carry spears or trays or jars, quietly launching themselves into battle with their thick lips and long ears, marching through avenues of trees loaded down by parrots and monkeys. The little calves of the dense grey water buffaloes gambol in the dusk. Pia sits with her hand in mind, but no longer afraid. "I have understood it," she said, as we rose and began the long walk back to the waiting car.

Yes, I too had understood it; and in a certain sense it helped me rather to understand the rest—that long sad journey of the lovers and the calamity which followed on their heels. But the whole thing exists for me like a series of pell-mell cinematic images thrown down one upon the other. How the rains caught them unawares, how their car broke down in the jungle and how they found no help for a day and a night. And Trash's fever mounted until she was racked like a black silk golliwog and bathed in sweat. Some Belgians from a Catholic mission took them into their little cantonment and put them in a grass hut where the insects engendered by the new rain swarmed and pullulated. By the feeble rushlight the little Belgian priest kept vigil with Pia, nodding off to sleep. The rain thrust downwards. There could be no doctor until it stopped and the road was mended. But in two days the noble black heart of Trash gave out while she slept, her crucifix fell from her hand to the rush matting—that is how they knew she had gone. Her body was hurried into the damp black earth to become one with it. And Pia, after sorting out her effects and writing to her brother, wrote me a full account of everything in a tremulous but meticulous hand. It was not for my sake she did this, nor because she wished to plant darts in me, no. It was as if to make herself realise fully the fact of Trash's death, to let it impact on her, pierce the numbness. She described how Trash's little wrist-watch went on twitching all night until she could not bear it any longer and tore it off from her wrist. She ran out barefoot into the jungle with some vague idea of attracting a venomous snake to bite her. But all she collected in the streaming rain were the big white leeches the size of a human finger. When she staggered back to the mission she was covered in them. They would not let her tear them away with her fingers because that left a hole and often caused blood-poisoning or infection. But the little fathers came running with rock salt and poured small quantities of it directly onto the nauseating animals. The result was extraordinary. They explode, releasing all the blood they have drunk, and wither away like a toy balloon. Soon she was freed by this method, though covered in gouts of blood—her own. "I drank a great deal of whisky to try and gag the nerves," she said. It didn't work, it never does.

I realised when I read the letter that for me the paint was still fresh, her memory green. They say that when you love someone, absence and presence partake of one another; and that you cannot really lose each other until the mainspring, Memory, snaps. Lies! Sophistries! Inventions! When I read this long letter which ended, "You will never hear from me again. Your Pia," I felt like an old blind dog which had lost its bearings—the dog in the memoirs of Ulysses perhaps.

First I tore the letter across in a fury; then realising that it was certainly the last I would ever receive from Pia I tried laboriously to stick it together again, thinking that it should be placed with the others in the little leather writing case which had once been hers. I read it over slowly again. She had taken over so many of my tics! For example when she got deeply nervous, as I did when I was working on a book, a sea of prohibitions overwhelmed her and she could no longer write cursive; she was forced to print. But this new reading only reignited my fury. I took it to the lavatory with some vague intention of flushing it away forever, but a sudden ridiculous and involuntary impulse took hold of me so that I tore it up and ate it.

Well, it is deep night once again, and here I am in this rotting city on the snatching curving medieval river. I walk about it sometimes with distaste and boredom. A man sitting at an open front door playing a violin. The Grey Penitents awash from the overflowing canal. An old sexton digging to bury the screams of the dead. And very old people, frail dry-points, in grooved clothes. It makes one think of old civilisations where puberty was treated with tact and custom sheltered sex, aware of its preciousness. Sitting in the leafy square by the Monument des Morts and finding the women grow more desirable with every *pastis*. Perhaps I will turn pederast and go for some slender woolly Negro boy from softest Africa *gekommen*.

Woman the most perishable of the vertebrates but so much more hard-wearing than man; somewhere in the kingdom of the fossils there will be an inventory of all this, printed in mud and then rayed upon a stone, to bite slowly into it over countless ages. The big defeats cut so deep that one sees nothing on the surface except the smile. And the big definite experiences come only once, alas!

Yes, you only have one bite at the cherry. The long night is coming and the darkness is explicit. It drinks as tigers drink, in stealth.

If I am still alive tomorrow I shall write to the duchess.

The thought brought with it no consolation but I set it down here for what it is worth. The act of sexual congress as the spirit-developer, the idea-hatcher, is the source of all science, all art, all information which the spirit needs as its aliment. Psychic growth is nurtured by it. Purifier of mind, sharpener of intuition, procurer of the future. But to fulfil itself and do its job it must be part of a double act, a chiming act. It is strongest when practised by the beast with the two backs. I am not being waggish—look around you at the army of the sexually defeated. Look at Rob. We impotents are great collectors of *objets de vertu,* snuffboxes, musical boxes, knick-knacks. "There's the rub!" As Hamlet says.

Then along comes Uncle Joy and tells me about the great separation from the teat and the mother which echoes on and on like sobbing in a darkened room. Poor Rob has become the champion of waiting on empty sidings, deserted railway stations, bus shelters in the rain, desolate cafés, midnight airports. . . . Waiting on in an agony of apathy and thinking that Trash with her skinny legs had the walk of a senior microbe.

The art of prose governed by syncopated thinking; for thoughts curdle in the heart if not expressed. An idea is like a rare bird which cannot be seen. What one sees is the trembling of the branch it has just left.

They say that if you can get bored enough with calamity you can learn to laugh. Comedians are the nearest to suicide.

> Grief clothed in days, in hours
> In places things and situations
> Grief thrown out of the trains
> Or emptied from sturdy dustbins
> Overboard from ships in sea-cremations
> From eyes or lips or refuse-tips
> Sliding like coals in chutes
> Grief thrown into disuse by miner's time
> A dustbin full of memories' old disputes
> And then to see sorrow come with its
> Stealthy foreclosing, final demands, the grave
> While super-silence hovers like a nave.

On the dark lake a boat by moonlight with its load of shadows—mounds of black grapes a-glister. Somewhere from an alp, white with spring snow, the sound of a bugle. I thought of Pia's piano teacher Mr. Valde-gour, a Russian prince down on his luck. He made her play with him. He played the piano the while to allay suspicion. Later he said that it was like sinking into yielding masses of music heaped up like snow or water or cloud. Cancer of the prostate and so on . . . Suppose, Suppose, *Suppositoire,* eh doc?"

"Life," said the little tedious priest, "is always point-ing in the right direction, it is always bliss-side up if only we know how to take it." Perhaps. Perhaps. But to take it you must begin by giving, and this is hard to learn.

Ah the specialised kindness of taut Christian phari-sees, les *pince-fesses* who fart like tent-pegs.

Pia, that last Christmas, the tree with its withered finery. Trash in her fur cape looked like the back legs of a pantomime bear, and Pia like a small lioness in spurs. The night a necrospasm—a unique depression follows, based on reproof, rebuke, self-reproach. Yet when I was ill she looked after me like an investment. Tenderness of a gundog.

There is mystery in the fact that if you repeat some-thing meaningless long enough it begins slowly to gather significance and meaning as a needle on the disc gathers fluff. It becomes a *mantram.*

I tell everyone that Bloshford was operated on for hernia by a French doctor who left a pair of garden-ing gloves inside him—or at least that is how he looks. Alternatively in certain lights he looks like a stage policeman who has swallowed the pea in his whistle.

The long suit of literature? Think of the impact of Melville's years of massive silence.

Bloshford does something quite hard to do—he trivialises reality. He does not feel the need for the monotony so essential to the creative spirit. I must be very jealous of him to go on like this. Bloshford! Gr . . . Gr . . . Woof! Woof!

In the Merchant Navy an expression signifying "to go mad" is wonderfully expressive. "Riding a corkscrew" it is called.

Tall and willowy, she was one of those pretty Swedish tubes into which one empties oneself in the desperate hope of getting a good night's sleep. (Régine.)

On gazing at my reflection in a mirror: "Even a god can be the victim of binocular vision."

Flesh-hating zealots avaunt! I am for all the soft collisions I can get. I have been decocted. Soft as a boxing glove by moonlight. Houris! Hear my call to prayer!

Roheim tells us that the Central Australian mother eats every second child, sharing it with the older baby. He adds that they are "all heroes" and "as happy as wolves" and goes on to attribute their idyllic characters to the fact that they have suffered no weaning period and no sex-repression (latency period). A link with gnostics? Hum. "We are born mad," writes Dr. Eder. "We acquire morality and become stupid and unhappy. Then we die."

MONSIEUR

The deliberate practice of helplessness in saints and women elicits sympathy and wonder.

Toby, in a flash of sincerity, said: "I have never spoken a truthful word in my life and I have always given several conflicting accounts of the same incident—so aware am I of the relativity of knowledge and the distortion of human vision. I am a born historian, so to speak."

Trapped between conflicting notions of rest and motion, man panics his way into the tomb, rest never bringing him the peace and reassurance he needs, motion only sterile change and ideal sorrow. O! Time the great Howler!

Mille baisers, Trash, *gelatineuses et patibulaires. Va caresser un chameau, Garce.* I am an old elephant and my back legs need polishing.

They were actually connected by the empty space between them, the interstices between felings so to speak, which set up this electrical impulse called desire.

SUPPOSED POEM FOR PIA

Sweet valves, in breath you will correct
The soft ellipses of my husband's sleep,
And the dull *Quand?* Repeat the
Chink-Chink of the French town's little clocks
In bogus belfries on a sour note of final
Twang. Clang! Was that someone at the door?

Today he drank pints of decorated wine,
Rods of gold wine all prizewinners.
Could one presuppose that the death
Of an ageing writer somewhere alters
Reality, diminishing a space the size of him?

It is not possible to contrast man's view
Of himself with the reality he presents
And not to feel sick unto death at such
Pretensions of a complacent little ape.

And we who say we love—how much the worse
For us and for those who possess us. Think.
Rain on my fingers, the smoke of Ithaca,
An old blind dog waiting at a garden gate.

Last night he dreamed a Negress for me, another Trash,
Took her in a thicket of whispers with a smile
That smelt of freshly turned earth, the open grave.

Pia writes: "The old Asian doctor had the face of a
wistful cobra, but the mind was worn like the coping-
stone of an ancient well; the ropes had grooved the
stone. The well of knowledge is deep and the thirst
of men is endless. But they know that the wells are
drying out, the levels falling."

Mirrors were originally invented to capture the reflection of flying swallows." (Sylvie. She had read it
somewhere no doubt.)

As Thoreau nearly said: "Most wives live lives of
quiet disapprobation." A well-furnished mind in an
ill-starred codpiece. (Toby.)

MONSIEUR

The wind whistles in my crows-nest of bones
In the conning tower of the skull
The sharpshooter's ambush of the eyeball.
Death will be only a change of code, of zones.
The python sadness shuffles in to claim . . . etc., etc.

A kid I fell into milk. I married and was a *coq en pute*.
A writer big with books I hurried to Orta like a harvest in peril. To salvage a general principle from a mass of conflicting evidence can be both science and poetry.

Toby gorged on corybantic Cambridge Sausages. Marsupial dons bellying out like sails. Galleons of furry gowns.

Les grands sensuels agréés comme moi, Robin
Les sensuelles ès Amour comme elle
Dans des jardins d'agrément jouant
Comme des poules dans les basses cours
Sont plutôt agronomiquement acariatres
Selon les pédérastes, les putains et les pâtres.
Mais ce soir si ce joli temps permet
Si l'équinoxe persiste
Nous allons entendre chanter tous les deux
La petite doxologie des toiles d'arraignés.
Éplucher le gros oignon de l'univers
Nous deux cachés par l'éventail de la nuit.
Écoute, c'est le temps qui coule
C'est la nuit qui fuit. A moi Bouboul!

I have shifted this huge weight
By only a hair in half a lifetime

Of dead breath and sinew, to somewhere else,
Merely a shift of weight, you'd say,
Though it might be heavier than air
But slow to grow as mammoth's teeth or hate,
A lifetime of nails growing on after death;
Yes, I have moved this huge weight,
By less than a weightless breath
And with it the weight of my afterlife
And massive, the weight of your death.

Something has collected around this long silence,
Pia, the pearl of silence formed round a grain of sand;
the golden embryo of the inner mind promised to
the gnostics. They say there is nothing like love to
develop the spirit except grief, sweet grief. *Ah! Ce
beau temps où j'étais malheureuse,* sighed Madame
to Staël.

What would we not give for Byron's ruthless charm?

Calm and fearlessness at birth should be the natural
attributes of man, but entering the gear-box of process
he has been twisted out of true, out of camber.

A wooden leg, a dimple filled with pus, a wart with
an eye.

Ah! The milky bagpipes of the latent wish! Tonight
Sylvie dragging and sucking at Chopin on the piano,
while I read a book about India—the smoked dung
of merchant enterprise.

Prose should have a gleam in it like mica. The glint
of nervous insight. That moonlit night in the trenches
the dead were hanging on the barbed wire like
sperm in a girl's bush.

Today I have been working under high pressure
weaving my necklace of suppositories. I have come
to some conclusions, like sex is not an act but a

thought: a Tip Toe Thought. (Toby in a high state of suppressed sincerity.)

Bruce told me that when the nurse walked on Sylvie's right side she became invisible. Cranial hemiplegia? Apparently not however.

Pia said: "When Trash leaves me I run a temperature." And I? And I?

I am forever writing her a letter in my head which I know will end in the Dead-Letter Office, will fall *au rebut, en souffrance,* that is why I suffer from a profuse loss of calcium. I am learning to see dreams as the expiatory device which voids the antisocial content of wishes and allows them to act themselves out harmlessly—not from civic conscience but from fear of punishment.

Later comes an embryology of boredom, we topple into the law of inertia. The sluggish foetus which won't contract out of the cosy womb life. So process gets slowed down by cowardice and slowly ankyloses. Gangrene sets in. People are born with frozen affects, and stalk the planet like dead men. In cold blood. These are the faceless hominids who cause us so much trouble by acting out what we are repressing with such heroism.

Tobor the poet for example. His young wife fell into a volcano. He never married again, and the girl became dearer and dearer to him as she receded in time. He trailed his sorrow in poems which became as heavy as lead. Finally, having become world famous, he realised one day that what he owed to her was precisely this deliberate consciousness of her death. She could not have done this for his work by simply living on. It was her death which gave his poems pith. He felt so ashamed he stopped writing.

Trash's body was a breathing bas-relief which might have appealed to a corkscrew on shore-leave. Her red mouth was a sabre-cut of laughter, like a duelling scar. Discussing me with Pia she said: "He's the sort of guy always trying to make a silk purse out of a horse's ass."

If ever I said sex was funny it was only to emphasise the enormous fragility of the enterprise. Spare us this day our classical pruritus.

Have I no right to talk about it? Why, uxorious Raphael, how he loved the act which he did not find lonely—bathed in the candy-floss of women's bodies. Nowadays all that is needed is the leaden sperm of some deteriorated schizophrenic in order to make people feel at home.

Accused by Toby of deplorable political cynicism, I asked: "What sort of social conscience and political awareness would you expect of Robinson Crusoe?" No answer. He just sat there working his finger in his ear and his foot in his shoe like a sexually aroused tomcat works its tail paddle-fashion. He told me about a friend who left everything and went to Peking where he lived with a girl called Persistent Mosquito Net, a lightly toasted concubine. He beat her till she sang like a lark.

The last word pronounced by Buddha was "diligence." An uffish thought.

A Cinematograph Company has been pestering me for ideas and I have accordingly worked out an excellent subject: a film about the filming of the Crucifixion. The actual nail-up takes place away in the distance, like in an Italian painting. The three famous actresses who play the chief female parts are sitting under an olive tree playing poker on a collapsible green card-table. Like a scene transplanted from a *maison close* and dumped down here on the Mount of Olives. Their poor straw-rotted hair is tied up tight against dust in garish bandeaux. They have wrinkled skin like old elephants—years of make-up and whisky have made them patchy as a whitewashed wall in summer. They sit and grimly play, waiting for a cue. The world's girl friends—for this is a super production. They grin yellow, their teeth have been planted in their gums by surgery, but the gums are giving out, and increasing softness has given them precarious grins (pun). Like unreformed whores, New Testament whores so to speak, they wearily play on, waiting for a client to ring. In the far distance the whole sordid little Thing is taking place. A tiresome Jewish agitator is paying for his conceit. Judas sits under a tree nearby eating an apple. They have given him enormous canines and talons like Fu Manchu. The producer is a cripple, wheeled everywhere in a bath chair. He is epileptic and has frequent fits during the shooting. I promise to supply the subtitles later on.

Women who like furs like Pia show their hidden bent for rapine. A passion for tiger-skins reveals the father-eater. Women who train their hair back into their eyes in order to toss it back every now and then see themselves as ponies—they will ride their men. Pia painted her nails the colour of coagulated blood, Trash hers white.

A dry run for a love affair, a mock-up for a kiss, someone dying of postoperative shock. Love, the old corpse-reviver . . . Thoughts closely linked like chain-mail that arguments cannot pierce.

Once upon a time he had been much intrigued by the theories which have grown up around the idea of a "double." Once it seemed proved when she entered his room while he was in bed with a fever and said: "Yesterday you had no fever when I came to you— now your forehead is burning." But yesterday he had been away in another town. Someone had entered his skin during his absence. Who?

If man did not have his illnesses he would have nothing to shield him from reality—and who could stand that?

Dinner with Banquo in that run-down shadowy château in the hills. He appeared to live there alone on his holidays with one Negro retainer. Sabine was due to attend but did not turn up which caused the old man some annoyance. "She has become less and less fun as she has grown older and more serious, and I can't really count on her any more." He recalled with nostalgia her silly period just after university: walking into Maxim's with a young lion on the leash. Sitting beside the chauffeur of a prime minister dressed as a pantomime dog. Their love affair created an international scandal. Perhaps it was as well that this period did not prolong itself unduly. "A little celebrity and one subsides into being a character."

Said that Piers' uncle has inherited the key to a large Templar treasure, and will not surrender it to Piers, who does not know where to lay his hands upon it. He sighed when he spoke of the goodness and beauty

of Sylvie, adding: "Though she has very distinct
marks of madness in her look one always feels that
to call her insane would be to put all ontology to the
question." Smiling in the firelight I saw his brave old
face which seemed to have foundered on the reefs
of success, the disappointment which money-power
brings. He was courteous, he was weary, but he man-
fully entertained his daughter's guest, rather pleased
to have read one of my books. He offered me horses
to ride. But he was very English, very London. I
thought of the smoky old hotels where he lodged as
a penniless boy from Manchester—they line the Crom-
well Road today. Lighted all night. The same night-
porters walk the dusty corridors distractedly waving
enemas. Even today he slept with the same rueful
smile on his face. "Come back," he said. "I spent a
lot of time alone here. Company is good for me." I
said I would. I meant to, but summer passed and the
fireflies died and the harvest came and the rains
started. I only had one wish by then:

> to melt back into the faceless ground
> without a sorrow sight or sound
> or watch the rosy corpses play
> in cinemas by night or day.

Dinner at Quartila's

Blanford the novelist sighed as he separated the master copy of the typescript from the other two, and taking up a blank white sheet rapidly wrote down several provisional titles for this new and rather undisciplined departure from the ordinary product. After several faltering attempts he decided to give the devil his due, so to speak, and to call it *Monsieur*. Sunset had passed him by and now evening was falling in all its brilliant phosphorescence over the loops of the Grand Canal. He was filled with a vague sense of insufficiency at having at last decided to say goodbye to his creations—they had been together for a couple of years now and he had, inevitably, become fond of them and reluctant to part from them. Besides, had he said all that there was to say about them? There were so many corners he had left unexplored, so many potentialities undeveloped simply because he had firmly decided not to write "the ordinary sort of novel."

That blasted Sutcliffe—he had grown fond of him; he had enjoyed even being pilloried by him under the disgusting name of Bloshford. Perhaps he should sue himself for libel?

Tonight he would have the first opinion on the book from the old duchess to whom he had sent the third carbon as well as many of the scenes from his notebooks which had not found their way into the definitive text. Never had he been more uncertain of a piece of writing, never had he needed advice and guidance more. Yet he implored her to say nothing until she received his telegram and the invitation to dinner at Quartila's silk-lined cellar where he would listen to her in all humility, in order to discover what he had, in fact, done. Several beginnings and several endings buzzed around him like mosquitoes as he sat on his high balcony above the water and turned the pages of his notebooks. The suicide—was that right? And he felt that he should perhaps offer a final summing up from the diary of Bruce, let us say; something like this: "The year is on the wane, the month is already November. I have let a number of weeks slip by without making any entries in my diary. I have only a few pages left, just enough to summarise briefly the final history of Verfeuille and its owners. I have decided to cease keeping a diary altogether, to lapse into silence; too much paper has accumulated around us during this long history. 'It is presumptuous to wish to record,' writes Sutcliffe somewhere and goes on. 'Anyway it is too late to alter anything; one has started to appear as a name on the death-map, as if it were among the credit titles of some shoddy film.' He is thinking of the map of Piers' where death assumes the shape of a constellation hanging in the sky—the great serpent Ophis we had once seen in old Macabru. How far away it seems now, watching the rain falling among the silver olives."

Blanford re-read these words with a pang which translated itself into an actual touch of angina as he sat in his bath chair, high over the lagoons, and let his melancholy eyes wander along the delectable con-

tours of dying Venice—the orchestra of divine buildings hallowed by the opalescent water-dusk. Soon he
would have done with the book, done with the masks
under which he had so successfully disguised his
weaknesses and disappointments and misadventures.
His cat slept with one paw still on the white Ping-
Pong ball, eloquent and slim as the devil himself.
He had chosen for his epigraph the well-known quotation from Shagbag: "The Prince of Darkness is a
Gentleman." He felt ill and yet elated by the nostalgia
of this farewell. Bruce's journal was to continue thus:

"The last few weeks at the château were long and
burdensome to live through, so impregnated were
they with the sense of our impending departure;
mind you, we worked hard, and even sang while we
worked at the olives, but it was a pretence for we
were all of us heavy-hearted. It was cold, and some
days we were greeted by heavy cloud and skirls of
young snow falling straight out of heaven, only to
melt as it touched the grass. In the short brush there
was often rime. Soon the colder December weather
and the snowfalls on the high *garrigues* would drive
the hungry wild boars down towards the lowlands
where they could be hunted. With the first frosts
thirst would set in, and game birds could be lured
by simple tricks like leaving a mirror in an open field
to suggest a pool of water. The shortsighted wood-
cock always came down to inspect it, whirring into
the shooter's range. Hares left their snug 'forms' in
the cold grass. Ah, Verfeuille! It was hard to imagine
any other sort of life, so fully had we lived this one
among the green hills and soft limestone river-valleys.
We did not know who the inheritors would be; but
we knew that the long-promised financial calamities
had fallen upon the place in the wake of Piers's death
and partly because of it. Only a huge fortune could
save the place. Mortgages had come home to roost,

contracts now had to be met. It was obvious that by Christmas the whole place would be boarded up, given over to the field-mice, its life extinguished. Moreover those of us who were left would also be dispersed. Toby, for example, had decided to take his now finished and indexed masterpiece to Oxford to touch up the delegates of the press and arrange for its publication. With all the privileged matter he had found among the Verfeuille papers his book planned to overturn many accepted theories about the sin of the Templars. It was now clear that the original de Nogaret had become a Templar himself in order to penetrate the order and destroy it more completely from within. The role of Judas suited him admirably, and like Judas he went mad and at last hung himself. All this new evidence caused quite a throb in scholastic circles—for in order to drive Babcock mad with apprehension Toby had leaked some of his material to learned journals. Now his triumph over pedantry was to be complete. But he himself had decided to leave.

"On his last day we walked over to the Pont du Gard and sat in an icy wind on the honey-coloured stone which we thought that we might never see again, so definitive did this ending of the Verfeuille story seem to us. It was almost a relief to be done with the lame affectionate conversations and to climb at last onto the windy platform of Avignon to await the train. But inevitably we had one last drink at the café by the hideous and funny Monument des Morts with its cheap tin lions we had come to love so much. Winter had unstitched the planes and the leaves rained down in drifts scattering and swirling around our ankles. Yet it was warm for the season, autumn had been delayed. Toby blew his nose a good deal to hide his emotion. We promised each other that we would meet again very soon, and our warmth was effusive and genuine—but how heavy our hearts were! Then the long slowcoach of a train wound out across the darkness and I thought with a sudden jealous pang of Paris, and all the rich anonymity of a big city in contrast to this little town which lost all reality in winter; where the inhabitants stayed lost in their summer memories, listening to the iron mistral as it climbed the battlements, shivering their shutters as it passed.

"As for me, Bruce, I know that I cannot leave Avignon as yet—indeed if ever. I have taken a couple of rooms in the Princes Hotel, directly above those in which Piers . . . They are cheap. Here I propose to 'tread water' this winter—to use the rather disapproving phrase of Rob Sutcliffe. Already, when Toby's train had borne him away, I felt a strange sort of disorientation setting in. I walked back to the hotel on foot deliberately, precariously almost, listening to my own footfalls with deep attention. In my nameless furnished room with its ghastly walpaper I sat listening to the silence and drinking small whiskies out of my toothmug. A vast paralysis had seized everything; I was caught like a fly in a chunk of amber. To shake off this feeling of unreality I turned to sorting my clothes and papers, and to entering these last details in the little diary.

"The rest is soon told. Before the château was closed and boarded up I had the contents of the muniments room transferred lock, stock and barrel to the local museum—including the heavy and copious files and notebooks left by Sutcliffe. Among them are several unpublished books and stories and essays, as well as all the letters of Pia. One day they will presumably be sorted out and see the light of day. Meanwhile his publishers have commissioned a biography of him from Aubrey Blanford, a novelist for whom he had scant respect, but who will be coming down after

Christmas to examine all this material at first hand. Of course Rob Sutcliffe would have been horrified—but I do not see what I, ignorant as I am, could do to avert this fate. I suppose publishers know what they are doing. I do not feel this is any part of my business. Rob knew that one day he would have to face the undertakers of the literary trade. Anyway there is no such thing as absolute truth, and inevitably he will become a half-creation of the novelist. Who will ever know him as we did? Nobody.

"The sleepers in the Nogaret vault are to remain there; but the place is to be bricked in definitively, and a high wall constructed around it before the château is handed over to the new owners—whoever they will be.

"Finally there is Sylvie—my one remaining link with this ancient town and indeed with reality itself, or the small part of it which we can share. I have lived a whole privileged life of concern for her beauty and of that I cannot complain. I cannot imagine how things could have fallen out differently, or made more sense. We have come full circle, she and I." If I close my eyes I can see the dark Sylvie that Bruce must continue to visit every day till death us do bloody part etc. She sits at her green baize card-table wearing tinted glasses to disguise the lines of fatigue under her eyes. Even though a woman be mad, some traces of concern for her own looks remain. Here she plays hand after hand of solitaire, her forehead smooth and unruffled. She whispers to herself and smiles very often. She is aware of his presence though she does not always recognise him—she calls him Piers sometimes. "But my silent presence sees to be comforting and sometimes dropping her cards she will sit and hold my hand for an hour or more, quiet and happy as a plant. When I leave her I usually go to the station on my way home and wait for the last train to come in from Paris. There is never anyone on it I know—how should there be? Often it is empty. Then I walk about the town at night with a sort of strenuous numbness, looking keenly about me, as if for a friend."

Blanford went to the bathroom on a sudden impulse and took off his glasses to examine his face in the mirror. A trifle sardonically—or perhaps the impression was caused by the fact of a small strabismus, a half-squint—the sort of thing which would force one to become a sort of self-deprecating type of humorist. He regarded himself and then winked sadly at his reflection.

"Strenuous numbness," he said aloud, finding the phrase a trifle mannered. He went back to the balcony moving with his swayback hesitation caused by the paralysis which always afflicted him after a day of sitting and writing with the light drawing board across his knees; soon Cade would come and massage him before he set off with the two linkboys to the cave where the duchess awaited or would be awaiting him. She had already sent him a telegram signed by Sutcliffe which showed that she had read the manuscript to the very end, for the text read: "Refuse to be rushed off the planet in this clumsy and ignominious fashion. Kindly arrange to have me die by less theatrical means. Rob." Perhaps the duchess had not grasped the little twist about the *saut mystique?* He would see.

It is still a moot point whether Socrates, in fact, existed as something more than a character in a novel by Plato. And what of me? he thought. Am I possibly an invention of someone like old D—the devil at large? He hummed an air he had made up to accompany the riders who left the Canopic Gate, etc.

It had not found its way into the text. It was a plaintive little home-made air they sang in the desert.

> ALL: Long long ago in time
> Far faraway in space
> When health and wealth
> And slimth and stealth
> Were *données* of the case

> PIERS: There dwelt a man de Nogaret

> TOBY: So overbred
> So overfed

> PIERS: Who threw his life away.

It might have been fun perhaps to print it with the music. He would reflect on the matter. He played abstractedly with the little cat Satan, as he waited for the valet. He supposed he was simply another vainglorious fool of a writer with insufficient courage to tell the whole truth about life. Always gilding the nipple, sugaring the pill. But after all what was the truth about these inportunate, nagging people of his, trying so hard to get born and achieve the fugitive identity of a penurious art? He thought long and sadly of his dark wife, Livia. Crumbs of her had been used for Sabine (the looks and the slashing style) and for Pia, and even a certain disposition of the eyebrows (when she was lying) which was one of the features he "saw" every time he put down the name of Sylvie. "How real is reality?" Blanford asked his cat which gazed back at him unwinkingly, unseeingly—like Livia saying: "Of course I love you, silly." By a singular paradox (perhaps inherent in all writing?) the passages that he knew would be regarded as overtheatrical or unreal ("people don't behave like that") would be the truth, and the rest which rang somehow true, the purest fabrication. He wondered if in the next book about these people he could not cut down a layer or two to reveal the invisible larval forms, the root forms which had given him these projections? Like an archaeologist cutting down through successive cultures until he reached the Neolithic stage of his people, their embryonic selves? He had half decided to let Sutcliffe finish and print his *Tu Quoque* if it could be found among his papers. "Poor Bruce," he said aloud picturing the boy wandering the windy streets of Avignon in the rain, waiting for him to arrive on the night train one day.

In a passage in one of the unpublished notebooks of Sutcliffe he had written: "How can Bruce, a so-called doctor, not be aware that he and Piers between them brought about Sylvie's collapse, the downfall of her reason? The division of objectives in loving is something woman finds impossible to face; it threatens the fragile sense of her identity, the unity of her vision of things seen through the unique lens of human love. Once this sense of uniqueness is put in doubt or dispersed the self breaks up (itself the most fragile of illusions) and all the subsidiary larval selves, demons and angels, come to the surface to splinter and confuse the central ego."

Perhaps he should have included that? He felt so close to these people, he saw them everywhere; yesterday he had lunched at Sardou's right behind Sutcliffe—at any rate it was the back of his head. At the end of the meal a hunchback woman came in to speak to him; she was very striking and resembled Sabine —except for the disability. This version of Sutcliffe picked his teeth with a silver toothpick of great beauty and wore a green baize apron with metal buttons— was he a hall-porter from the Majestic Hotel? He looked such a *savant* from behind.

Where was Cade? Night was falling and the plaintive rivercraft crossed and recrossed among new shadows. The real Sutcliffe, so to speak, who had loaned a physical wardrobe and a few light touches to the book Sutcliffe, had indeed committed suicide but only after a great nervous upheaval. For some reason he had not wanted to deprive Rob of his reason before despatching him. "I wonder why?" he asked the cat. "Perhaps I didn't want to steal thunder from Sylvie?" He riffled among his notebooks and recovered the passage on the Bridge of Sighs, and the nervous breakdown which prefaced the final act—so theatrical, so Byronic: yet this is precisely what Sam (the original of Sutcliffe) had achieved in reality—that word again. . . .

"He was filled now with a delicious vertigo, the winged consciousness of freedom which heralds general paralysis—liberty without precariousness or guilt. The kiss of euphoria. Death was no longer even an event. He existed adjacently to it, could reach out and practically touch it, it was so real. Hurrah. He heard his mind turning smoothly like a motor; it gave him powerful traction. Yes, he would go to India for a year. Learn Sanscrit, write out a cheque for a million, apologise to God. To laugh aloud suddenly and for no reason in a crowded restaurant was delectable. He found he was being naughty, mischievously eating matches or tearing up paper napkins; but he was soon coaxed to behave more correctly. When reproved he would stand up and offer a very stiff arm for a handshake. Sometimes he was forced to hide his smiles in his sleeve. His eyes seemed to have pupils of different sizes. At the café he calls for a paper and proposes to read it aloud but all that results is a deep humming noise. Nothing really outstanding; a little compulsive talk and laughter. And in the evenings in his shabby *pension* some silence, moodiness, followed by catatonic stupor."

Poor Sam, poor Sutcliffe, which version . . . ? So many of these states were interchangeable, particularly if you took drugs. (Sometimes under the influence of the drug he found the taste of mineral water altered so much that he had the illusion that he was drinking warm flannel. Next morning, however, a burnt mouth. . . . But he was an honourable morphinomane as Brutus was an honourable man; his back was still a mass of shrapnel from a low burst. They had not dared remove most of it. So he was the man with the iron spine, dwelling in the shadow of multiple sclerosis which was held at bay by the stubby fingers of Cade.)

Where the devil was Cade?

Blanford rolled his way to the balcony and stuck his head over it, calling out as he did so: "Rob! I say, Rob Sutcliffe!" A few faces in the street below turned up a vague white expanse whose curiosity soon evaporated. "You see?" he said to the cat. "Rob doesn't really exist." In every rainbow there is a gap which one must leap in order to slide down to the pot of gold on the other side.

He heard the whirr of the lift rising to his floor. This would be Cade coming to set him to rights— his Fletcher. The door of the flat was open, it only needed a push. Cade had been his batman during the war and had stayed on afterwards—from sheer lack of imagination. What a cross he was to bear with his insane hatred of foreigners and their ways. The pale soapy face with its skull almost shaven, though with a water-waved spitcurl over his forehead. He was sanctimonious, superior, disapproving. He had no sex, never frequented bars or brothels; did not drink, did not smoke. And spoke so very carefully in his low Cockney whine that you feared he would sprain something by making the mental effort. When he was abroad, among "them foreigners," he always wore a peculiar expression—a slyly superior look; and his nostrils were narrowed as if he could smell the carrion. Blanford always wondered in an amazed way why he went on keeping Cade in all his loutish ungraciousness.

The valet came into the room and without a word started to clear up with a wooden methodical air. He made the bed, tidied the bathroom, and gathered up the notebooks and placed them in a cupboard. If Blanford addressed a remark to him he did not reply but simply went on with his work with the air of someone fulfilling hs destiny, an insect of utter rectitude. He had been extremely cowardly in action, and hardly less objectionable in civil life. But he was a good masseur and grudgingly did what was asked of him in the ordinary affairs of everyday life. Yet . . .

"Cade, I am dining with the duchess of Tu tonight," said Blanford rippling the irresistible Ping-Pong ball along the terrace. Cade without a word laid out a clean suit and went on with his mysterious operations inside the flat. The flowers were dead and would have to be replaced. The whisky decanter replenished. When he had finally completed his work he sidled out onto the terrace with his cunning ingratiating face set in a half-smile. His fingernails were bitten down to the quick. But he put a hand upon Blanford's forehead and reflected gravely. No word was said.

They breathed quietly and evenly—Cade like some heavy mastiff. "No fever," he said at last, and Blanford added, "And no cramps last night, thank God." For a long time they stayed like this, master and bondsman, unspeaking. Then Cade said, on a note of command, "Go limp, then." And Blanford allowed himself to flop. Cade picked him up by the armpits and with surprisingly agile movements, like a lizard, wangled him into the bedroom and laid him down on the bed. He was to be massaged, bathed and then dressed— Blanford always thought: "Just like a lovely big dollie, with a D.S.O. and Bar, and a spine full of shrapnel fragments, and a male nurse for a mama."

Cade dressed him with method, moving him back and forth like some ungainly lobster; Blanford stayed with his eyes closed inhaling the grubby smell of tobacco and boot polish which his batman gave off when he worked. He chewed quids of tobacco, did Cade, and spat black and viscid. "Got the crutches back, shod with rubber," he said, but Blanford replied: "I won't need them tonight at any rate. I'll take the rollchair and the sedan."

"Very good, sir," said Cade.

Within the hour he was suitably washed and dressed for his dinner engagement; Cade helped him into his light wheelchair and thence into the lift which deposed him two floors down almost into the arms of Guido and Franzo the linkboys. It was a pleasant fancy of his to travel by this old sedan chair with its brass polished lamps, swung on the shoulders of the two linkboys. The distances were short, and it saved his energy for better things. He abandoned his wheelchair and limped the few yards to the chair, greeting the boys as he did so. Quartila's was not far off, but he directed them by a slightly circuitous route in order to enjoy the movement and noise of the canals, now settling fast into their night routine.

The old duchess of Tu still went on sitting in the once fashionable inner room of the place whose walls were lined with opalescent satin and where the lights, tamed by oval mirrors, were kind to her wrinkles and her fine white hair. A famous beauty in her day, she stll had young hands, the celebrated swan-neck and eyes of sapphire blue which quizzed a world grown stale and old with an unrelenting candour, and without vainglory. Once they had been famous, those extraordinary arched brows, the expression at once pious and mischievous, devout and impudent. She was waiting for Blanford now as she smoked her slender gilt-tipped cigarettes in a little jade holder and sipped absently at the typescript and notes which lay before her. She smiled as she did so—perhaps a little sadly. She had been his friend and reader for a lifetime, remaining always astonished by the quality of his work and disappointed by its shortcomings. "I finished this morning, Aubrey," she called to him as he came limping over the floor towards her—having abandoned his sedan outside in the street. And as he kissed her hand and sank into his place she added, "I have ordered a well-earned champagne." He thanked her and fell silent, holding her hand. He had decided not to talk about the manuscript unless she did. He had not come to dine with an old friend in order to cross-examine her. But she said: "Did you get my telegram about Rob—he was awfully like Sam, I had to laugh. But to go so near the truth . . . ?"

Relieved, the writer said: "In the case of Rob, it was literally him or me. We couldn't both commit suicide. Composite he may be but a large part is not Sam, it's me."

She paused and thought about her husband for a long moment with narrowed eyes. Then she quoted:

Huddled in dirt the reasoning engine lies.
These are the pearls that were my father's eyes.

And without giving him a chance to catch up with her train of thought she added: "What laughter must have echoed in heaven when Sutcliffe went to the altar. It still rings in my ears."

"It did in his, as it still does in mine. In the *Tu Quoque* he re-enacts all the great roles of the race with himself in the part, starting with the role of Jesus—the famous film script he wrote which caused so many suicides that they had to stop turning it. You remember—how could you? I haven't written it yet. When the door of the tomb was rolled back they found that the body was gone, but on the stone floor were patches of bloody hair and chewed bones which suggested that the disciples had had a midnight feast in the dorm. Or dogs perhaps?

"Men or dogs.
Gods or Men,
Take your choice.

A girl comes through the wood singing:

" 'Of which wood of woods was the True Cross made?
Tell me, tell me, my pretty maid.'
'I'm going a milking, Sir,' she said.
'Be he alive or be he dead
I'll grind his bones to make my bread.' "

They sipped quietly at their champagne and watched the coming and going of other guests; soft and decorous was the place, while from the invisible canals came the soft discreet lapping of water and the distant chaffering of the marketplace. "It's strange," he said, thinking of her husband—his friend Sam— "that we hardly ever spoke much about him until I told you my plans for this book." She had never quite managed to disguise the transitory expression of hurt which crossed her face at the mention of his name. "You were going to try and bring him back to life— that's why." She made some purely mechanical gesture to recover her poise. "The kiss of life so to speak."

All of a sudden he felt that he had failed her—for his Rob Sutcliffe was not Sam to the very life. "My writer inhabited a different, a humbler world. He could never have played the kind of trick which Sam was famous for; I mean, like putting on a Guard's tie and a bowler in order to make the sentries at Buckingham Palace present arms when he passed. Rob would not have thought of that."

"No. Nor Sam thought about Jesus."

"It was essential for Rob the writer to measure his stature, or the lack of it, against the big models."

"But Jesus," she mused, smiling at him.

"The first version of Hamlet," said Blanford with some small asperity. "Nailed to the mother cross he was a good symbol for the inversion which ruined his life and Pia's, as well as Livia's and my own. Don't look hurt."

"Livia was my sister, I rather loved her," said the old duchess softly. "Whatever she did to you: and it wasn't right or good, I know that."

"I am sorry," said Blanford warmly, and meant it, as he thought of his wife (Livia), that "lay figure" as it might be laughingly called. He lit his pipe and said: "In my panic I got all my symbolism mixed up —everything to do with our personal *consummatum est* as you might say; the pretty little *non lieu*."

"You were hard on her rather," she said with a far-away hint of tears in her voice. "Not really," said Blanford, thinking of the sufferings of Sutcliffe. ("The smokeless cartridge of the nun's kiss.")

"It was better when you got on to Hamlet," she said. "Really it was, Aubrey. I don't know why Livia played you that dirty trick."

"In Hamlet," he said soberly, "it was not only an Oedipus situation, but something more complicated; he discovered that his Ophelia and Laertes were lovers. To be or not to be, really meant 'Should this marriage go on or not?' Ophelia had already told him that Laertes must be the master-mistress of his passion. It was the pressure of this guilty knowledge ('I'll fit you') that bore down on him, and then, through him, on her and made them see that there was no way out of the problem except madness. Which is never any solution."

"Never."

"Never."

Their waiters came now and provided the bill of fare; they chose with care and discrimination from it, arguing and bantering as old friends will. Then the wine steward brought forward his wines but they elected to stay where they were with a fine French champagne, and the compliment touched him coming from her. It was a little gesture which proved that she thought that, in spite of deficiencies, his book had come off. A sudden elation filled his sails. "It was not only poor Livia, poor Livia," he said, "it was also my mother's death which came right with it, alongside it."

"But Livvy got all the blame."

"Yes," he said, "it's true. She had discovered that to be adored by men she only had to simulate sharing in the man's wholehearted adoration of himself. Tick, Tock, to cut a long Tory short she laughed in her lilywhite sleeve and said to herself in the mirror: 'People with weak bladders should not climb up high ladders.'"

The duchess smiled sadly and shook her head as he went on, quoting from his own book. "The sponge-rubber heart, the prestressed concrete soul, the glass-fibre emotion . . . No, my dear, books are finished."

To his surprise she shook her head vehemently and denied it, saying, "No, the book will not lose its place or its preciousness for it is a privileged communication between two spirits and the link it forges is vital to the culture of the heart and mind, and hence to man. The contact is between two lonely and desperate souls united by an embrace. No mob-throb here! My complaint was only on behalf of Livia; I thought she could have been comprehended more."

Blanford quoted, mimicking the very accents of Stekel: " 'The homosexual neurosis is a flight back to one's own sex induced by a sadistic predisposition towards the opposite sex.' " After Vienna I really comprehended the lot, but none of my new knowledge served any purpose, he told himself, and then went on aloud, "I studied Livia with all the anxiety of a man in love, and I finally managed to arrive at an interpretation of her which met the facts. That marble beauty and silence, that reserve. I had been puzzled by the role of the wedding ring in all this—for Livia was honest and truthful as girls go. It was old Uncle Fred who set up the skittles differently for me by his animadversions upon the male lesbian type who, like the male counterpart, will often welcome the wedding ring which disguises her private proclivities, and at the same time gives access of approach to unsuspecting wives and adolescents of undetermined sex. That was Livia's line. And by it of course the man is overthrown. It is precisely this sort of girl who becomes a man-eater for pure window-dressing. But even in sex her aim is to overthrow the hated male." He broke off with a short and bitter laugh. "In the powder rooms of the world's great hotels when male lesbians meet they show each other their wedding rings and burst out laughing."

"O come, my dear," said the duchess compassionately, and put a hand on his sleeve to calm him down. "Poor Livia. I am glad you cut out the blue pages from the book, about the caresses of the mantid. After all she is dead now." He took the blue pages from her and read them again slowly: "The dry marsupial's pocket of that unused vagina might have made him awake to the enormous and beautiful clitoris. Painful to penetrate, but expert in many ways, yet shamming her orgasms very often, perhaps thinking of someone else whose memory had worn thin? He didn't know. (Sutcliffe.) But then the ring—was that finance or status or what. . . . ? They told him in Vienna. Male lesbians like to conquer married women and the ring excites them for they are at the same time cheating the man and aping him, replacing him."

He gathered the whole mass of papers together and drank the last of his champagne. "*Une belle descente de lit* was Livia to me." One day he had woken up to the fact that she was servicing a whole county of unsatisfied wives. No, he had not been hard on her. It had not been fair to entrain him in this adventure which led nowhere except to mutual despair. Because love did come at last, and as always rather too late to change the course of events. "The green ink, the lucky charms . . ."

The duchess nodded a little with fatigue.

"I realise that you are right," he said at last, "and that is why I cut those passages out of the text; my arraignment of Livia drew its force from the unconscious springs of inversion in myself—my mother fixation, my woman-what-have-I-to-do-with-thee? complex; in all these bitter animadversions I was really standing on the high cliffs of my mother's death, on the plinth of the monument of words which I have set up to her memory. I understood this when Livia died—but thanks to Uncle Freddy (Freud) who taught me about this great landslide in the affairs of men. A huge chunk bitten out of the heart, a cliff subsiding into the sea after an earthquake. I knew it all, of course, without recognising it. Its impact was retroactive. I saw myself once more (forever) standing on the cold grey asphalt of the crematorium. In the nearby airfield the wind socks hovered in the western wind which doth the small rain down shall rain, etc. I am standing there stiffly, head on one side, listening to my cardiac murmur; the faint gurgle of mitral stenosis—I am inventing this, hoping to punish myself with an illness. The pulse which was set going in the belly of the whale is not as yet at rest; death had simply detached it from the mother pulse, the mentor, the tutor. Now all it could feel was the swishing of the primordial waters as they closed over my silent mother. The real self-starter in this homely old country bus of the body is the shared orgasm— hence the importance of the love artifact. I saw myself walking about in ever-diminishing perspective like some consecrated pig with a tiny mistress like a pinch of snuff. The amazing thing was that (as Pia said in her letters) love had come, real love, that passeth all understanding. She had experienced a successful passion before Rob—it was marvellous for the complexion. It gave her whole skin a gloss like new paint. The skin itself was derived from the marble pallor of Livia who always wore the shy silenced look of a wasted childhood—of someone who had never had a birthday party, nor any shadow to cast before her parents. Yes, you are right, when she died it became necessary to invent her just as if she had never existed. That was when the big ennui set in."

"Ennui?" said the duchess on a sighing fall.

"It's when you find yourself saying: 'If I can get through the next ten minutes I won't do it.' Feverishly you concentrate on a book of political cartoons."

The smoke of their cigarettes curled lazily skyward; they stared into each other's eyes, devoured by private memories.

"Once Livia and I spoke about suicide in low voices so as not to wake the sleeper in the curtained bed," said the duchess slowly, as if trying to settle something in her own mind. "About the mysterious veil of amnesia (about seven years old?) which rubs out memories, making them hard to recover in full focus. Well, I compared it to a comparable veil which seems to supervene before death arrives; perhaps to cradle one by its insulating power against the foreknowledge of departure. Everyone dies blissfully, calmly, humble and hopefully. At the end a sweet amnesia dulls the effects of pain or drugs. There comes a secret lapsing, a not-caring to go on living. Now we often get a simulacrum of this state while we are fully in life, living it fully. One becomes death-prone, accident-prone, swollen with the luxury of the idea, careless, exposed. The primordial attachment to breathing is compromised. Nor do you need any special excuse to go out, though of course people blame love or money just as duellers choose their weapons. No, simply catch flu and make no effort to fight it; founder with all hands in a smiling silence. *Sérénité . . . Pérennité . . . Mortalité . . .*"

"That is the moment Akkad watched for," he said. She opened her handbag and took out a letter with an Egyptian stamp on it; it was not difficult to recognise the beautiful precise handwriting on it as Akkad's. It was addressed to her at the country estate. The envelope had been slit with a paper-knife. He knew what was written on the single page of notepaper inside. One day he would presumably receive such a letter himself, delivered by a flesh-and-blood postman. He suddenly remembered a remark of Akkad quoted by Sutcliffe—was it in the book or not? He had forgotten.

Akkad had said: "You can't explain symbols beyond a certain depth; after that you have to live by them in order to understand them. They sidetrack the conceptual field and become part of the blood beat.

In this domain one can really say 'I know' without the onus of proof, and in default of reason."

Back in the flat Cade lit a candle, put his spectacles on his nose, and opened the Bible which he read each night, his lips slowly moving over the words and forming them as he read. He would if necessary wait up like this all night for his master. When he heard the feet of the linkboys he would take the lift down and open the front door. Apart from the Bible there lay a half-darned sock of Blanford's and a few pages of heavily corrected typescript which he had saved from the wastepaper basket, and would to-morrow take round and sell to a collector for a good sum. It was an excised part of the new book. It read: "As for Toby, who thought that alchemy and astrology were the remains of an ancient, vanished neurology, the problem of the Templars seemed no problem at all. They had gone too far, clear beyond the Orphics, beyond the double sex, the gnostic two, Tiresias and all that bedlam. They lost their balance and plunged into this new and terrifying darkness where they could realise all flesh as excrement only, decay as the only truth, death as the great Motive of the usurping god-head. Cannibalism and cabeiric orgies overcame their reason. So they came to the eatable foetus of the gnostic cults—the horror of sows gobbling their own litters for which the wine sacrament was so imperfect a surrogate. Eating and defecating at once they remained blind and earthbound—were carried into the chthonic darkness of unreason. And with them the destiny of man in Europe."

Cade folded the paper and stowed it in his pocket; then he turned back to the story of Job in the silence of the Venetian night.

It was late when Blanford paid the bill and said goodnight to the duchess; wearily the waiters hovered round him. They had come to respect this distinguished elderly Englishman who came so often to spend the whole evening talking in whispers to an empty alcove—for it was some time since the name Duchess had appeared on the death-map of the stars. The yawning linkboys would be sitting about in the dark street waiting for a signal to being the bath chair in and roll him out to the sedan. In it perhaps he might find a letter with an Egyptian postmark. Or it might be at this moment lying on the table with all the other correspondence, in front of Cade who read on and on into the momentous night.

Envoi

So D.
  begat
    Blanford (who begat Tu and Sam and Livia)
      who begat
      Sutcliffe
      who begat
      Bloshford
  Piers and Sylvie and Bruce
    who begat
    Akkad
    and
    Sabine
    and
    Banquo
      who begat Pia
      who begat Trash
      who begat . . .